The Dragon Within

The Dragon Within

CINDY LYLE

iUniverse, Inc.
Bloomington

The Dragon Within

iUniverse books may be ordered through booksellers or by contacting:

iUniverse
1663 Liberty Drive
Bloomington, IN 47403
www.iuniverse.com
1-800-Authors (1-800-288-4677)

ISBN: 978-1-4759-2464-0 (sc)
ISBN: 978-1-4759-2465-7 (hc)
ISBN: 978-1-4759-2466-4 (ebk)

Library of Congress Control Number: 2012908412

Printed in the United States of America

iUniverse rev. date: 05/24/2012

Thanks for your support!
Cheers!
Cindy Lyle

Prologue

Fitch

Daring the wrath of the weather outside, I cautiously stood in front of my window. The old oak trees, usually proud and tall, bent and submitted to the frightening force of the wind. It was dark, the kind of dark that lived in your nightmares, escorted by vicious lightening and deafening thunder, making me shudder deep inside my soul. The very foundation of my simple home trembled in fear, echoing my human emotions. This was the second storm of this nature this week, and I knew it was not natural.

What were *they* up to, and how far were they willing to go to find me?

Then, with a sudden, furious crash, the window gave way, knocking me to the ground and showering me and everything else with water and debris. My few belongings churned about the small room, crashing against the walls and landing in ruined heaps. I lay there for a moment cursing, trembling with my eyes squeezed shut, and then there was silence.

Slowly opening my eyes, I sat up and looked around my ruined home. The storm had left me shaken and worried. The elements knew I was here, and they were angry; I had failed to protect my kind—had failed *her*—and now they were through waiting. They had found me, and now it was time to find out what they wanted.

I pulled myself up off the wet floor using the window ledge as leverage. I straightened and brushed the splintered wood off my robes and then held out my hand. A small blue glow began to form in my palm and continued to grow until it was the size of an apple. I stared intently at the dancing orb, tempted, but I quickly swallowed the urge to do more and forced my neglected powers back down into my battered soul. I sighed heavily and gently placed it in the middle of the room and began the task of cleaning my ruined living space.

Pushing my broom absently around the room, I tried to stay calm and objective, but when one was dealing with the forces of creation, that task was always nearly impossible. I was a pawn to more than one, and I was tired of my loyalties under scrutiny. Fury began to burn a hole in my belly as I thought about protecting her alone, without being able to ask any of them for guidance, leaving me feeling abandoned and vulnerable to mortal emotions.

I gripped the wooden handle of my broom and snapped it in two as a wave of pity and hatred washed through me. I heaved in great ragged breaths as I tried to control the creature inside me. I wanted to be free, I wanted my life back, but none of that would ever happen if I couldn't protect her. She was everything, and protecting her was now all I knew.

Taking a deep, cleansing breath, I let the mortal feelings wash away. It would do me no good to dwell on the choices I had made in the past, choices that weighed heavily on my conscience. I did what had to be done, and now was not the time for human guilt.

I tossed the broken broom into my fire pit and tried to clear my mind but froze in place. A strange sensation tingled throughout my body, and I gasped in surprise. She was using her powers without her knowledge, and my own reaction to the charge in the air came forward again. The storm once more gathered power, assaulting the rest of the kingdom where she no doubt lay sleeping and unaware. They also knew who she was. I had no choice; I needed to tell her what was going on, even though it would be hard for her to accept.

Reaching inside my wet robes, I brought forth a battered, hollow wooden tube. I uncapped one end and shook out a tattered piece of parchment. I did not need to unroll it to know what was written there but did anyway, just to remind myself that this was real, that I was really going through with it. I held it up so the unnatural blue light of my orb cast its magic on it and showed the writing written in blood, my blood.

*Let it be known that a child will be born bearing the mark
of creation upon her body. This child sent from the god Ashia
will restore balance and all that has been lost.*

*However, that child will not know who she is or what
she is capable of. This child must undergo a quest to recover
what has been stolen. Only then will this child unlock the
secrets buried deep within, unleashing the power of the gods.*

*In addition, she will restore the freedom we have long
lived without.*

I carefully rolled the slip of parchment back into its protective
case and slipped it into the confines of my robe. I sighed. As far as
prophecies went it was a good one, but there was so much more
to the story, so much more that even I did not fully understand.
Nevertheless, I guess I had no choice. If I was to discover her true
form and reunite her spirit with it, I needed help, and the prophecy
had done its job well over the past 300 years.

Coming back to stand in front of my broken window, I stared
into the cold black night and looked to the unsettled skies. I was
not ready for this, but if I ever wished to see my kind, I needed to
be ready.

I turned my bright golden eyes from the night and began to
prepare.

*

The Elements

The two beings conversed along the shore of the river, careful not
to draw attention to themselves. They listened to the chaos of the
storm and gazed toward the castle that kept their treasure hidden.

"It's her—we've finally found her. After all these years of
searching, we've finally found her again. He's very good at keeping
her hidden."

"Yes, that is what we wanted—but what do we do now? We can't interfere. Even being this close to her could alert Mother to her presence."

The river gathered speed in response to the beings' agitation.

"We're not going to do anything for now. It is time we put our plan into motion. All of our pieces have been set. It is time we started playing the offensive. The mortals will help her; they have no choice."

The dirt along the shore slid down the embankment and fell into the river. It formed a tiny island and drifted downstream toward the sea. The river held it close and kept it safe.

"I'm frightened, sister. I don't want to do this anymore. I want to rest."

The current of the river slowed, and the two beings held each other.

"Don't be, brother. She will not fail. She will fulfill her destiny, and then we can all rest. We can all have peace."

CHAPTER 1

Karah

Cold, wet, and very tired, I trudged forward on weary legs. I didn't know where I was, but the sounds of pursuit haunted my footsteps. I heard the horses' hoof beats getting closer and felt the ground tremble with their approach. I was running out of time, but there was nowhere to go, nowhere to hide in this unfamiliar landscape. These were not the hills of Aserah, my home, but a forest thick with vegetation.

It was dark, well past midnight, but I could still make out the trees stretching silently to the skies. I heard a creek nearby and a sudden pang of sorrow touched my heart. This place felt like a sanctuary for me, my peace when there was none to have, but that was impossible. There were no large forests of this kind in Aserah. It was a farming land filled mostly with fields and hills, but every fibre of my being was telling me I knew this place, loved this place even though I had never been here. Everything I touched or smelled gave me waves of memories. Memories that were not mine, memories of a love that had ended in betrayal, a love that had cost me my very soul.

Sounds of crashing through brush suddenly brought my attention back to my immediate problem. I needed to get out of here before my unseen enemies found me.

I pushed my weary body toward the creek and cringed at the sound of something scraping against the bushes, screaming out my location. I looked down toward the sound and realized I carried a short sword in my hand. I admired the simple blade and tightened my hold on the worn grip. The blade gleamed in the moonlight and my face was reflected on its edge. I stifled a gasp of horror as I studied the image staring back at me. It was not me. I stared into my own frightened eyes but my appearance was different. My hair was not my fiery red but a dull brown and my skin was much too dark. I was somehow looking at myself in a different body. I had morphed into this girl but I didn't understand why.

Shouts pierced the solitude of the forest, and my feet lost their hold on the ground. I started running, no longer in control of my body. It had no trouble finding a familiar trail that led to my destination.

My pursuers were getting closer; I could hear their voices now, no longer trying to conceal them. They had dismounted and were continuing on foot. I ducked behind a large tree and tried my best not to breathe.

Their voices drifted through the dense night.

"Where is she? She couldn't have come much farther. There is nowhere to hide out here."

After a pause, loud, cursing voices came nearer.

"If we don't bring her back, the Master will flail us and feed us to his hounds—not to mention that horrible creature he keeps as a pet! He should have sent *it* out here, not us. Why do I have to be out here in woods, traipsing around in the dark? She is just some girl who our lord wants dead."

I heard a gasp in surprise and the sound of a blade drawn from its scabbard. "It would serve you well not to talk poorly of your commanding officer or our lord in my presence. Your whining and lack of conviction is grating on my nerves. I should slit your throat here and save him the trouble. Now quit complaining and find the girl."

There were only two of them, thank the gods, but I recognized the harsh, uncaring accent of the Dark Lord's legions. I did not know how or why I knew this, but there was no doubt in my mind that Dark Lord soldiers were after me. The question was why. One other thing disturbed me and sent shivers of fear and foreboding through me: Why did I feel as if this had all happened to me before?

The two henchmen made their way past my hidden location and searched along the creek for any signs of me. I thought for sure

2

that the pounding of my heart would give me away at any moment. I listened to their words while trying not to breathe.

"Do you see any sign of her?"

Brush snapped and gave way with the force of their search.

"None. It's as if she just vanished. Maybe the Master is wrong, and maybe she is just a girl. You can't seriously believe any of that garbage that we have been told."

"Don't be a fool; you know the stories. She's the girl from the prophecy, and it's our duty to find her. Whether you believe in magic or not, you cannot deny the words of our lord. She's here—I can smell her fear."

Prophecy? What prophecy? And magic? How is this even possible? I'm just a girl living in the king's court, my lady's handmaiden. I can't even boil water for a stew without burning myself.

Movement caught my attention again, and I heard them moving farther along the bank away from me, so I made the decision to make a run for it. If I stayed here any longer, I was going to be discovered.

I steeled myself and prepared to make my escape, but as I turned around and prepared to run into the safety of the forest, I stumbled right into the point of a blade. My own sword dropped uselessly to ground as sharp pain racked my body. I tried to pull away, but the sharp edge drove deeper into my body. I looked down at the red blossoming on the front of my shirt and then looked up into the eyes of my killer. They were cold, black, and evil. They were eyes I had seen before, I was certain of it.

They were the eyes of the Dark Lord.

His voice echoed throughout my soul as he towered over me. "We meet again, my pretend goddess. This time will be the last."

As I slumped forward, leaning my weight against the evil man, I began to fade from this world. Commotion and shouts of alarm erupted around me. I heard swords clashing, and then a bright, brilliant light encased me.

The Dark Lord screamed in outrage. The sound was terrifying and inhuman.

The sword was ripped from my abdomen and blood flowed from my body. I fell to the ground and listened to the struggle going on around me. I felt the wind pick up and debris flew around as if a giant bird was flying overhead, but I had no strength to look up. My body turned toward the creek, and I saw figures engaged in combat.

Then one of the mysterious newcomers stood before the water and began saying words I had never heard before. The water from the creek started to move faster and faster and then shot out of the creek bed into the sky like a great geyser emptying into the night.

I heard that same horrible shriek and then the wind died down. Strong arms lifted me from the ground and carried me away.

"You are safe, my lady. You shall be reborn again. I only regret that we have not yet found a way to return you to yourself. I will not give up. Please have faith."

My rescuer looked down at me with eyes full of pain and sorrow. They were so familiar, but I could not remember why.

As the noise began to fade and the darkness of death closed around me, I heard the man who had killed me. There was such rage and contempt in his voice that I was sure I would hear his words for eternity.

"There is nowhere you can hide her where I will not find her! She will be mine, and this pathetic little game will end!"

I tried to stay conscious, tried to understand what was going on, but darkness claimed me, and I was no more.

*

Gasps of horror filled my bedchamber again, the third time this week. I clutched my knees to my heaving chest. It took a few seconds to realize that I was safe in my own bed and not dying in the middle of some forest. Sucking in deep ragged breaths, I tried to calm my racing heart. What had just happened? Being plagued by bad dreams ever since I could remember was nothing new, but during the past month my dreams had become much more vivid and frequent. Tonight felt like no dream I'd ever had; it felt like a *memory*, and that terrified me more than anything. How could that be possible? How can you have memories of things that never happened?

I lowered my head and rubbed my temples. Another headache was coming along with the feeling that someone had a hold of my soul and was trying to rip it from me. It was not a pleasant feeling.

Without lifting my head, I glanced over at my window. The moon was hidden behind large dark clouds. A storm had just blown through; I smelled the dampness in the air. I had not been asleep for long and sighed as yet another night was ruined for sleep.

I shook my head, stretched my legs, and tried to get the tendrils of sleep to let go of my body, but a sudden cold feeling came over me, forcing me to retract my legs again to keep warm.

From the corner of my eye, I could just make out a shadowy figure standing close to the curtains. I focused my full attention on it, but it disappeared. Knowing what it was, I relaxed. Sprits were a common occurrence for me, although I never understood them. It was bad enough my dreams kept me awake at night, but I was also "lucky" enough to be subjected to visits from the dead. They always appeared right after I had one of my dreams but rarely stayed longer than the blink of an eye. Spirits were not uncommon, especially in an old castle such as this, but it almost seemed as if they were trying to tell me something or that maybe they wanted something from me. I felt sorry for them. No one really knew much about *him* or *her*, except that before the Dark Lord, spirits did not exist. Memories of my dream and the evil overlord suddenly came flooding back, and I forgot all about the lost soul.

I looked around my dark room. Everything seemed different, and nothing felt like it was my own. I lowered my head and tried not to cry. I felt lost and confused. I didn't know how much more I could take.

Before I had a chance to collect my thoughts, Queen Anora, my adoptive mother, bright eyed and beautiful as usual, came into my room. My room was adjacent to hers, so unfortunately, my midnight terrors often woke her up.

She silently glided over to my bed and sat next to me, smoothing my hair back out of my eyes. "Are you all right, Karah? I heard you screaming again. Was it another nightmare?"

The sense of fear and evil started to dissipate with her kind words, but the confusion remained. I couldn't manage to speak much above a whisper. "It was, but this time it was different. I remember so much of this dream. I remember it like it really happened to me, like a *memory*. There was a creek and a forest that I know in my heart I have been to, but I have never in my life seen it. I also wasn't myself. I looked different but I still knew it was me"

I had started to tremble with cold. I was still wet with sweat, and the memories of my dream were making me shiver.

Anora placed my blanket around my shoulders and asked me to continue.

"I was been chased by the Dark Lord's soldiers, and I swear it was the Dark Lord himself who tried to kill me this time. I don't know what he looks like, but I looked into this man's eyes and just knew it was *him*. They were the very definition of evil; they were not human."

Anora straightened and looked concerned. "The Dark Lord? Are you sure? He has not yet become a threat to us this far north. Perhaps you were mistaken."

I shook my head and began to regain the strength in my voice. "No, I'm sure, it was him. That part confuses me the most. I know we are safe here, but in my dream, I wasn't in Aserah. I was somewhere else, but it was home to me; I could feel it."

I looked up and locked eyes with Anora. "There was something else too. They mentioned a prophecy and my having some kind of magical powers. I thought magic died when the gods disappeared along with the mages and warlocks. Do you know anything about this prophecy? Do you know why I am dreaming of it?"

Anora looked stunned and very frightened but quickly recovered and put on her "court face." I could hear the lie in her words. "It was just a dream, Karah, nothing to worry about, but I think in the morning you should go see Fitch. He may have something to help you sleep better at night. Talk to him about your dreams, and maybe he will have some answers."

Abruptly and without another word, she got up, gave me a quick, reassuring hug, and returned to her rooms. Never in my eighteen years of living in this castle had I ever known Anora to dismiss someone that abruptly, especially me. Something I said had gotten to her, but I didn't know what.

I got off my bed with my blanket still clutched around my shoulders and shuffled my way over to my dressing table. The castle's cool stone floor chilled the soles of my feet, and I quickly made it to the soft rug that my table sat upon. Splashing water on my face from my washing basin helped clear my mind, and I let my blanket fall so I could see myself clearly in the mirror. My green eyes were shining with the light of my candle, and it almost seemed as if I was looking at tiny pools of water dancing in a breeze, but I blinked and the illusion was gone. It was too bad I couldn't blink away the mess on my head that some people call hair. Me, I call it a curse. Its thick and wavy locks were never manageable, and I happened to be the only redhead in the whole kingdom, which used to get me a lot of unwanted attention. I asked Anora about it once and she had told me that many years ago there was a group of tribes' people living deep in the Kanarah woods. The Dark Lord had wiped them out, and now none exists. The Kanarah people had hair like mine, and that was also how she came to name me. She said it was a tribute to the poor souls who had been killed without cause or reason.

Everything about me looked the same but I felt so different, as if I didn't even know who I was any more. Vivid images of the girl in my dream—who looked nothing like me but I knew was me—plucked at the strings of my sanity, making my headache worse. I needed to find out what was going on before I went crazy.

I got up, crossed the room to my window, and stared out into the night. The thunder rumbled in the distance and made my body tremble. Glancing down into the courtyard, the evidence there had been a storm was confirmed. Debris was everywhere, along with soldiers and servants trying to clean it up. The storm must have been another violent one. How I'd managed to sleep through it was beyond me. The weather lately was frightening, and there had been too many freak storms to be natural. The worst was when the ground shook and threatened to bring the whole castle down upon us. It seemed as if the land was angry, but no one knew why.

My gaze went past the courtyard walls to the outer ward, and I noticed that light came from some of the houses and shops. If this storm was anything like the one we'd had a few days ago, those houses were probably filled with scared children and adults trying to put their simple lives back together. There was so much confusion and chaos right now.

There was not just the problem of the storms; our crops this year were not as bountiful. Several sections of farmland just refused to grow anything, and then in other parts the harvest was small and sparse. The King and Queen were having a hard time keeping their people from panicking. They desperately needed answers.

Beyond the castle walls, I could just make out the hillsides and the never-ending farm fields and I could hear the river gently flowing. I liked listening to the water; it was calming and gave me a sense of peace, of belonging. The city was surrounded by water. The river stemmed from a large lake off to the east and it snaked its way almost completely around the kingdom. It then flowed for a few miles west and emptied into a small cove. The cove then led out to the vast expanse of the Forever Sea.

I longed to be able to travel out into the open waters of the sea, but Gareth had no ships capable for the journey. The small port was used primarily for trade with Clorynina, a large port city far down the coast, but even that arrangement seemed to have stalled for reasons I was not aware of.

I didn't know much about this world, and there was so much I wanted to see. The King told me that most of the realms we knew were controlled by the Dark Lord and were not safe. He said that only here in Gareth were we truly safe from the Dark Lord's reach. I thought back to my dream and a sliver of doubt crept through my bones. How could anyone be safe with that man alive? Why was here any different?

I hugged myself and looked into the dark, forbidding sky. What was out there? What was trying to make me remember things I had never seen or done? In my heart, I knew that somewhere out there were my answers—and my enemies. Even now, staring out into the blackness of the night, I could see that man's cold evil eyes staring at me from across the world. I still felt the pain of the sword plunged into my abdomen, and looking down, I half expected to see blood flowing from my body, but there was nothing there. I shivered and closed the shutters.

I turned away from my window, retrieved my blanket, and lay back down on my bed. There was no sense in trying to sleep, but the castle still slept so I had to wait until dawn. After my morning chores, I planned to go see Fitch.

Fitch was a strange man who lived on the outskirts of the city. He has always been kind to me and always been there when I needed something. Some people believe he is magic, but there was no more good magic in the world, only the dark power the Dark Lord and his followers possessed. Good magic hadn't been seen for almost 300 years, and really, I doubted it had ever existed.

Maybe I would ask Fitch about it tomorrow. Maybe he knew about magic and our missing gods and the answers to all of my questions. Maybe he knew why I felt like someone else.

Chapter 2

Warm sunshine filtered in through the cracks of the shutters, warming my face. I smiled, rolled over, and stuck my head under the soft pillow. I felt at peace and probably would have fallen back to sleep if it were not for a loud, insistent pounding making its way to my ears. It sounded like a very angry bear was outside my door trying to get in. Dread filled my bones as I sat upright, causing me to feel light headed. I jumped out of bed, threw on my robe, opened the door, and came face-to-face with my "bear."

Well, maybe not a real bear, but Gladice was definitely mad as one. The head of the servants, and technically my boss, stood before me with her arms crossed, breathing heavily. My room was near the top of the east tower, so I'm sure she was not happy to have gone in search of me this morning for me to do my morning chores.

"Why my Lady puts up with you I will never know. Get dressed and get downstairs. Breakfast doesn't cook itself, you know." Gladice turned and stormed away, grumbling under her breath the whole way, leaving me to smile at her back. Gladice could be a bit overbearing sometimes, but the woman had taken care of me since I was a babe and I loved her for it.

I quickly shut my door and began the task of getting ready for the day. I didn't have much in the way of clothes, but what I had was nice. Sorting through my wardrobe, I grabbed a clean, cream-coloured wool work dress, tied my apron, found my worn leather shoes, and then attempted to do something with my hair. A quick look in the mirror confirmed that my hair was a lost cause, so I twisted it up in a knot and stuck a stick through it.

There. I was finished and in record time. I ran to my bedroom door, threw it open and ran straight into a wall—the wall being Prince Elric. I rubbed my forehead as I listened to the laughter in the young prince's voice.

"Good morning, Karah, late again, I see. You'd better be careful or old Gladice will tan your hide."

I stepped back a little and looked up into Elric's amused face. "Yes, well, she would have to catch me first, and we both know who would win that race. What are you doing here anyway? I thought you were out on a hunting trip with your father."

Elric's face became dark, and a bad feeling crept into my bones. "We returned late last night during the storm. We came across a group of Dark Lord soldiers by chance just outside the nearby village of Holsten. There were maybe ten of them and appeared to be a scouting party. My father wanted us back here nevertheless, to prepare our men—just in case."

I was a little shocked for a moment. The Dark Lord's lackeys were here, in Aserah? It had to be a coincidence. I felt faint all of a sudden and had to grasp Elric's arm for support.

Elric gently led me back into my room and sat me on a chair. He handed me a glass of water. There was concern in his eyes.

Prince Elric was a year older than I was, but we had grown up together. After the king and queen had found me on their doorstep, they had decided to keep me and raise me as one of their own. Elric and I used to get into all sorts of trouble, which was usually my doing. I used to sneak away and watch his sword practices, until he caught me one day. He then proceeded to tell me that swords had no place in a woman's hand and that I should be back in the kitchen listening to Gladice teach me the ways of the fire pit. That conversation lasted about as long as it took me to kick him in the shins, wrestle his practice sword out of his hands, and make him say "mercy." After that, he taught me how to protect myself with a sword. I was quite good at it and became almost his equal. I always considered him my big, annoying brother. He had his father's good looks and hardnosed attitude, but every once in a while his mother shined through him—he was kind and caring.

I looked up at him now and saw in his eyes that he was genuinely concerned, and something stirred in me. I pushed the feeling aside and regained my composure. I tried to focus on his words again.

"This morning I was speaking to mother, and she told me you had another nightmare last night and that this one was a bad one. Are you all right?"

I gripped my metal cup a little tighter and resisted the urge to rub my arms, which were now covered in goose bumps. I nodded but didn't remain looking at him. My eyes dropped to glance at the cup in my hand and I remembered last night's terror.

"Yes," I whispered, "it was a bad one. It was like no dream I'd ever had before. It was so real. Anora thinks I should go and see Fitch today, and see what he says, although I don't know what help he could offer." I sighed and put my head in my hand. I could feel another headache coming, and it wasn't even midday.

"Do you want some company? I have the day to myself before heading out again. I need to go to city for a few things anyway."

I couldn't imagine what a prince would need to go into the village for, but I decided not to argue the point. Truth was I wanted his company. This dream had me more spooked than I cared to admit. I told Elric I would find him after lunch—that is, if Gladice didn't kill me first.

*

The rest of my morning played out the same as any other. I helped prepare breakfast and clean up afterward, the whole while listening to Gladice gripe about my tardiness and how if things were to be done properly, she may as well do them herself. I loved that woman dearly, but sometimes she really got on my nerves.

After I was done in the kitchen, I went in search of Anora. I wanted to see if there was anything she needed me to do before I left for the city. She was not in her rooms so I went down to the garden where she sometimes went to get away from things. On my way, I passed the king's study and heard Anora's voice. She was having quite a heated discussion with her husband. I don't very often hear them argue, so I sneaked closer and held my breath so I wouldn't be discovered.

"She needs to be protected. I simply can't send her away. I think she may be close to remembering who she is and that may be a key to unlocking the prison she is trapped in. I can't ignore the prophecy."

That was Anora's voice, but she sounded so tired, she must not have gone back to sleep last night after I woke her.

"But she is putting us—our son—in danger. What if she does remember? Then her power will attract the Dark Lord like bees to honey. I have seen his men with my own eyes just outside our borders, looking for something. What if they already know she is here? I have heard what happens to those who harbour the child from the prophecy, and I will not let that happen to my people."

King Edwin sounded angry and very frightened. This made no sense. Who were they talking about? Surely not me.

"I told her to seek out Master Fitch today. He will have answers; he will tell her what to do. We must wait until we hear from him. Please. Do not turn your back on her as you have so many times to others in the past. She is not some stranger; she is family, and like it or not it is our duty to protect her." The anger in Anora's voice was surprising. I had never heard her speak that way to the king before.

King Edwin's voice was equally enraged, his tone unfriendly. "He is the man who got us into this mess in the first place! I should never have let you and Fitch talk me into this—and do not speak to me as if I don't know what's at stake. I'm trying to protect *my* family, as I always have. You have no right to question my methods. Now because I gave in during a moment of weakness, everything I worked so hard to protect could be ruined. We would have been fine; no one would have noticed us." King Edwin sighed heavily.

"But she was just a baby; how could I have said no?"

I couldn't listen anymore; I felt numb. They *were* talking about me, but I didn't understand any of it. My dream that was supposed to have just been a dream was becoming more real by the hour. What prison were they talking about and what power? How could I be putting anyone in danger?

Now more than ever I needed to find answers, and apparently, Fitch had them.

Silently I moved away from the study and started to make my way out of the castle. I was so consumed in my thoughts that I ran into Prince Elric again.

"We do really need to stop running into each other this way." He laughed, but the smile left his face when he realized my mood. "What happened? You look like you've seen a spirit."

I almost laughed at the irony of that comment. Elric didn't know I could see spirits, and I wanted to keep it that way. "Maybe I have. That would explain a lot."

I thought I was going to start crying but realized that would solve nothing, so I shouldered past Elric and told him to follow. I guess he listened but I didn't stop to find out. I was getting angrier by the minute. What was the big secret everyone was keeping from me? Who was I? And why in the name of the gods did the Dark Lord want me dead?

I'm not sure how long I walked staring down at the ground, but when I finally stopped to look around, we were outside and headed toward the village.

Elric gently knocked my shoulder to get my attention.

I stopped walking and turned to him. "Tell me how much do you know about me before I came to live at the castle."

Elric shrugged a confused look on his face. "Not much. Just what I was told—that you were dropped at our doorstep and that my parents took you in. Not much to tell, really." He started to walk toward the village again. I fell in step beside him.

"Well, it seems we have both been lied to," I shot back.

"What do you mean? What are you talking about?" Elric stopped again and turned to face me with suspicious, questioning eyes. The thought of his parents lying to him was obviously bothering him. It bothered me too, more than I cared to admit.

I decided to tell him the whole story. I told him of my dream, about the man who had killed me and the man who had tried to save me. I also told him what I overheard in his father's study between Anora and Edwin.

14

Elric shook his head. "I don't believe it. Are you sure that's what you heard? It sounds so unbelievable. Maybe you heard what you wanted to hear to make sense of your dream." Elric was stunned; he couldn't wrap his head around this any better than I could.

"I didn't imagine anything. I am not who I thought I was. I don't know who or *what* I am." At this point I really did think I was going to cry, especially after Elric put his arms around me. I felt safe, and he was the one certainty in my life. I was suddenly very thankful for his presence. That feeling made me feel joyful and uncomfortable all at the same time. I really couldn't deal with this right now.

Without removing his arm from my shoulder, Elric pulled me toward the village again. "Come on, let's go talk to Fitch and see if we can figure out what's going on. It'll be all right, you'll see."

I wanted to believe that but knew deep down that nothing would ever be all right again.

CHAPTER 3

It was early afternoon by the time we reached the outskirts of the outer ward. Evidence of last night's storm was everywhere. We stopped often and heard the horrific tales of nature's fury, and we helped out where we could. People were scared, and I couldn't blame them. Elric gave reassuring words where he could, but even he didn't believe in what he was saying.

We were very close to the river that flowed steadily under the bridge that separated Gareth from the rest of Aserah. The body of water had grown swollen and its current flowed quickly, but to me it was peaceful and soothing. Not like the chaos I felt inside my mind or the trouble that once again seemed to be plaguing this city and its people.

The city of Gareth came with a tragic past. Gareth is the biggest human settlement in Aserah, and second only to Clorynina, far to the south. The two cities are the only two major settlements left in our world of Eiddoril, the rest having been destroyed or made slaves by the Dark Lord.

It was here that that King Edwin's ancestor King Gareth led his people after a long-fought battle and stalemate with the Dark Lord's army. Both sides retreated with heavy losses, and Gareth made the decision to move his people north across the mighty river Haltek and to the farming hills of Aserah. Ever since then, people fleeing from the south and from the Dark Lord usually ended up here, where we were safe for now.

Gareth was a thriving community. We supplied the surrounding villages with food, and in return they traded to us what we needed. Livestock farms thrived to the east of us along the shores of the Lake of Tears, and farther north, near the mountains, was the mining village of Sunder, where we got most of our weapons and iron materials. It was a good system that benefited many.

Fitch lived in a fairly small home with a well-kept yard—that is, usually well kept. It looked as if a cyclone had blown through his yard. The huge oak trees outside his house had just started showing signs that autumn was approaching, but broken branches and leaves were scattered everywhere.

Fitch must have heard us coming, because before I even stepped foot on his pathway his front door swung open. He smiled at me warmly. "My lady, I have been waiting for you."

My concern for his well-being quickly vanished and was replaced by my hot-headed temper. His strange comment didn't even penetrate the angry fog that clouded my mind. "Great—then maybe you can tell me what in the name of the gods is going on."

And with that I pushed my way inside and flopped down on one of his chairs.

Elric stared at me, and Fitch looked worried. They both followed me into the house and Fitch shut the door behind us. Elric pulled up a seat beside me, and Fitch disappeared into the small kitchen at the back of the house.

"That was subtle. You might want to think about curbing that temper of yours if you plan to get any information out of him. Look around at his house. He has obviously been through a horrible night."

Elric was not happy with my behaviour and was looking at me with a scolding glare. That only succeeded in making me angrier, but I did look around, and what I saw made me regret my earlier attitude. I could tell that Fitch had tried to clean up, but there were still bits of broken window and other furniture lying around the small room. I felt my face turn red, and I turned my eyes away from Elric. "I know, I'm sorry. I'm just so frustrated. I don't even know where to start."

"Try the beginning." Fitch was suddenly at my elbow holding out a steaming cup of tea that smelled like raspberries.

I took the cup, sucked in the delicious aroma and instantly felt calmer. Fitch also handed a cup to Elric, took a seat opposite me and waited for me to begin.

I looked up from my tea at the man I had known my whole life. Fitch wasn't a striking man, but he held himself with a confidence I had never before seen. He was of average height with a head full of long, greying brown hair that was always tied back. He was constantly dressed in plain brown robes, which I supposed contributed to the magic-user rumours, but today he seemed dressed for travel, wearing leggings and a worn tunic. He was always kind to me but never hesitated to tell me if I was doing something stupid or when to keep my mouth shut. He must have been as old as the king, but he didn't show it, except in his eyes. His eyes seemed older than the world, and sometimes there was great sadness there. It was his brilliant blue eyes today that drew me to him; they were eyes I had seen before, not here but in my dream. His eyes were the eyes of my saviour, the eyes of my mystery.

I told Fitch about the dream and lastly of the conversation I had overheard. "It was you I saw last night in my dream. You tried to save me from the Dark Lord. But you looked different. I was different, but we were still us." I sighed heavily and stared into my cup. "What's going on? Why am I having dreams of another life? Who am I and who are *you?*" The last bit came out in a whisper. I had lost myself and needed him to find me.

Fitch sat back in his chair and seemed to age 50 years right in front of me. His shoulders slumped, and when he looked up at me, his eyes were filled with pain and something else I couldn't explain: belonging. "I am sorry, child, but I was hoping a solution to your problem would have been found already. To tell you the truth, this is the first time this particular problem has ever arisen, and I am not quite sure how to handle it. What I am about to tell you you were never meant to know and you may not believe, but I swear it is the truth. Please don't hate me."

I sat back with a sliver of fear slowly creeping into my bones. "Hate you for what? And what exactly is my problem, besides my bad temper and poor cooking skills?"

Fitch took a deep settling breath and shifted in his seat next to me. He stole a glance at Elric, perhaps trying to decide if he should speak in front of the prince, but his gaze didn't linger long on Elric. He fixed his piercing blue eyes on me.

"Tell me, child, how much do you know about our gods, and what do you know of their disappearance?"

I didn't see the point in discussing my faith, but Fitch had such an intense look about him that I found it hard to refuse. "I don't really know much. I know their names. Mareth was the god of death, and Ashia the god of life, and one day they both just disappeared, leaving the Dark Lord to consume us. Our faith was forgotten, and now we live day by day, wondering when and if our gods will return and stop punishing us. I have tried several times to find books or papers—anything that could tell me what had happened—but there are none, or no one knows where they are. Do you know why? Why is our past such a secret to us?"

Fitch turned away from me for a moment and seemed to stiffen. When he glanced back at me, his whole posture had changed. He was angry and very guarded. "There are written histories of our past and of all of the different races that lived here, but they are locked away deep in a temple within the Kannarah woods. Three hundred years ago the Dark Lord removed the final obstacle to his controlling all of Eiddoril. He then overpowered the temple and ordered the books inside destroyed. He then banned writings of any kind under the penalty of death, which you already should know, so that is why there are few if any records in our households."

I reddened at the comment. I did know that. It was something every child is taught by the time he or she is able to speak. Reading and writing was forbidden, causing damaging effects. People had no idea what happened in our past except what we were told. Without knowledge we were powerless and were slowly losing ourselves to the Dark Lord. Of course, there were some that refused to give up the right to pass on knowledge, and reading and writing was taught in secret. We learned deep in the woods through scratching on the ground or in the dust of a dark room. It was not much but it was something.

I lowered my gaze and heard Fitch's voice soften a little. "The Dark Lord has done irrevocable damage. Whole generations have lived and died never knowing the joy and power of the written word. Everything is passed on by word of mouth, and what is written down is so secret many do not deem it an acceptable risk to read." Fitch paused and turned to Elric, changing the tone of his voice. "What King Edwin has in his library is the largest collection in all of Eiddoril, besides what was left in the temple. Most were smuggled here when King Gareth came here all those years ago, and they have been locked away since. Every king thereafter has been too afraid to find out about its past, so it remains forgotten and unimportant, like his views toward the rest of Eiddoril."

I stared at Fitch in shock. His callous opinion was so unlike him.

Elric, sitting beside me, bristled, and his face became flushed with anger. "Who are you to speak ill of my ancestors' decisions, or my father's? You were not there; how could you possibly understand the pressures of keeping a community safe? And how do you know all of this? If what you say is true, how did you come to possess this knowledge when no one else seems to know?" Elric was sitting on the edge of his chair with "challenge" written across his face.

A look of rage passed in Fitch's eyes, making them seem to glow a bright gold, but the illusion passed and he took a deep, steadying breath. He bowed his head deeply toward Elric, but I could tell the gesture was forced. "I am sorry, my young prince. There is much you do not know, which, in part, is my fault, but the blame can also be laid at others' feet. If you will permit me, I will try to explain."

Elric stared at the older man for a moment more but nodded and sat back in his chair, crossing his arms.

Fitch turned his attention back to me, and I suddenly felt sick to my stomach. I wasn't so sure I wanted to know the answers any more.

Fitch reached out and held my hands in his. "You, my dear, are a being of great power who, for the last 300 years, has been trapped in a human body, doomed to never remember who or what you are."

I just blinked and stared at Fitch open-mouthed. I guess he took that has a sign that I was incapable of thought because he just kept right on speaking.

"All those years ago the gods made a decision to leave this world and let us govern ourselves, which you already know to some extent, but what you don't know is why. You see, our gods did not originate from this world; they were immortal travellers from another plane of existence."

My eyes bugged out, and I inhaled to ask a slew of questions, but Fitch cut me off. "Please do not interrupt. I know a lot of this will make no sense to you, but I promise I will explain everything in time. None of what I am telling you has been heard or taught in centuries, but please let me finish and I will do my best to fill in the holes."

I shut my mouth with difficulty and kept my green eyes fixed on him. Fitch released my now-sweating hands and tucked his own into the sleeves of his long robes.

"Now, as I was saying, these travellers were immortal, meaning they could not be killed by anything natural. So compared to the rest of the species living in Eiddoril at the time, these beings were the dominant power. They could never grow old or become sick, and they had the ability to wield magic." Fitch paused and took a sip of his tea. He took a quick glance at me to see if I would interrupt, but I was biting my tongue so hard I think I tasted blood.

Fitch actually grinned a little and continued. "The inhabitants of Eiddoril quickly grew accustomed to the newcomers, even going so far has to worship two of the immortals as their gods. Ashia and Mareth gladly accepted their new positions and began to teach the mortals how to use magic, spawning mages and then the warlocks."

"As you can imagine, the two immortals were not friends, and Eiddoril was quickly divided. Some followed Mareth and his dark power while others followed Ashia and her teachings of peace. Eventually their inability to get along caused a war that almost succeeded in destroying Eiddoril."

"This is all very fascinating, and I'm sure this *tale* greatly entertains children, but what does any of this have to do with Karah?" I had almost forgotten Elric was still in the room.

Fitch whirled on the young Prince. "Oh I assure you, Prince Elric, this is no tale, and if you are done with your ignorant questions I will continue."

Elric said nothing, but his posture was tense. I wasn't even aware that the two of them spoke let alone had this much animosity toward each other. It was something that bothered me deeply.

Fitch took Elric's silence as a sign and ignored him. "Mareth and Ashia and the immortals who followed them chose to return to the immortal realm where they could fight out their differences and not destroy the home they had come to desire. However, Mareth and Ashia each had a plan of their own, which was not discovered until after all the travellers had left Eiddoril. That was when the Dark Lord and you were discovered to be among the mortals."

Fitch paused and set his intense gaze on me. I felt as if he was looking directly into my soul, and I had to fight to keep control of my rising anxiety.

"Balance was held for a time, but it did not take long for the Dark Lord to proceed with a plan that his master had left him. It was during the great battle with Gareth's army that the Dark Lord and his warlocks placed a spell on you that ripped your sprit from your body and trapped it in a human one, therefore rendering you mortal. That was the only way you could be killed. Once you died in that human body you would be gone from this world, and any memory of you would be wiped from history. However, your followers, mages of great power, interfered with the spell and added a loophole. Even though your human body could die, your spirit would find another host, so long as someone was there to guide it. Unfortunately, they were not able to allow you to keep your memories or keep everyone else from forgetting who you truly were. They were also not able to rescue your true form. The Dark Lord did not have the power to destroy it but he hid it from them, and even after all these years no one has been able to recover it. The mages barely escaped with you in your new human host, and they went into hiding."

I stared intently into Fitch's eyes and realization hit me. "You are a *mage*! You were there that day and have been there ever since . . . but how is that even possible?"

Fitch's eyes softened a little and I could hear regret in his words. "Yes, I was there and have been with you up to this point. After that day, many other small battles between the Dark Lord and the peoples of this world have been fought and lost, and for 300 years he has steadily been gaining everything his master wished him to. He never gave up searching for you and found you several times. Eighteen years ago was our last encounter, and it was also when I became your last sole protector."

Fitch stopped, reached out for my hand and held my gaze with his own. "So you see, that is why you're having dreams of different lives that seem so familiar to you. You have lived all of these lives for the past 300 years, but each time the Dark Lord finds you and kills your human body, your memories of that life disappear and a new one begins. I have been searching all of these years for answers, a way to break the spell and find your true form, but every time I get close the Dark Lord finds you and I must start again somewhere new. Even though you are not aware of your power you use it unconsciously, and he can sense it. That is how he finds you. I can cloak it for a time, but I am just one mage and all that is left of my line."

Fitch paused and looked at me. I stared back. I think I must have turned green because Elric passed me a bowl that was on the nearby table. Elric spoke before I had a chance, which was just as well because I did think I was going to be sick.

"You can't be serious. Karah is not some being of power, she's just a girl. I've known her my whole life, and she has never displayed any kind of power. She can't even fry an egg."

"Thanks," I managed to muffle from inside the bowl.

Fitch controlled his anger better this time, but there was no hiding his frustration with Elric. "I assure you, everything I have told you is the truth. I wish it were not so, but this is the true story of Karah's life—and her deaths."

I lifted my head out of the bowl and looked up at Fitch. I could see it in his face that he was telling me the truth, but there were still things that did not make sense. "You said I can never remember my previous lives, and that no one remembers I even existed, so how is it that you know of me? Because last I heard mages were supposed to be human. And why I am remembering my past lives now?"

Fitch got up and started to pace, something I had seen him do many times when he was frustrated. "I don't know. It could be that the life you're living now is the longest you've lived in a human host. Maybe it's a key to breaking the spell; maybe your powers are trying to fight back. I just don't know."

Fitch and I stared at each other for a moment, and I could tell he was trying to decide whether or not he should tell the rest of his story. His eyes softened and he sighed. He turned his back to me and looked out the window, staring off into nothing, remembering another time and place. "I remember you because I am not mortal either. I came through the gate with the others, but I chose not to assert my powers over the races. Instead, I became a teacher of magic. Ashia never fully trusted Mareth, or anyone for that matter, so she left me and the other mages to protect you."

Bitterness laced Fitch's words and I could see him tremble with rage. He took a few steadying breaths and lowered his head to look at the floor. "I was the most powerful and the one sworn to protect you personally. My link to you was the strongest. That is why I remember you and why I still have some magic left." He turned, and I could read on his face that there was more he was not telling me, but I decided not to press the issue.

Instead, I asked about my adoptive parents. "Do Anora and Edwin know about all this? From what you've told me, they cannot possibly know who I really am. How did you convince them to take me in?—which I assume you did."

Fitch had a look of guilt on his face. He reached into his dark robes and pulled out a small wooden tube. He placed it in my hands. The small wood cylinder was warm to the touch and my hands became itchy and irritated, as if I had just been bitten by a bug. I turned it over a few times and found that one end sported a cap. I gently popped it off and shook out the contents into the palm of my now-shaking hand. It was just a piece of old parchment, but the vibe I got from it was eerie, like the feeling I got when there were spirits around. I gingerly held the tattered parchment in my hand and turned my questioning eyes toward Fitch.

He again took a seat next to me and gestured that I unroll the parchment. I was only vaguely aware of Fitch speaking again as I stared at the strange words drawn in what looked like blood. Fitch's voice brought my attention back to him, but I didn't stop staring at the words I held in my hands.

"No, the king and queen do not know who you truly are; they can't. Your part in history has been erased from mortal minds. However, I knew that I had to try to keep your memory alive in some way, so I created a prophecy. It told of a being who would be sent from the heavens to save humankind from the Dark Lord and redeem them. This being would be trapped in a human vessel and would not be released until her true power was discovered. She would come in the form of child with the birthmark of creation on her body, and a great quest would be undertaken to free her. I convinced the king and queen that you were this child, just as I had convinced many before them, and that you needed to be protected."

I dragged my eyes from the mysterious words in a language I could not read and stared blankly at Fitch. "What prophecy? Why does everyone know about this damn prophecy but me? And what birthmark? I don't have a birthmark."

I stood up and proceeded to inspect my body, unaware of how uncomfortable I was making Elric feel.

He turned his reddened face away and shook his head. "Really, Karah, you do need to learn a little modesty. And didn't you listen to anything we were taught? I have heard that fairy tale since I was five, and that is just what it is—a fairy tale. You can't really expect us to believe that Karah is a protector from the gods—gods who probably never existed. Even if there had been, how could they have just left us to the mercy of that monster? Why didn't they teach us to protect ourselves? If you ask me, they were nothing but selfish children playing with power. Prophecies are nothing but fools' errands. No one actually believes in those stupid things." Elric was no longer sitting. He had walked over to the only front window and was watching the sunset.

His sudden burst of anger surprised me. I didn't know he felt that passionately about our faith.

Fitch came over to me and retrieved the prophecy scroll. He placed the tube carefully into his robes and then reached his hand out and placed it gently on my forehead. A warm tingly feeling ran through my body, and a strange blue glow covered his hand and spread out over my face, causing me to shut my eyes, and then it was gone. When Fitch removed his hand, he led me over to a large bucket that I assumed he had used to clean up rainwater from last night's storm. He gestured toward it and I hesitantly peered into the water.

At first I didn't see anything, but as my eyes adjusted I began to see my reflection—and what I saw made my breath catch in my throat. Covering almost the whole of my face was the most beautiful marking I had ever seen. It was the sun and moon combined into one, surrounded by beams of light. The individual beams sprouted from the central image in the middle of my forehead and snaked around my face, but it was not overbearing. It looked like it belonged there, as if it had always been there.

"Where did that come from? How did you do that?" Elric was back by my side, his warm hands on either side of my face. The warm tingly feeling was back but I don't think it had anything to do with magic.

I quickly turned my reddened face away and stepped back a few paces. When I trusted my voice, I turned back to Fitch. "Was that magic? Was that my magic? Why is this the first time I am seeing this mark?" I pointed to my face and at the obvious marking that now covered it.

Fitch gave me a small smile. "It is in a way your magic. My power is connected to you. When we are close it is the strongest but not nearly as powerful as it was. Your power is too suppressed, so my skills and spells are limited, but I can still perform simple concealing spells. I hid the mark after I convinced the king and queen to protect you. No one could know you were in this region. That symbol Ashia herself placed upon you. No matter which body you inhabit, that mark follows you. It is your link to her."

Fitch and Elric stood there and stared at me. I hugged my arms around myself and made my way back to my seat.

So there it was. My completely unbelievable life spread out in front me. How was this possible? Did I really believe I was who Fitch said I was? I am not even human; I'm immortal, and Fitch—someone I had trusted and known my whole life—was not human either. How does one wrap her head around that? Nothing I believed about myself was real, but I felt in my heart that it was true. I was humanity's hope for the future, the key to destroying the Dark Lord. Some saviour though. I couldn't access my power or remember who I truly was.

I lowered my head and stared at the floor. "What is my true name? What was I called before everyone forgot I existed?" I barely spoke above a whisper but somehow Fitch heard me. I don't even know why I asked that question; it seemed so unimportant at the moment, but I felt I needed to know. I needed some small recognition from a life that I knew nothing about.

Fitch came around, knelt down in front of me and held my hands in his. He placed his hand on my chin and lifted my face so I could look into his eyes. I saw comfort there, and love, and pride, but I was not sure for what. "Your true name is Ililsaya, but your name does not matter, nor does the body you are currently in. You are the same loving, caring, spiritual being you have always been. Your different lives have varied so much over the years but you have not changed, your spirit has not changed, and no matter how hard the Dark Lord tries he can't take that away from you."

I stood, closed my eyes and took a deep breath. *Ililsaya.* It was a pretty name, but I felt no connection to it. Maybe Fitch was right. It didn't matter what my name was or what I happened to look like at this moment. I was still the same person, and right now, I needed to know what to do next.

I rounded on Fitch with determination. "Now that I know who I'm supposed to be, how do I fix this? There must be some way to break this spell on me. How do I find my real body?"

I started to sit back down in my chair with a hundred more questions in mind, but I noticed that Elric was back at the window. His rigid stance and intent gaze was unsettling. Fitch had noticed too, so we both joined him at the window. It was almost completely dark outside, well past the dinner hour. Gladice was going to be furious—I could just hear her now—but something wasn't right.

As my eyes adjusted to the fading light outside I could just make out the other houses starting to light lamps and usher children inside for the night. Everything looked as it should, but then it caught my eye: just over the hill, beyond the castle walls and the river, a strange orange red glow snaked its way toward us. Then I felt something deep in my soul. It was as if I was being held by a string and was being pulled toward something. It felt like a pulse; a deep steady beat reverberated in my heart.

I understood what it was now. Fitch and I locked gazes, and I knew we were thinking the same horrible thought. I knew that sensation and recognized it from another life.

It was the Dark Lord feeling my power.

It seemed he had found me once again.

CHAPTER 4

The Dark Lord

The giant warhorse snorted and pawed at the earth. Its stance was rigid and its ears pricked back and forth, listening to the sounds of the forest. I was listening too, but not with my ears. Months of searching in this cursed land had passed and it was wearing thin on my nerves. It was so cold here, not like home. The towering craggy mountains and tar pits of the Barren Wastes called out to me. I missed the poisonous air that spewed from the bellows of my lair, and most of all I missed the feel of my own skin. There was too much green here, too much life. It irritated me.

I had almost given up hope of ever finding what I sought until a week ago, during a violent storm, when my persistence paid off. Her magical scent laced the storm clouds and was leading me north, deep into the realm of Aserah, which by a wonderful coincident is the home of the kingdom of Gareth. I would greatly enjoy crushing the life out of every last one of those treacherous mortals. My black soul soared at the thought of revenge, but I had to be patient. Their time would come.

Ducking, I avoided a large tree limb from taking my human head off. The trees in this area were enormous, and I inwardly cringed at the distant sound of flowing water. It was no wonder I could not sense her before now. This land was riddled with water, which caused me great pain and interfered with my magic. Her protector had chosen well.

I tried to stretch atop my horse to find a more comfortable position, but it was useless. I wanted off this horrible beast. I would have preferred to fly but a monstrous creature darkening the skies tended to draw some attention, which for the moment was something I needed to avoid. I hadn't shown my true form to the mortals of this land for nearly 300 years, not since my forced retreat by Gareth's army and the botched demise of Ashia's consort. My race was nonexistent in this world now, our memory lost in shadows, but that too would soon change. I did not want to destroy my secrecy now, even though it was costing me my dignity to remain in this useless form.

Letting my mind drift back to that fateful day when all of my careful planning had blown up in my face still angered me, but remembering it also assured that I would never fail again.

We had been fighting for days all those years ago, and with the help of Ililsaya's elemental artefacts and her mages, the mortals were gaining ground. Ashia had armed her minion well, and she was proving to be quite a nuisance. Ililsaya's power resided in the power of creation, so she could manipulate the four elements, water, fire, earth and air, whereas mine came from death and the life energy that flowed through all mortals.

Using the powers of creation, Ililsaya created four weapons: a sword, shield, a ring and arrows, each imbued with one of the four elements, to help her mages and her human followers against me. None of the artefacts alone could kill me. Only another immortal could accomplish that, but if I were to be attacked simultaneously with all four of those weapons I could have become severely weakened, and an easy attack from Ililsaya would have been possible.

My army's lack of success was taking a toll on my soul, but then the prize herself had been brought before me on her knees. I remember looking down on her, trapped within her human form, resenting every moment she lived. She had so much power, so much promise, but she insisted on wasting it on her mortal slaves.

I wanted what beat deep within her soul, that same intoxicating power that called to me now, and I would stop at nothing to possess it.

Putting my master's plan into action, I infused my warlocks with as much dark magic as their fragile bodies could hold. Their job was to channel my power and perform the spell that would trap her, but somehow those insufferable mages got their hands on a very powerful crystal, which they used to drain my warlocks of their magic and life energies. To this day, it remains a mystery to me as to how they acquired it. Few know the art of my specific magic, and that crystal was not of their making. The mages were able to disrupt and change the spell, leaving Ililsaya a way to survive. My warlocks were destroyed, were left as useless hunks of flesh, but the activation of the crystal left the mages vulnerable as well, and I pressed an attack on them. Ililsaya was now trapped in a human body, so they received no help from her. Some of the mages did, however, manage to escape with her human host and left the rest of the battle to Gareth's army. They were able to force me to retreat, due to the loss of my warlocks and my own fatigue from giving them so much of my own power to trap Ililsaya.

I had failed. The words still seemed foreign in my mind; after all, I am the Dark Lord. Nonetheless I *had* failed, and my army was greatly depleted. Most important I lost *her*. My master, Mareth, was most displeased with that failure, and I vividly remember the punishment.

Ever since that day I have been rebuilding my army and training new warlocks right under unknowing mortal noses. I had even laid siege to the temple of Ashia in hopes of finding the crystal and the artefacts, which had nearly defeated me. The remaining mages that were left to guard the tower had next to no power, and her other disciples had been no match. I had won the tower but had found nothing—nothing that is but books, thousands of them. I remember the joy I felt as I made the mages watch my slaves destroy hundreds of them and desecrate their precious temple right before I slaughtered them all. I had succeeded in scattering the mage order to the winds and successfully stopped any new followers from being trained. A wicked smile spread across my lips as that memory flitted through my mind. Many lives had been destroyed and my soul fed deeply that night.

I marvelled at how easy it had all been. How easy it was to take control. Eiddoril was all but mine, and few obstacles now stood in my way. I was grateful that the human race is as pathetic as I knew they were. Ashia's followers were furious and despondent when she abandoned them and left no one to guide them. Most just stopped believing, and the memory of Ashia burned along with everything she believed in. Of course she had left Ililsaya, but thanks to Mareth's spell she had never existed in mortal minds. Most of the mages' recorded history of what really happened was destroyed, and my iron-fisted law of no writings of any kind assured my dominance and power over the weak-minded mortals. Generations of the stupid creatures have grown up never even knowing how to spell their own names. I would not be surprised if the humans had completely forgotten what I truly looked like and what had happened all those years ago. Even the humans I enlist in my army had no idea what I truly was or what I was capable of. In their blind need to escape the past they sealed their fates, and with no knowledge of the power they once had, they were doomed. What senseless creatures. I really couldn't wait to see them erased from this world.

The wind picked up, bringing me out of my musings, and I felt . . . something. The storm clouds far to the north carried her scent, and my soul hungered. I felt her presence now, much stronger than before. Her mage had chosen well to hide her in Aserah. The entire region was snaked with rivers and streams, all steaming from that blasted Lake of Tears. All that water shielded her existence from me, but that too was weakening.

That pathetic excuse for a mage is the last of his order, and his power is coming to an end. It has puzzled me how he'd managed to survive this long. He was no mere mortal, but he had also been Ashia's favourite, so who knew what kind of magic she helped him master? I longed to be able to drain him of his life, to feel what power lay beneath his skin, but even that once-powerful human was losing his magic. She would find no help from him.

A dark shadow covered me, and I felt a wave of pleasure. I looked into the sky and saw my most trusted companion, Reaper. Today he was in the form of a great Ristiaper, which was his favourite form when traveling. Ristiapers were massive winged birds, with wingspans up to 50 feet. They were found only along the coast of the Forever Sea and dwelled in the caves that lined the sheer cliffs banking the vast body of water. They are the colour of the mist that constantly clings to the waters and lower levels of the cliffs. They are fierce hunters with large serrated beaks useful for tearing flesh, and long, sharp talons for catching their prey.

But Reaper truly did not belong to this particular species. He was a Hautur, a shape-shifter much like myself, a creature able to transform into any living thing it comes in contact with. They are a strange breed of mortals, keeping to themselves and shunned by the rest of Eiddoril. It had not always been that way, though. They were once a strong and respected part of society, but like so many other races, they became victims to hate and mistrust when Ashia left. It was easy for me to gain their trust and soothe their battered souls. I had offered them acceptance and revenge, two very powerful emotions. They were an invaluable tool against the races of this land. I employed many Hautur in my army, but Reaper was special. He was the one who'd enabled my plan to destroy Ililsaya come together.

What a thoughtless being she had been. Ililsaya was powerful but she had too many of humanity's flaws. She was too trusting, and most of all, her capacity for love blinded her. It was so easy for Reaper to change himself into the human male she had fallen in love with and lure her away from the protective circle of her mages. Still, my plan had been foiled in the end. No matter, I was a patient being and soon my reward would be my hands around that filthy creature's neck, watching as the life drained from her eyes, her soul destroyed forever.

A scout I had sent ahead of the party returned, disrupting my thoughts. I glared at the hapless mortal and smiled inwardly at the discomfort I caused him. "Master, the city of Gareth is less than a two-hour ride from here, but they have raised their defences. They know we are here." Slither respectfully bowed his head and awaited my next command.

He was a Litui, a strange reptilian creature with a large bulbous head and insect-like eyes. Their species was not native to this part of Eiddoril. They came far from across the sea. A ship full of the creatures docked in Clorynina, intending to sell slaves. The king at the time was aghast and had no idea what to do with them, so I graciously took them off his hands—at no charge, of course.

They were average in height compared to a human being, but their arms almost dragged to the ground and their knife-like claws covered webbed feet and hands. Their skin was like armour and because of their bodies, they were good soldiers on land or in the water. They required little to sustain them and were highly intelligent. Litui made perfect weapons in a fight but the horses were scared to death of them. I had to fight to keep control of the stupid beast I was riding. Oh how I hated horses. I was looking forward to ripping this one to shreds later.

"Excellent, we will proceed as planned. I only want the girl; I am not interested in starting a war with these people yet. My army is not ready for the final assault on Gareth as intended. They may have escaped 300 years ago, but their peace will soon end."

"Yes, master." Slither trotted off and resumed his position at the front of the party.

I did not bring many troops with me, just what I needed to protect myself while in this form. I didn't want to draw unwanted attention, but it seemed that my party had been discovered anyway. Ililsaya and that wretched mage must have felt my presence. No matter; the end result will be the same. I can finally see the end to this tiresome game of cat and mouse. Every step I take I can feel her power drawing me on, teasing me with its promise of absolution. But I need to hurry and get this finished because if I can sense her presence this strongly, that can only mean that her power is starting to resurface and her little mage puppet is no longer able to hide her from me. Ililsaya was never meant to survive this long in a human body, and I had no idea what that meant for the spell. Something inside her was changing. I could feel it.

By nightfall I will have reached Gareth's outlying farmlands, and there I will have a little surprise for the peoples of this land. No one defies the Dark Lord, and no one can hide from me forever. This would all be over soon, and then I could go back to the task of opening the door between the mortal and immortal realms.

Mareth is not as patient as I, and he is eager for his return. What a glorious day it will be when he finally returns to this world. Then everywhere on this accursed continent would be home, everywhere would be death.

CHAPTER 5

Karah

We pretty much ran all the way back to the castle. Fitch insisted on coming too, so I had to stop a few times to let him catch up. Elric didn't bother to wait for us, and by the time Fitch and I reached the inner ward the alarm had been sounded, and everyone was busy preparing for the impending encounter with the Dark Lord. We hurried into the main hall of the Keep and found Anora, Edwin and Elric conferring with some of the army's commanders. A scout ran in ahead of us and reported directly to the king.

"The prince's reports are accurate, Sire. There is a small group of about fifteen headed toward us, but I did not see the Dark Lord. He does not appear to be among them, but there are Litui."

"Send a detachment to the bridge and stop their advance there. Since they did not bring a large company I don't think this is an attack, but be ready for anything. If there are Litui, chances are his Hautur are there as well, so their numbers could be deceiving."

King Edwin turned at the same time as Anora to see Fitch and I enter the front hall. Our reception was not a warm one. Edwin was furious, and the look on his face made me feel like I was the Dark Lord himself.

He stormed across the foyer, but Anora reached me first and threw her arms around me as if she was seeing me for the last time.

Edwin stared, but his anger loosened his tongue. "*You,* this is your fault. I should never have allowed you sanctuary here. You have brought the Dark Lord to our doorstep and put this entire city in jeopardy. I should throw you out and let him have you. I have kept your secret for too long and now it may have cost us our safety."

That last comment wounded me deeply. I considered King Edwin my father, and to have him cast me away as some disease was heartbreaking. Although I could understand where he was coming from; I would be angry too if the people I was sworn to protect were being threatened from within.

Anora pushed herself away from me and looked like she was about to strike at her husband, but Elric was suddenly between us.

"Father, enough! You can't possibly be blaming Karah for what's happening. She didn't ask for any of this. Do you honestly think the Dark Lord would have left us alone forever? She was only told this afternoon that she isn't human, that she is trapped in a human body with no memory of who she is. How is any of that her fault?" Elric looked at me and then back to his father. "Karah and Fitch came to you for protection, and this is how you repay them? By spouting insults and threatening to end it all by handing her over? Do you not see that that would be the end? The Dark Lord will have won, and everything you worked so hard for would be destroyed. Karah needs us, and we need her."

Elric stood between his father and me, so luckily he didn't see my face beam with hope and then redden in embarrassment. What was I thinking? Elric was not my knight in shining armour come to save me. This was my mess and I had to fix it myself.

I gently placed my hand on Elric's arm and nudged him aside so I could face his father. He was still angry, but the look of hatred was gone from his eyes. Now there was only fear and uncertainty.

"I am truly sorry I have brought my dilemma to your doorstep. I am so grateful to you and Anora for taking care of me and loving me for the last eighteen years, but you are right. I am a danger to you and this village. I have to turn myself in to the Dark Lord, and maybe he will leave you alone. You have survived for 300 years without me. I cannot see what possible difference I can make."

Elric spun me around to face him. "No, I can't believe you're giving up. What happened to the girl who used to follow me around everywhere and get us into all sorts of trouble, and who made me teach her how to use a sword? What happened to the girl who used to pretend to fight shape-shifters and Litui? You are a fighter. You have fire in your blood, so don't give up now."

Elric held me at arm's length, but I wanted nothing more than to close the gap and let him hold and protect me, but I shrugged his hands away and moved closer to Fitch.

"I'm not strong enough to be the person you want me to be. Those were just games we played when we were young and naïve. I'm a nobody who is lost and alone and will just cause pain to the ones I care about."

Fitch squeezed my hand to reassure me. "You are not alone, my lady, you have never been alone. As long as I still breathe I will be with you. But enough talk of surrender. That is not an option. You may believe there is no hope, but you are Ashia's champion and we must not give up on our quest. We must find your true body and return you to it before it's too late."

Elric turned toward the old mage. "So does this mean you have a plan? Because back at the house it sounded like you had no idea what to do." Elric had his arms crossed over his chest and was looking very sceptical.

Fitch shot him a scathing look and turned his focus on King Edwin. "Yes, I believe I do. At least I know where we need to start looking for answers. I need to get Karah to the temple of Ashia. I feel that Karah's powers are starting to resurface. I believe that because she has remained alive for so long in a human body, the spell is starting to weaken. We need to get to the temple so she can try and communicate with the lost God of Life."

Fitch paced between the King and Elric, which only made me feel more nervous. "Unfortunately, shortly after Karah was being spelled, the Dark Lord laid siege to the temple and ran the mages and others followers out. He's had control over the temple ever since, and I'm not sure how we're going to get in—if there's anything left to salvage. Who knows what the Dark Lord's minions have done to desecrate the interior? I'm afraid that this is our only option, and we must leave right away."

Fitch stopped pacing and levelled his gaze at me. "The Dark Lord knows you're here, and I'm afraid that with the spell holding you captive, acting the way that it is, I may not be able to transfer you to a new host if he succeeds in killing you again."

My little makeshift family was staring at me, waiting for me to make a decision. I felt so tired and lost; I could feel in my heart that I wanted to stop running. I needed to fight back. I looked at them all in turn, willing their faces to stay in my memory. I did not want to forget these people no matter what fate befell me. How many people throughout my lives have I forgotten? How many people had sacrificed them to protect me? I wanted to remember. I needed to remember.

"All right, let's do this. I am tired of running. I need to know who I am. I need to finish this."

"Great. When do we leave?" Elric smiled at me. It was one of those mischievous smirks, like the ones we used to give each other when we were kids.

"What? No. I can't ask you to put your life in danger. Besides, I thought prophecies were fairy tales and fools' errands?" Now it was my turn to cross my arms.

Elric ignored me. "First, I don't need your permission, 'my lady,' and second, did you really think I would just let you leave with only an old mage to protect you? What kind of prince do you think I am?"

King Edwin cleared his throat and brought our attention back to him. "You are the kind of prince who has a duty to his kingdom and his troops. You are my most skilled officer. You cannot just pick up and leave whenever your heart desires. This kingdom needs you, especially with a war possibly pending. You have no idea what it is like out there beyond the borders of Aserah. It is dangerous and cruel. There is nothing out there worth fighting for; it is our home that needs you."

Everyone stared at the king, all of us probably thinking the same thing. How could the ruler of such a grand kingdom be such a poor judge of reality? It hurt me to know he would not lift a finger to help the other people of this land if they reached out to him. It made me wonder how many had fallen because this too-proud king would not help.

I took a quick glance at Anora and was surprised to see fury in her eyes. She stood tall and rigid, staring straight at her husband.

I was thankful when Elric broke the suffocating tension. "Father, you know I'm their only option. We need to sneak out of here and past the Dark Lord undetected. A small group is the only way to do this, and I am not trusting Karah's safety to another officer. I am an adult; I do not need your permission, but I would rather go with your blessing."

The two men faced each other. Eventually Edwin sighed in defeat and turned away from our group.

Fitch took the opportunity to continue with his plans. "Then it is decided. The three of us shall leave immediately, but there is one more thing that I have forgotten to mention that you must know before we leave."

Fitch had a peculiar look on his face, like he had just bitten into a lemon and was going to be sick. "Karah and I have no doubt that the Dark Lord himself is out there with his men. The reason you do not recognize him or know if he is there is that he can change his form, much like the shape-shifters can. He is most likely in the form that we all know him, which is a human general. His true form is that of a giant winged serpent, but he has not used that form for centuries."

I noticed that he neglected to inform everyone that the Dark Lord was immortal, but I guessed it didn't really matter. If he decided to attack, Gareth was in serious trouble.

"What in the gods' name are you talking about?" Elric took a step toward Fitch, but I put a restraining hand on his chest.

"How could you forget to mention that a giant disguised snake was on my doorstep? I'd heard stories passed down from generation to generation about this creature, but I thought it was just something used to frighten children. I had no idea it was true. How do we defend against that?" King Edwin had returned and was right in Fitch's face. My old friend did not even flinch, which is something I had to give him credit for. I think I would have sooner stared down a bull.

"I'm sorry, but I was so involved with Karah that I didn't have a chance until now. The Dark Lord has not shown his true form since his defeat by Gareth's army, so it does not surprise me that very few people—if any, for that matter—know what he truly looks like, but there is some hope. His powers are greatly weakened away from his home in the Barren Wastes. He draws his power from there. In addition, natural sources of water are deadly to him, so the river that surrounds this city will be an advantage. I do not think he will show his true form, he has kept it a secret for this long and must have his reasons. All he wants right now is Karah; once she is away from here and no longer protected by water, he will follow."

King Edwin rounded up a couple more messengers and sent word to his men about what he had just learned and that the water could be utilised as a defence if necessary. He rounded back on Fitch. "Now you listen to me, old man. I do not trust you, and I know there is more that you are hiding from us. If anything happens to my son, it will be me you will be fleeing from, not the Dark Lord."

The two men stared at each other and came to a mutual understanding.

Fitch nodded once and cleared his throat. "Now, King Edwin, we need to get out of this city. Is there another way out of the castle?"

"I can help with that, Master Fitch." Anora silently glided over to the mage. "There is a secret passage through the kitchen that leads to an underground tunnel. It will lead you to the back of the castle and out to the farming fields beyond. I will make sure horses will be waiting for you."

I had forgotten Anora was even still there. She had remained very quiet throughout our conversation.

She faced me and placed a gentle hand on my shoulder. "Go and collect what you need and meet me there when you're ready. I will have Gladice prepare road provisions for you." And without even a look at her husband she turned and headed for the kitchen, leaving the four of us alone. Elric and Fitch also took their leave to prepare for our journey, which left me alone with King Edwin.

"I guess I should go change and pack, I'm not even sure what to take. I . . ." I suddenly didn't know what to say. My throat closed up, and tears formed in my eyes.

Edwin suddenly took me into his arms, and for a moment I felt safe, the way a child feels safe in her father's arms. "Please forgive me for what I said earlier. I didn't mean it. It's just that everything seems to be falling apart, and I'm the only one standing in front of the landslide. I'm very proud of what you're doing and of the woman you have become. I do not regret your coming to us, or the decision we made to raise you. I couldn't have asked for a better daughter. Please take care of each other, and no matter who you turn out to be, please come home to us and don't blame me for the decisions I've made."

Edwin gave me a final squeeze and then turned and walked away, leaving me alone. I stood there for a moment wiping at my eyes. That last part about forgiving him about his decisions had me worried, but I couldn't put my finger on it. I decided to let it go and started toward my room, with King Edwin's words lying heavy on my heart.

CHAPTER 6

I reached my little corner of the world without running into anyone, which I was grateful for. I didn't think I could handle any more goodbyes. I washed up as best as I could and quickly changed into a pair of riding leggings and a plain shirt. I found one of my tunics and threw it over my head. I packed a few other items of clothes and my leather armour in my pack and searched around for my boots. I had just sat down to put them on when there was a knock on my door.

"Come in, it's open."

Elric came in carrying a sword in a scabbard in one hand and a beautifully tooled belt in the other. He had his own sword strapped to his back along with his shield. His pack was slung over one shoulder, and he had put on his leather armour.

"I brought something for you. I was going to give it to you on your birthday but since it seems that you have a need of it now. I thought you might like it. Besides, I can't do all the fighting by myself." Elric spoke softly and looked uncomfortable. I had never seen him act this way. He was always so composed and sure of himself. It seemed I wasn't the only one who didn't know how he felt.

I had forgotten about my nineteenth birthday. It seemed so unimportant now. I didn't know what to say, so I reached for the belt first and ran it through my fingers. It was soft and supple but very strong. It had beautiful leaf-like designs throughout the leather and was braided along the edges. I strapped it around my waist and then took the sword from Elric's hand. As soon as I pulled the sword from its scabbard, a spark ran through me. I swear I could hear water slowly lapping at a shore, and then it began to grow in power until it sounded like there was a waterfall crashing in my skull. I shook my head to clear it and the feeling vanished. It was such a simple-looking short sword made of iron and sharpened to a point, but I knew there was much more hidden inside. The cross guard was made to look like crashing waves coming together in the middle where a bright topaz stone was set. The pommel was made from polished quartz and glittered as I moved it through the air. It was beautiful and felt so right and surprisingly light in my hands. The scabbard also caught my attention. The design on the outside was something I had seen before. It was the sun and the moon as one surrounded by beams of light, just like the mark that covered my face.

"But how? We only saw this mark today. Where did you get this?"

Elric nodded with a look of wonder on his face. "I know. I was just as surprised as you. When I saw that mark appear on your face earlier, I was stunned. I bought this sword a few months back when we were on a scouting trip. We had to ride through a small village, so I stopped to get supplies. There were old women selling items of clothes and leather apparel. That is where I saw the belt, sword and scabbard and thought of you. When I asked about them one of the old women said that they had been in her family for centuries. Times were tough this season and her family needed the extra coin, so she had decided to sell them. I told her I wanted to buy them for a friend, and the woman said that she felt I was meant to have them now and that whomever I gave it to would know their story. She had said that it had come to her in a dream one night during a violent storm. It didn't make any sense to me at the time. I just thought she was a crazy old woman who was trying to get rid of some old junk, but obviously, they were made for you. Do you remember them? Do you remember who made them for you?"

I shook my head. I didn't remember the scabbard or the sword, but when I touched them, I felt something familiar. The memory was there, but it was locked behind iron doors. Gods, this was frustrating. I couldn't go on like this. I felt the memories and emotions bubbling at the surface, screaming to be released. I had to do something before I went insane.

"Thank you for the gifts, Elric. They're beautiful. Let's just hope I don't have to use them much. Practicing against dummies is one thing, but actually trying to kill someone is frightening. I feel sick just thinking about it." I attached the sword to my belt and was amazed at how right it felt hanging from my hip.

"If it does come to that, I know you'll do fine. Your instincts and drive for survival will take over. You are a skilled swordswoman, and when the time comes you will know what to do." Elric paused and suddenly looked very nervous. "There's something else I need to say to you."

He placed his hands on my shoulders and looked into my eyes. "I know I was sceptical about Fitch's story and about your true nature, but I just want you to know that it doesn't matter who or what you are, I will always be there for you. I will not fail you. We will see this through to the end no matter the outcome."

I stared at him a moment not knowing what to say. Ach, why did he keep doing this to me? I felt like a little girl trying to deal with her first crush, not a being of power about to take on the Dark Lord. I turned my blushing face away and tried not to look uncomfortable. "Thank you, that truly means a lot to me, but let's get going to the kitchen. Everyone is probably waiting for us."

I let Elric lead the way out of my room for the last time. I turned to take one quick glance around and then shut the door. I couldn't keep myself from thinking that I had just shut the door on another forgotten life.

The kitchen was expectedly quiet for this time of night. There were no servants running around, and Gladice was not barking out orders. The mood was sombre and quiet when Elric and I walked in. Fitch was already there, and the only other two occupants were Anora and Gladice. As soon as I came within arm's reach, Gladice collected me up in a bear hug. After a few moments, she released me and tried to speak. I had never seen her at a loss for words. At any other time, this would have been very amusing.

"I just want you to know that even though you are terrible cook and horrible at following the rules, I will miss you and am proud of you." Gladice gave me one more hug and a hug for Elric too and then disappeared into the hallway, her loud sniffles carrying down the hall.

Next it was Anora who took both of us in turn into her arms. She grabbed us both by the hand and held her head high. "You must take care of each other now. Watch each other's backs; the world outside these borders is a very different place. You will constantly need to be vigilant, and please return home to me, my dear children. Be safe and know that I love you both very much." Anora released our hands, gave a bow to Fitch, and she too was gone.

The three of us stared at each other not knowing what to say, so I gathered the provisions Gladice had prepared for us and waited for Fitch to open the secret passageway. Elric and I helped shove aside a large storage cabinet, and I watched as Fitch pressed on one of stones on the wall and a section silently slid aside, revealing a dark passageway beyond. Fitch said a few words that I didn't understand, and a small blue orb appeared in the palm of his hand. He stepped into the tunnel with Elric close behind.

I went to follow but a spirit suddenly appeared, a look of fear in its eyes. I could barely make out the faint outline of its shape, but its eyes were bright and aware. It came in front me, blocking my way forward into the tunnel, and it seemed to be warning me not to go. But before I could say anything to my companions, it vanished, leaving a cold, empty feeling inside me. I absently reached up and rubbed at my face that now held my new birthmark.

Well, this adventure was starting out great. I decided I'd better get moving before any more bad omens appeared. I took a quick glance around the kitchen and at the life I was leaving behind. I said my silent goodbyes, hitched up my pack and stepped into darkness.

Chapter 7

The Dark Lord

Night had fallen when my minions and I came upon the bridge that led into Gareth. It appeared we were not alone. A detachment of the king's army was blocking the bridge, and I was quite sure archers would be hiding amongst the dark empty farmhouses across the river. It was quite a reception. It was good to know that my reputation had preceded me.

I called my troops to a halt a few hundred yards from Gareth's soldiers and stayed well back from arrow range and that blasted river. Reaper landed beside me and quickly changed into one of my human soldiers. The form of the Ristiaper seemed to liquefy into a black puddle of blood and then slowly the form of a man grew, forming tissue, bones and skin, and finally the end result.

I gestured toward the rabble that blocked me from my goal. "Come, let us get this over with; my patience is wearing thin."

I dismounted, and Reaper and I made our way to the main bridge that separated the farmhouses and their land. The bridge itself was a remarkable piece of artwork, and I found it hard to believe mere humans had constructed it. It was made from solid stone and was supported underneath by several stone pillars. It looked as though a lot of time and care had gone into its creation—and I couldn't wait to tear it down.

Reaper and I approached the bridge cautiously and in a non-threatening manner. I had no doubt that the soldiers would attack if provoked, but all I wanted to do at the moment was talk. Besides, they had no idea it was truly the *Dark Lord* coming to speak to them.

Reaper held his hand up in greeting and proceeded to make my demands. "Soldiers of Gareth, we speak on behalf of the Dark Lord. He wishes no confrontation this night, only that the girl from the prophecies be delivered to him. We have been tracking her for months and believe she resides in your city. We demand access to search for her and take her into custody. Such heretical behaviour is forbidden and it would be wise to let us handle her. If you surrender this girl, the Dark Lord will look favourably upon you and may consider letting you keep control of your city. If you do not comply, he promises that when his army moves north, the city of Gareth will be destroyed. Choose wisely. My lord is not one to make an offer twice."

I tensed in anticipation. Finally my revenge would be sated. Surely these human cowards would not risk their own safety for one being.

One lone soldier, who I assumed was the commanding officer, stepped forward to address us. "I too bring a message. I am Duncan, the commanding officer of my lord's men. King Edwin knows who you are and is not fooled by your attempt at mercy. The woman you speak of is no longer in this city. She has been gone for days, and her whereabouts are unknown. You are greatly outnumbered and stand no chance of winning an attack. The king wishes you to leave this area and know that we are prepared to defend this city by any means necessary."

My soul filled with fury! No, this was not possible. They had to be protecting her. I reached out with my powers and faintly felt Ililsaya's presence, but the officer was telling the truth—she was not in the city. I could feel her off to the west just behind the castle walls. She was escaping, and unless I did something fast I would lose her again.

I opened my mouth and let out a cry of fury that had no business coming from human lips, and before the soldiers' eyes I revealed my true self to the poor pathetic creatures. My body began to stretch and split, exposing black scales underneath. Bones snapped and reformed into much larger ones. My neck elongated and a fearsome reptilian head exploded from its human shell. A long spiked tail stretched out behind me while my torso grew until I was the size of a large house. Two massive wings pierced through my back and I stretched them out to their fullest.

I turned my head and gazed at the humans with death and hatred in my eyes. I opened my mouth again and let out an inhuman scream.

The humans were terrified and did everything but dive into the water to escape me. I would have enjoyed watching them flail around in terror but had a task to complete. I took to the skies, knocking men into water with the force of the updraft from my wings. At the same time, Reaper returned to the rest of the group and ordered my men to attack.

*

Karah

We emerged from the tunnel into the crisp autumn night air. I heard the river close by, quietly soothing my nerves. I was thankful to be finally out of the dark, dank confines of the hidden passageway. I sucked in a huge mouthful of air and smelled *smoke*. Something was burning. We quickly found the horses that Anora had left for us, tethered by the river's edge, and rode to the top of a small hill. We had a perfect view of the castle and the city beyond. I saw the river stretching from east to west, and then, just beyond, that the fields had been set ablaze, the fires rapidly spreading. The three of us watched as the sky was filled with deadly missiles from our archers, but they never reached their targets. The arrows caught fire in mid-air and changed their trajectory, caught in a sudden gust of wind. They landed in the middle of the fields, well away from their intended targets, and crops that were to be harvested for the winter quickly became ablaze.

I pivoted in my saddle and found Elric's eyes. "This is my fault! Their crops will be ruined more than they already are from the recent storms, and they will have nothing to last them through the winter. What do we do? We need to help them!" I started to push my horse back toward the city, but Elric grabbed the reins and yanked me back.

"Be still, and don't be foolish. The burning fields are not their only problem. Duncan and his men are under attack by . . . something. I can't tell what they are. They look like monsters."

Elric had a spyglass in his hands and quickly passed it to Fitch to take a look. The old mage sucked in a breath, and worry etched his face. "*Ngogars*. The Dark Lord must have brought shape-shifters with him. Those beasts are not found outside the Barren wastes." He looked up from the spyglass and shook his head. "Duncan's men will be hard-pressed to win this fight. The Ngogars are fearsome creatures with armoured bodies with a massive horn on the end of their snout. Large fangs almost drag on the ground, and their strong stout legs resemble small tree trunks, more than capable of supporting their massive bulk. A Ngogars' only weakness is the light. They cannot see in the brightness of the day and will become disoriented and stampede. However, because they are shape-shifters, they will simply transform into another being if their currant shape becomes compromised. There is something else too . . . no it can't be . . . it's impossible."

Fitch lowered the spyglass and the look on his face frightened me, but before I had a chance to ask him what else was wrong, Elric spoke.

"Well, we need to do something. I can't just leave my people alone; we need to go help them. There must be something you can do with your magic."

Elric had his sword drawn and was becoming increasing agitated. I felt so helpless and angry. I should be able to do something, but without proper use of my powers, I was just another useless girl trying to act brave.

Fitch furiously shook his head and attempted to grab hold of my reins. "As much as I admire both of your courage, and I do wish I could help, but what little magic I have left I need to conserve to defend Karah. There is nothing we can do. We must flee before the Dark Lord knows we have escaped."

I was so intent on listening to Fitch's words that I didn't notice that the night had suddenly become silent. We were all too busy looking at the fields ahead that we did not bother to look into the sky. Dark ominous clouds had started to roll in, and the wind had substantially picked up. Another vicious storm was coming, but there was something else. I felt terror in the sky seeking a way into my soul. I began to tremble with fear and it took all of my strength to control the terrified horse underneath me. I didn't understand what was happening, and then the Dark Lord's vicious scream tore through the night as he suddenly came into view a few hundred yards away.

I froze in terror as I gazed at the monster flying toward us.

"Move! Run toward the water and back to the castle; it's our only chance!" Elric smacked the flat of his blade against my horse's rump, which was more than enough encouragement, and it tore off down the hill toward the water and the safety of the hidden passageway.

Elric followed closely behind, but Fitch broke off from us and headed toward another smaller bridge that led across to the fields.

The Dark Lord saw what we were trying to do and increased his speed. We were not fast enough. The Dark Lord landed between safety and us, causing the horses to buck and rear in terror. I was thrown from my horse and landed close by the river's edge. Elric landed not too far from me, but I had no idea where Fitch ended up. My head throbbed and my body ached from the impact, but at least the crippling fear that had gripped me had dissipated.

Elric was holding his head in pain. "What's that noise? Can you hear that strange humming sound? It sounds like a tuning fork."

I tried to pinpoint the sound, but a vibration beside my thigh distracted me. I reached back to rub my leg and brushed against my sword. It was the cause of that vibrating and that annoying humming, but I didn't have time to contemplate what it meant because my attention was drawn to the huge, very angry lizard coming toward us.

The Dark Lord lowered its massive head to my level and looked like he was smiling, if a giant monster is capable of such things.

Everything at that point happened very fast. The Dark Lord sucked in his breath and let forth a stream of some form of liquid straight toward Elric and me, but it didn't hit us. Elric had jumped in front of me and slammed his shield into the ground, creating a barricade for us to hide behind. It shouldn't have worked, and I was furious at the prince for recklessly putting his life in danger, but the strangest thing happened. Elric's shield expanded and became solid stone, at the same time causing the ground to shake, and a large fissure started to spread toward the Dark Lord. It forced him to jump out of the way, and his spray splashed harmlessly around us, hissing and popping against the hard stone of the shield.

I stared at Elric in disbelief. "Well that was interesting. Any more tricks up your sleeve?"

Elric shook his head and stared at his shield in wonder, which had returned to normal. "No, but we'd better think of something—he's coming back for another attack, and I don't think we'll be so lucky this time!"

Elric pulled me to my feet and we prepared to make another run for the hidden passage. But then, out of nowhere, a brilliant light illuminated the sky, piercing through the dark gathering storm clouds, turning night into day. A tremendous thunderclap rocked the skies and they opened up, drenching everything in sight. I watched the river start to swell and rush faster by us.

Then a huge wave that reached as far as I could see rose from the water and slammed into the side of the Dark Lord, sending him sideways across the increasingly muddy ground. The Dark Lord roared in frustration and pain as he lost his footing and crashed down on his side.

I stole a quick glance across the bridge and saw that the rain was putting out the fire, but Duncan and his men were still under attack. The shape-shifters had done what Fitch said they would. The bright light had blinded them, and they were now in mid-change, transforming into something else. Duncan pressed his attack before they could fully change into something even more dangerous.

The unnatural bright light was starting to fade, but it was being replaced with constant brilliant flashes of lightning. Flash after flash slammed into my senses, and I became increasingly aware of every sensation around me. My head pounded in time with the thunder and my skin felt like it was on fire even though I was soaked through. The symbol that dominated my face was glowing a brilliant blue almost as brightly as the lightning. I could see it reflected in Elric's astonished eyes.

Uncontrollably I raised my arms, and bolts of lightning crashed down, creating a circle around me, forcing Elric to jump away from me. I felt charged and powerful, but it was also frightening.

"Karah! Watch out!" Elric's urgent voice cut through my haze like a blade and he dived in front of me, right into the path of the Dark Lord. The monster batted him out of the way as if he was an insect, and he collapsed in an unmoving heap.

Something inside me snapped. The Dark Lord came within striking distance of me, lowering his massive head to look into my eyes. I felt him trying to invade my mind, trying to reach my soul. He had triumphed, and it was written all over him, but still he did not move in for the kill. He was tormenting me, making me suffer in fear, but I refused to move.

I was shaking all over, and all around me the storm raged on. Hatred like I had never known filled me and I directed all of it at the creature who had tried repeatedly to ruin my life. I drew my sword and noticed that it too had transformed into something more. The blade looked transparent, and the fading light reflected on its surface. It rippled when I moved it and it looked like I was holding a piece of the ocean in my hands.

When the Dark Lord saw the sword, his black eyes bulged in surprise, and he paused.

That was the break I needed and I used it to my advantage. I dived forward and to the side in a tight roll, springing up underneath his extended left wing. Without pausing, I struck up at the exposed membrane with my sword. The blade may have looked like it was made of water, but it was stronger than any material I had ever seen. It sliced through the thin membrane that covered his wing almost down to the tip, as if it was butter, splitting his dark wing almost in two. Dark thick blood sprayed everywhere, and the Dark Lord reeled back in pain and struck out with his tail, sending me flying through the air again. I landed hard, and the wind was knocked from me.

All the power I had been holding inside me was released into the night sky. Several more bolts of lightning struck the ground, trying to hit its target, but the Dark Lord was already retreating. My head was swimming; I could feel myself losing consciousness.

Arrows suddenly flew through the air from atop the turrets and castle walls, pelting the Dark Lord. The king must have sent archers to protect us. The Dark Lord bellowed in rage one last time and then changed back into his human form, clutching his shredded left arm to his side.

I saw through blurry eyes a huge bird fly down and carry the Dark Lord away in his claws, cursing my name until he was out of sight.

Then everything was quiet. The storm passed, and I let the darkness take me. Everything went black, and then I dreamed.

CHAPTER 8

The same familiar forest surrounded me and calmed my racing heart. I was not running for my life this time, but I felt an urgency in my soul that I couldn't explain. It was a strange feeling to know that I was in another part of my past and not just a dream. I decided not to fight the vision and see where it took me; maybe I would find a clue to unlocking my repressed memories.

A well-travelled footpath appeared along the ground, beckoning me toward the creek. I could hear it in the distance, gently calling me forward and setting my fears at ease. By now I had realized that I definitely had some kind of magical connection to the water. It seemed a part of me, just like this forest and even the ground that I walked on. I listened to birds, other small animals go about their business and felt the wind gently caress my bare arms. I looked down at them and realized I was still in my current human host body. I wondered what I really looked like and hoped I was not a monster like the Dark Lord. Even though Fitch was immortal too he did not posess the ability to transform into something monstrous, and I hoped I didn't either. It was something I needed to remember to ask about when I was conscious. Something about the Dark Lord's true form bothered me though, while some part of my mind tried desperately to fit the pieces together, but every time I reached for one, it disappeared. The Dark Lord's form was so familiar to me, but I had no idea why.

Pulling my attention away from my body, I began to travel along the path again. As I got closer to my unknown destination, I spotted a figure by the water's edge. His back was away from me so I couldn't tell what he looked like. I tensed and wondered fearfully if this was a trap by the Dark Lord, but something inside told me I knew this person. Knew him and loved him very deeply. I swallowed my fear and continued toward my rendezvous. The distance closed, and I noticed the way he moved and held himself. He felt so familiar, but it couldn't be anyone I knew; this had to have been part of my past.

The man must have heard me coming because he suddenly turned to face me, and my heart jumped into my throat. I was looking at Elric. I knew it couldn't possibly be him, but he looked almost identical. He had the same dark hair and beautiful grey eyes, which were looking quizzically at me. His body structure was the same except for maybe a couple of inches, and when he smiled, he had the same dimple in his left cheek. He was dressed differently though. The style of armour he wore was not familiar to me, but the family crest stamped on the front was, and so was the shield he wore on his back. It belonged to the royal family of Gareth.

I ran toward him and he caught me in his arms. He kissed me deeply and I didn't want to pull away. I felt so safe and loved, but he gently pushed me back until I was at arm's length. He looked down into my eyes and smiled, but this time it was not friendly. All of a sudden, I could sense great evil. I pushed him forcibly away and turned to flee, but two other figures appeared out of nowhere, blocking my escape. I knew from my memories that they were warlocks, and I was glad they no longer existed. The pair knocked me to the ground and then clamped iron shackles around my wrists. Calling to my power, I raised my hands to defend myself but nothing happened, and the man who had betrayed me laughed. Whatever they had placed around my wrists was blocking my magic. The two warlocks hauled me back to my feet and brought me to my betrayer, forcing me to look into the eyes of the man I loved, but the eyes I had known were gone.

I watched in horror as his body started to ripple and change. He looked like a living pool of blood thrashing around like a fish caught on a hook. The creature settled on the form of a Dark Lord soldier and backhanded me across the face, making me see stars. I fell to my side, but I was quickly brought back up to face my adversary.

"What a stupid little creature you are. Ashia was truly a fool to place her trust in you. You have sealed this world's fate by your silly human tendencies. My lord will rule, and all that you love and hold dear will perish. This war is at an end—along with your pathetic existence."

The shape-shifter turned his back on me and proceeded to lead us out of the forest. I struggled to get free from my captors but it was futile. I turned my gaze to the ground in despair and noticed something strange discarded among the foliage along the path. Getting closer, I realized it was a pair of boots, and those boots were attached to a body, a dead body. The shifter turned his gaze back toward me and realized what I was staring at. A wide evil grin spread across his face as he called our procession to a halt.

"Forgive me, my lady, where are my manners? I should have at least let you say goodbye to your lover. He put up a brave fight, but like you, his foolish human emotions got the better of him. The world will be a much better place without the son of King Gareth and his useless concubine."

The son of Gareth. No wonder he looked so much like Elric. I dragged myself over to the lifeless body of the man I had loved and stared into his dead eyes. This was my fault. He was dead because of me. I sobbed, and as I looked at my lover's dead body, it began to change. He was no longer the prince of Gareth from long ago; he was Elric, covered in blood and gore. I started to scream. It was too much. The shifter'd had enough and punched me in the face. I collapsed, and as the darkness started to claim me again I was haunted by the shifter's evil laugh and Elric's dead, accusing eyes.

*

Waking with a start, I bolted upright, which was a big mistake. My head felt like it had been trampled by a horse, and my body felt no better. My cry of pain and sudden wakefulness immediately brought Elric to my side. I tried to shy away from his touch but he gently laid me back down on my makeshift pillow and took a look at my current condition.

"Nice to see you could join us. You know, when I agreed to come with you on this journey, I didn't know I would have to carry you the whole way." He smiled at me, the way he always did to make me feel better, and my gut twisted. All I could see was his body dead in the bushes somewhere because of me. I couldn't let that happen.

His smile faded when he saw the look of pain on my face. "Joking aside, how are you feeling? You have been out for the better part of the day. I was starting to get worried."

Elric reached down and brushed my hair out of my eyes. His fingers lingered on my cheek as he traced the lines of my symbol, and in his eyes I saw safety and belonging, but then I remembered my dream and recoiled from his touch. It broke my heart to see the look of hurt and confusion on his face, but it was better than the alternative. I tried to quickly change the direction of the moment and make Elric think about something else.

"What exactly happened last night? I don't remember much after the Dark Lord sent you flying. Are you all right? Where is Fitch, and what happened to Duncan and his men?"

Elric sat back a bit and picked up a nearby stick. He looked away from me and started to scratch mindlessly at the dirt in front of him. "I have a nasty gash on my arm but I'll survive. I came to just in time to see you slice open that bastard and then go flying through the air yourself. My father had archers on the castles walls, so the Dark Lord left pretty quickly after that. You and Fitch left him badly injured, and he didn't have much choice. I don't think he expected a fight, from you or our people, but he will not be so foolish as to make that mistake again. Once I was sure the snake had gone I checked to make sure you were breathing and then hunted around for your mage."

Elric paused and glanced over at me, but I quickly pretended to have a headache. I placed one hand over my eyes and with the other rubbed my temple. I don't think the ruse worked though because I heard him sigh and continue his recap in a much more guarded tone.

"I found Fitch collapsed close to the river's edge. Calling up the rage of the river and turning night to day took quite a toll on him, but thanks to his efforts, most of the farming fields were saved, and it gave Duncan and his men the advantage they needed to defend themselves. Our people will be hard-pressed this winter, but they will survive. I was able to rouse him after a few moments, but he refused to stay where we were. He insisted we leave immediately so he made sure you would be all right to travel. Then we found our horses."

Elric again paused and looked at me, but I quickly turned my gaze back up to the sky. I flinched inwardly at the angry tone he took in his voice.

"I'm afraid that most of what happened last night I am at a loss to explain; I know nothing of magic and leave that to Fitch, but good luck getting anything out of him. He hasn't spoken two words since we fled Gareth. I think there's something wrong, but I'll leave that to you to discover."

Elric stood and looked down at me. The caring, concerned look was replaced with a guarded one. "Now, if there's nothing else I can do for you, I need to tend to the horses. I'm sure Fitch will want to get underway as soon as possible once he knows you're awake. I'll go find him."

Elric's abrupt dismissal hurt, but I deserved no less. What was I going to do? I had already lost my body and now I was in danger of losing my heart and soul. I regrouped my thoughts. I needed to speak to Fitch.

I sat up, much more slowly this time. I looked around and discovered we were in a small clearing in the woods. I had never ventured outside Gareth so I had no idea where I was. The trees were beautiful. They were so tall, like giant sentinels watching over me. They stretched high into the sky and their top branches formed a canopy to keep us hidden. Birds flitted and small animals scurried from branch to branch, adding their own voices to the busy forest clearing.

The earth beneath me was soft and as I dug my fingers in to push myself up, I felt a slight humming in the ground. I quickly pulled my hand back and felt the skin on my face start to burn. It was not uncomfortable, just different. An idea formed in my mind. I reached for my sword, which was close by, and drew it from its scabbard. It was not the piece of the sea that I had seen earlier but its smooth, flawless blade gave me the perfect surface to see my reflection. My facial marking, which had been a light golden colour was now a brilliant blue. Against my better judgement I hesitantly placed my hands back on ground and felt the vibration again. It felt as if it had its own pulse and was beating in time with my own. I closed my eyes and concentrated, and all of a sudden, everything around me seemed to come alive. A gentle wind picked up and started to blow my hair back. I felt it swirling around me, caressing me, trying to hold me the way a human would. The life in the soil called to my soul. I felt the grass roots that had gone dormant with the approach of autumn and the flower seedlings awaiting spring release. I reached out to them and caressed them, nurturing them back into the world.

My surroundings quickly disappeared, and I felt the power around me. There was an energy that crackled in the air, begging me to use it. I thought I could hear someone shouting and the high-pitched whinny of a horse, but none of it mattered right now. I was completely engulfed in the rapture of power pouring into my body.

I sensed everything in the ground beneath me, including the insects, worms, tiny microorganisms, and even the rock far below. It all had a life of its own, calling out to me to be used and needed.

The heat made me feel uncomfortable, like I was sitting beside an open fire, and it caused me to feel dizzy and nauseous. Then I heard my name being called from a great distance. I heard fear and awe in the voice. Insistent and agitated shouting tried to penetrate the fog I found myself drowning in. I heard Fitch screaming at someone to *release me,* and I tried to answer but couldn't find my voice. The power was so strong, and it was pushing at me from all directions, trying to find a way inside my body.

I began to tremble uncontrollably, and I felt like I was being shaken apart. The voice returned, and this time it was strong enough to break through my walls. My eyes flew open and I took in the scene around me. Surrounding my body where I had been sitting was fresh grass and field flowers. A sapling had even started to grow. The wind was whipping my hair around my face and I felt like I was on fire. Everywhere around me was chaos, and from the corners of my vision I could see spirits everywhere, crowding and pressing toward me. I had never seen this many before and I shrank back in fear.

Fitch knelt in front of me, fighting the gusting winds. He grabbed my hands. His grip was strong and his very presence commanded attention. He looked into my eyes with his own now strangely golden ones and I saw mine reflected in his. They were pools of water thrashing about in my sockets.

"Fitch, help me, please. What's happening? I can't control it. It hurts so much." A small whimper escaped my lips as I franticly pointed around me. "They're everywhere, can't you see them? They want something from me. Make them go away." I was becoming hysterical.

Fitch dragged my attention back to him and yelled to be heard over the wind. "It's your magic. It's too strong for your human body. You must let go or *they* will tear you apart." Fitch squeezed my hands until they hurt and continued to look into my eyes.

I felt his strength and power. He was trying to draw it out of me and I let him. I released the magic and let it flow into Fitch like an open levy. I saw him stagger at the sheer force that knocked into him, but he didn't let go. The wind died and my body started to cool. We were both panting, trying to stay upright. The feeling of power was gone, leaving me feeling empty and cold. I collapsed in a heap into Fitch's lap.

CHAPTER 9

Night had fallen again when I began to stir. If I kept this up, I was going to sleep through this whole journey. I could hear Fitch and Elric across a crackling campfire having quite a heated discussion. I lay there for minute listening.

"I demand you tell me what's going on, old man. Karah looked like a demon earlier. I need to know what's happening or I can't protect her. I don't know what I'd do if anything happened to her, but seeing her like *that* scared me. She's not the girl I once knew." Elric sounded so lost. I didn't know if I could take much more of this.

"No, she's not the same girl, and I'm sorry for what you're going through. When she awakens I will attempt to explain what is happening to her, although I am afraid you will not like the answer." Fitch sounded annoyed, but I couldn't be sure if it was because of me or his strange dislike of Elric.

I wanted to go back to sleep and pretend that none of this had happened, but the vision of myself earlier that day came into my head and I quickly decided against it. I cleared my throat and gently sat up to look across the campfire at my companions.

Fitch reacted first, although I noticed that Elric wanted badly to say something, but he remained quiet. I hated what I was doing to him but I had no choice.

"Karah, how are you feeling? Are you able to eat? We prepared some rabbit stew while you were unconscious." Fitch stood up, brought over a steaming bowl of stew and sat down next to me. I took in the delicious aroma and immediately my stomach started to clamp. I hadn't realized I was so hungry, but I really couldn't remember the last time I had eaten anything.

I took the bowl and began spooning large amounts of stew into my mouth. It tasted so good. I reached for the offered bread and emptied the rest of bowl in happy gulps. When I stopped to breathe, I looked up from my bowl at Fitch and Elric's stifled laughter. I smiled sheepishly. "Sorry, I didn't realize I was so hungry. Excellent stew, by the way, my compliments to the chef."

I blushingly handed my bowl back over to Fitch and took a drink of water from my water skin.

Fitch took my bowl, placed it by the fire and focused his attention back to me. "Well, I suppose that answers the question of how you're feeling. If you're well enough to eat like that, then it's time we got on with things. We have lost enough time already and our journey has barely begun. Now, I know you have questions, so ask away and I'll do my best to answer."

I looked at Fitch and could tell he was ill at ease. He looked like he had aged since our encounter with the Dark Lord. His hair looked greyer and his frame thinner. Maybe it was just my imagination.

Fitch sat back and looked expectantly at me. I didn't know where to start, so I just started spitting them all out. "What happened to me today? Why did my magic act like that? I thought I couldn't access my powers. And where did my sword and Elric's shield come from? Is that my magic also? And—" I sucked in a breath to blurt out more but Elric was laughing at me again and Fitch was staring at me open mouthed.

Elric came closer to me carrying my sword and his shield in his hands. He placed them between us and sat down, giving us both some space. "Perhaps we should deal with one thing at a time. I also would like to know the story behind our weapons. Let's start there, shall we?" I could tell he was uncomfortable and not at all happy with my current attitude toward him.

If Fitch noticed what was going on between us he made no inclinations. He instead reached out for my sword, held it carefully and ran his fingers across the symbol tooled on the scabbard. For a moment, he looked very sad, but he masked it quickly and handed the sword back to me.

"Yes, well, fortunately, that is the easy part of the explanations. I must say I was quite surprised to see both of you had in your possession two of the elemental weapons that had been forged centuries ago. *You*"—he nodded at me—"had them made for King Gareth and his army in the hopes that they would aid them in the fight against the Dark Lord. The sword you carry is embedded with the element of water, and Elric's shield has the power of the earth. There was also a ring with the power of fire and a set of arrows with the might of wind. I'm not quite certain of their capabilities, but they are very powerful. After the war, the artefacts disappeared and I never knew what became of them."

Elric shifted uneasily beside me. "Why do you speak of the elements with such reverence? What do they have to do with magic?"

Fitch lowered his gaze and swore under his breath. He abruptly rose and walked away from us, seemingly trying to control his anger. He turned on us and his words were filled with passion. "I speak of them with reverence because that is what they deserve from me and all the mortals who inhabit this world. The elements are your *true* gods and the source of everything you see around you."

Elric and I stared in stunned silence, which prompted Fitch to start pacing around our campsite. "There is a lot about magic and this world you both do not understand, so I will try to simplify it as best I can."

Fitch paced to the other side of the fire, causing his shadow to grow. It almost looked like it didn't belong to him, that it was part of some other creature. I stared, mesmerized, trying to figure out why it looked so familiar, but he crossed back over to our side and started speaking again, shattering the illusion.

"First, our world's magic comes from the four elements of nature and creation: fire, water, earth and air. They have a life of their own and are living entities that shape our very existence."

"Yes, okay, so where are they? Why is it that no one has ever seen them or spoke of them before?" I was confused and really not in the mood for these word games.

Fitch, on the other hand, looked annoyed that I had interrupted. "The elements have been a presence since the birth of this world, but most mortals just did not know how to listen to them. The elements do not communicate as we do, cannot form words or any form of speech, but they can understand us. They speak to us through images and feelings."

He moved closer to the fire and crouched in front of it. "For example, if you were to stare long enough into this fire, and if the element chose to make itself known, you would be able to communicate with that element." He rose again after a few moments, looking frustrated, and resumed his pacing. "There are also certain races that were chosen to be certain elements' avatars, but most as far as I know have gone into hiding or were completely wiped out during the wars that plagued these lands.

"Humans have always had the most difficulty communicating with the elements. They did not feel the need to show themselves because I suppose they felt that humans were not ready. Human mages were very rare, but the ones who did exist were very powerful." Fitch paused and took a drink from his water skin. A strange, unreadable mask came over his features, just like back at the house when he was telling me about my past. It made me feel very uneasy.

He continued. "What I know of the elements came from Ashia's teachings. She was very wise, and as soon as she arrived here she felt the elements' presence. She had no problems learning and using the elemental energy around her and teaching the skill to others. Are you both with me so far?"

Elric spoke for both of us. "I believe so. What you're saying is that our world was created by these four beings of power. Combined together they essentially make up life as we know it; they are the energy that flows through us and around us each day. Without them, we would have no fire for heat or cooking, no water for drinking and cleaning, and so on. We were not aware of them because we were ignorant and selfish and took everything for granted, traits that unfortunately have not left us. Why would the elements want to speak to us? We had not shown any interest, except in ourselves."

Fitch looked very proud of Elric at that moment. It was the first positive emotion I had seen him give the prince. "Very well said, my young prince, you would have made an excellent mage."

I gave Elric a small smile that did wonders for his attitude.

Fitch, on the other hand, seemed to become more irritated. He chose that moment to sit cross-legged directly in front of us, and his demeanour demanded my full attention. "Now, unfortunately for Mareth, the elements rejected him. They felt the evil in him and refused him access to their powers. This made Mareth furious; especially since, Ashia, seemed to have no trouble at all in gaining abilities that are more powerful with their aide. Mareth raged with fury and lashed out at the mortals, trying to force the elements to bend to his will, but it was to no avail. The elements ignored him and hoped the problem would go away on its own."

Fitch lowered his gaze to stare at his now-shaking hands. His voice lowered and I could tell he was holding back a lot of emotion. "However, those acts of ignorance toward emotions cost the elements dearly, because during Mareth's tirade against them he discovered another ancient powerful being that he could manipulate: *death*."

The cap on my silence broke. "Hold on a second. Are you trying to tell me that death is a being? I thought death was just that—death, the end." I was having a hard time wrapping my brain around this.

Fitch quickly raised his head, and I was surprised at the annoyance I saw there. "You of all people should realize that death is not a simple black and white situation. Look at how many times you have died and returned. And how do you explain the spirits that you see? Where did you think they came from."

I ignored the nasty tone in Fitch's voice and instead remembered those spirits crowding me today. I looked around the campsite expecting to see them, but they had disappeared. I shivered at that memory and forced it from my mind. Elric stared at me. I had never told him about my ability to see spirits; only Fitch and Anora knew.

He looked hurt again, and at this rate, I was going to lose him as a friend.

Fitch tried to look patient and started to explain more of what *death* was. "Being immortal and coming from another plain of existence allowed Ashia and Mareth to travel from one state to another. There are in fact four different planes of reality and magic: the elemental, mortal and immortal, and death's domain, called the *Duggati*. It is in this last realm that Mareth encountered his solution."

I leaned forward, hanging off Fitch's every word.

"Many people and creatures believe that when they die, that is the end, but it is just the beginning. When you die your spirit or life source returns back to the elements from where it came, and from there it can be returned back into the world to create something new." He waved his arms around our campsite, encompassing the area. "They recycle energy, never wasting and always using that energy to benefit the world around us. *Death* is the doorway from the mortal world to the elemental realm. It is the space where our energy is most vulnerable. It is the power of death that sends our life energy back home to the elements to be reused for something else. Death's job is to separate the good and the evil in the life energy."

Elric, being the well-mannered student between the two of us, gently cleared his throat before he asked his question. Fitch actually gave him an approving glance instead of the nasty glare he'd given me. Suck up.

"How is that determined, exactly? How does death know if particular life energy is good or evil? Many people have both in their hearts. How does it decide if it is one or the other, and why does our energy need to be recycled? Would it not be fair to let those spirits rest in eternity? Why can the elements not just make new life energy? They must have in the beginning, otherwise, where did it all come from?"

Fitch shook his head. "That, my dear boy, is a mystery even to me, and really, I have never really given it much thought. You do bring up a valid question though, one I'm not equipped to answer. I can tell you that energy cannot die or be destroyed, and when the elements created a life energy it was purely good and innocent. It is the actions of that individual that will determine what happens to it in Duggati. Originally the evil energy stayed in Duggati contained by death until it was able to cleanse it, and the good was sent back to the elements for rebirth, but Mareth found a way to manipulate death and forever change the system."

A dark look passed over Fitch, and a cold feeling in the pit of my stomach made me shiver. Fitch's words were shrouded in anger. "Death recognized Mareth as an immortal and accepted his presence in his realm. In doing so it allowed Mareth access to all the energy around him. He learned to absorb the life energy for his evil magic and for revenge against the elements he chose to use his new power to hurt their beloved creations. He captured some of the life energy and sent it back out into the mortal realm without a purpose, dooming it to roam the earth without a host—hence the creation of walking spirits."

That comment sparked my interest. At least now I knew where they came from and why they always seemed so sad and angry. I wondered if there was a way I could help them once I was back in my original body. Maybe that was what they wanted from me. I would have to remember to ask about it later.

I turned my focus back to Fitch and continued listening.

"Death discovered too late what Mareth was doing. Death was outraged; never before had it encountered betrayal or anger. It then did something it never thought necessary. Death closed all access into Duggati by any other immortal except himself. It knew that his realm would now become its prison, but death had no choice. He had to protect the life energy that came into his care.

"But Mareth had already learned what he needed and was now able to directly drain life energy from the living host in the mortal realm. Mareth kept most of the energy for his own magic, but sometimes there was a part that remained, which was then doomed to a life of no end or purpose."

This time when I asked my question I reached out and gently touched Fitch's hand. The cold look left his eyes and he nodded at me. "Why can't the spirits cross over? Why are they punished after being through so much?"

Fitch closed his eyes, and I regretted asking the question. His response was filled with sadness. "The spirits, good or evil, that had been drained by Mareth were tainted by his mark, barring them access into Duggati. Death would not allow the damaged souls through. That is why we have sprits that walk among us, and this never happened before Mareth's arrival." Fitch sighed and looked into the sky.

I wonder who he had lost who was now doomed to roam the world with no purpose. I suddenly felt very sad and wished I could sit closer to Elric.

Fitch came back from his memories and resumed. "When Mareth asked the Dark Lord to assume his position while he was gone, he was able to teach him the same abilities among others. The Dark Lord's powers come from death also. He is able to directly drain the life force from its victims, sustaining his life and fuelling his powers just by touching them."

"What are his powers? He tried to cover us with what looked like some form of explosive acid during his attack. What else is he capable of?" Elric, being a solider first and prince second needed to know exactly what we were dealing with, but I was afraid that no amount of research would prepare us in a fight against the Dark Lord. We got lucky the first time, and I doubted it would happen again.

"When he is in his original form he can do that, yes. He can also project fear and other emotions directly into mortal minds. He can completely incapacitate an individual just by making him or her too scared or hopeless to save himself or herself. His sheer size and lethal intent in his original form is a powerful weapon in itself. There are few things that can harm him when in that form."

Something did not make sense to me—well, actually, a lot did not make sense to me—but this was the most important, I think. "If the elements denied Mareth and the Dark Lord access to their powers, why are they still able to use some of their power in their magic? I saw fire appear out of nowhere, so how is that possible?"

Fitch remained silent for a moment, and the look of sadness deepened in his eyes.

"That is a very observant point. I'm glad you're paying attention, although I wish I did not have to speak of the answer." Fitch rubbed at his face, took a drink from his water skin and inhaled deeply.

I was suddenly afraid of the answer to the question I had asked. It was obviously something he did not want to talk about.

"While Ashia was able to teach mortals the ways of elemental magic, thus creating mages, the Dark Lord was able to create something else. You asked why the Dark Lord possessed the power of fire when by all accounts he should not be able to use any of the elemental energy; well, it was not his magic that you saw, it was a *mage*. During one of the Dark Lord's first attacks on you and the good peoples of this world, he captured some of our mages. He wanted to see, when he drained them of their life force, whether he could gain access to the elemental powers. He failed, but in his process he discovered he could drain just enough life sources from a human mage to keep him alive, but he would become a mindless obedient slave, an empty vessel, devoid of emotion and free thinking."

Contempt laced his words. "I am assuming the elements were not capable of telling the difference between these damaged mages and our own, so the corrupted mages retained their magical connection with the elements but they were now also infused with the Dark Lord's power and completely under his control." Fitch turned bright golden eyes up to me, and I fought the urge to look away from the anger I saw there. "That is how the warlocks were born. That is the source of the elemental powers that you saw last night. The Dark Lord must have discovered rogue mages in hiding and turned them into his warlocks. A human being able to use the elements for magic is very rare in these times, and I foolishly believed none still existed. The Dark Lord made it known that any human found displaying magic would be captured. That is why mages and warlocks were considered an extinct breed. People were too afraid to nurture their abilities, especially with no one to teach or guide them."

Fitch's eyes returned to normal and he regained control over his emotions. "I thought we had set all the mages free when we drained them of their powers and remaining life source all those years ago, but if the Dark Lord has one in his possession, chances are good that he has more, which means there are humans out there capable of magic, and we need to help them."

"How did you drain the warlocks of power? I thought only the Dark Lord possessed that ability."

Fitch gave me a strange look, and I knew he was hiding something. "The Dark Lord is the only one who can do it naturally, but it takes a lot of effort and is very time-consuming. When Ashia found out what Mareth had learned and then passed on to the Dark Lord, she asked the elements for assistance. I have been told that that they convinced death to help her. It created a crystal that was able to drain and hold life essence. We used it to drain the warlocks, and later we released them. It meant that they were now trapped on the mortal plane, unable to return to the elements, but at least they were no longer under the Dark Lord's control."

Fitch fished around in the front pocket of his travelling cloak and produced a small crystal. It was beautiful. It reflected the firelight and seemed to glow with an inner light. "This is the crystal we used. It is also the means I use to transfer your life spirit from one host to the next. Without it, you would have been lost a long time ago."

Fitch placed it back into his pocket and stared off into the fire. I knew how he felt. It was not easy watching people you care about suffer because you were unable to do enough to help.

"So now that we know all of this, how do we use it to protect Karah? How do we keep her from doing whatever it is she did today?" Elric and I stared at each other and I could see the uncertainty in his eyes.

My little discovery stroll down elemental lane today still had my body reeling. The knowledge of what I had caused that day was sobering. I felt awful but at the same time, I was in wonder. What else was I capable of?

Fitch smiled a little as he looked at me. "Karah, when Ashia asked you to help her while she was gone, she chose well. You are a very powerful being. We all have the ability to control the elements, but only one at a time, for the sheer power is too much for us all at once, but you are different. You are a living conduit for all the elemental powers, so you are able to manipulate all of them at the same time. You are the only being I know of who is capable of doing that; not even Ashia was that strong. For this reason, you were targeted as major threat to the Dark Lord and his master's plan. Unfortunately in your current human form you cannot withstand their full power." Fitch shook his head. "What you did today . . . I don't know how to tell you to control it. You're not even supposed to able to access the powers of the elements. The only theory I have is that the constraints on the Dark Lord's spell are weakening for some reason, thus allowing the elements to sense your presence. Every time you use your power in this form, you risk the onslaught of the four elements. It will tear you apart unless you discover a way to control it."

Elric stiffened and quickly became alarmed. "But you helped her today. I saw you. Why can't you simply do whatever it is you did again?"

Elric moved closer to me in a protective manner. He moved close enough that only our shoulders were touching, but it was enough to calm me and make me feel safe. I knew I should have pushed him away, but I needed him now more than ever, and I wasn't sure if I was strong enough to resist that need.

I settled my gaze on Fitch. "Elric has a point. I felt you draw the power out of me and into you."

"Yes, which is something I don't think I could do again. When I connected with you, all four powers slammed into me and nearly destroyed me. The only reason I survived is that I was Aisha's first and most powerful student, and I am more capable than most."

Fitch suddenly stood up and looked out into the night. There was something nagging at me, something I couldn't quite put my finger on. Fitch was not telling me everything; he was hiding something, that much I was certain of.

After a few moments, he turned back to us. "I am done with the lessons for tonight. I'm afraid they've taken a toll on me. Tomorrow at first light we head south, close to the coast toward the Wild Plains. The temple lies east of there in the heart of the Kanarah woods. It is a long journey so I suggest we get some sleep." Fitch said his goodnights and retired to the other side of the camp, leaving Elric and me alone.

I didn't know what to think. I just had so much information thrown into my lap that I was feeling overwhelmed. The thought of me being capable of so much power, and to be able to do all of the things I was told I could do was frightening but at the same time exhilarating.

I turned my attention back to Elric. He was staring off into the fire watching the flames dance and crackle in the pit. We sat in silence for a while, just enjoying our surroundings and each other's company, but then Elric shattered it.

"I need to ask you something, and I want you to be honest with me." Elric was very quiet and kept his gaze on the fire.

My body tensed and my heart sank in anticipation of his query.

"Are you angry with me, or did I do something wrong? Ever since you woke from our encounter with the Dark Lord, you have been different toward me. I know a lot has happened and things have changed, but I thought we felt something toward each other. Was I wrong? Please tell me and I'll try to stop feeling the way I do."

He turned toward me and looked into my eyes. He looked so vulnerable, so uncertain. He sounded very young as he spoke to me. "I know all of this has come has a surprise. Heck, it even surprised me. I had no idea I had these feelings for you, but I do and I'm not sure what to do about it."

I hung my head down so that my red locks covered my face. What could I tell him? How do you tell the person you care about most in this life that you can't care the way he wants you to because of fear? I would die if Elric were hurt protecting me, just as I knew I died inside when King Gareth's son perished trying to protect me. I couldn't even remember his name, which tore at my heart even more.

I looked up into Elric's face with tears in my eyes. He brushed them away with his gentle touch and waited for me to say something. He deserved to know the truth.

I couldn't lie to him. I drew in a steadying breath. "When I was unconscious after the Dark Lord's attack, I had another dream. It was a vision from my past. It was the day that I was captured and had my body stolen from me. A Dark Lord shifter had been the one to trap me. I had gone into the woods to meet someone, a man I had fallen in love with and he me. Our affair was not welcomed because we were so different and because he was a prince, so we met in secret.

"Somehow this shifter discovered our relationship and sabotaged it. When I got to our meeting place, it was the shifter who met me there, not the prince. It wore his skin so I had no idea until it was too late. It and some warlocks captured me and led me away in shackles, but before we left the woods, the shifter showed me the body of my dead prince. He was covered in blood. He had died because he cared for me. I . . ." I couldn't finish. All of the stress and anguish from the last few days overwhelmed me. I broke down in Elric's arms and cried for everything I had lost and couldn't remember. I cried for a long time while Elric held me and stroked my hair.

I eventually stopped and gulped in a few calming breaths. "I'm sorry; I didn't want you to see that. It's just . . . I'm so emotionally exhausted. I don't want to hurt you and am afraid that if you get too close to me that that is exactly what will happen. One prince already died because of me, I can't let it happen again."

Elric pushed me up out of his arms and turned me to face him. "Is that what you think, that you're the cause of this man's death?"

I nodded, not able to do much else.

Elric shook his head. "You didn't kill that man, the shifter did. You can't condemn yourself over something you had no control over."

I tried to protest but Elric wouldn't let me. "Listen, this man loved you. It was his choice to do so, no one else's. You can't avoid caring for someone for fear that one day something bad will happen. You will only die alone and afraid."

I just stared at him, a fire starting to burn in my chest. I couldn't keep the heat from my words. "But that's just it. I can't die. When I am reunited with my true form, I'll be immortal, a freak being of power. I won't be the person you care about now. I'll be forced to watch everyone I care about die while I continue on. I can't do it, not again."

I stood up and started to walk away. I was getting angry. Why couldn't he see this from my point of view?

Elric grabbed me by the arm and spun me around. "I understand you're scared, so am I, but we don't even know if it is possible to get you back in your body. Maybe you are going to die an old mortal woman, or maybe we are all going to die at the hands of the Dark Lord. We just don't know, but that is the gift of life. You can't go around regretting the past and fearing the future because you just end up missing out on living, which is truly the most important part." He gently pushed my hair behind my ears, "No matter what happens it is not going to change the way I feel about you. You could sprout three heads and a tail and I would still follow you to the end of the earth. Please, let's just deal with the present. We have a job to do, so let's do it together."

Elric smiled at me and gave me a quick kiss on the cheek, which melted my anger instantly. "That is for your birthday. See you in a few hours; wake me up for second watch. Fitch needs to sleep more than I do." He then walked over to his bedroll and lay down while I stared off after him with what I'm sure was a very stupid look on my face.

I guess I had first watch. It's not as if I was going to sleep anyway.

I went back to my own bedroll and sat cross-legged listening to the night. Some birthday. I only hoped I'd live to see another. Despite everything that had just happened, I felt better. At least Elric and I knew the truth about our feelings and both had a better understanding of what we were dealing with. I only hoped that we could figure out some way not to hurt each other and come out of this with our lives. I could only wish that the days to come would bring answers and that the Dark Lord remained wherever he was.

Chapter 10

The Dark Lord

A scream of pain and torment echoed through the dark damp walls of my lair. I dug my claw deeper into the chest of the pathetic mortal pinned beneath my front foot and relished in the fear and agony emanating from my victim. However, no amount of torture would sate my need for revenge. I ended the Lituis's life with a quick thrust that sent my claw through its body and into the rock beneath it. I felt the rush of life energy enter me, and after a few moments, I tossed the gore-soaked body onto a growing pile next to me.

After my encounter with Ililsaya and that damnable mage, I had been left weakened and significantly damaged. My left wing still throbbed with pain, but it was in one piece again. Memories of that night caused my anger to boil in my stomach and rise up my throat, leaving a foul bitter taste in my mouth. I shook with a rage that brought the remaining victims in the room to their knees. Turning my massive reptilian head to the ceiling I screamed my anger, causing the very walls to tremble.

My tail swung back and forth in agitation as I paced the length of my cave. Where did they get those weapons? I had ransacked Ashia's temple looking for them and had found nothing. How could they have gone unnoticed all this time?

Consumed in my destructive tirade, I didn't notice the electric charge in the air that would have given me warning. Instead, I dropped to my stomach in agony. I writhed around on the ground struggling for air and clawing at my head. Razor sharp shards of pain lanced through my mind, and just when I thought I would not see another night the pain stopped and left me quivering and panting like a newborn. I struggled to raise my head but a presence in the dark confines of my mind forced me to lower it again in reverence.

A powerful voice echoed in my mind. *"Greetings, my fanged brethren, I trust you are in good health?"* Mocking laughter filled my mind along with more pain, but I dared not breath.

"Mareth, my master, I am honoured." I bowed my head deeper to the cavern floor and waited obediently for a reply.

"My time and patience are short so I will make this quick. Let me see your progress."

I continued to show reverence with my eyes squeezed shut against the pain. What I saw before me was only an image of my master in my mind provided by our powerful blood bond, but I was still awed by the sheer power and menace emanating from my master's form. I spoke mentally to his dark visage while fighting through the steady stream of agony that his communication caused.

"Yes, my Lord." In my mind, I relived the past many years since last I communicated with Mareth. It had been nearly 100 mortal years, but time passes differently in the immortal realm. Lifetimes flit by in mere hours while time here in Eiddoril drags painfully. My anger got the better of me when I came to my most recent defeat at the Gareth castle. I felt my master bristle with anger, but no more pain followed. If I had not been afraid to breathe I would have heaved a sigh of relief. Instead, I waited patiently for my fate. I did not have to wait long before Mareth's voice drove fear into my blackened soul.

"Can you explain why you are still trying to kill Ililsaya? I would have thought after our last encounter that my wishes were clear. Do you not understand what I am saying, or are you trying to betray me?"

My heart froze in my chest as I stammered over my words. "No, Master, I would never betray you. I just thought . . . well, it had been so long since last we communicated I wasn't sure if your wishes were still the same. I wanted to eliminate her to protect your return, that is all."

My passion for killing that wretched creature consumed my every thought, and truthfully, I thought my master's reasons for keeping her alive were foolish, but I took care to keep those feelings well hidden. Apparently, it was not well enough. Mareth saw right through the lie.

"You're lying. Your hatred and jealousy for Ililsaya run deep. You did this for your own purposes and you could have jeopardized everything I have worked so hard for. I will not tolerate this kind of insubordination; perhaps I was wrong to trust you to bring me home."

Mareth's deep red eyes pierced my mind and left me nowhere to hide. The pain intensified until I felt I would break apart into a million bloody pieces.

"No, Master, you were not wrong, I will bring you home and will make myself worthy again. There will be no more mistakes."

"You are right, there will not be, and if you fail me again you will learn that the pain you felt in your mind was the least of your problems. Now, you must stop your attacks on Ililsaya. I need her alive."

My sudden outburst of rage and disbelief caused another wave of punishment from my master. The pain rocked my very bones and I fought to control the nausea I was feeling.

When my master spoke again, I made sure to keep my emotions and thoughts in check. *"Do not question my motives, slave! My time to return to your pathetic world is almost at hand and I need Ililsaya alive! I need the power that flows through her soul, or I will be stuck here for good."*

I shook my horned head in disbelief, not caring what punishment Mareth wanted to inflict. "I do not understand. It has been my sole purpose in life to end that wretched creature's life for you and now you're telling me I have to keep her safe! Forgive my questions, Master, but I didn't understand then nor do I now."

I also did not agree but would deal with that later.

"You don't need to understand. Just do as I say and all will be revealed in time. My plans are almost complete and when I return there will be nothing to stop me. Eiddoril will burn, and from the ashes, I will create a new world with me as its one true god. You must trust me; together we will rule this world and all the pathetic mortals who are left standing."

Mareth's form started to fade and I could feel his hold on my mind start to slip.

"I have very little time left, so listen carefully. Ililsaya and that puppet of a mage are nothing but predictable. He will take her to Ashia's temple in the hopes of finding answers and to no doubt try to communicate with her. Send someone there to wait for them and then bring Ililsaya back here."

"No, Master, I will go myself. I need to feel her fear clutched in my claws."

"I know, and you will after I am done with her, but I need you here to finish the preparations of our army. They must be ready."

I bowed my head in defeat. I could wait. "As you wish, my master. I'll send Reaper. He is my most trusted officer, and he fooled her before. It should not be too difficult to do so again."

"Excellent. Now I must go. These communications are taxing on my power. I will speak with you again soon with my final wishes. Do. Not. Fail me."

White-hot pain shot through my mind, and then it and my master were gone. I stood there for a moment perfectly still while I regained my control. When I again opened my eyes, they were filled with hate and determination, which I turned on my prisoner chained at the far end of my lair.

It held its head high in defiance and stared right back at me. "You should have listened to me. I warned you that Mareth would not be pleased. You are as stupid as you are blind."

I snatched the mortal into my claws, pulling on the chains that held it to the wall. Its arms pulled back at an agonizing angle, and I curled my lip with pleasure.

"It would do you well to remember your place, *mortal*. I have been easy on you over the last 100 years and I would hate to break my favourite plaything now."

I squeezed painfully one last time and dropped the limp body at my feet. I smiled a toothy wicked grin, gave a mock bow and then turned and left in search of my commander.

*

The Barren Wastes, pitted with tar and lava pits, were my dominion. Fissures of steam snaked through the rock, and thick, acidic, ash-filled air covered my realm. The sun could not penetrate the clouds, so during the day it was desolate and grey, filled with oppressive heat from the volcano that rested in the heart of the wastelands. Not many creatures were strong enough to survive here, which is why I chose this place as my home. I wanted to be surrounded by survivors, cutthroat individuals who would do anything to stay alive.

I emerged from my lair deep underground into the stale, dead air. The opening of my cave emerged on to the edge of a cliff, leaving me an excellent view of my home below. I looked down and saw my various units training for the upcoming invasion. Those poor pathetic mortals who lived elsewhere in Eiddoril had no idea what was about to happen to them. I have been forcing them farther and farther north for years, and the towns and cities that remained were either under my control or had been wiped out. Now I had my eyes on the prize: *Gareth*. Nothing was going to stop me from that sweet revenge, not even my master.

I stretched my wings and winced a little at the pain that still bit at my left wing. A momentary rage gripped me but I quickly regained my composure. I had a job to do; I would have my revenge in time.

I took flight and scanned the land below for Reaper. I quickly found him doing drills with a squad of Litui. I circled once, allowing them to see me, and then I touched down next to Reaper. I let my dark gaze fall upon the kneeling Litui and gave Reaper an approving glance.

"You are dismissed. I am in need to speak with your commander." My unspoken mental command filled every solders' mind.

"Yes, my Lord," the Litui said in unison, and they quickly dispersed.

Reaper remained where he had been standing with his head bent low in respect. He was in the form of a human soldier today, which he was quite comfortable in. I did not understand this. I

79

hated being in human skin. I always felt weak and small. However, Reaper was by no means a small human. He was well more than seven feet tall and was built like a mountain. His black scale armour fit like a second skin. He chose to keep his head clean-shaven, but most of his exposed skin, including his face, was covered in tattoos. He was modeled after one of the wild tribes that had inhabited the wild plains years ago. They had been wiped out after the Battle of Gareth. I had hunted down and destroyed all of Gareth's allies, making sure that when I attacked them again they would have no one to ally with.

I lowered my massive head so I could see my minion's face. I also continued to speak to him mentally so I did not blow out his eardrums with my native language. *"Why do you insist on taking the form of these pathetic humans? You're better than that!"*

Reaper raised his head, and his black eyes glittered with malice. He replied aloud to the mental question. "My lord, although most humans are what you say, the Kanarah tribe were fiercely strong warriors and I respect that. Also, it is easier for me to lead this rabble while in human form. They are not as threatened by me."

I feigned surprise. *"This is non-threatening? I would be interesting in seeing what you consider threatening. I almost feel pity for them—almost. But there is a reason I have come to you today, my friend. I need you to do something for me that is of the utmost importance."*

Reaper knelt in front of me and bowed his head. "What is your will, my Lord?" he asked.

"I need you to go to the temple of Ashia and capture Ililsaya."

Reaper glanced up at me with undisguised hunger and delight in his eyes. "My Lord, I am honoured to be given this task, but why are you not going? I would have thought that revenge would be fresh on your mind. Are you still injured?"

I gave Reaper a stare that would intimidate death itself and sent a crippling wave of fear and dread into Reaper's mind. He cowered and lowered his head in fear while I spoke.

"Don't assume that I'm not capable of doing this myself. I would love nothing more than to rip her still-beating heart from her chest and swallow it whole, but my master has given me special orders and I'm

needed here. That is why I chose you to do this for me. Do not make me regret it."

The mental intrusion screamed in Reaper's head, adding to the pain he felt from my attacks. I released the incapacitating fear that held Reaper in thrall and allowed him to regain himself.

Reaper stiffened and his form rippled and shimmered with his emotions. He kept his head bowed and hid the hatred in his eyes. "Forgive me, my Lord, I meant no disrespect. I know that I'm privileged to complete this task for you and I accept with great anticipation."

Reaper turned his masked eyes up to me and saw that I was cutting my wrist with a sharpened claw. Reaper obediently tipped his head and opened his mouth. Three single drops of my blood fell and then burned down the shifter's throat. I waited as he fought hard not to gag on the fire that coursed through his veins. The sensation faded quickly and he was able to swallow again without feeling as if he was digesting razors. This was something he and I had done many times. It was a variation of the blood bond I shared with Mareth. It was by no means as powerful, but it was useful. With my blood in his system, it formed a connection between us, allowing us to sense each other and briefly communicate no matter where we were, but the effects did not last. A week, maybe a few days more was all the magic my blood would provide.

I motioned for my servant to rise. *"Excellent. I have no doubt that you will not fail me, but remember: I need her alive. I don't care what you do with the rest of her companions. Prepare what you need and take a small group with you. There is already a detachment set up at the temple, but I want to make sure she does not escape again."*

I turned my back to the shifter and spread my wings. *"I must travel to the outskirts of the Barren Wastes, where our human allies are camped. We will be moving out soon, and I must make sure all is prepared. I'll be in contact with you in a few days. Be well, my friend, and do not come back empty-handed."*

With that I took to the skies and headed back toward my lair, leaving Reaper alone with his thoughts, and my commands.

CHAPTER 11

Karah

I had never ventured outside the borders of Aserah—well, not that I could remember, anyway. Fitch had told me we have travelled all over Eiddoril fleeing the Dark Lord. It made me wonder how many different people I had known, how many different people I had lost. Fitch had stayed with me through it all, protecting me and making sure my soul lived on. I was grateful, but it made me wonder why—and I was afraid to ask. Whenever he spoke of the past, he looked so sad and lost. Whatever I went through so had he, and I had a feeling there was more but didn't know how to broach it.

We had been riding for a few days now, stopping only to eat and rest. My body ached everywhere and road rations were rapidly becoming my least favourite thing.

Elric, on the other hand, seemed to be thoroughly enjoying himself. He and Fitch were constantly talking about the world around us, the different sections it had fractured into and magic. Elric was quite fascinated with his shield and was determined to learn more about it. Fitch was also trying to teach me how to control my own magic. Whenever we stopped to camp for the night, he would take me aside and explain how he used the powers of the elements. Our lessons were brief because of the fear of the Dark Lord's ability to track me, but it was a necessity. He taught me how to relax and just sense what was around me. He taught me not to just use my eyes but my hearing, touch and smell.

If my mind stayed still long enough I felt the power deep inside me. It felt as if I had a small burning flame trapped inside a steel cage. Tiny pieces could filter through the cracks in the bars but it longed to be free, to be used. Whenever I touched upon it, it threw itself against its prison, but I couldn't break the bars. I felt the pain and loss of it like it was loved one trapped and being tortured.

In those rare moments when I did touch my magic, if only briefly, the elements instantly knew I was there. Their behaviour was strange, though; they approached me hesitantly as if afraid, not like before. Fitch had told me they were not capable of emotion, but that is all I felt from them. Fear and anger were prominent in their touch, but I couldn't discern the reason. Communicating with the elements was overwhelming. It was hard for me to grasp the thought that fire was alive, that it could think and react. I had never given much thought to the elements around me; they were always "just there," giving me what I needed when I needed it, but now it was hard not to be awed by them, not to cower in the face of creation itself. It was all very humbling.

We had been heading south along a river into the realm of Chanadar, leaving Aserah behind. Now from what I remember from my lessons, which wasn't much, Chanadar was mostly sparse fields and a few forests. I could tell that the land had been used for mortal needs, but there were no major settlements in the area, just scattered villages here and there, and I wandered why. Fitch told us as we rode through the desolate land that all of Eiddoril was once populated with dozens of different races of man and creatures, but for some reason the population was steadily decreasing. I thought this pattern was only a problem in Gareth, but the signs of Eiddoril wasting away seemed apparent everywhere. It was unsettling.

It was nearing midday on a particularly gloomy day and I was quite fidgety. I glanced over at Elric but he was no help. I don't even think he noticed me. He was too busy staring off in every direction, keeping a constant watch on our surroundings.

I moved my horse, who was acting rather strangely herself, beside Fitch. He seemed lost in thought too, but when he saw me, a small smile creased his mouth. I knew he knew I was bored, and the smile was an invitation. I wanted to know more about Eiddoril so I asked about the other races he so often spoke of.

He decided to tell me about a mysterious tribe called the Ywari. They were a nomadic people keeping to the plains and grasslands farther south. They had a unique ability to blend in to their surroundings, and you would never know they were there until it was too late. I asked him why he kept referring to them in the past tense, and his face became clouded with anger, his words passionate.

"The Ywari were a very proud and independent people. They thought highly of honour, and when King Gareth approached them for help in his battle against the Dark Lord, they gladly agreed. After the battle that changed your life forever, King Gareth made the decision to uproot his people and flee to the north. That decision affected more than just his people. King Gareth had formed strong alliances with the surrounding races in his fight against the Dark Lord. Most viewed his leaving as a betrayal, and they were left to fend for themselves. Many of those people were wiped out or forced into hiding because without the aid of the king's army, the Dark Lord and his followers were able to pick them off one by one." He sighed heavily. "I don't know if any of them still exist. If they do, you can be sure you will not find them unless they want to be found."

I couldn't understand how anyone with the Gareth name could be so callous and deceptive, but Fitch explained that the loss of his only son, and his kingdom in practical ruin had driven him into despair. All he wanted was to lead what he had left to a new land and start over. The king had never known what had happened to his son and blamed Ashia and the rest of the gods. My involvement had been erased from his mind, so he had no knowledge of the love his son and I had shared, or what had happened to his son because of me. That made me feel sick inside, so guilty. I not only got the man I loved killed but had a hand in destroying a father's spirit. I suddenly wasn't feeling so bored anymore and lost myself in self-loathing.

Fitch called a stop. I had lost interest in our surroundings being consumed by guilt, but glancing around I saw we were about to head into a forest. I also noticed that it was very quiet and didn't hear any of the usual sounds that came with being outdoors. No birds singing, the bugs were eerily silent and even the wind seemed to stop rustling through the tall grasses. The horses' ears twitched back and forth as if trying to hear anything, and they tensed with anticipation. Something felt very wrong.

I pulled my horse to a stop alongside Elric, who had dismounted and was scanning the perimeter of the forest. I did the same and watched Fitch farther up ahead sitting very still with his eyes closed and his head slightly cocked, as if listening to something.

Then I heard it too, something like a high-pitched whistling, but before I had any time to wonder, I had my answer. Arrows flew out of the trees too fast to be humanly possible and completely surrounded Elric and me in a perfect circle, cutting us off from Fitch.

The horses panicked and bolted, but no matter which direction Elric and I turned to try to evade our circle, we couldn't pass the barrier. Then, to my amazement, a wind kicked up around us. It followed the circle of arrows and continued to grow higher and faster. We were trapped inside a wind funnel. I tried to see through the swirling dirt and debris in search of Fitch. He had dismounted and was attempting his own magic to bring down the wall of wind that separated us. Too late. Figures moved in behind him, and then I saw him fall to the ground.

Elric was shouting, but I couldn't hear him over the roar of the wind and the insistent ringing in my ears. He pointed at my face. I gingerly traced the pattern that covered most of it and felt the heat under my fingertips. My mark, the one that proclaimed me immortal was glowing so intensely that Elric had to shield his eyes. I closed my own and tried to calm my thoughts.

The wind pushed at my senses, willing me to open up and let it inside me, but I was afraid. What if I hurt someone? What if I couldn't stop? I started to falter, and this time I heard Elric cry out. The circle was constricting us, forcing us closer together. Unless I did something, we would both be crushed. I refocused my attention and ever-so-lightly reached my senses out to the wind that surrounded us. The magic slammed into me and I staggered, but Elric was there holding me upright. The element of wind flowed through me and caressed me like a long-lost lover. It was intoxicating, but I knew I had to let go or I would lose myself. I concentrated on the wild magic and forced it back up into the skies, into the air where it belonged.

I could feel that it wasn't happy but it obeyed, and with a sudden powerful gust it was gone and everything went still. I collapsed into Elric's arms, breathing heavily. I took long steadying breaths and tried not to pass out. Soon the dizziness subsided and I was able to stand on my own again.

Elric lifted my chin and pushed my damp hair out of my eyes. "Are you all right? Your nose is bleeding and your eyes are bloodshot. Can you hear me okay?" Elric stared at me with a cross between amazement and fear in his eyes.

I wiped at my nose with the sleeve of my tunic and rubbed at my temples in pain. "Yeah, I think so, but I feel like I smacked my head against a wall. Where's Fitch? What in the blazes happened?"

I followed Elric's gaze and noticed we were no longer alone. We still stood in the ring of arrows, but now that the wind was gone I could see what I had only caught glimpses of before. We were surrounded by people. Well, they looked sort of like people. They were much shorter than the average human, maybe standing four feet tall, and they were thin, very thin, not an ounce of fat adorned their small bodies, but their limbs were corded with muscle. I had no doubt they were much stronger than they looked. They were covered head to toe in strange markings, some red, some green, but the majority of it was black. Their hair was very long and black and they all wore it braided down the length of their backs. Their faces were oval shaped, and two large dark eyes dominated their features. They were not wearing much clothing, and I shivered just looking at them. Autumn was not yet in full swing and even though it was still warm during the day, it wasn't that warm. Not one of them seemed impressed to see us. They had arrows notched and ready, pointing straight at Elric and me. Fitch was on the ground holding his head in his hands.

I inched closer to the group and kept my hands palms up in front of me, to show that I was unarmed and meant them no harm.

One of them shouted at me in some strange langue and pointed his bow right at my head. I stopped. I felt Elric tense and reach for his sword.

"No, don't. The only way we're going to get out of this is if we figure out a way to communicate with them. We're not here to fight."

Fitch looked up at me and risked speaking. "Be careful, child; these are the Ywari. I can't believe we have stumbled upon them, but be cautious—they will not be happy to see us."

One of the Ywari standing next to Fitch cuffed him in the back of the head, silencing him. I focused my attention back on the man who had me pegged as a target, and the look on his face said he had seen a spirit. The strange man was staring at my face with wide, almond-shaped eyes. I felt my face glowing again; not has brightly as before but it was enough. His eyes widened and he dropped to his knees. The others saw it and did the same, all the while chanting in some foreign language I did not understand. I did, however, pick up one word: Ashia.

"Oh no, no, no . . . I'm not Ashia. Stop that, please. Can you get up or something? This really isn't necessary."

I tried to get their attention and weaved in and out of the stooped people, but they were having no part of it. They kept their heads bowed, chanting and completely ignoring my futile efforts.

Fitch raised his head out of his hands and looked up at me with a smile. He rose slowly and made his way toward me, smiling the whole way. I really did not understand what was so funny. This was embarrassing, and they were not going to be happy when they found out I was not who they thought I was. Elric was smiling too. They were both having quite the chuckle at my uncomfortable situation and my lack of anything useful to say.

"This isn't funny. How do I get them to stop? I need to explain myself before they start expecting to see 'god stuff' or something."

Fitch just looked at me dumbfounded and shook his head. "God stuff? Really? What exactly is god stuff? If you're referring to your magic, then yes, they may expect to see that, but I do not think they are referring to you as Ashia. You look nothing like her right now.

I merely think they recognize your mark and believe you're here to save them or give them a message. It can't be a coincidence that we have run into these beings. The elements must have had a hand in this; we must not ruin this opportunity."

I threw up my hands in frustration. "Great, so now what do I do? It's pretty hard to tell someone anything if you can't communicate. How are we going to do that?"

A new voice quickly grabbed my attention. "Some of us can understand you, and please stop talking about us like we're not here."

I whipped around to see the whole group of Ywari rise as one, and then most of them disappeared right before my eyes. I hadn't noticed before but their clothing and skin blended into their surroundings, making them seem invisible.

They retreated back into the forest and the surrounding tall grasses without a sound. The one who had spoken remained standing where he was with two others, and I assumed they were their leaders. I was relieved to see they had put away their weapons.

The older looking one of the three slightly bowed his head. "I am called Yaleon, and these are my sons, Ossian and Deneoes. I am sorry for our attack, but these are dark times and our trust has been diminished. Please accept our apologies and tell us our prayers have finally been answered. Has Ashia returned? Has she come to save us?"

I looked down at their delicate forms. I could read so much in their faces: mistrust, fear but also hope. Hope that I was here to save them, hope that I had the answers they so desperately wanted. But I didn't have them; all I had was more questions and a fear of my own, the fear that I could not live up to all of these people's expectations and that I was going to fail.

Elric placed his hand in mine and gave it a gentle squeeze. I drew strength from his touch and found my voice. "I'm sorry too. I'm afraid I'm not who you're hoping for. Ashia did not send me, nor do I have the power to save you."

Yaleon frowned and pointed at my face. "But you bear her mark; you controlled the power of wind. How can you not be sent from Ashia?"

I self-consciously rubbed at my face. "That, my friend, is a long story, and if you will permit me, I'll do my best to explain it. Please know that we mean you no harm and that you can trust us. I give you my word."

Yaleon turned to his two sons and conversed in their language. When he turned back to us, he was guarded but not hostile. "Come, you will eat with us this evening and tell us your tale, and then I'll decide if you are worthy of our trust." He paused and gave Elric a hostile glance. "Don't think I don't know where your companions come from. I see the emblem of Gareth, and I have no love or trust for them. We will not make that mistake again."

With that he turned and led the way into the forest. One of his sons—I think Deneoes—came and collected the arrows that were still in the ground. He placed them reverently back in their carrying case and took up a position behind us. Together we walked into the woods and disappeared from sight.

CHAPTER 12

The Ywaris's home was not what I had expected. For one, I thought we would have been led to a clearing in the woods where we would find their encampment, but to my surprise Yaleon led us into the heart of the forest where very little could be seen through the thick cover of trees and brush. The trees here were enormous, towering over us at least 50 feet. I stared up in wonder and was humbled by the sheer beauty and power of the elements' creations. I found myself standing in what must have been the very centre of the forest. The towering limbs all but blocked the sun, leaving the ground shrouded in shadows.

Yaleon led us to the base of one of the mighty tress and waited while we tethered our horses. I searched the shadows for any other sign of life but nothing around me suggested a group of people lived here.

"Welcome, child of the sun and moon, to the home of the Ywari."

Yaleon looked expectantly at me, and I in turn looked around. I saw the trees and brush and the occasional bird but no home suitable for a group of people. I also noticed that Yaleon's two sons had disappeared.

Elric looked around as well, and I could tell he was just as confused as I was.

Fitch on the other hand was unusually silent and regarded me with a look that I should know what was going on.

I turned back to Yaleon and got the sinking feeling that I was about to fail some test. "Ah . . . I'm sorry, but I don't see anything here but trees. What exactly am I looking for?"

Yaleon regarded me with disappointment.

Yep, apparently I'd failed. I was never very good at tests.

"Perhaps I was wrong to bring you here; maybe you are not the one we have been hoping for. Please collect your horses and follow this trail. It will lead you safely out of the forest to the other side. Travel safe and be well." Yaleon turned and simply disappeared into the surrounding trees.

Now I was angry. Okay, so maybe I wasn't the most observant person in the world, but I'm not exactly in my element, and a lot had happened over the last week. I threw my arms up into the air and stomped over to where Elric and Fitch were standing. "So now what do we do?"

I waited, but neither of my companions wanted in on my tantrum. That was fine.

"Yaleon's son obviously has the element of wind in his possession. If we could just get him to speak with us maybe he would help us, but they insist on playing games with me. How do I see something that isn't there? Why are they being so unfair?" I crossed my arms and stared at Fitch, waiting for him to answer.

He stared back with those strange golden eyes that I kept forgetting to question him about. "Are you quite finished with your childish tirade?" I didn't answer, so he continued. "It's clear that you have a lot to learn, and I apologize for waiting this long to teach you. Now, if you will curb that temper of yours and look around, you will find what it is we seek."

I raked my fingers through my hair in frustration. "Why can't you just tell me? I'm tired of these games and people expecting me to know things I don't. We don't have time for this."

Elric came forward to stand beside me. "She's right. I know you're trying to teach her something, and me as well, because I can't see what you want us to see either. If we don't keep moving, the Dark Lord will track us down again. Karah had to use her powers back there to save us, and if he's still out there somewhere, he will have sensed her. As annoyed as I am with these people right now, I don't want to cause them any more harm than what they already blame us for."

Elric had remained relatively quiet during our trek here and was quiet and subdued. I think the Ywaris' lack of trust and open hostility toward the Gareth name had deeply wounded him.

Fitch on the other hand was not so relaxed. He squared his shoulders and looked me straight in the eyes. "Listen to me. I know you're doubting yourself right now and that you would love nothing more than for me to tell you the answer, but things are only going to get worse from here. You need to accept who you are and rely on yourself." He pointed a finger at my chest. "You are a strong, smart, independent woman, and I know you can do this. We need the Ywari help, and if you can't see what they wish you to see, then they will never trust you and our quest will become that much harder." Fitch placed both hands on my shoulders and lowered his voice. "Close your eyes and clear your mind, use what I have taught you. You do not need magic; just listen, and you will find what you are looking for. I know you can do this; you must do this."

I continued to stare into his eyes for a few seconds, and then I sighed in defeat.

I walked a little from where Elric and Fitch were standing and did what I was told: I closed my eyes. I took several deep steadying breaths and focused my attention on the sounds of the forest. At first I couldn't hear anything except the hammering of my heart, but I forced myself to calm down and let my ears find my answers. It took a few moments, but I heard the many different birds calling to one another, each call or cry echoing in my head. Many of the birds' song I didn't recognize but the ones I did I recalled what they looked like and I pictured them in my mind. One of the birds was my favourite, mostly because of its colour. It was called a blood wren. It didn't have the most appealing name, but it was a beautiful bird. Its feathers were completely red except for the tip of its tail, which was black, and the sound it made was musical, almost like listening to the notes from a flute. I followed its flight with my mind's eye and was amazed at how I could almost actually see it.

Next I listened to the insects singing all around. They were everywhere, and my mind's vision quickly filled with the buzzing and humming of hundreds of the creatures. I inhaled deeply and took in the rich aroma of the forest. I could smell the heavy cover of leaves that surrounded us along with the sweet tinge of natural decay found on forest floors. Wildflowers added their own unique scent and their colors suddenly burst forth in my mind.

I listened to the breeze softly rustling the foliage above and around me. Everything I heard was soothing, like a lullaby, and I became more relaxed. I let the music of the forest take me and guide me through every crevice and brush against every creature. More pictures began to form in my mind and I recognized the forest. I was seeing everything in my mind through the sounds and smells, as if I was looking around with my own eyes. It was amazing.

I stood there for several minutes lost in the glory of creation when a peculiar sound caught my attention. It was a sound that had no business being in a forest in the middle of nowhere. It was a child's laughter, which was quickly muffled. I pushed harder with my senses and heard other sounds as well: a creaking of wood, like an old bridge, the gentle flap of cloth in the breeze, the shuffling of feet across a wooden floor and the collective breathing of a large group of people. I smelled smoke and the enticing aroma of roasting meat. This was confusing to me because everything I was hearing and smelling came from above me, in the trees. So with my mind's eyes I looked toward the sky, and I gasped.

There, nestled among the treetops away from harm and practically invisible was the Ywari encampment. I opened my eyes and smiled. I saw everything clearly now and felt foolish that I had not seen them before, but I had never thought to look up into the trees.

I locked eyes with Yaleon, and he gave me a warm, thoughtful smile. I guessed I passed the test after all. Yaleon and a few others threw down what looked like rope ladders, and then they scaled down the trees like a couple of giant spiders. They touched down gracefully a few yards from where I stood and casually walked over.

"Your friend is very wise, and I'm glad you have seen with your heart and not your eyes. Come, we have much to discuss. It's not safe to be on the ground at night. I hope you and your companions are not afraid of heights."

I glanced up into the towering trees and then back to Yaleon. "Well, I'm not, but I'm not sure about the other two. Thank you for allowing us into your home. It is truly amazing."

I turned around and saw Elric staring up into the trees in amazement. "How did you do this? How do you live among the trees like that? It's unbelievable."

Yaleon shrugged and coldness replaced the welcome in his eyes. "Yes, and it is that shallow thinking that we really heavily on. As long as you don't know we exist, we will survive. It is your blindness of the magic that surrounds you that keeps us safe."

Yaleon and Elric were at a standoff. Elric towered over the smaller leader but it was he who looked away first. "I'm not your enemy. I had no idea what my ancestors did to you and your people. It wasn't taught and I intend to remedy that. Do not judge me on my ancestors' mistakes. I'm not King Gareth, and you can trust me."

The Ywari leader made no move to be persuaded. "We shall see. Come, you may use the ladders to climb up to the platforms above. One of my people will be waiting and will guide you to where we can eat and talk."

Yaleon and his companion turned and headed back up the side of the tree the way they had come down. No wonder they looked so strong. I couldn't imagine the strength they must have in order to scale a tree like that.

I turned to Elric with a smile, but he just turned away and went to check on our horses before we ascended the tree.

I started to follow him, but Fitch stopped me. "Let him be for a moment. He's wrestling with emotions he's not accustomed to. He has lived his whole life believing that his father and his legacy were solid and true. This news is hard for him to swallow."

I shook my head in anger. "As it should be. Why were we not taught any of this? Why is there no recorded history after that battle? We should not have forgotten these people. Just because I was forgotten shouldn't have meant that everything else was has well."

Fitch looked ashamed and tired. "There are recorded histories at the temple and at my home, as I have told you before, but we lost the temple to the Dark Lord's attacks, and what I could save I brought with me into hiding." He looked away from me. "I'm just one person. I know I'm immortal, but the task that was set upon me was too great. I could not keep you and the books safe at the same time, so I chose you. It was an easy decision, but I see now that it has done great harm. I just wanted to keep you safe. That is all I cared about."

I had never seen Fitch look so vulnerable before. I felt pity for him and anger toward myself. I was always so worried about myself and what had happened to me in the past 300 years, but what Fitch had gone through was equally painful if not worse.

I tried to comfort him as best as I could. "Look, if anyone knows about self-pity, it's me. You've done the best job you could do under the circumstances, and I'm so grateful that you stuck by me through the years. You are not alone anymore—together we will figure something out, and starting today, with the Ywari, we will set things right. Now let's get going before they change their minds about dinner. I'm starving."

Fitch smiled and the shadow of pain and the past left his eyes. Together we walked over to the ropes that hung from the treetops and prepared to climb. Elric was there waiting. As I approached he gave a quick grin, but I could tell it was forced.

"Are you two ready for this? It's a long way up and I don't think I can carry you."

I shoved him, trying to knock him off balance. "Listen, Your Highness, I can climb circles around you, so how about you just shut it and get going. I need to eat before I get cranky."

Elric laughed, which made me smile, and started up the ladder. I took my place next, with Fitch close behind, and together we climbed into a completely new world.

CHAPTER 13

Exhaustion plagued me by the time we reached the top platform. Elric practically dragged me up over the side, and I lay there panting, trying to calm my racing heart. Man, was I ever out of shape! Elric looked a little winded too but then Fitch crested the platform without as much as a trickle of sweat on his brow. I was speechless . . . almost.

"How is it you look to be more than twice my age, but you having the stamina of a teenager who's just gone for a morning stroll?" I managed to gasp between large gulps of air.

Fitch quickly turned away and spoke excessively fast, as if he was hiding something again. "I am immortal, remember, plus I work out. You should think about doing the same."

Before I could point out that even a seasoned soldier like Elric was having a hard time and that I really didn't think being immortal meant you can climb trees without breaking a sweat, Deneoes and Ossian appeared beside us. Ossian proceeded to pull up the rope ladder while Deneoes offered his hand to help me up.

"Nice job. Ossian and I had a bet you wouldn't make it up. This is the first time we have ever had outsiders in our home."

I reached out for his hand and gripped it tightly. He pulled me to my feet quite easily and smiled up at me with a mischievous look in his eyes.

I smiled back. "So which of you bet against us? Who won?"

He thumbed toward his brother. "Ossian is the one who said you probably wouldn't make it half way, but I knew you would. Whoever can control wind like that must be strong. Trust me, I know." He gave the arrows slung across his back a quick pat, confirming that

I had been right: Deneoes had the elemental arrows. Maybe there was hope after all.

Ossian pushed past and started to walk across a bridge that spanned to another tree. "Enough talk, come. Father will be waiting for us. Let's finish this as quickly as possible so that they can go back to where ever it is that they came from."

Well, I guess not everyone was happy we were here. I turned back toward Deneoes and gave him an apologetic shrug. He just waved me off.

"Don't mind him; he's very much our father's son. He doesn't trust any of you and was against your coming here."

I raised my eyebrows. "But your father does trust me."

Deneoes shook his head. "No, he trusts in his faith for Ashia and the elements. He sees this as a sign—something my brother does not believe in."

"And what do you believe?"

Deneoes looked up at me and stared into my eyes. He cocked his head a little, studying me, and then he laughed aloud. "You're a hard woman to read, my fiery friend, and that I'm not used to. I'll let you know what I think after I hear your story, but I'll tell you one thing. I'm sick of hiding, and I see that in your eyes as well."

He walked past me and waved us forward. "Come, let's go before my big bother starts howling. Watch your step and stay on the bridges. It is a long way down."

Fitch quickly fell in step behind the young Ywari, and I hung back a little with Elric so we could talk. We took in our surroundings for a few moments, just enjoying the pure awe that came from being in this place. It was a completely new perspective of looking at things. The trees were surprisingly dense up here, and it was easy to trick yourself into thinking you were strolling through the woods on the ground. Bridges spanned everywhere, connecting the small community like a spider web. Small huts made of twigs, leaves and animal hide were scattered about the strong limbs of the trees. Small children no taller than my thigh and even some adults stopped what they were doing and watched us pass with curiosity but also anger in their large, luminous eyes.

Elric took it all in silence, and the farther we walked the more tense he became. "These people hate me; they hate my father and everything I've been taught to believe in. I don't blame them, really. I don't know how I would feel if I were in the same situation." Elric rubbed his hands over his face. He had not had the chance to shave since we started our journey and the hair on his face was growing in. His brilliant grey eyes were tired and full of doubt, but he still carried himself like a prince, with strength and confidence. He looked like his father—and another thought suddenly jumped into my mind. I squeezed my eyes shut, willing the image to fade and was jolted out of my memories by Elric grabbing me around my waist and hauling me to a stop. My eyes flew open and I realized I had almost fallen off the bridge. I let him hold me for a minute and then gently wiggled from his grasp. I brushed my red hair out of my eyes and turned my equally reddened face away.

"I'm sorry, I wasn't paying attention to where I was walking, I . . ." I stopped talking and actually think I stopped breathing too, because there in tree limbs not ten feet away from me were the two largest eyes I had ever seen staring out at me. They were easily the size of a large fist and were bright orange with a black slit for a pupil. The eyes stared at me with intelligence, and it made me want to turn and run as fast as I could. I started to back up, but I had forgotten Elric was standing right behind me, and I bumped into him again. He could tell that something was wrong.

"What is it? What do you see?"

Without taking my eyes off the strange pair of eyes that seemed to be floating in the leaves, I pointed with my left hand and rested my right on my sword. I instantly felt a humming in my head and the mark on my face was getting warm.

Before either of us had any time to react the creature launched itself out of the leaves and gracefully landed on the bridge directly in front of us. It was the most intriguing and beautiful creature I had ever seen. It was feline in nature but was bigger than any I had seen. Its sleek muscular body was covered in fur that looked like soft silk, but the remarkable thing about its fur was that it shifted and continually changed colours to match its surroundings. Its tail was easily as long as its body, and it twitched back and forth.

I stared into those eyes and again was struck with an intelligence that I had never seen in an animal before. It twitched its large tufted ears as if it was listening to something, and then it simply sat back on its haunches, licking its mouth, revealing a huge, healthy set of sharp teeth. I didn't know what to do. It seemed to have no intention of attacking but also seemed to have no plans to move so we could pass.

Elric tensed behind me and started to try to shift his way in front of me. I blocked him. "No, wait, stop. I don't think it wants to hurt us. I think it's just checking us out."

Elric scoffed at my words. "Yeah, right, checking us out for dinner maybe; you can't be serious. That is a mist fang cougar. They are called that because all you see before they attack you is their teeth and nothing else. That thing is not friendly."

At the mention of its name the feline tilted its head, watched us and then lay down and began grooming its huge paws—which, by the way, were endowed with massive claws. I even think I heard it purring.

I crouched in front of the beast and studied it cautiously. My sudden movement brought its head back up, and a low growl escaped its throat.

Behind me, Elric drew his sword and prepared to defend us. I reached back and put a restraining hand on Elric's leg and then I felt the marking on face get warmer. From the corner of my eye I caught the familiar blue glow of magic.

The cougar was also looking at my face, and then our eyes met, and just for an instant I heard its thoughts—well, feelings really, its emotions. I felt no malice or anger, just a curiosity, loyalty and friendship.

I reached my hand out to the cougar against Elric's sharp warning and let the animal sniff me. Elric sucked in air, and I heard behind me others who had gathered to watch the scene play out. The beast timidly took in my scent and without any warning stood, padded the rest of the distance between us and lay its head on my lap so I could stroke its soft fur. My symbol faded and my connection to the cougar was broken, but I didn't need it anymore; she was no longer a threat.

I looked up at the sound of a low whistle and was surprised to see we had drawn quite an audience. Deneoes strode up the bridge and stopped a good distance away from the cougar. Apparently, this was not a common occurrence. "Well, aren't you just full of surprises, Red?" He pointed toward the animal. "We live in harmony with the mist fang because these trees are their natural habitat. They leave us alone and we leave them alone, but never in my or anyone's life have we been able to tame one. What did you do?"

I looked around at the people gathered, including Elric and Fitch, who were all looking at me with awe, and it made me feel very uncomfortable. I stood, straightened out my tunic and pushed my hair behind my ears. The cougar took a step next to me and sat as well, regarding the rest gathered with indifference.

"I didn't do anything, I just listened to her. She won't hurt anyone, but I'm afraid she won't leave my side either. I think she has appointed herself as my bodyguard. And my name is not Red, it's Karah."

I placed my hand on the big cat's head, which was chest level, and scratched behind its ears.

Deneoes smiled from pointed ear to pointed ear. "Now this is definitely worth my waking up this morning. I haven't had this much excitement in years." He gestured me forward again. "Come on, we're almost at my father's home, and I can't wait to see the look on his face when he sees . . . that . . . and just so you know, that was the first time you told me your name, but I still prefer Red."

Deneoes turned, and we all followed him toward his father's hut.

Elric slipped past me and gave me a smile. "No offence, but I'll walk with Fitch. Your new pet makes me nervous."

I glared back at him and gave him a playful shove, falling in behind him with my new shadow close behind.

It did not take us long to reach Yaleon's home, and we were greeted by quite a crowd, although I had the feeling that they were not there to see me but rather my new furry companion.

Yaleon was waiting for us outside the entrance to his home, along with Ossian and a woman I assumed was his wife. He stood facing me with amazement written across his face. "Are you certain Ashia did not send you? For someone who claims she has no powers, you seem to be doing some extraordinary things."

Fitch thankfully answered before I could, taking the unwanted attention off me.

"Karah does have ties to Ashia, but not in the way you think. Please, we are tired and weary, and if you permit us we will gladly fill you in on our journey and how it involves not only your people but all of races in this land."

Yaleon nodded. "Yes, of course, please enter. My wife, Emtai, will seat you. First we'll eat and then I will listen to your story, but I'm afraid that you will have to leave the beast outside." He directed this last part at me.

I looked at Yaleon hopelessly. "And how do I do that? I doubt she is going to stay like a trained dog."

Yaleon shrugged and went inside with the rest. I turned to the cougar, who was patiently waiting for another scratch, and attempted to tell it to go home or hunt or whatever it is that giant cats do. It looked at me once as if to say it understood, and then it shifted its colour to match the surrounding foliage and leapt silently away into the trees.

I entered through the animal hide flap that was used as Yaleon's front door and was amazed at how warm and cozy the interior felt. There were no tables or chairs to speak of, just furs piled up in various spots of the home. One large tree branch off to one side served as a bench. The top of it had been levelled to make sitting or storing items on it easier. The wall and roof were made entirely of branches grass, leaves and other natural materials. I placed my hand against the wall and instantly felt a connection to everything around me; it was if the hut were alive, which I guess in reality it was. I removed my hand and made my way to the centre of the room, where my companions and hosts were seated around a cooking fire.

"Are you not afraid the fire will destroy your village? How do you keep it contained from spreading?" Elric asked.

101

I quietly took a seat next to him on a pile of furs and watched the fire dance in the pit in front of us.

Yaleon's voice carried through the hut. "We have no choice but to use fire; it helps keeps us alive. Long ago, we learned that if you heat up certain materials, like clay or sand, they become hardened and can be used for pots or in this case, our fire pits. We meticulously watch over the fires and deeply respect the element. Our kind has always worshipped the elements. They have always taken care of us and even in these dark times they have never abandoned us like they did some." Yaleon gestured above his head. "We have made small holes in our roofs where the smoke rises and can escape. The thick cover of leaves and branches hides the smoke well so passersby on the ground would never know we were up here. It is the threats from above that we must be wary of, but we have not had to be concerned about that for a long time. Though I have a feeling that the news you bring us tonight will change that."

Yaleon leaned back and allowed his wife to circle our group, handing out steaming bowls of what smelled like some kind of stew. My mouth started watering, and as soon as I was sure everyone had some I gladly dug in and enjoyed every last drop. I wasn't sure what the meat was in the stew but was also pretty sure I didn't want to know. It tasted good, so I left that little curiosity alone.

I sat and listened to the idle conversations around me. Elric, Deneoes, and Ossian were discussing the defence of their homes while Fitch, Emtai and Yaleon spoke about the recent violent storms and how it had been quite dangerous and frightening. Many of their homes had been destroyed and lives had been lost. Fitch also spoke of the attack on Gareth by the Dark Lord, but he left out the part about why. Fitch's face became more and more concerned as the conversation went on and I choose that time to mention something I had heard earlier that was quite puzzling to me.

"Yaleon, earlier you mentioned that you had only to worry about the threat from the skies. Are you referring to the Dark Lord? I was under the impression that he kept his true form hidden from mortals."

Everyone looked over at me at the mention of the Dark Lord, and I swear all the colour drained from Fitch's face. I thought he was going to pass out, but before I could ask him if he was all right Yaleon answered my question.

"Yes, it is true that the destroyer of nations has kept his true form hidden for the past several hundred years, but before Ashia and the others chose to return to their native realm, dragons were quite pompous and arrogant and would never stay in a mortal disguise for long. They considered it beneath them. Mareth and his followers would hunt us from the skies. Our lives were quite difficult back then."

I felt like someone had just pulled a rug from under me and I was falling into darkness.

CHAPTER 14

"What did you just say? Did . . . did you say *dragons?* There are no such things as dragons. They have been extinct for over 400 years" My voice was trembling as I spoke, and I felt my temper rising with each passing second. I turned my sharp gaze on Fitch, but he had his head lowered, covering his face with his hands.

Yaleon did not understand what was going on so he continued with his story. "Oh, I assure you, dragons are quite real. My ancestors kept detailed records of our histories, even going back as far as when they first came to us from their magical realm. You have seen the Dark One with your own eyes—what did you think he was? Did your ancestors not keep detailed histories? For a people who always considered themselves a superior race, I am quite shocked by your lack of information."

"You and me both," I said through clenched teeth, and I rose from my seat and left the hut for some fresh air.

The cool autumn night hit me but it did nothing to ease my anger. I felt so stupid. How could I not have put these pieces together? Yaleon was right; I should have known what the Dark Lord was. A dragon, a gods be damned dragon! Just thinking it sounded utterly insane. I couldn't believe it; I didn't want to believe it, and to add to my injured heart the one person I was supposed to be able to trust had been lying to me.

Leaning back against one of the rough trees I closed my eyes and took some deep breaths, trying to calm my anger. Minutes passed and I let my head fall forward as a gripping despair washed over me. Now what would I do? I didn't want to be a dragon. I had just barely come to grips with the fact that I was immortal. I had just assumed

I would be human looking, like Fitch. My relationship with Elric was lost before it even had a chance to start, and what had I been thinking all those years ago getting involved with a human? That relationship had been doomed from the beginning.

I felt the presence of my feline friend next to me and gently laid my hand on her strong back. I stroked her soft fur and drew comfort from her silent presence.

Raised voices coming from inside the hut brought my head up, and I listened as Elric and Fitch screamed at each other. An intense urgency made me leave the cat and see what was going on.

Walking back into the hut brought a chill to my bones. Fitch and Elric were yelling at each other, with Yaleon and Deneoes trying to calm them down, their weapons drawn. Fitch's eyes were a bright golden colour and I saw hatred as he faced the prince.

I bounded over the piles of furs and inserted myself between the two. "Enough, you're both acting like children. This is no way to gain these people's trust."

I glared at them, daring them to continue their argument, but it had thankfully lost some of its heat.

I grabbed Elric's arm and squeezed, making him stare at me instead of Fitch. "Let's sit back down and let Fitch explain himself. Maybe we'll finally hear the truth."

I bit out that last part with enough violence that it made Fitch flinch. The two males continued to stare at each other for a moment and then conceded. We all sat back down, but I chose to sit next to Deneoes. I couldn't bring myself to look at Elric right now. It hurt too much.

Yaleon, however, did not return to his seat, and he was clearly not pleased with the chaos that had just transpired in his home. "What's going on? I don't understand any of this. Who are *you* and why should I allow you to remain in my home?"

Yaleon locked eyes with me and I froze. I couldn't get out the words that I knew needed to be said.

Fitch could, however, and all eyes moved to him. Anger and resentment covered his face. He was not the same man I knew only moments before. "The human that you see before you is really the human vessel for the dragon, Ililsaya. She has been trapped in various human hosts for the past 300 years. It was a trap designed by Mareth himself and carried out by the Dark Lord. The spell took away any memory of her existence from mortal minds and erased her memories as well.

"For the last three centuries I have been her guardian from the Dark Lord, and I have had to watch her die on several occasions. Eighteen years ago, on his last attempt on her life, I became her sole protector and chose to flee to the city of Gareth. There I had hoped to keep her safe, but it was not to be. The Dark Lord has found her again, and this time it is different. The elements are involved, for reasons I have yet to understand, and the spell that has trapped Ililsaya for so long is weakening. She has started to remember things and her magic has slowly been returning to her."

He turned his sharp, now-golden eyes to the Ywari leader. "We were on our way to the temple of Ashia to find answers and hope, because if we cannot find her true form and release her from this spell, I am afraid our land will greatly suffer. The Dark Lord is up to something, I can feel it, and because I have failed to hold all the races together, we will not stand a chance. He has had 300 years to plan his revenge and it will be swift and severe; of this I am certain. I don't know when or if the other dragons will return, I only know that Ashia left Ililsaya here to protect you because she is the only one strong enough to do so. If I fail her this time, if I don't find a way to free her, then we will all be at the Dark Lord's mercy."

The silence in the room that followed was oppressive. No one spoke, lost in his or her own unbelievable thoughts. I knew how they felt. How could any of this possibly be true? I'm sure they all wondered how this young, fragile, hot-headed human could be the saviour. But as my eyes met Yaleon's I knew he believed it. Whether he was going to help still remained to be seen.

Yaleon tore his gaze from mine and faced Fitch. "There is still something I don't understand. You also look human, but from what you have told us you are more than 300 years old. Who are *you*, and why are you keeping it a secret?"

Fitch stared into the fire. I could see it reflecting in his eyes, which were now not human looking at all They seemed to swallow the fire to feed an inner light that kept growing and getting brighter. "My true name is Enthor, and no, I am not human, which you have already figured out. I am a dragon also, one of the original beasts to pass through the portal so many years ago. Some of us including Mareth and Ashia have the ability to take on human form. We did this so that we could control the mortal races better and to become your gods. Our Dragon forms were kept secret and no mortals knew of the deception except for a scattered few . . . or so I thought. Ashia begged me to stay behind and protect Ililsaya, so I shifted into this human form and pretended to be one of my mages. Dragons cannot sense each other when we are in human form, which allowed me to remain undetected."

Fitch lifted his head to look at me. "This is how I have stayed to keep Ililsaya safe. I haven't been in my true form for 300 years, and I haven't used my true magic in fear that the Dark Lord would sense it. And for 300 years I have pretended to be something I'm not."

I was speechless. I had no idea what he had sacrificed, what he must have gone through. I was still angry at not being told what I truly was, but under the circumstances, I wasn't sure I wouldn't have done the same.

Yaleon cleared his throat and faced me. "Many nights ago I had a vision. In this vision, I saw great beasts returned to our world, but what should have brought peace and harmony only brought death and destruction. Our world is unstable. There is a sickness plaguing it that is spreading every day. There is something driving it, a darkness that is foreign to us. It is affecting the water we drink, the food we eat, even the air we breathe." I nodded my understanding while he continued. "I believe your story and your plight, and I thank the elements for guiding us to this meeting today, but you must understand that we have survived all of the years by staying hidden. I'm not sure if it's the right choice for us to breach our silence now. Your presence here, combined with the vision I had, does not bode well for things to come." Yaleon stood, as did his wife and Ossian.

My heart sank with the depth of his words.

"We have heard much this night, and I am afraid I'm not quite sure what to do about it. What you have told us has grave implications on the future of our race. The three of you all welcome here for the night. My wife and I must now call together a meeting of our elders. There is much to discuss that is not for outsider ears. Please rest, and we will speak again in the morning."

Yaleon, Emtai and Ossian exited the hut, and at the last second Ossian turned back to his brother, who was still seated next to me.

"Deneoes, are you coming? This concerns you as well. Do not get lost in your delusions of adventure. You are a member of the council; your presence is required."

The younger brother shifted a little and started to poke absently at the fire with a long metal pole. Without taking his attention off the fire, he answered his brother. "Relax, brother, don't worry; I know *my* place in the grand scheme of things. I will be there shortly. I don't need to hear the first part anyway. I already heard it." Deneoes gave his brother a wicked grin, which only caused Ossian to leave grumbling to himself.

The young Ywari turned his bright, wide eyes to me. "Family. Aren't they wonderful?"

I just shook my head not knowing what to say.

Elric shifted across the room and coughed. I had almost forgotten he was there. He had been so quiet.

Deneoes suddenly stood up and headed for the door. "I'll let you get some sleep. I just wanted to let you know that no matter what the council decides, I'm coming with you—that is, if you want my company."

I smiled. "I would be honoured, and thank you, I know this is not your fight."

"Ah, but that's where you're wrong, Red. It's everyone's fight, we have just forgotten that." He left, leaving me alone with my two companions.

I looked back and forth between the two and got a horrible feeling in my stomach. I didn't know who to speak to first; neither conversation was very appealing to me right now.

Elric spoke before I had the chance. "I know what you're going to say and I want you to hear me out first." He paused and breathed deeply. "I am not going to pretend that I am not freaked out about what just happened. Honestly I'm not really sure how I feel right now, but like I said before, it doesn't matter to me what you are or what you look like, it doesn't change the way I feel about you."

Elric gazed at me from across the fire, and I could see in his face that he meant every word.

I lowered my head and let my thick red hair fall to hide the tears that were rapidly forming in my eyes. "How can you say that? You can't possibly know how you will feel once you see me as a monster."

I felt a warm gentle hand on my chin lifting my face up so I could see. It was Fitch, regarding me with concern and pain.

"You are not and never will be a monster. You are a magnificent, beautiful creature, and I am deeply sorry I have caused you so much pain. I just couldn't bear to tell you the truth. I did not want to see your heart broken again."

I looked at Elric and knew that Fitch was speaking of the prince I had fallen in love with all those years ago. My eyes found Fitch again, and I tried to ignore the pain in my heart. "You knew?"

Fitch nodded but made no move to explain the situation, for which I was grateful.

I reached out and held my friend's hand. "It is not too late, you can tell me now. Tell me our story, the real story."

Fitch rose and turned his back to me. I didn't think he was going to say anything, but then he spoke, and it sounded like thunder rolling. I covered my ears and squeezed my eyes shut trying to block out the deafening words that I couldn't understand. Then everything went deathly still.

I opened my eyes and found that everything was gone—the hut, the trees, Elric, the forest and Fitch. I was now sitting in an open field with burnt grass and dead flowers all around. Everywhere I looked, I saw death and devastation.

A booming scream from above snapped my attention to the skies above where I saw dozens of dragons locked in combat. The noise was deafening and I was terrified. A sudden familiar voice drifted through my mind, causing me to yelp in surprise.

"Don't be frightened. What you see are just images from my memories; they are not real. I wanted you to see the story of dragons with your own eyes."

I stared at my friend and pointed dumbly to my head.

Fitch smiled and took a few steps away from me. *"Ah, the mind communication, I forgot that it must seem quite strange to you. I apologize but that is the only way I can communicate with you in my natural form. If I were to speak to you in my natural voice I'm afraid your human ears would burst from the sound. Mortals were never meant to hear our true voices."*

Then, before my eyes Fitch's kind, elderly visage vanished and was replaced by a huge dragon. He was around the same size as the Dark Lord but that was where the similarities stopped. Where the Dark Lord was stocky and bulky, Fitch was longer, looking graceful, more like a snake than lizard. He was covered in deep blue and sea-green scales that caught the sun and shimmered like raindrops. Two large golden horns spiralled from atop his head, and his massive wings nestled gently at his back. He was the most beautiful creature I had ever seen, and I felt such guilt at being the cause of his hiding his majesty all these years.

I looked around nervously at my surroundings and then back up at Fitch. "You didn't really just transform in this tiny little hut did you? Because I think Yaleon might be a little upset."

Fitch chuckled in my mind and lowered his great head down to my eye level. *"No, child, we are still sitting in his hut around the fire, all of what you see is in your mind through my magic."*

"But you are using your *own* magic, not the elements'; won't the Dark Lord know you are here?"

"Yes, but I can't hide any longer. My selfish, stubborn nature has caused enough problems. It is time I started to fix them."

I sat and listened, mesmerized, letting his magic take control and play our past inside my mind.

*

The mortal world of Eiddoril was not the first design to be created by the elements. Many have come and gone throughout history, and unfortunately, this may not be the last. It was during their first attempt at Eiddoril that the elements created their first being, dragons. Hundreds of the beautiful, terrifying creatures once gracefully glided through the skies, adding their stunning uniqueness to the landscape.

The elements moulded dragons in their image—timeless, strong, powerful, superior beings that nothing could challenge. However, with that came arrogance, hate and greed. A great need burned in their souls. They were never happy, never satisfied, their thirst for power and dominance dwarfed everything, which eventually led to the Dragon Wars. Hundreds of dragons perished in their self-inflicted genocide, and the world the elements held dear suffered greatly.

The elements realized what dragons had become, and although it pained them to do so, they created a prison, another state of being, and banished them there. The immortal plane was now their home.

The elements left dragons enough energy in this prison to keep them alive, but it was not enough for them. They continued to fight amongst themselves, battling over the limited energy that flowed through their state of existence. Being immortal could not save them from each other, and their numbers diminished almost to the point of extinction.

Many years passed, and their once mighty race had been dwindled down to few dozen. Their realm was dying from their abuse and they had no way to stop it. However, two of their most powerful kind, Ashia and Mareth, had discovered the way in which all of the planes were connected, magical lines that connected and held all of these different states together. But these magical lines or pathways were sealed from dragons with doorways that required a vast amount of elemental power to open. They were designed to be only accessible by the elements but once again, dragons outsmarted their makers and discovered how to get the power they needed—by mating.

When two dragons mate, they combine everything, their power, minds and souls. They essentially become the same being in two separate shells. So out of necessity and not desire the two most powerful of their species mated, and together joining their own powers combined with every bit of elemental magic left in their realm, they were able to open a portal and travel the magical pathways.

They searched for a long time, becoming lost in the endless pathways and pockets of magic. They discovered other areas in the immortal realm. Each one they went to they encountered new beings, some that not even nightmares would welcome, and others that were just trying to survive. They learned that the world they had once lived in had been reborn several times. The elements had been busy, trying to accomplish whatever it was that they had planned, but it seemed that dragons were not their only failures. For reasons no one knew they had banished each creature, and dragons could not find the elements.

Traveling within the pathways was draining and was costing more and more power from Aisha and Mareth. There was not enough elemental energy left on these other pockets to keep replenishing themselves. They decided that they would open the portal one more time in hopes that finally they would be reunited with their makers, and it turned out that they were rewarded. They came to Eiddoril, finally breaking free, returning to the mortal realm, and they knew as soon as they crossed the threshold that they had finally come home.

*

The images changed and I was through the dizzying magical pathways and back home. It was nowhere that I recognized. It seemed so alive and peaceful, not like the Eiddoril I knew, my home that was dying and being torn apart by war.

I watched with wide eyes as two dragons came into view. The first was a creature from nightmares. Mareth was black, but it was deeper somehow, as if you were looking into the deepest part of the night. He was also enormous. He easily dwarfed any of the other dragons that existed. His massive head was protected by a huge bony crest that looked like hundreds of spears were jutting from his head, and his eyes, which were the colour of blood, bored deep into your soul.

The other was Ashia, who was the colour of dawn, and her golden, orange and red scales shined with their own brilliance. She was half the size of Mareth but was no less intimidating. She also had two horns spiralling out from her crest but hers were platinum and they twisted back together at the top to form a single point. It was not hard to see why she had been thought of as a god; she was glorious.

Fitch let me take in the images for a moment and then shifted back to human form, letting his magic fade some. We sat in silence for a few minutes, still sitting somewhere in my mind. Our location changed but we had not returned back to Yaleon's hut; instead, I found myself sitting by a creek, the same creak I realized was painfully familiar. I didn't understand why my mind had chosen here to listen to Fitch but I ignored the ill feelings and paid attention while he began speaking.

"When we finally came back to this world we could feel the soft caress of our makers all around us, but they did not welcome us like we had hoped. Eiddoril was different now, and we sensed no other immortal souls, only something new and foreign to us. For reasons we never discovered the elements gave up creating immortal energy and instead adopted the system of recycling mortal energy. It made no sense to us, but we still found a way to exploit it. Many of us had changed over the millennium we had spent searching. We were still arrogant and smug but understood that we couldn't be the same creatures we had once been. We wanted a home and wanted to survive.

"However, others like Mareth and the Dark Lord had not changed. If anything they had become worse. The elements made a decision to let all the dragons stay, but only a certain few would be allowed access to the elements for magic. Mareth was not one of them. Unfortunately, in doing this they also abandoned Ashia as well because she and Mareth were linked through their mating bond."

Fitch shifted restlessly beside me. He let the images play out around us, but I could tell this part of the story was difficult for him. He looked down at his hands, which were folded in his lap. "Ashia pleaded to the elements to release her from the bond that she shared with Mareth, but it was not something they could undo. The elements did have a solution, but it came with a price. In order to break the mating bond she had to give up her soul, had to give up the life energy that Mareth and she shared. In doing so she was also giving up her immortality."

A frown crossed my face, and I shook my head. "I don't understand. How do you live without a soul?'

Fitch lifted his head and regarded me with patience. "I know this is difficult to grasp, but the world of magic is very complicated. A dragon's life energy is ageless, a onetime thing. It is not like a mortal that can be recycled back into the world once its host has expired. The elements were unwilling or perhaps unable to give her new immortal life energy, but they did not want to lose her completely. Death removed her combined sprit that she shared with Mareth and gave her a mortal one. She would still live for a very long time but was no longer invincible. She could die now like any other mortal and she could *feel*."

A sad smile crossed his face. "Ashia changed after that. During the transfer, she lost all of her memories of her life before. The elements and others did the best they could to help her remember who she was, but she was never the same. She developed emotions that none of us had ever experienced before. She felt joy, regret, belonging, sadness and love. Ashia became an outcast among our kind, preferring to spend her days with the different races that now worshiped her, finally becoming what the elements had hoped for in our species all along, but you need to understand that Ashia did not make this sacrifice lightly. She did it, yes, to break her bonds with Mareth and regain her elemental powers . . . but she also did it to protect you."

The images around me faded, and I was left feeling light-headed. I was back in Yaleon's hut, and to my surprise Elric was still there as well. We locked eyes.

"Did you see? Were you here the whole time?" I managed to whisper.

"Yes, I saw." That was all he said, all he could say, really.

"Fitch, what did you mean she did it to protect me? Which dragon was I? Because I really felt no connection to any of the ones I saw."

Fitch, who was still standing in the same spot as when his tale began, came over to kneel in front of me. He reached out his hand and traced the symbol on my face with a shaking hand. "That is because, my dear, you had not been born yet. You are Ashia and Mareth's offspring."

CHAPTER 15

Of all the thoughts and emotions I had running through my mind, *Oh* was all I could muster. I was the daughter of our gods—one of whom seemed bent on my destruction—and I all I could do for the moment was breathe and try to not pass out. I was vaguely aware of Elric standing up and moving to confront Fitch.

"Why? Of all the things you've kept hidden from her—why tell her this now? Why add more pain and confusion to what she's already experiencing?" Elric was rapidly losing his cool.

Fitch stood still and faced Elric's outburst. "She has a right to know where she came from. She's strong enough and can handle it. Besides, she wanted to know the whole truth."

"But why now? Haven't you done enough damage today? Do you enjoy watching her suffer?"

Fitch was on Elric so fast I barely saw him move. He slammed Elric against the wall, which made the hut shudder. He pinned Elric's arms down by his sides and glared him in the face, contempt and anger dripping from every word. "Do you think I don't know what I've done? Do you think I wouldn't give anything to reverse what's happened to her and to *me?* She is not my true daughter, but I have loved her as such for longer than your short-sighted mind can imagine. So do not presume I don't care. You have no idea what it's like to live with failure for an eternity."

I came up behind Fitch and placed my hand on his shoulder. He was breathing heavily, and I now knew *what* he was trying to control inside his fragile human shell . . . his dragon. He slowly dropped his head and shook. Releasing Elric, Fitch stepped back and allowed Elric to breathe again.

The prince was stunned and wisely wary of the dragon, but he did not press his argument. "I'm sorry. I didn't mean anything by what I said. I'm just frustrated and overwhelmed."

Fitch ignored Elric and grabbed my hand, holding it for few moments and then releasing it. He again looked up at Elric. "No, it is I who should apologize. I lost my temper. I know you are acting out of love, which is, unfortunately, sorely misplaced, but that is a conversation for another time. I am not accustomed to having all of these feelings, let alone sharing them with another being. I have been alone in this for so long."

I cleared my throat and got the attention of my two companions. I needed to change the subject. "So the god of light and the god of darkness are my parents. What does that make me? Where do I fit into all of this, and what did I do to make my father hate me enough to want to kill me?"

Fitch led me back to the circle of furs. The fire was starting to fade, which meant we had been talking for a long time. It would probably be dawn soon, and the decision of the Ywari people would be known. I took a seat in the soft warm furs and Elric sat down beside me. I knew I shouldn't but I leaned my body against his and let him support my weight. I needed his strength and compassion.

Fitch didn't return to his seat. Instead, he paced to the window and stared out into the night. My eyes closed and I listened to the sound of Fitch's voice as his words told the story of my birth.

"Shortly after we arrived in this new world, Ashia discovered she was with child. Ashia saw what Mareth was becoming, had watched him grow more powerful and more evil every day, but she had hoped that when they finally found the elements again, his attitude would have changed. However, it didn't, and then the elements punished him and others by removing their own magical influences, making him an even more dangerous partner, especially after he had learned how to manipulate life energy. Ashia's instincts screamed at her to protect you, and that is why she sacrificed her immortality."

Fitch's voice lowered to what sounded like a growl. "Mareth had known that Ashia was with child, but once she received her new soul, he could not sense her any more. He was outraged and demanded he be the sole source of your upbringing, but Ashia somehow managed to convince him that she had lost the offspring during her soul transfer. Mareth almost killed her that day, and he would have it wasn't for others' interference. He never spoke to Ashia again after that day, and it still puzzles me as to why he had even bothered to be concerned about you."

I cracked my eyes open a little. "So she managed to keep me hidden from him. How? I thought we could all sense each other in our natural forms."

Fitch turned from the window and nodded. "We can. We can't pinpoint exactly who we are individually, but every dragon's life energy gives off the same aura. When we are in human form, that aura is masked, and our natural powers are muted. We have to rely heavily on outside forms of magic, which for us was the elements."

Fitch returned his gaze to the window and I shifted closer to Elric. I watched Fitch as he spoke about my real mother.

"Your mother was a powerful dragon, and even with her new soul her own magic, which had nothing to do with the elements, was very powerful. She managed to disguise your hatching, and as soon as you were old enough she taught you to stay in human form. I didn't even know of your existence until many years later."

Fitch smiled a little at some memory, and it was good to see that he actually had some good recollections from that time. When he started speaking again his voice had changed. He was more sombre, and a look of longing crossed his face. "During the time that everything was somewhat peaceful in this world I became very close with Ashia. Our experiences and interactions with the other races, especially the humans, were beginning to wear off on us. We started to understand and even developed positive emotions, such as happiness and love. Most of the dragons were content to live here now; we had found a home, and there was no more fighting.

"I worked closely with Ashia, teaching the other races how to use the elements' powers, and our feelings for each other grew daily. It was right before Mareth started the war that I discovered Ashia had had an offspring." He smiled at me. "You stayed in the forests surrounded by animals and the few other races who called it home.

You had an acute affinity with the creatures around you. You could read their thoughts and you kept them safe. This was where you were most comfortable, where you felt safe, so you thought that it would do no harm to roam free in your true shape confined in the safety of your wilderness."

He shook his head. "You were so young, so naïve. I happened to be hunting that day and sensed you. You seemed so familiar yet different. I flew down to a clearing and that was when I saw you for the first time. You were lying next to a small creek. You were shaped longer, like me, more like a snake than dragon, but you were larger. You had deep red and golden scales, but the boney spikes that led from the tip of your crest to the tip of your tail were the colour of midnight. Two silver horns jutted from your head but curved into the shape of rams' antlers. Your eyes were the colour of the deepest forest, but it was the odd marking that dominated your gracious head that caught my breath in my throat."

I reached up and traced the now-familiar lines that covered my face, and Fitch nodded at me. "Yes, it resembled the sun and the moon combined with rays of energy streaking gold down your face. There had been no doubt in my mind that you were Ashia and Mareth's child—darkness and light combined."

Fitch paused and took a deep breath. I could tell he was weary. None of us had slept much in the past week, and I was beginning to think that I was doomed to never sleep peacefully again. "Fitch, I know you're tired, but there is one more question I'd like to ask."

"Go ahead; your insatiable appetite for knowledge was tiresome even back then."

He gave me a little smile and I stifled a yawn as I shifted my weight against Elric. Throughout the course of Fitch's story, I had somehow ended up curled up beside Elric with his arm gently supporting my head. If I had been more awake, I would have moved, but apparently, my body doesn't listen to my brain very well.

"Why did all of the dragons leave? Why not just Ashia and Mareth? And how did they open the portal again? They were no longer mated, so how did they have enough power?"

Fitch laughed, which was a deep rumbling in his chest, and shook his head at me.

"That, my dear, is more than one question, but I'll answer anyway. What I told you a few days ago about the two dragons deciding that they need to leave to settle their differences was not the truth. The elements forced them to leave. The elements had no intention of losing another world of their creating to the greed and selfishness of dragons. So they gave us a choice: leave and settle our differences elsewhere or stay and get along, but if we chose to stay and if any dragon broke the truce the elements would have no choice but to banish us all for good."

Elric shifted so that I was no longer lying on his arm and sat up a little straighter, flexing his hand as if it had fallen asleep.

"There is something I don't understand. If the elements cared so much for Eiddoril and its creatures, than why did they let dragons take control in the first place? Why did they allow them to be worshipped as gods and cause all of these problems?"

Fitch's eyes flared gold once and then returned to their human brown colour. He was angry—but at who, I couldn't tell. "I do not pretend to know the motives or actions of the elements. Soon after dragons returned they almost completely disappeared, leaving Eiddoril to our mercy. It wasn't until Mareth started another war that they chose to interfere again."

Fitch shook his head. "All the dragons had agreed to let Ashia and Mareth be the ones to return to the immortal plane to fight out their differences. None of the other dragons wanted to go. Some had had offspring and they were quite content at staying behind and abiding by the elements' wishes, but something had happened to change their minds. I tried to speak of it with some of them, but they refused to talk about it and only said that they had no choice. In the end, dragons were once again absent from the mortal world, or so was thought. The rest of the story you know."

I did, mostly. I didn't yet know how our alliances and friendships had become so fractured over the years and how we stood a chance of fixing all of this, and I didn't understand why the elements had not stopped the Dark Lord from completing his evil plans, but my brain couldn't handle any more tonight. I was exhausted.

"Thank you, Fitch, for telling me the truth. We'll get through this, and you'll see Ashia again."

A single tear rolled down his cheek, which he angrily wiped away. "You're welcome. Now both of you get some rest while you still can."

As I rolled over and closed my eyes I was expecting to be plagued with visions and dreams of my past, but all I saw were my mother's golden dragon eyes and then only darkness.

Fitch

Standing there watching her sleep curled up beside a human sent waves of disgust through me. I was tempted to end the distraction now, but I knew how that would play out and I was not willing to jeopardize my goals any further . . . for now. Despite my dragon instincts, I did care deeply for her and believed deep down that I was doing the right thing.

Quietly, with stealth born from years of practice, I emerged into the waning night. I left the Ywari hut behind and travelled down one of their many bridges. Coming to a relatively secluded spot, I sat cross-legged on the worn wooden planks and attempted to call *them*. I needed to know what they were up to and why they had suddenly broken their silence. I needed them to stop playing games with me.

Closing my eyes, I reached deep inside myself, being careful not to use too much magic. The response was almost instantaneous, which I was not used to, and my eyes flew open to see a shadowy presence lost among the foliage. It was not who I had expected, which I suppose did not surprise me; they were never reliable, but if he appeared instead, there was definitely something wrong.

My voice carried softly through the trees. "Why are *you* here? I've kept up my end of the bargain, thanks to no help from you or the others. You risk too much by coming here; they must not know of our involvement."

A feeling of dread stole across my soul and I became very cold. I clenched my human teeth tightly and fought the pain the other was inflicting. Its voice echoed through the night and left all the hair on my body standing on end.

"Do not forget your place, immortal, and do not forget who you are speaking to. I have come because the game has changed and it does not bode well for our arrangement."

My anger flared. "What are you talking about? I have done nothing but follow your wishes—and let me tell you, it has not been easy. Why is she so important? What is it she has that you wish to possess so badly?"

I stifled a gasp as I clutched at my chest trying in vain to stop my life energy from leaving my body. My head dipped and I inhaled deeply, waiting for the sensation to pass.

"As I said, the game has changed. The elements are no longer happy with your progress and have decided to take matters into their own hands. This does not please me, and if you want what I can give you, I'd suggest you discover a way to fulfil our plans."

Resisting the urge to flee as fast as I could I lifted my head and stared into the dead of night. "The elements trust me so have no fear from them, but I have also noticed changes and am well aware of the urgency to complete our plans. I will deal with it just as I have always done. I will not fail."

Warmth crawled across my skin again as my co-conspirator left me alone with my thoughts. Sitting deathly still I took stock of my situation. I knew I was not being told everything from both parties and it bothered me. There was more to Ililsaya than what I had been told, and I was determined to find out one way or another. I was tired of playing by the rules; it was time I found some answers before I made any more mistakes.

CHAPTER 16

Dawn arrived too soon and I was awakened by a soft nudge. I opened my eyes and gazed up into Deneoes's amused face.

"Do you know you snore?" he asked me with an amused face. "I am surprised they didn't figure out you were a dragon long before this. I've heard thunder quieter than you."

I took a swing at the young Ywari, but he easily sprang out of the way. I rubbed at my still sleep-weary eyes and tried desperately to find something to throw at the little bugger. "I don't snore. And didn't anyone ever tell you it's impolite to watch someone while they sleep? Not to mention creepy." I stood and stretched, trying to get the last tendrils of sleep out of my bones. I glanced around the small room and noticed that I was alone with Deneoes.

"Where are Elric and Fitch? You didn't throw them off a bridge, did you?"

Deneoes laughed and headed toward the door. "They woke about an hour ago. They told me to let you sleep for a little while longer." He started toward the canvas doorway. "We're gathered in the meeting room. Wash up in the back and I'll take you to them, but I have to warn you—you're not going to happy with what they have to say."

Before I could ask what he meant, Deneoes exited the hut and gave me some privacy while I attempted to make myself presentable. As soon as we were back on the ground, I really needed to find somewhere to take a bath. Maybe Deneoes could show me where the Ywari bathed, but I suppose that is a luxury that will have to wait. I finished quickly and found Deneoes waiting for me outside with the mist fang quietly waiting beside his feet. As soon has the big animal saw me, it silently padded over and stuck its large head under my hand, demanding to be stroked.

Deneoes shook his head, turned and headed down the bridge. I fell in step behind him with "Fang" close behind.

Deneoes led us across several other bridges before we came to what he had called the meeting room. Food smells wafted out of the cracks and my stomach growled. I told Fang to stay outside, and then Deneoes and I entered the large enclosure. It was not like Yaleon's hut. There were no comfortable furs around anywhere, just several benches laid out in the middle of the room, making it feel practical but not very inviting. It was larger than Yaleon's home, quite capable of holding a dozen or so people.

I found my companions quickly and sat next to them near the front of the room. Elric handed me some food on a clay plate, which consisted of fresh berries, vegetables and some kind of dried meat. It was delicious and did wonders to heal my sleep-deprived body.

Looking around the room, I noticed several other Ywari I had not yet met. I assumed they were the elders Yaleon had spoken of yesterday. I found him, his wife and his son Ossian at the front of our gathering. Deneoes curiously stayed near the back, which was causing rather hostile stares from his father and brother.

Yaleon picked up a small horn that was lying beside him and blew into it. A low sound echoed throughout room, and everyone stopped talking and waited for Yaleon to speak.

"I won't delay this any longer. Last night I met with the elders of our tribe. We discussed what I had learned last night at great length and in great consideration."

He directed his full attention to me. "You have brought us dire news, which we require more time to study. I know you were hoping for assistance in your quest but I can't safely condone it. We have remained undetected for centuries and the best course of action for us right now is to remain so. I won't risk betrayal again. I am truly sorry but I must ask you to leave. Perhaps our paths will meet again when Ashia returns, and perhaps then we can repair what has been broken."

Before anyone had a chance to stop me, I sprang from my seat and approached Yaleon. Ossian drew his knife he wore at his side and pointed it at my throat, but Yaleon placed a restraining hand on him.

I approached the Ywari leader with my hands held out in front of me. "May I speak? I promise I'll leave with my companions after I say what I must." I waited and held my breath. I didn't think he would grant my request but he surprised me.

"Go ahead, but my decision has been made. I won't change my mind."

I lowered my hands and looked down at Yaleon. "I understand, but there is something you all need to hear. Can you please translate to the rest of your people? I'd like them to understand my words."

"I'll do it." Deneoes was suddenly at my side, glaring defiance at the rest of his family. He nodded at me and I took a deep breath and turned to face the gathered crowd.

My voice was stronger than I felt, and I hoped my words would not be ignored. "I know I have come to you as a stranger, a threat to your peaceful existence, and I'm deeply thankful that you took us in and trusted us enough to hear our tale. However, if you think you can hide forever, you are sorely mistaken. I have been hiding my whole *life*. I don't remember any of it but I can feel it in my soul, and I'm tired. I'm tired of being scared, tired of not knowing when the next death blow will fall, but most of all I'm tired of not living my life the way I was meant to. Ashia may never return, she may not even be alive, and dragons may never again grace the skies of Eiddoril. Ashia hid me here to protect you, to keep you safe from the Dark Lord and his army, but I can't do it alone."

I faced Yaleon. "I want to be the protector that I was meant to be. I know that mistakes were made and I know that we have so much work to do, but if we don't stand together now the Dark Lord will win, just as he has for the past 300 years, and If I don't stop him now there is nowhere in this world you will be able to hide. He will destroy everything that is good, and you will be powerless to stop him."

I knelt in front of the proud Ywari leader and bared my soul to him. "Please, don't do this for me or Gareth or Ashia, help me for you, and help me for the right to live free and in safety."

Deneoes finished translating, and I heard murmurs all around the room. Standing, I glanced back at Fitch, who regarded me with pride. I at least had tried; now it was up to them.

Yaleon looked at me with a deep sorrow in his eyes, and I knew I had not won my case. "I'm truly sorry child, but I can't help you on your journey. We are too few and I must think about my people. If you can accomplish this impossible quest, we will wait for you to lead us against the dark one. We will come when you call; this I can promise you, but I can't help you get there. I'm sorry."

"You are as stubborn as you are foolish. Your prejudiced ways will be your undoing." Elric rose and stormed out of the room.

I turned back to Yaleon and looked down at the Ywari leader. "I hope it will not be too late then. Be well, and may I see you again in the future under better circumstances."

I turned to leave to find Elric, but Deneoes stopped me. He gave me a strange, mischievous smile and then addressed his father. "My position still stands, Father. I'm going with Karah and her friends. I believe in their quest, and I for one am tired of hiding."

"You can't leave! You're the only one who can use the wind arrows. How can you leave your people unprotected to help a couple of charlatans and a treacherous human?" Ossian was right in his brother's face, and I was afraid that things were going to come to blows, but their father came between them and pushed them apart.

"Enough! We have heard enough of this argument last night. Deneoes, you must do what you feel is right, but please know once you leave this village you are not permitted to come back; it is too dangerous for us."

I stared open mouthed at the Ywari leader. How could he just turn his back on his son that way? But Deneoes didn't seem to care.

"I understand, Father. Perhaps someday you will see me as the son you always wanted me to be and not some hot-headed child playing with magic."

Yaleon looked wounded at his son's comment but did not reply to it.

Instead, his mother came forward and placed a gentle kiss on his forehead. "Be safe, my son, and may the elements guide you."

Deneoes nodded at her but did not take his eyes off his brother, who continued to glare at him.

Ossian snorted and then turned and stalked out the back with his mother and father.

The other Ywari had all left as well, leaving Fitch, Deneoes and me. The young Ywari looked up at me, eager to be going, but I could see the hurt in his eyes.

"Well, let's get this show on the road. I already have supplies waiting for us down by your horses. I'll go find your moody prince and then we can make our way down."

Deneoes left and I looked at Fitch. "Hey, I'm sorry about what I said about Ashia. It sort of just came out."

Fitch kept his face a blank mask as he spoke. "Do not apologize. What you said was true. She may not be alive, but I still have hope, if nothing else. I have always had that. I am proud of you, and she would be too."

He forced a smile, which made me feel odd. The old dragon had changed, and I wasn't sure what that meant for our friendship.

*

The trek back down was so much easier than the way up, but my muscles were still screaming by the time I reached the bottom. Deneoes was already down strapping additional supplies to our horses. I was the first to reach the ground so I took the opportunity to ask my new friend some questions. I pointed at the tree I had just come down and stared up into the dizzying heights.

"How do you do that? I know you're strong, but how do you seem to stick to the trees like little insects?"

Deneoes held up his hands, palm out, and told me to look closely. At first I didn't see anything unusual, but then tiny little barbs emerged from his fingertips and the perimeter of his palm.

They looked like tiny little fishhooks. I went to touch them when they disappeared back into his skin and he withdrew his hands.

"We have them on our feet too. Makes climbing easier, and it comes in handy in a fight."

My dangerous curiosity got the better of me and I blurted out a personal question.

"Speaking of fights, what is the deal with your brother and father? It doesn't seem like you have the best relationship with them."

Deneoes's eyes flared with anger for a moment, and I was afraid I had overstepped, but he quickly masked it and gave me a shy smile. "That, my fiery friend, is a long story, but I can give you the simplified version."

We continued to pack up the horses as he spoke. "My father's line has always been leader of our people, dating back to our creation. We have always been the leaders because we were always the only ones in our tribe who yielded magic. For some reason the past hundred years or so magic has not blessed our family or any member of the Ywari. We grew fearful that the elements were angry with us and were punishing us. Anyway, when my brother was born the tribe all had high hopes that he would manifest the ability to wield the elemental arrows, breaking the curse sent upon us."

He reached back and gave his arrows a loving pat. "As you can see, that didn't happen. Since the day I was born my mother said she could feel the elements with me, and by the time I reached the young age of five, I had the power to wield the arrows. My brother never forgave me for it, especially since he was the eldest and most likely to replace my father. His jealously quite often clouds his judgment and we have caused much grief to our parents with our constant bickering. I think my father secretly regrets my place in the tribe as well. My brother has always been the good student and loyal follower, but I was never one to follow the pack. So I guess you can say that none of us really see eye to eye, but they are still my family and I will do my duty to protect them and my people."

Deneoes fell silent and continued loading the horses. I let the conversation drop and instead turned my attention to Elric and Fitch coming down the ladder.

Elric reached us first and brought up a good question. "Ah, we only have three horses. I don't mind riding double, but it may slow us down a little. Is there anywhere close to here that we can acquire another steed?"

Deneoes shook his head. "No offence, but I'd rather run and keep close to the forests. I can keep up; and besides, animals don't like me much."

Then an answer to our problem literally materialized out of the bushes, causing the horses to nearly pass out from fright. Fang appeared, and without a pause walked up behind Deneoes, stuck her head between his legs and easily threw him onto her strong back, causing Deneoes to yelp in alarm.

I laughed. "Well, I guess Fang is coming too, and I don't think she wants to travel alone. Can you handle that or do you still want to run?"

Deneoes gave me a withering look, but I could see a sparkle of anticipation in his eyes. "This will do, I guess, but we'll have to stick to the trees and tall grasses. Your beast is scaring the horses, so I think that will be safest for all of us. Can you do me a favour?"

I mounted my horse and looked back with humour in my eyes. "What's that?"

"Can you please tell her that I am not a snack? I don't think I taste very good. There's no meat on my bones."

We all laughed, which was good to hear.

"I think you're safe. Just hold on and try not to fall off."

With that, we headed out of the woods and left the peace of the Ywari home behind.

CHAPTER 17

The Dark Lord

Cowering in my lair, the echoes of my pain bounced off the cave walls. My claws dug deep into the stone beneath and my mighty head pushed into the floor trying to bury itself to get away from the pain. At last, the pain in my mind started to ebb and I was able to focus again on my master.

Mareth was still angry, but he was back in control. *"When did you sense this other dragon? How long has he been there?"*

I swallowed the dryness in my throat as I tried to explain my sudden communication with my master. "Just last night, and I went into deep thought to try and contact you as soon as I realized its presence. I can't tell if it is male or female, but there is definitely another dragon traveling with Ililsaya."

Mareth's eyes shined bright with hatred in my mind. *"It's a male. I know who it is. I was a fool; I should have seen this before. It is Enthor, Ashia's puppet. When he did not follow through the gate with the others, she had said he had perished during the war—and I believed her."*

A roar filled my thoughts and I tried in vain to block out the sound.

"It doesn't matter; I am not concerned by his presence. I still have the bargaining chips. He can do nothing, but we must speed up our plans. Commence the march on Gareth. It is time we crush them and all those that stand in our way for the last time. I trust you are ready."

I straightened and bowed to my master. "Yes, Master, my army is ready and I have been in contact with Reaper to let him know of Karah's location. But what about the elements; will they not try to stop us?" A pang of fear escaped my thoughts and I was immediately punished for it.

"Do not cower in the face of those pompous beings. They will do nothing to jeopardize their world. They are tired of rebuilding and know I will tear it apart if they stand in my way. I hold all the pieces to this puzzle, and it is time we put them into place, starting with the annihilation of the human race."

That thought brought great joy to my heart. "Yes, Master, I will launch our attack immediately. But what of Ililsaya? Where do you want her brought once Reaper has her?"

"Bring her back to Gareth. That is where the portal will open. I need the power she holds inside to sustain it and keep it open long enough to finish my plans. This world does not stand a chance. Contact me when you are in position, and do not fail me."

With a sudden final flash of pain, Mareth disappeared from my thoughts.

I remained where I was for a few moments, regaining my strength. My master's plan to start the march on Gareth was unexpected, but I was ready. My army was the strongest they had ever been, and Gareth was alone. I had worked hard through the years to isolate them. They had ignorantly thought they were safe, but soon they would bend in fear.

I had to admit, though, that I was gravely disappointed in my failure to figure out that Ililsaya's mage had really been a dragon all this time. I remembered Enthor and looked forward to the time when I would come face-to-face with him and we could end our dispute the way we were meant to, in the skies.

I swept across the expanse of my lair and headed out to call my army to arms, but I paused in front of the pathetic mortal chained against the one wall. I bent my massive horned head to stare into her eyes.

"Don't worry; it will all be over soon. My army is headed for Gareth, and Ililsaya is walking into a trap. There is nothing you or anyone can do to stop this. Mareth will return, and then this world will be his."

I left, leaving the poor creature alone in the dark with only her tears to comfort her.

*

Standing on the outskirts of the Barren Wastes in my human form, I looked out at the scene before me. My army spread out, numbering in the thousands, forming a blanket of death that would soon cover Eiddoril. Humans and other creatures sworn to me awaited the signal that would tell them to move out toward their destination. I had sent out the call to arms as soon as I was done speaking with Mareth, but it had still taken almost a week for my army to gather. I wished Reaper were here to see all of his hard work come to pass, but he was at the temple waiting for Ililsaya. I had not had any contact from the shifter in days, relaying my last message as to Ililsaya's whereabouts to deaf ears, but I was not concerned, I had faith in my officer and knew Reaper's hatred for the lost dragon burned brightly and painfully in his soul. He would not fail.

A Litui general came to stand beside me and lowered his head in reverence. "Master, your legions are ready. We await your orders."

I looked down at my minion and smiled. "Is the precious cargo prepared and ready for transport?"

"Yes, my Lord."

"Good. You have done well, General Qued. You have my orders to proceed with the invasion of Gareth. I will follow you after I take care of a few loose ends. Take the most direct route to Gareth." I reached for a map and spread it open so that my general could see it. "There will be small towns and farms along the way that will aide in your efforts. They are under orders to do everything in their power to help you reach your destination. What you do with them when you are finished is up to you." I rolled the map and handed it off to the Litui. "Do not bother trying to mask your march. I want Gareth to see their doom coming. I want them to realize that they are alone and that no one is coming to rescue them this time."

"As you wish." General Qued produced a horn and blew long and hard into it. The low sound echoed throughout the crags and pits of the Barren Wastes and was answered by a thunderous, chilling yell. The Dark Lord's army moved out as one, soldiers, beasts and war supplies all massed together like a flowing tide of death. General

Qued bowed to his master and then skittered off to join the ranks of his army.

A wide, evil smile spread across my lips, and after one last look at my masterpiece, I turned and disappeared among the rocks.

CHAPTER 18

Karah

We had been riding hard for only a few days when we came upon a small lake. We were still in the region known as Chandra, but we had veered slightly west away from the coast south toward the Kanarah woods and the temple of Ashia. I reined my horse to a stop and looked at my companions.

Deneoes came out of the bushes and looked at me happily. His demeanour reminded me of a little boy who had just received a new toy. He was enjoying himself immensely, but unfortunately, our furry companion was scaring the horses to death. My horse started to jump and shy from Fang, causing the other two horses to react the same. I ignored the curses coming from Fitch and Elric and dismounted, taking the gentle horse's face in my hands and stared into its eyes. I instantly felt the connection between us and felt its fear and need for flight. I gently sent waves of peace and safety through the horse. I sent feelings of trust and friendship toward Fang into its mind and began to sense confusion at first and then acceptance. The horse calmed and stopped fidgeting. I released its head and watched as it began to graze on grass. I followed the same procedure with the other two horses, and by the time I was done all three were happily grazing next to a purring Fang.

"Now that was impressive. Why didn't you do that before? And why did we stop? It's not even midday yet." Deneoes had gotten off Fang and he went over to Elric's saddlebags, producing an apple.

"Yes, why have we stopped? We need to keep moving and gain as much ground during the day. I don't think it is safe for us to travel at night." Elric scanned our current position and waited for me to answer.

I put my hands on my hips and glared at my male companions. "I stopped because I need a bath. I don't know about males and their hygiene, but I have not bathed in days, and frankly, I can't stand myself anymore."

I motioned behind me, irritated. "This lake looked like a safe spot." I started rummaging around in my pack, muffling my words. "I'll only be a few minutes but I think it might benefit everyone if they did the same. The Dark Lord can probably smell us coming."

Deneoes gave a snort and laughed at Elric's horrified expression.

Fitch dismounted and led his horse over to me, looking especially irritated. "Is this really necessary? We don't have time for this."

I glared at the older dragon and grabbed my personal saddlebag. "Yes, it's necessary. I'll only be a few minutes, I promise." I ignored the glare, proceeded down to the bank and started to walk down the shoreline.

"Wait—you can't go alone. What if something happens?"

I turned and saw that Elric was already half way to my position, when realization hit him and his face reddened in embarrassment. He looked very uncomfortable and I hid my smile. I also noticed that Fitch was watching us, trying to mask his fury. He really was taking this too seriously. It was just a quick dip; what could possibly happen?

I tried to hide my amusement as I spoke to Elric. "Don't worry, I'm not alone, Fang is with me. Trust me; I'll be fine. Go wash up with the boys. I can take care of myself."

At the sound of her name, Fang shifted her camouflage and became the colour of the sand. She sat on the small beach and gently growled at Elric, telling him to let me have my privacy.

"All right, but yell if you need help, and don't be long. I have a bad feeling about this." He turned and walked back up the embankment to find our companions.

I walked a little farther down the shore and found a larger patch of beach that was hidden by some overhanging trees and brush. I was just thankful that the farther south we seemed to travel the warmer the temperature seemed to get. It still was not as warm as our summers, but at least I wouldn't freeze to death while bathing. I glanced around quickly to make sure I was alone and then quickly stripped my clothes. Stepping into the lake I only paused for a moment before I dived under, completing covering my body with the cool, clean water.

I stayed submerged for a moment just enjoying the feel of the water around me, when I felt something brush past my leg. I broke the surface of the lake with a gasp and swam back to where I could touch the sandy bottom again. I looked nervously at the water around me, trying to see what it was that had touched me but nothing moved, and all I could see were weeds. It must have been the plant life or a fish or something, but nevertheless I decided it was time to get out, just in case it was a poisonous or dangerous animal. I started to swim back toward the beach when I noticed Fang pacing back and forth along the bank. Her hackles were up and she was growling, and then I saw off to the side shadowy figures in a copse of trees.

Wonderful—spirits. This was not going to end well. I was nearing closer to the beach when something grabbed my ankle and pulled me down beneath the water. I heard Fang's muffled roar as I was pulled deeper into the darkening water. I kicked franticly at whatever it was that held my leg, but it was strong. Desperately I tried not to panic and I focused myself. The water was murky, making it difficult to see, but as if in response to my dilemma, my symbol started to glow, filling the water around me with a strange light.

The creature that had a hold of my leg suddenly released me and came to face me. I had never seen or heard of anything like it. It was humanoid in shape, but where arms should be were two long tentacles on each side and its legs were in the shape of a fish's tail. Its torso was the form of a female, but instead of skin she was completely covered in blue-grey scales. Her face was quite stunning. Long golden hair fanned out all around her while she stared at me with large, lidless dark eyes.

We stared at each other for a moment, but I was running out of breath and my curiosity was not enough to keep me alive.

The creature seemed to sense this, and faster than I cared to think about it, she touch both sides of my face with her tentacles. I was immediately assaulted with images I could not understand. They were all jumbled together, and I couldn't make sense of what I was seeing. I stayed there motionless in the water as wave after wave of information was thrown into my mind.

I was starting to lose consciousness, and when I felt the last bit of air leave my lungs, something large swam beside me. The creature released me and released a high-pitched scream as she swam out of sight.

I closed my eyes, and right before I passed out I felt myself being cradled against a large body and speeding out of the water.

Coming to, I started to cough uncontrollably, causing me to jerk my body up and to spit out water. I heaved a few more times and then shakily lay back down, and that was when I realized I was still naked and probably surrounded by my male companions. My eyes flew open, and thankfully I had been covered with a blanket, but I was still very naked.

Fitch knelt down at my side, looking worried. "Are you all right? How do you feel?"

I rubbed at my temples, willing the headache that was starting to take hold of me to vanish. "I feel like a soggy piece of bread, and my head is pounding. What happened? How did I get out of the water?"

Deneoes came around and stared down at me. "Red, you missed it! It was the most amazing thing I have ever seen. The old man turned himself into his big toothy self and dived right into the water and brought you back out. I hope you are nice and clean 'cause there is no way him and mister soldier boy are ever going let you back in the water."

He chuckled. "All kidding aside, I'm glad you're all right. I really didn't want to try to explain to that cat of yours that you were not coming back."

I suddenly realized Fang was curled up beside me, quietly watching the water and growling every now and again. I propped myself up on one elbow and tried to see over the top of my big guardian. I saw Elric sitting away from us with his arms crossed over his knees. He was looking out over the water too but I don't think he was seeing it. I wanted to go over to him but Fitch interrupted my thoughts.

"What happened, child? What did the Ridyhkin tell you?"

"The what? Oh, you mean the scary fish lady. Well, she didn't really tell me anything, she just shoved a whole lot of images into my head. I have no idea what she was trying to do but, she almost killed me." I shivered and sat up pulling the blanket closer around my body.

Fitch regarded me impatiently. "The Ridyhkin are messengers for the element of water. They are generally docile creatures but can be very nasty if provoked. Can you remember any of what she showed you?"

"Yes, but it doesn't make sense. In one image I saw a dark cave with dozens of large rocks nestled in the centre of a crater, and then she showed me a portal ripping open in the sky and shadows spilling from it. The next image was of a huge army preparing for war and then a dark mass of some kind blocked out the moon and chaos reigned from the skies. Do you know what any of this means?"

The colour drained from Fitch's face. "What did the rocks look like? Can you tell me more about them?" He was staring at me with his dragon eyes with such intensity that I felt he would burn through me.

My voice shook with the cold and fear. "They were all different colors and seemed to glow with an iridescent light. They were quite large, and now that I think about they looked more like—"

"Eggs." Fitch sighed, and he stood up and walked away from me. It took me a minute but I grasped the thought. "Eggs? You mean dragon eggs? But where are they? It didn't look like they were in an ideal place. It felt wrong, it felt evil."

Fitch whirled on me with fury in his eyes. "I am so blind; I should have realized it then. Do you remember when I told you that the other dragons at first didn't want to return through the portal, but something had happened to change their minds?"

I nodded.

"I believe Mareth must have found their eggs and stole them, threatening them with destruction if they didn't obey him and follow him through the portal. He raised an army against Ashia right under our noses. She would not have had a chance. However, the question is, why he has waited so long to return? What else is he planning?"

Deneoes shook his head. "I don't understand. Why don't the elements simply stop this big dark nasty? They have the power; why haven't they used it?"

Deneoes brought up a very good point, something I had been wondering about myself.

Fitch was already heading back up the embankment and barely took the time to answer the question. "I don't know. I've been asking that question for years, and they have refused to answer. However, I am afraid this information holds little hope of Ashia's return. There is no way she could have withstood our kind in that number, and it also leaves the question as to why Mareth has not returned. My only guess is that the elements have refused to open the portal again to let him back through, but that does not mean he will not try. There is much more going on in this than we know. We must get on the move again. Time is wasting, and I'm afraid that we may have very little left."

"But what about the army? The only possibility is that The Dark Lord is planning an attack. We have to do something." I huddled back into my blanket, fearing the hostility in Fitch's words.

"I have no doubt that the Dark Lord is preparing an attack, but frankly, it doesn't concern me right now. If we want to find the answers we need, we must gain access to the temple. I need to know the truth! Get dressed and meet us back at the horses; we can talk on the road."

Fitch hastily disappeared behind some trees, leaving Deneoes to hand me my clothes. We exchanged glances, and I read the uncertainty in his eyes that I felt in my heart. I no longer felt I could call my friend by his human name. He was no longer a human to me; he was the dragon Enthor, and I was frightened.

I glanced over at Elric, who was still sitting staring off at nothing, and I turned my questioning gaze to Deneoes, but he just shrugged and went to follow Enthor.

I carried my things behind some brush with Fang close at my heels. I doubted that the big cat was going to let me out of her sight again either. Some great idea I'd had. My nice refreshing bath ended up being a disaster. My hair, not to mention other parts of my body that I would prefer not to have sand in was full of sand, and I'd had to have my neck saved again by use of magic that we were supposed to be hiding. I was definitely not cut out for this quest business.

I walked back to beach and strapped my sword back on. I told Fang to stay and quietly walked over to where Elric sat and joined him, pulling my knees up and hugging them.

We sat there for a minute, but me and uncomfortable silences did not get along. "Hey, listen, I'm sorry about the whole 'getting clean' idea. I need to start keeping my dumb ideas to myself. Next time I'll—"

Elric turned his bewildered gaze to me. "You're sorry? I'm the one who should be sorry. If it were just my responsibility to keep you safe, you would be dead. I was the one who heard Fang and I was the first one to the water, but I couldn't see you." Panic and fear showed in his grey eyes. "Fang was pacing back and forth along the water's edge but she wouldn't go in. I finally figured out that she was afraid of the water and that you were somewhere in there." He pointed toward the hateful lake and sighed. "I was about to dive in and search for you but Fitch thundered past me in his dragon form and dived straight in. He knew exactly where you were and had you out in a matter of seconds. If he had not been there you would have drowned. I hesitated and it nearly cost you your life."

Elric paused and turned from me to look back out across the water. "I have grown up my whole life believing I could do anything—be a hero, a prince worthy of leading a country, but all this quest has proven is how horribly inadequate I am. I can't protect you. You are a dragon with incredible powers surrounded by other beings with skills I don't have. I can understand Fitch's hostility and impatience toward me. You don't need me; I'm only in the way."

I stared at him open-mouthed. I couldn't believe a strong man I had grown up with and depended on for most of my life thought he didn't matter, that he wasn't important. But in a way I guess that was partly my fault. I was scared and even now, staring at the man who would do anything to protect me, I was unsure what to say.

I shifted my body so that I was sitting directly in front of him, and I placed my hands on his face. I lifted his head so I could to look into his eyes and was shocked at how hurt he was, how vulnerable. "How could you ever think I don't need you? I have never needed you more. I may be a dragon, but my spirit is human, my flaws and emotions are human."

I rubbed my thumbs gently across his cheekbones. "You are the strongest, most compassionate, honourable man I know, and I don't know what I would do without you. You save me every day from myself. I need you with me, I want you with me; please don't make me do this alone."

I had tears in my eyes and Elric gently brushed at my cheeks. He leaned forward so that our foreheads were touching, and he searched my face for the truth in my words.

"Thank you; I needed to hear you say that. I'm sorry, and as long as I still breathe you will never be alone."

We stared into each other's eyes for a moment, and I felt as if we were the only two beings in the world. I listened to my heart hammering in my chest and closed my eyes, breathlessly waiting for the outcome of our moment in time. However, it was shattered by Deneoes's sharp yell.

"Hey, you two, let's go. Your dragon friend is about to rip something apart and I would rather it not be me. Let's wrap up the lovers' drama and get moving. If we hurry we should reach the Chanadar and Quahril border by nightfall."

I heaved a rock at Deneoes's head, but the snickering little fiend had disappeared.

Elric and I stood and brushed the sand off ourselves. We smiled at each other, and together with Fang, we headed up the embankment and continued on our journey into the unknown.

Chapter 19

We pushed on through most of the remainder of the day, stopping only to grab a quick bite and to rest our mounts. We came across small clusters of homes and farms here and there but no major settlements. Enthor steered us clear of those. He said that we would not be welcomed and I didn't argue. It seemed that most of the outlying lands considered the people of Gareth traitors and cowards. King Edwin had always told us that we were a haven for outsiders who wished to leave the iron grip of the Dark Lord, but it seemed that most everyone else considered us a place to hide and wait out the inevitable—the Dark Lord's total control. How were we ever going to repair this mess? We had strength in numbers and in skill, but our different lands and races were so fractured, so mistrustful that we would never work together. We were digging our own graves.

The more I travelled through this land the more despair and corruption I saw. Elric and I had no idea that things outside our city were like this. Even when Elric had gone on his scouting parties with his father they had never travelled this far. It became more apparent that the king had deliberately kept things from his son, and it was making him a very moody companion.

It was approaching dusk when Enthor called our procession to a stop. We reined in beside him and Deneoes jumped off Fang to give her a bit of a rest. The elder dragon gathered us close together.

"We will be approaching the town of Delroth within the next few miles, and some cautionary tactics must be employed. Delroth is a mercenary town filled with cutthroats and fiends for hire, but it is also an excellent spot for information if you have enough coin. It is a mostly human controlled town but there may be other beings as well, namely the Hautur. We need to disguise ourselves as best we can, get supplies and info and get out."

Enthor turned to me. "Karah, I will need to cloak your symbol again, and I need you to keep your hair tied and hidden at all times while we are here."

I self-consciously ran my fingers through my hair. "Why? What does my appearance have to do with anything?"

"The Dark Lord would have sent out descriptions of us by now and you stand out the most. I can make subtle changes to our appearances but it would be best if I used as little magic as possible, so we need your flaming red hair kept hidden."

I nodded reluctantly. "All right . . . well, what about Elric and Deneoes?"

Enthor remained silent for a moment, thinking. He nodded toward Deneoes. "As much as it bothers me to split up our group, I think it would be wise if our young friend circled around Delroth and waited for us. I will not be able to mask his height, and no one will believe we would be travelling with a child."

Deneoes bristled at that comment. "Look, I may be the height of a human child, but I assure you that I can take on anything you throw at me. You need me. I came here to help, and I'm not going to be shoved into the background because you think I can't handle myself."

Deneoes's eyes burned with resentment, and I wondered how much of his life he had spent in someone else's shadow. I sympathised with him but could also see Enthor's point.

"We must convince them that we are just common thieves for hire looking for jobs, and we can't do that if they think you are a child." Enthor placed a strong hand on the young Ywari's shoulder and softened his tone. "I want to keep the identity of your race a secret. You could put your whole tribe in danger if someone figures out what you are. I know you're quite capable of taking care of yourself, which is why I want you to cover our escape. We need you and Fang to remain a secret just in case things go wrong and we need out fast."

That seemed to calm Deneoes considerably. "Fine, but Fang and I are sticking close. She can hide herself and so can I; we won't be seen. We'll wait for you just outside the town. Here, take this—" and he handed me a small wooden hollow stick.

"Blow into it if you run into trouble. It has a high-pitched sound that only I can hear. I won't be far. Good luck and don't take all night." Deneoes hopped onto Fang's back, and together they disappeared.

It amazed me how Fang always knew exactly what we were talking about and how majestic she was. I felt a pang of worry for her and Deneoes but I pushed it aside and focused on what needed to be done.

Enthor looked at me with worry in his eyes. "I wonder if maybe we should have sent you with him. This is going to be highly dangerous and I have no doubt the Dark Lord has set traps for you. I have never put you in this much danger before. I have a bad feeling about this."

Elric moved his mount closer to me. "She'll be safe. You are not alone any more, my friend. I will not let anything happen to her, and besides, I think we both know that neither one of us would let her be out of our sight. She's a trained fighter, and she'll be all right."

I reddened at Elric's concern, and the look of worry in Enthor's eyes deepened, but he quickly masked it. "All right, now I can change the appearance of Elric's armour to hide his families crest and colours, and as for myself, I can shift to make myself look younger."

My eyes widened in disbelief. "How are you going to that?"

Enthor shook his head in annoyance as he dismounted and came to stand beside Elric. He held out his hands for the prince's shield. Elric handed it over and I watched as Enthor placed his hands on it and it became just an ordinary defence weapon. The emblem of Gareth, which was a single black rose wrapped around a short sword, was replaced with simple tarnished wear. Then he did the same to his armour, and Elric was now dressed as a common sword for hire.

Next he made himself look younger. His form shimmered for a moment and his kind, elderly visage was replaced by a much younger and stronger-looking man. He had changed earlier in the day into leather riding pants and shirt. He produced a sword and strapped it to his back, and two throwing knifes were skilfully tucked into his boots. The kindness was removed from his eyes and was replaced with the hard cold look of a man who was used to fighting and killing.

I didn't like it. "Where did you get all that stuff from? You look like you've done this before. Will I be able to change my appearance like that too when we find my dragon form?"

"I have had to be many people over the years to protect you and I came prepared, and as far as I know I am the only dragon who can change my appearance when I take human form. That is a skill that is unique to my magic. It also allows me to mask or hide others' appearances as well. When other dragons take on their human forms, they are always the same. Our magic takes care of weapons, clothes and other accessories, and before you ask, no I don't know how it works."

I closed my mouth and pouted.

"Now let's do something about you." He placed his hand on my forehead, and a warm sensation flowed through my body. When he removed his hand I knew my symbol was again hidden, just like before, but I could still feel its presence. I had only known of its existence for a little while, but it was a part of me now. I pulled back my hair and placed my leather helm over my head. I had also changed clothes earlier and had put on my leather armour.

Enthor gave us all a once over and then we quickly remounted. We were ready, and pushing our doubts aside, we started off down the road toward Delroth.

*

Twenty minutes later we came into view of the mercenary town. The glowing lamps and fires from the town lit up the night. We slowed our horses to a walk and rode up to the front gates. There were two guards stationed that we could see, but I had no doubt that there were many eyes on us as we came to a stop. I remained behind Enthor and Elric and tried not to look terrified.

A huge hulk of a man who must have stood at least seven feet tall stepped forward. His head was clean-shaven and he was built to fight. Twin swords were strapped to his back and I was quite sure he had other weapons stashed on his body. He did not look friendly, and I was rapidly having second thoughts about this whole plan.

With his arms crossed over his chest and his legs spread in a fighting stance, he addressed us. "What business do you have here? We do not welcome outsiders."

Enthor didn't miss a beat, and I was impressed at how easily he took on the part of a cutthroat criminal. "Now that's not what I have heard. Everyone has a price, even the famed thieves of Delroth. We have merely come to replenish our supplies and possibly find some work. Things have been slow lately, and we were told this is the place to come for mercenaries looking to find extra coin. We will cause no trouble—that is, of course, as long as no trouble finds us."

The big brute looked us over critically, and as his eyes met mine a *memory* hit me smack in the face.

*

A dozen men and women stood in front of and behind us, their flaming red hair whipping around them in the wind. The strong warriors were the only thing standing between death and me. We had been trapped, with the Dark Lord's soldier encroaching from both sides, and I knew our luck had run out. Glancing down beside me, I saw that I was with someone who was broken and bleeding and knew he would not last much longer. My own body screamed in pain as I held my sword against my chest.

I had no more strength to fight as I heard the call to attack, and dropping to my knees in fatigue I could only watch in horror as my valiant protectors battled terrible odds.

The fight came down to just one woman, who stood over my now collapsed body, swinging a blade of fire over the top of her head.

The lone women with hair that was has red as blood and eyes that were a brilliant lavender stood bravely before the oncoming attack, daring the remaining soldiers to strike, but the Dark Lord's men parted—and in strolled the evil beast himself, along with another who I recognized as my beloved murderer. It was the shape-shifter who had captured me and started this whole nightmare.

The Dark Lord stepped forward and ignored the woman guarding me, setting his gaze on his prize. "At last, my weak brethren. It is finally time to end the pathetic game we have been playing. Reaper, come and dispose of this useless mortal who dares stand in my way of revenge. I do not wish to dirty my hands with her blood."

Reaper turned toward the Dark Lord. "But, Master, she has fought bravely in the face of difficult odds. She would be a great asset to you if she were to swear her allegiance with you."

Something in the Hauturs voice seemed so odd to me, and the way he looked at my protector made me wonder if they knew each other.

The woman straightened and spit at the foot of Reaper's human form. "I would rather die than stand in allegiance with a monster." I could tell those words were meant for Reaper, not the Dark Lord.

Reaper's eyes burned with regret, but before he could say anything the Dark Lord stepped in front of Reaper and with one deadly swipe of his sword, decapitated the young woman. She collapsed in front of me, leaving her head to roll and come to rest at Reaper's feet. Her open dead eyes stared at Reaper accusingly, and I wept for another sacrifice made in defence of me.

The shifter turned his gaze on me, and if I could have shrunk into the shadows I would have. I had never seen such hatred or pain before, and it was all directed at me.

Reaper took a step toward me, but a bright flash appeared between us as if a lightning bolt had just struck the earth. Dirt and debris filled the air, and I could not see two inches past my face. Someone grabbed me from behind, and we made our escape through the sand storm. The last thing I heard as I was pulled away from yet another dance with death were the screams of an angry dragon and the cry of a wounded heart.

*

I was jolted out of my memory by Elric roughly shaking me. I realized I must have blacked out, but it could not have been for more than a minute. I shook my head and realized he was staring at me suspiciously.

I masked the fear in my voice. "Back off before I make you wish you hadn't woke up this morning."

I put on my best tough, "don't mess with me" face and held my breath, waiting for our cover to be blown. The guard simply gave me one final stare and then turned, said a few words to his companion and waved us through. We started forward, but just as I was passing through the man grabbed my reins and put his massive hand on my arm.

"If you are a mercenary, then I am a whore for hire. Watch your back; there are worse types than me in here." He released his grip on me, but not before I noticed the sparkle of something on his hand. It was a ring, and it was glowing like a summer flame in the dark night.

CHAPTER 20

We rode along the main street and quickly found a stable where we could keep our horses for a little while. Elric slipped the stable boy two silvers, which was probably more than the poor thing had ever seen in his life, and told him to guard our mounts. The boy beamed with pride and told us our horses would be safe with him. We left the boy to take care of the animals' needs, and as soon as we were out of earshot, both Elric and Enthor stopped me and demanded answers.

"What happened back there? You could have gotten us killed. Remind me to never sign you up for a part in a play. You are horrible at acting—and lying for that matter."

I gave Elric a withering look and glanced around to see if anyone was listening. Most of the town's residents were either busy closing up shop or hurrying on to other destinations for the night. People glanced at us, but for the most part none gave us a second look.

I still kept my voice lowered, though. "I know. I'm sorry. I'm not very good at lying, but this wasn't my fault. I was hit with another memory when I looked at that man. I have seen his people before in another life. I was cornered by the Dark Lord again, and his people were defending me but they lost."

I lowered my eyes in regret. As soon as I got my memory back, I was determined to remember everyone who had sacrificed his or her life to protect me. I planned to write them all down on some kind of memorial so they would never be forgotten again.

Enthor's eyes softened as he regarded me. "What else did you see? Maybe I can fill in the blanks."

149

I didn't know how much I wanted to tell them. I was still confused about Reaper's involvement with the young woman who had died. I decided just to tell them about the battle and the Dark Lord. "I'm not sure where I was, but I was not with you. Another man was with me, and we were both gravely wounded, him more than I. He was unconscious beside me, and we were surrounded by people who had made a protective circle around us. They were all the height of giants, even the women, who were at least seven feet tall. They were fierce warriors, covered in black tattoos. Some of the men had clean-shaven heads but most wore it long, and all of them had red hair."

I unconsciously went to run my fingers through my own hair but remembered that I was wearing my helmet. I lowered my hand and scratched at the hidden symbol on my skin.

Enthor looked lost in thought. "They were the Kanarah people who used to dwell deep in the Kanarah woods close to the temple of Ashia. I remember that battle. We had been separated and I lost a dear friend that day. I thought the Kanarah people had been wiped out by the Dark Lord's army, but if the man we saw today triggered that memory there must be some sort of connection there."

I nodded. "There's something else too. When we passed through the gate, he stopped me and gave me a warning to watch my back. He knows we're not who we say we are, and he wears the elemental ring of fire."

Enthor's golden eyes widened in surprise. "Are you certain? I haven't even told you what it looks like."

"No, you haven't, but when we touched, my face instantly became very itchy and I saw the stone glow. It looked like a tiny flame had been placed inside a crystal. I have no doubt in my mind that it is the ring. I just feel it."

Elric crossed his arms in front of his chest. "I believe her. If anyone would know how to recognize the elements, it would be her. Everything elemental is drawn to her right now, like a bloody magnet.' He shifted uneasily, staring into shadows "Maybe we should just leave. This is becoming entirely too risky. If that man knows we're frauds, what's to stop him from turning us in to the Dark Lord's men?"

Elric brought up an excellent point. Even though he carried the ring, who's to say he knew what it was capable of or even if he had good intentions?

Enthor shook his head fiercely. "No, we need to stay. There is a pub not far from here where we can get information. Those images were sent to Karah for a reason. The elements are reluctant to get involved personally, but they are doing their best to warn about something. If there is an army poised for attack, this is the place to find out when and where, and we'll also be able to discern what we can expect at the tower. I know the Dark Lord has men stationed there, so maybe someone here knows someone who's there or who has been there."

Enthor turned from us and started walking down the dark street. "We'll go, have something to eat, ask a few questions and get out. I want to be away from here before dawn anyway."

Elric and I quickly moved to catch up with Enthor. I tried not to meet anyone's eyes, and for the most part it was easy. Delroth was not a friendly town, and I could smell the mistrust in the air. Everywhere I looked I saw boarded-up windows and heavily locked doors and it made me wonder why anyone would want to call this home.

We made it to the tavern, which just so happened to be called the Black Dragon. Elric and I exchanged amused glances and I just shrugged. We entered the dimly lit structure, and I was immediately assaulted by strong aromas: the stench of ale and sprits was everywhere, but so was the pleasant scent of spices and fresh bread. The large room was filled with tables in various conditions of disrepair, and toward the back the bar and kitchen could be seen. It was still early in the evening, so the place was not yet crowed with the late-night drunks.

We found an empty table near the back in the corner and waited for the barmaid to greet us. It took a few minutes but the young woman, who could not have been much older than I, came by and happily took our orders. She returned with three ales and a large plate filled with roasted potatoes, meats and bread. She took the silver, which Elric discreetly gave her, gave him a much too long playful look and disappeared back into the kitchen. I was not a drinker but needed to keep up appearances, but I was definitely hungry so I wasted no time digging into the food.

Elric snorted and just shook his head at me. "Your appetite amazes me. Where do you put it all?"

I smiled at Elric with a mouthful of bread and kicked him under the table.

Enthor rose and looked down at us. "You two stay here. There is a Dark Lord soldier sitting at the bar. I'm going to see what I can find out. Don't talk to anyone and try not to cause a scene."

Enthor headed over to a nearby stool beside the soldier. It did not take him long to engage him in conversation. Maybe we would be out of here fast after all.

I was trying to choke back a mouthful of ale when Elric gently nudged me under the table. I followed his eyes to the front door and swallowed my cry of surprise. The man from the gate and two others, a much shorter Dark Lord soldier and a woman who was almost the same height as the Kanarah male were coming into the tavern. It did not take them long to see us and start making their way over to our table.

I started to panic. The bastard had turned us in. I didn't know what to do that wouldn't cause a worse situation. Elric placed his hand on mine and willed me to calm down. I took a deep breath and managed a scowl at our unwelcome visitors. The woman sat next to me while the man from the gates and the Dark Lord soldier sat on either side of Elric.

The towering woman spoke first. "Evening. My friend here tells me you're looking for work. If you're not afraid to get your hands dirty I may have a proposition for you."

The woman stared directly at me with intelligent lavender eyes, and my heart jumped into my throat. I realized I was staring back and quickly turned to Elric, who thankfully was not similarly tongue-tied.

"We are, and what did you have in mind? But I must warn you our services do not come cheap."

The Dark Lord soldier leaned forward, resting his arms on the table. "Oh, we know, anyone who flaunts around that much silver is either very good at what he does or is an idiot trying to get himself killed."

Elric stiffened, and I knew this was going to end badly.

The woman quickly intervened. "Nalin, enough, please do not antagonize our guests." She turned intelligent eyes toward me. "I will tell you what the job is, but not here. I prefer to conduct my business in private. Will you and your companions join me in my home? It's not far from here, and I think it would benefit us both if you did not refuse."

Again, the woman was addressing only me. I didn't know what to do and spoke without thinking. "Yes, we'll come with you. The sooner we get out of this town the better. I prefer the open road, but if you don't mind, I would like my other companion to come along too. He's over at the bar; I'll go get him."

I started to rise but the woman grabbed my arm and pulled me back down. "No. Nalin will go and get him and he can meet us later." She started to rise. "Now let's go quietly before you attract any more attention."

She was right. The tavern was increasingly filling up and many eyes were directed toward our table. I nodded once and Elric and I gathered our things and rose with the two larger humans. We headed toward the front door, and as I glanced back at the bar, I saw the Dark Lord soldier who had been sitting with us approach Enthor and the soldier he was talking to. He met my eyes for a brief moment and then I was pushed out the door and into the dark night.

*

The woman was right; her home was not far from the Black Dragon, but it was not off the main road either. Our two would-be employers led us through a series of back allies into a rather dirty part of town.

The homes here were run down, and garbage and filth lined the allies and roads.

We came to a small shack with shuttered windows and a barred door. The woman took the time to unlock the front door and then ushered us inside like a couple of escaped prisoners. There were no lights on in the small room but I could tell the space was sparsely furnished. The man, who still stood directly behind us, pushed us over to two wooded chairs and then shoved us into them. The fear and anxiety I felt in my stomach was making me sick. I took a couple of deep breaths and tried to calm my racing heart. This plan was not going very well.

The big man stayed near the door and stood staring at us. I was uncomfortable with the lack of light in the room but the mysterious woman soon had a couple of lanterns lit and then came to stand directly in front of me. "Take off your helm."

It was not a request and I shakily obliged. With my helm removed, my curly red hair flowed out around my face and rested on my shoulders. The women's eyes bugged out in shock and then tears filled them. I was completely confused.

She regained her composure quickly though and her eyes became hard again. She then removed her helm as well, and although her hair was shorter than mine was, it was the same fiery red. "I don't believe it. You've finally returned to us, but why now? We are nothing now thanks to your mage and his promises."

Venom filled her words, but I could see the hurt and the loss in her eyes. She had been through a lot and I knew I had somehow been a part of it. I swallowed the lump in my throat. "I'm sorry, but I don't know what you're talking about. I have never seen you before. Please, if you let me explain, maybe we can still help each other."

A series of soft knocks interrupted our conversation, and the big man by the door opened it and let in two newcomers. It was the Dark Lord soldier and Enthor. The elder dragon did not look harmed, but when he saw the woman standing before him, surprise and then coldness lit his eyes.

"Miara, it has been a long time. I'm glad you are well."

Miara scoffed at his concern and stalked over to her friends by the door.

Enthor came over to us. He looked agitated. "Are you both all right?"

Elric stood before I had I chance to answer and got in Enthor's face. "No, we're not all right; we're both confused as hell. What did you neglect to tell us this time? Because it seems you forgot to tell us something pretty damn important again, right?"

Enthor's eyes glowed in warning, but he did not strike at Elric like before. He looked between us and the group standing by the door, sighing he looked back at me. "The woman you see over there is Miara, and beside her is her mate, Jaitem. They are as you suspected, part of the Kanarah tribe."

My eyes widened in surprise and I watched Miara eye Enthor with hate. "We *were* part of the Kanarah tribe. We are all but wiped out, no thanks to you." Miara pushed herself off the wall and stood beside the dragon. Enthor was tall in his human form but this woman was at least a foot and half taller. She looked down on him with anger.

I spoke quietly but my words echoed eerily in the small enclosure. "But what do they have to do with me, and why didn't you say something at the gate?"

Miara dragged her vicious gaze from Enthor and looked at me. "You never told her, you smug bastard. You never told her the story of how she came to be in that body, the body of my dead sister's child?" She returned her focus to Enthor. "Why? Was Turias sacrifice not good enough for you? Were you shamed to have her knowing whose body she took?"

Miara was in Enthor's face, and he clearly didn't like it. He turned bright red and the anger in his gold dragon eyes matched Miara's lavender ones. "Do. Not. Push me. I have my reasons for doing what I did, which I now see caused more harm than good, but I am through apologizing for my actions. I did what I had to do to keep her safe." His intense gaze took in all of us, "Now sit down so I can explain this as quickly as possible. None of us are safe here, and there are grave matters we need to discuss."

"But what about him? He is a Dark Lord soldier. We can't trust him or these people." Elric stood close to me with his hand on his sword. He was right. We couldn't trust any of these people.

At the mention of him, the soldier came over to us with his hands extended. He stared at me with a strange look on his face. I couldn't tell if he wanted to strike me or hug me. "You can trust me. I am not a Dark Lord soldier. I merely pose as one to get inside information to warn others, and I am not the only one. We are part of a secret organization, called the Order of Freedom, whose main purpose is to spy on the Dark Lord's army." He turned his dark eyes to Elric. "The humans in the south do not enjoy their freedom as you do in the north, so we do what we can to warn surrounding cities and villages of the army's activities. It is dangerous and not very significant in the grand scheme of things, but we do save lives which otherwise would be crushed under the Dark Lord's boot."

Elric eyed Nalin suspiciously and refused to let down his guard. "How do you know that we are from the north? And why did you single us out?"

Nalin laughed, as did Miara and Jaitem. "You're kidding, right? The two of you stick out like sore thumbs. You carry yourselves with pride and have an ignorance that surrounds you. No one from the south holds his or her head that high; it's been beaten out of us. Even mercenaries for hire do not act as you did, and no one has silver, and if they did you can be damn sure they wouldn't be throwing it around like it was sand. If it had been your friend there alone, I would have believed it. He has had many years' experience lying and deceiving people."

There was such hatred in Miara's eyes that it scared me. What had Enthor done?

Elric remained silent but did not relax. His skin was indeed getting tough, with stone after stone being thrown at him about our upbringing. *We have so much to mend,* and my heart sank deeper at the thought of it.

Enthor just glared at the defiant Miara as he responded. "About eighteen years ago I and another mage by the name of Faleva were on the run from the Dark Lord. We had been staying in the port city of Clorynina on the edge of the Forever Sea. We were the only two protectors left and had just failed again. Your life energy was safely contained in the crystal, but it cannot survive for long that way. The crystal was designed for transfers only, it was not meant to hold life energy for long. We escaped the city but could not lose our pursuers. They chased us to the cliffs of the Forever Sea and had us trapped. We would have been lost if not for the intervention of the Kanarah people. They saved us and destroyed the Dark Lord's men."

I shook my head in confusion. "Hold on a second—why were these people at the cliffs? I thought they were forest dwellers."

Enthor was about to answer my question but Miara jumped in. "As much as I would love to reopen old wounds and explain how my people were forced from their homes and into hiding, we really need to decide what to do with the lot of you."

As if in response to Miara's statement, everyone in the room hushed, and we listened. I could hear men shouting orders and the distinct sound of slamming doors. Miara and Jaitem ran to the front window and peeked through the shutters.

A slew of curses flowed from the Kanarah woman's mouth and she turned on us, lavender eyes glowing. "Looks like the party's over. Dark Lord soldiers are searching the houses, and my guess is they're looking for you. I don't know what you've gotten yourself into this time, but I'm done throwing my life away on empty prophecies. You're on your own. Don't take it personally, but I have survived too long to be taken down like this."

Miara pushed past Elric and me and headed for the back of the house, where I assumed was another exit, but Nalin of all people stopped her. "Wait. You can't just leave her like this, she could be killed. There must be a reason she's here, why she has appeared again after all these years." He paused and glanced at me. "I've heard the rumours through the ranks, and if this is indeed the girl they are looking for, we must protect her. We have worked so hard for too long; please don't make that all in vain. Please do it for our people. Do it for your sister."

Miara whirled back on him at the mention of her sister and stared at the smaller male. She was breathing hard and seemed to be wrestling with inner emotions. Nalin stood his defiant ground, matching her challenging stare, and it was Miara who finally looked away.

A loud bang on the front door and shouts for it to be opened rang through from the other side. Elric and I drew our swords and prepared for the unavoidable attack.

Miara looked at Nalin and then at Jaitem, who gave her a quick, stiff nod, and then as quick as a cat she was between the front door and us again.

Miara looked back over her shoulder and spoke to me. "I hope you're worth all this trouble and for all of our sakes I hope you have some tricks up your sleeve because this is going to get messy."

She turned to Nalin. "Nalin, how many are out there?"

Nalin took another quick glace outside while drawing his sword. He had removed any distinguishing armour that would place him has a Dark Lord soldier. It left him fairly unprotected, and I hoped he was good with his sword. "It looks like only eight. There is not a large detachment here at the moment. Most of the soldiers have been called to arms—we have new marching orders."

He threw a pointed glance at Elric and me, and I could see pity and fear in his eyes. "We can take them, but we need to do it fast and without any escaping. If word gets back of my involvement it could put our whole operation in jeopardy."

Another series of pounds rained on the other side of the door. They were done waiting; the door would not remain on its hinges for much longer.

"All right, here's the plan. Nalin, take rich boy out the back and circle around to flank them. Watch your backs because they probably have men back there already. The mage and the girl can stay here with us and we'll meet in the middle. Go quickly. We need to finish this and leave the city before too many people see us. Good luck, my friend."

Miara and Nalin grasped arms, and then he proceeded out the back with Elric in tow. Miara and Jaitem went on either side of the door, leaving Enthor and me in the middle as bait. I was so nervous my hands were shaking. Enthor placed a reassuring hand on my arm and I took a deep breath.

A loud male voice sounded from outside. "That was your last warning! Break it down! If the girl's in there, I want her alive. Kill the rest."

With one large crash, the Dark Lord soldiers had the door battered in, but they didn't come through; instead, one lone figure walked in. He wore a dark cloak that covered him from head to foot, and his head was lowered so we couldn't see his face, but we could hear—and what we heard sent chills down my spine. He was chanting under his hood and I could feel the magic charge the air.

The two Kanarah warriors raised their weapons and started for the dark man before Enthor or I could call out a warning. The lone figure threw his arms out straight to the sides, and Miara and Jaitem were thrown across the room by a sudden gust of wind that slammed them against the walls, temporarily stunning them. In the same moment a wall of fire suddenly appeared, circling Enthor and me. The figure raised his head and lowered his hood and I looked into the dead, uncaring eyes of a warlock. I had never seen a warlock before except in memories, but even then it had not prepared me for what stood before me.

What once was a human man now stood an abomination. His eyes were glazed over and his too-pale skin clung to the bones in his face. His mouth was a thin, blood-red line that barely moved except when he was chanting. His clothes hung from him, barely held up the sickly stick body underneath. Bony hands pointed at us and instantly the flames grew higher. I felt as though I was staring at death itself and I was terrified. We were in serious trouble.

Enthor's eyes were on the magic wielder as well, and he began to shimmer. The two Kanarah warriors were already back on their feet and fighting the Dark Lord soldiers who now came in through the broken door.

The heat of the fire was oppressive, and if we didn't get out of here soon the whole house would collapse on us. I tried to concentrate but my head was ringing and my face was so itchy. The sword that I clutched in my hands had transformed into the beautiful transparent look of water, just as it had during my battle with the Dark Lord. Without thinking, I slashed at the wall of fire, dousing the flames. The warlock, however, did not seem to notice. He resumed his chanting and the fire was replaced by more. I kept dancing around our circle, but no matter how many times I struck the fire it just kept coming.

Enthor's eyes were glowing and I was afraid he was going to shift right here, but then I heard a deep rumble of thunder reverberate through my bones. I wasn't sure if it was him or if a storm was brewing outside. Then in answer to my question a lightning bolt tore a hole through the already fire-damaged roof and struck the floor between the warlock and our confinement. Bits of splintered wood flew everywhere, narrowly passing through the flames, missing us and becoming tiny flaming missiles. They struck everywhere, causing multiple smaller fires in the already burning home.

The warlock was thrown back out of the door, breaking his concentration. The wall of flame dropped, but it was too late. The house was on fire all around us. We needed to get out fast, before we were burned to a crisp.

Enthor followed the downed warlock out into the night and an elemental battle ensued. The warlock threw fireball after fireball at the dragon but he deflected every one and returned them with a blast of wind that carried the evil magic user out of my line of sight. Enthor followed and I lost track of them both. A huge ceiling beam crashed down not five feet behind me and forced my frozen legs into action.

Miara and Jaitem were still fighting off soldiers. Two lay dead at the bigger male's feet but he was still locked in combat with another, his twin blades slashing.

I watched memorized for just a second because his blades were on fire. I had thought it was just a trick of the flames that were now consuming the house but no, his blades were actually on fire and the ring he wore was glowing with its own inner flame.

A cry from across the room dragged my focus back to Miara. Two soldiers were bearing down on her. She was fighting with a pole arm that was sharpened with steel points at both ends. She moved it gracefully, deftly blocking the attacks from the soldiers, dancing a deadly rhythm, but one got through and a deep gash down her left arm pumped blood onto the floor.

I dodged burning debris and thickening smoke and made it to her location. The soldiers were not expecting me nor did they hear me through the crackle of flames or the roar of the storm that was now bearing down outside. I came up behind the first soldier, letting my adrenaline take over, and sliced at his side under the protection of his armour. The momentum and power of my magic caused the blade to slice cleanly through him. He cried out in surprise and pain, dropping his weapon and grasping at his side trying to hold in his internal organs. It was a useless effort and I watched horrified as he collapsed with his lifes blood pooling around him.

The man beside him stared in disbelief, which gave Miara the opening she needed. She blocked his sword strike, and then in one smooth movement turned in a circle, bringing her deadly weapon in for striking position and skewered the Dark Lord soldier in the throat. She pulled back, and the man dropped dead to the ground right on top of the soldier I had killed.

I just stood there staring at the man I had attacked. I had never seen anyone die before, much less be the cause of it, and I was quickly overcome with nausea and panic.

A wicked smile spread across Miara's lips as she grabbed me, and together we ran outside to the fresh air of the night.

The night air did wonders to clear my smoke-filled lungs as I choked and hacked.

Chaos surrounded us everywhere. Fire had broken out in several other locations, lighting up the dark in a ghastly light. Lightning flashed, illuminating the separate clashes of steel against steel.

I spied Elric and Nalin not far from me, and between flashes I watched the pair fight back to back against the Dark Lord's men. We were outnumbered, and then something came to me in my smoke-filled brain. I had forgotten about Fang and Deneoes. I pulled the whistle from around my neck and blew into the thing as hard as I could. I didn't hear a damn thing, but I remembered the little Ywaris explanation of how he would be the only one to hear it.

I blew into it a couple more times just to be certain than I tossed the piece of wood to the ground and stifled a yell as I was suddenly hit from behind and collapsed into the mud face first. I tried to rise but a boot landed in the middle of my back and pushed me back down. My face was submerged in the mud and rainwater and I desperately tried to rise so I could breathe.

The attacker kicked me in the ribs, and I blew out my remaining oxygen; bright white spots filled my vision. I rolled over on to my back and saw that it was the warlock who was inflicting me with so much pain.

Fear for my life gripped me as I groped for my sword, but I couldn't see anything. I sucked in huge amounts of air trying to clear my head so I could see, but my eyes and mouth were filled with too much mud and water. I hacked up mouth fulls of muddied water and clawed at my eyes managing to clear them, I looked up just in time to see the warlock standing above me with his arms raised. I started to back pedal, pushing my damaged body along the ground trying to find purchase in the slick mud. I opened my mouth to shout for help but something flew into the side of the warlock, knocking him to the ground. He lay there fighting off an unseen foe. Blood poured from everywhere on his body, and his mouth opened with an inhuman scream, making the blood freeze in my veins. Then I heard the distinct snapping of bones, and the unholy sound of the dying warlock ceased. The space above the dead warlock shimmered, and there with her jaws firmly locked around his neck was Fang. She turned her intelligent eyes toward me and then disappeared, gone off to find another victim. The screams of men being torn apart was the only clue I had as to her location.

A strong hand grabbed my arm and hoisted me to a kneeling position. I came face-to-face with Deneoes.

"I told you you'd need me, Red, and I'm a little disappointed you waited so long to call me to the party."

I scraped the mud off my face and gave my friend a small smile. "Yeah, sorry about that. Have you seen Enthor? I lost him." I searched around trying to see through the rain but all I could see were my friends still fighting in front of burning buildings, which thankfully were starting to die out due to the rain.

Deneoes shook his small head. "No, but you go look for him. I can handle this lot." He jumped away with the grace of a cat to where Elric and Nalin were fighting.

The attention was off me for the moment so I stood and retrieved my sword. I scanned the darkness again, and then there, lying in a heap against a broken building, was Enthor. I ran toward him but slid to a stop as a Dark Lord soldier intercepted me. I raised my sword to block his attack just in time to avoid being decapitated. We parried back and forth while I matched him blow for blow, but I was hurt from the warlock's attack and was quickly losing ground. He finally got in a hit against my leg and I cried out in pain as I fell to one knee. Blood ran freely down my leg and mixed with water and mud.

This particular soldier seemed to be ignoring his orders which I had heard spoken back before the fighting began because with an evil grin on his face he moved in for a killing blow. I raised my sword in defence, but the Dark Lord soldier suddenly flew backward with the force of a storm gale and was impaled on the building, two arrows protruding from his chest.

I swung my body around to see Deneoes wink at me, and then he was off again in Elric's direction. I took a steadying breath and crawled the rest of the way to where Enthor lay.

The storm was dying down, and all that remained was a slow gentle rain that washed the blood and dirt from me. As I drew closer to my friend, I could see that he was still breathing but wasn't moving. I wondered why he hadn't transformed into his dragon form. I reached him and slowing turned him over so he was lying on his back. He had returned to the form I knew him best. The cold lines and hard muscles of a killer were replaced by the kind old man I had known my whole life.

He groaned, and I helped him into a sitting position.

"What happened? How did the warlock get the drop on you?" I waited until his head cleared and his eyes became focused and full of anger.

"I was too preoccupied with fighting the warlock and wasn't paying attention. Being a human for so long has made me weak. One of the soldiers managed to get behind me and slap this around my wrist."

He held up his right hand. I saw a thick silver band inscribed with symbols and other markings I didn't recognize—or wait, yes I did. I had seen them before. It was the same kind of restraint that had been placed on me when I was captured and brought to the Dark Lord. It had blocked my powers, so I assumed the manacle that was now on Enthor's wrist was doing the same.

"I recognize it. I had a vision not long ago of the day I had been captured. It blocks your powers, yes?"

He nodded grimly. "Yes, and until I get it off, I am completely useless. The Dark Lord knows I am with you, otherwise they would not have bothered with this primitive device, and there is no way that us running into this many soldiers was an accident."

I was about to argue with him, but the sound of booted feet running toward us brought my attention back to our situation. Fortunately, it seemed that it was just my companions, who had all made it through this confrontation with their lives. They were all bloodied and bruised but at least they were still standing. The rain had almost completely stopped and the night seemed eerily quiet compared to the chaos we had just gone through.

Elric reached me first and I hugged him before I could stop myself. He held me for a second and then pulled me up to my feet. I winced a little at the pain in my leg from the wound I'd received and from the beating the warlock had given me.

Elric looked at me with concern. "Can you walk? We need to leave now. There are more coming. This was a trap; they knew we would be here."

Miara came up beside him. She stared at my face with shock and I realized with Enthor's powers being blocked my symbol was no longer hidden. The Kanarah woman blinked a few times but otherwise seemed to ignore me.

"An alarm has been raised; it will not take long for more people to get here. I know where we can hide, but we need to leave this city. Can the mage walk, or do we have to carry him?"

In response, Enthor rose and glared at the taller woman. "Let's go. There is much we need to discuss. Lead the way."

"But what about our horses and supplies?" I asked.

"Leave them; I know where we can get more. Now let's get out of here!" Miara was in no mood to listen to any more protests, and she turned and headed toward the back allies that had led Elric and me here earlier. Elric ripped off some of his shirt and wrapped my leg as best as he could to stop the bleeding, and then we all followed the Kannarah woman into the night.

CHAPTER 21

We travelled swiftly and silently into the forests that bordered the city of Delroth. Each step for me was agony; bright hot pain stabbed through my leg with every footfall, and by the time we reached a small clearing filled with tents I could not stand anymore. I collapsed in a heap and shook with chills.

Elric was by my side in an instant, propping my head up and pouring cool water down my throat, but I couldn't make my mouth work and ended up choking. Rough hands grabbed my face, and my eyes were pried open. I tried to struggle but it was like fighting my way through a swamp. I felt like I was being sucked under murky water with no room to breathe.

"She's feverish. Was she wounded?" The voice sounded like it came through a deep fog. The words were mumbled and I couldn't focus on them. Someone must have shown the newcomer my leg because white-hot pain shot up my limb and into my brain, causing me to yell.

"The wound is infected and needs to be stitched. Bring her to my tent; I have herbs and salves that will help. Quick now, before she gets worse; I will not harm her."

Gentle arms lifted me and I was carried a short distance. I could vaguely tell through my pain-soaked mind that I was inside a tent. It was warm in here, making me sweat even more. I started to shake uncontrollably, and then I was placed on a bed of some sort. I moaned at the shift of my body and at the cool hands that were touching my forehead. A blanket was placed over me and I tried to remain conscious. Something warm and pasty was placed under my nose on my upper lip, and I could smell menthol and other herbs.

I started to relax and the fog in my mind started to recede. A cool cloth was placed on my head, and then my healer spoke words that I didn't understand, but it was what she said after that made my heart leap into my chest.

"Hold her down. I am afraid this will be very painful."

I didn't understand what was going on. I opened my eyes and looked up at Elric, who was carefully pinning his weight against my shoulders. I was going to ask what was happening when pain tore a scream from my throat. My whole body contorted, making Elric fight to keep me still, and then I slipped into sweet oblivion.

*

Time slipped unknowingly by as awareness slowly returned to me. Cracking my eyes, I turned my head slightly without raising it and looked across the small tent into the gaze of a woman. I started a bit, causing my ribs to throb a little, but it was nothing compared to the pain I had felt earlier.

The older woman gazed at me with a mix of curiosity and something else I couldn't place, resentment maybe, but for what reason I couldn't be sure. She was an older woman with deep lavender eyes and bright auburn hair with streaks of silver in it. She was not has tall as Miara but the resemblance was unmistakeable.

The Kanarah rose into a crouch and came across the small space that separated us, like a cat stalking its prey. I couldn't quite put my finger on it, but something about this woman made me ill at ease.

She peered into my eyes and then placed a worn hand on my forehead. "Your fever has passed. How do you feel?"

I wanted to say "awful," but I found myself wanting to impress this woman with strength that I didn't have, so I gritted my teeth and forced a small smile. "Better, thanks to you, I'm sure. Thank you for saving my life."

The woman scoffed at my gratitude and returned to her spot across the tent. She did not, however, remove her condescending gaze from my face. An uncomfortable silence followed, and I wasn't quite sure what to say, so me being me I just started belting out questions.

"Where are my friends? How long have I been unconscious? What is this place? Are we safe . . . ?" I would have asked more but my quiet companion was staring open-mouthed at me with a strange look on her face. I wasn't sure if she thought I was crazy or just plain rude.

I snapped my mouth shut and tried to sit up a little. The pain in my left side where I had been kicked was sore but manageable and I gingerly moved the blanket off my leg so I could get a better look at it. My riding leggings had been removed and I was now wearing a pair travelling pants. They were not mine and were very loose. I carefully pulled up the bottom of my right pant leg to just below my knee and saw a long gash down the outside of my calf. Someone had cleaned all the blood away and it had been stitched up quite professionally. It was still red and angry looking, but I could tell that no more infection was present.

I rolled my pant leg back down and shifted my attention back to the older Kanarah woman. She was still regarding me with a cool expression, but pride of her handiwork showed on her face. Movement outside the tent stole both our attention and then the flap was moved aside, letting in the cool night air.

Miara bent her tall frame and entered through the opening, letting the tent flap fall behind her. She crouched beside the older woman and gave me a small smile. "I'm glad to see you're awake, little one. You gave your friends quite a scare, especially your prince."

My eyes widened at that comment. I would have thought Elric would want to keep his identity a secret for the time being.

Seeing the surprised look on my face Miara smiled and nodded. "Yes, I now know who you *all* are and where you came from. We have discussed much while you have been asleep, and let's just say that I have been persuaded to help you on your quest. Your mage—or should I say *dragon*—has always been rather convincing, and now that I know what he is, I understand why."

That comment got a withering look from the older woman but she remained silent.

"As soon as you are able we must leave. We have spent most of the night packing up our encampment. It is no longer safe for my people to stay here. My brother will lead them to a safer location while I, Jaitem and Nalin go with you to try and save this wretched land from extinction."

I didn't know what to say. I had so many questions swirling about in my mind that it was making me dizzy, but I decided to keep my mouth shut for now and get moving.

Miara turned to leave but the older woman's voice stopped her. "I will be coming with you also, my child. I imagine you will be in need of a healer and I am the best in our tribe."

Miara turned on the old woman with fire in her eyes. "Mother, you can't be serious. I know you're a capable warrior and your skills would be greatly appreciated, but we are going on some fools' quest that may or may not be a death sentence. I can't allow you to put the safety of our tribe in jeopardy. They need you more than I."

"Do not talk to me as if you have the right to tell me what to do. I am fully aware of my responsibilities as leader of this tribe. I will leave your brother in charge, and stop rolling your eyes. You know he is quite able to lead our people. You can't deny me the right to avenge my daughter, your sister. I'm coming, and arguing really is a waste of your time."

The two women stared at each other for a moment, and then, without another word, Miara left the tent, leaving me alone with her mother.

I busied myself with trying to locate my personal pack and the rest of my belongings. I found them next to the foot of the bed and began rummaging through my pack for a pair of pants that fit. I quickly changed, being careful not to reinjure my leg, all the while under the strange scrutiny of Miara's mother. She worked in silence, packing up herbs and salves and other things I didn't recognize. She did it with the speed and precision of someone who has had to leave in a hurry many times before.

I was strapping on my sword and getting ready to test my weight on my leg when Miara's mother was suddenly at my side, holding me down by my shoulder. She stared at me for a moment with intensity. I squirmed under her tight grasp but she possessed a great strength for a woman her age, and she was making me very nervous. Then, just as abruptly, she released me and sat down beside me, looking off into the tent—at what I couldn't guess.

"Do you know the true story of your host body, child? Are you aware of the tragedy that surrounds it and this tribe?"

I swallowed hard and looked down at my hands. I wasn't sure if I really wanted to know. I had witnessed so much pain already, but I felt I somehow owed this woman so I shook my head. "Not all of it. Miara and Enthor spoke some of it back in Delroth, but we never finished the conversation. I'm aware that this body was her sister's child, but I do not know the circumstances leading to my possession of this body."

I hugged myself, rubbing my arms. I suddenly felt very cold. The reality of my being no more than a parasite invading someone else's body was starting to weigh on me. I felt like an intruder in my own skin and despised the feeling.

If the woman beside me noticed my discomfort, she paid it no attention. Instead, she began to speak without emotion, as if she was reading a page from a book. "Your possession of my grandchild's body was not the first time someone in my family sacrificed herself for you. My ancestor also believed that you could save us from the Dark Lord, and she died at his very hands while trying to protect you."

A flash of a memory flew across my vision, and I quickly masked the recognition in my eyes.

"You disappeared after that, and my tribe had no knowledge whether you lived and if her sacrifice had not been in vain. We were all but wiped out after that encounter, and our memory faded from mortal minds. Then, many years later, about 18 years ago, our fates brought you to us again. We had found sanctuary in the cliffs, but not even that could keep us safe from fate and the *dragon*. As usual, chaos followed him and Miara was forced to dispatch the Dark Lord soldiers that pursued him and his companion—only the beast survived the encounter."

Hate and anger seeped into her words, making me feel on edge. I felt the strong desire to flee and every instinct in my body told me I was not safe. I swallowed the dryness in my throat and willed my body to stay still, while the Kanarah's voice continued to fill the tent.

"Miara invited your mage back to our home and it was there that I recognized him for who he was. His appearance was slightly different but he matched the description passed on by Mother. The only thing that confused me was the absence of you, but that was also explained. He claimed that your spirit was trapped in a crystal and would not survive without another human host. He spun his fantastic prophecy of treachery and hope and everyone once again was dragged into his net of illusion. I was the only one against him but my protests remained unheeded. My husband still lived at that time so I was not yet leader of our tribe, and his word swayed our people. The mage had asked if any of our people would be willing to sacrifice themselves for the greater good, but his task was made easier by the sudden cries of my eldest daughter, Turia."

The older Kanarah woman paused and turned her penetrating gaze on me. "Turia was with child, and it had decided to come early. It was a very difficult birth and even with all of my experience, I could not save her. The child, a baby girl, was born but she was weak and there was no way she would survive without her mother. There was no hope for either of them, and my daughter knew this. On Turia's dying lips she made me promise to let the mage place your soul in her child's body so that she may live. I knew it would be a mistake but I could not say no to my daughter."

She looked away from me, and bitterness dripped from her every word. "So that is how you came to be. Your mage placed your soul in Turia's daughter, healing her and making her strong, and she was able to see and hear her own daughter cry before she passed on. It made her happy, and she died with hope in her heart, but I knew it would not last. As I suspected, your mage betrayed us again. Two days later we woke up and the two of you were gone, sneaking away in the night, and once again our tribe was left wondering."

Miara's mother stood and continued gathering her things for our journey. I sat stunned with tears in my eyes. This was the first time I had ever heard of how my spirit had moved from one host to another. I felt dirty, I felt evil.

I took a steadying breath, wiped at my eyes and tried to speak without a tremor in my voice. "I know you won't believe me, and I truly don't blame you, but I'm deeply sorry for all the pain I have caused your family. I don't know why our fates are so closely entwined but I will do everything in my power to justify your daughter's sacrifice." I sighed and looked down at my hands. "My choices have not been my own, and I have been forced into this prison of pain and deceit, but it will stop, it has to stop or nothing will matter any more."

The old woman looked back into my eyes, and I couldn't read anything in them. Her lavender orbs were devoid of emotion. She nodded at me once and handed me a strong carved stick.

"Use this to support your weight. Your leg is not yet strong enough to support you fully. If you reopen your wound, infection will sweep in again. I have what I need. I will meet you outside with the others."

I sat there for a moment staring at the carved piece of wood in my hands. I felt numb. My emotions had been stretched to the breaking point and I was also exhausted. I felt like I hadn't slept in weeks.

I felt rather than heard movement to my right, and then a massive feline head materialized in my lap. I stroked Fang's smooth strong head and listened to her purr. I wondered how long she had been there silently watching the past events unfold. When I made no move to get up, she gently nudged my leg and manoeuvred her massive body so I could use her as leverage to stand.

"I take it that's a hint? I don't suppose you could teach me to disappear too?" Fang looked at me with those intelligent green eyes and growled a little.

"No, I didn't think so. Well, I guess I'd better get this over with," and with the Fang's help I stood up and began to make my way outside.

The pre-dawn air was crisp and refreshing. I quickly scanned my surroundings and noticed that the small camp that we had arrived in earlier that night had all but been packed up.

As soon as Fang and I were a safe distance from Miara's mother's tent, two Kannarah men swiftly moved in to disassemble and pack it up with the others, all the while keeping a wary eye on my feline protector. They must have known of her because they did not seem too surprised to see her, just cautious. It did not take long for one of my friends to see that I was out of bed, but unfortunately, he was not the one I most wanted to see.

"Red, it's about time you got up! It figures you wake up just when all the work's done. You know, for a dragon you really are pretty lazy." Deneoes smiled up at me and I took the joke for what it was. I could see the concern for me on his face and I smiled back at him, but I knew it didn't reach my eyes.

The smirk on my little friend's face vanished and worry creased his features. "Are you all right? What happened in there?"

He pointed behind me at the space where the medicine woman's tent had been. A shudder ran through my body but I pushed those feelings away for now. I had more important things to deal with. "I'm all right, my friend, just a little shaken up. Where are the others? Where is Elric? I need to know what has been happening since I have been out."

The scowl on Deneoes's face deepened, and I became worried when he did not answer right away. "We have a problem. Well, more than one, actually, but if you don't talk some sense into that pigheaded prince of yours he is bound to go off and get himself killed."

Before I could ask what he was talking about, shouting broke the stillness of the air. I turned in the direction of the noise and saw Elric astride a new mount getting ready to leave. He was having some trouble though because both Enthor and Jaitem had a hold of the reins, preventing the poor animal from moving.

It was not hard for me to approach the group unnoticed. I stood in the background and listened.

"You cannot leave. I know you feel the need to be with your people but what about our quest, what about Karah?" Enthor was red in the face, and if he could have, I think he would have transformed and sat on the stubborn prince.

No one had yet noticed I was there, so I walked up as best as I could to Elric's horse and put a steadying hand on its head. I looked up and caught Elric's frightened, determined eyes in my own and held them for a moment. His restlessness eased somewhat but he seemed so angry, so lost.

I spoke normally, but it seemed to cut through his frustration. "What is going on? Why are you leaving without me?"

The world had fallen silent, and it was as if everything and everyone else had disappeared. My companions backed away and simply stood waiting to hear what would happen between the Elric and me. I wasn't sure if I was using magic or if they recognized the fierceness in my voice but I felt different, I felt charged with energy that I had never felt before. I felt powerful, and my aura demanded answers. I had been through too much this night to put up with foolishness.

Elric regarded me with astonishment, and then it was quickly replaced with a guarded look. He dismounted and came face to face with me. I almost lost it then. My heart ached with the need to have him hold me and never let go but I kept him at arm's length. His guarded stature also shattered when he looked at me. The kind, caring eyes of the human prince I fell in love with stood staring at me with fear and pain lining his features. He started to reach for me but then stopped, pulling his hand away as if afraid he would break me.

"I'm glad you're okay. I was so worried, and that giant hulk of a woman wouldn't let me near you. A lot has happened while you were recovering. Gareth is in danger. Your vision was right; The Dark Lord has sent out his army to attack our people, and my father has helped seal his own doom. He has isolated the kingdom from the rest of Eiddoril and now, when he desperately needs it, there is no one he can call on for help. I know you want me to stay but you have others who can protect you. I must try to warn my father, and I must try to find someone who will stand with him and our people."

Elric took an exhausted breath in and scanned the rest of our group. "Don't any of you understand? I am the prince of Gareth. It is my responsibility to help my people. I have no choice." The last of his words came out as a whisper, and he lowered his head to stare at his clenched fists.

I stepped forward, closing the distance between us, and grasped his hands in my own. He looked up and we found strength in each other's eyes.

"I understand, and if I have learned nothing else over the last few days, I learned the importance of trust and sacrifice. You are not going alone. They are still my people too and my family is there. I will not stand by and run again while others are killed because of me. My own problems can wait. I haven't been a dragon in 300 years, so I think I can handle a few more weeks."

Elric fiercely shook his head. "But we need you as a dragon; you are the only one strong enough to defeat the Dark Lord. You have to go on to the temple and learn what has become of your true mother and your true form. Eiddoril needs you."

It was my turn to shake my head. "I don't care what Eiddoril needs. This world has been suffering for too long, and not all of its problems stemmed from me. None of the races trust each other, and even within our own race there is no loyalty. If I have any hope at all of defeating the Dark Lord, we need to fix that first, because through all of our faults we have one thing that he will never have: love. Love for each other and for the world we live in, and that is more powerful than any dragon."

Elric kissed me then and broke whatever hold I had on my surroundings. Everything suddenly came back alive and the mood was not a pleasant one. I turned to face the group behind me that was now talking all at once.

Enthor's voice boomed over the rest, and he came forward to face me. "What do you think you're doing? This is not part of our plan. You can't just go off and do whatever your little heart desires." He pointed his finger and stabbed me in the chest with it. "You have a responsibility to this world and its inhabitants. I won't allow you to go running off with a human lover who in the end will cause you nothing but pain."

I don't know what Enthor saw in my eyes, but it caused him to back up a step. I limped my way to stand directly in front of him and glared my defiance. "I appreciate everything you have done for me over these years. I would not be alive if not for you, but I'm done taking a back seat in my own life. This was never *our* plan, it was yours. I have never been given a choice; everything has been written for me. I'm going to make my own decisions and won't stand by and watch others fight for me any more."

My voice shook with passion. "You can't ask me to turn my back on people who have taken care of me for the past 18 years. I know that you are a dragon and you want me to act and think like a dragon, but I'm *not*. I don't even know if I *want* to be. I'm a human being and we don't just think of ourselves, we take care of our own, and I intend to remind everyone of that. It is a strength that we have lost and if we have any hope of winning this we need to get it back."

Enthor remained where he was, fighting an internal battle with his emotions. His words surprised me. "You, my dear, are more like a dragon than you think, but you are right, even after all these years I do not understand what it is to be human. I know that has caused more problems than it has solved. But are you serious? Do you truly not wish to be who you were born to be?"

I looked away from Enthor and back at Elric, who had remained standing with his horse. I wasn't sure what I wanted. All I knew was that I needed some control, to figure this out on my own.

I turned back to my protector and friend and gave him a small smile. "I think I am who I was meant to be. I just don't look the same any more. I don't know which path I will choose when the time comes, but I want it to be my choice. I hope you can understand that."

Enthor nodded and reached for my hand. "I don't agree with this but I do understand, more than you will ever know. I won't stand in your way and will support you, but I can't go with you."

Enthor held up his other hand to silence the protests that were already forming in my mouth. "You need to follow your path and I need to follow mine. I have made too many mistakes over these past few years, and I too must now try to fix them. I will continue my journey to the temple. There are answers there, and it is the only place I can think of that may help me get this off." He held up his wrist, and the faint glow of the manacle he wore glinted in the predawn light.

He said, "I will meet back up with you as soon as I can in the outskirts of Aserah by the shores of the Forever Sea. Hopefully I will meet up with whatever aide you find and then together we can help save Gareth."

I knew that I would not be able to change his mind and also knew that what he was doing made sense, but I still did not want him going alone. "But you can't go alone. How are you going to sneak in there without being caught?"

Enthor smiled. "I'll figure that out when I get there. I may be old but I still have tricks up my sleeve." He released my hand and pointed to the rest of our party. "Now, enough of all this talk, your companions are waiting to hear from you. Time is not on our side and we must get moving."

Enthor was right. I took a deep breath and looked out over the faces that had chosen to stand with me. Could I do this? Could I be the leader I needed to be? I decided I didn't have a choice.

"First things first. I know the longer we stay in this spot the more danger we are all in, but I need to make a few things clear. I don't expect any of you to follow Elric and me. Things have changed and you all need to make your own decisions. I have only known some of you a short period but I know you are good people, and that no matter what is decided I will respect and honour your wishes."

Deneoes was the first to step forward, as I knew he would be. "Well look at you, Red, wearing the leadership pants now; it's about time. You already know where I stand. Oh, and don't worry about your grumpy old beast, I have no intension of letting him go off on some dangerous adventure without me. I couldn't sleep at night if

I knew I had let a senior go out all by himself wandering around in the dark. It just wouldn't be right."

I swear the ground shook with the growl that came from Enthor's throat, and the glare he threw Deneoes was hot enough to melt steel, but he made no protest. Perhaps he realized as I did that once our young friend made up his mind there was no changing it. I nodded and smiled my gratitude and then turned my gaze up to the strong Kannarah woman before me. She regarded me with respect.

"I will not lie and say that I agree with this plan of yours either, but at least it is an honest and direct one. You are right; the healing must start somewhere, and what better way to bring a world together than impending doom? Jaitem and I will help you against this army, and may I suggest we take the time to stop at the other Kannarah settlements in the cliffs? We are not far, and I am sure we can convince some of them to aide your kingdom as well. There is much unrest in our tribes and I know some are looking for a way back to their old lives. My brother will lead our tribe to safety and then meet us in Gareth with our warriors. There are small pockets of us all along the coast up into the region of Aserah so hopefully some will be swayed to our cause as well."

Nalin was at Miara's side too. "I'll stay. I can send word to the rest of my company. We use a special message system through the use of hawks; I can discreetly get word to them. We have men already inside the army that now heads toward Gareth, which is how I came to know of the upcoming attack. We also have a large company stationed in a village that lies in the direct path of their march. The Dark Lord believes he has control over that settlement, but it has been ours for quite some time. I will tell them what we have planned, and they will be able to let us know what is going on."

I didn't know what to say. I was not expecting so much from these people. "Thank you, Nalin; that is very generous, but how do you know they will even care about our cause? What makes you think they will listen?"

Nalin seemed to straighten a little, and then he gave me a mock bow. "They will listen because I am their commander. We have fought hard to stay hidden and do what we can for the people of these lands, but as you said, the time has come to stop hiding. We will back you when the time comes, I swear it."

Well, that came has a surprise. I knew Nalin was part of this secret militia, but I had no idea he led it. Maybe there was some hope, maybe.

Another thought came to me. "Nalin, do you have men stationed in the city of Clorynina? Since we're headed to the cliffs first anyway, maybe it would be worth seeing if we can find help there also."

I turned to face Elric. "Didn't your father sometimes trade with the Clorynina king? Do you think it would be worth a shot to ask him for aide? He is Anora's brother, after all. He has ships. Maybe he would send men down the coast and meet up with Gareth's army there."

Elric was already shaking his head before I had finished. "It's a good idea, but my father broke off trade with Clorynina about a year ago. The Dark Lord was putting pressure on the new king, my uncle, to stop trade with us. He said that he would continue trade if my father could guarantee safety for his ships and also have Clorynina's back if ever they needed help. My father refused, said it was too risky, and that was the end of their relationship. I still don't think my mother has forgiven him for abandoning her brother. I highly doubt that the king would be so inclined to stick his neck out for us now."

How could a king who had such good intentions go so terribly wrong? Why had no one seen the mistakes he was making? "Regardless, I still think it's worth a shot. You are not your father, and once your uncle sees that, maybe he will change his mind."

Miara also joined our conversation. "I also agree with Karah. This new king is not his father's son either. He has rectified many mistakes that its kingdom has made. He has no desire to be under the Dark Lord's boot either."

Elric said, "All right, but let's get moving. We're still closer to home than the army, even making these side stops, but I think we should get our plans in motion. I don't trust this good fortune. I keep expecting something to jump from the shadows and destroy us all."

Elric was right. I had the same feeling. I couldn't put my finger on it but something felt out of place. I kept thinking I was missing something but it was out of my reach, like the rest of my forgotten life.

We all separated and made final preparations for travel. It was dawn and the sun's rays gently started to peek in through the tops of the trees. I stood next to my new mount, debating on how I was going to get on top of it without hurting my leg when Elric suddenly appeared by my side.

"I wanted to thank you for your support earlier. I know it wasn't an easy decision. I'm grateful that I will not have to do this alone."

I put my hand on his cheek and gently kissed his forehead. "It was an easy decision. You dropped everything to come with me, so why wouldn't I do the same for you? I've had enough people making my choices for me. Its time I took control of my own life."

My thoughts drifted back to the conversation I'd had with Miara's mother earlier. I wondered anew how many bodies my soul had been shoved down, how many lives had given their own so that I could survive. I wouldn't let it happen again. This was my final human body. One way or another, this would be my last host.

Elric was staring at me with concern in his eyes. He carefully wiped a stray tear from my cheek. I didn't realize I'd started to cry.

"What's wrong? Are you in pain? Do you want me to get Avada?"

"Who's Avada?" I asked pulling myself together.

"Miara's mother. She never told you her name?"

I shuddered a little at the memory of that woman and shook my head. "No, she didn't. She had other things she wanted to talk about." I paused and took a steadying breath. "I need you to promise me something."

"Anything."

"I need you to promise me that no matter what happens to me you will not let Enthor put my soul into another human body."

Elric took a step back from me and looked horrified. "Why? Why would you want that?"

I looked down at my hands that were not truly mine and looked around the camp and at the people who were not truly my kind. I wondered if Turia's child would have survived and what kind of life she would have had.

I looked back at the man I loved and wondered if I still would have had these feelings for him if I were still just a dragon. "You need to promise me this because these bodies, these hosts that I inhabited are not my own. Do you know what happens to the soul that belongs to each body I possess? It dies. They sacrifice themselves so that I can live. They do this on blind faith based on a made-up prophecy, and worst of all, I can't remember anything. I can't even properly thank their families or loved ones because I can't remember."

My body started to shake and I fought hard to hold myself together. "Do you know what it's like to not have a choice in how you will live your life? I have been hunted and killed for 300 years and bits and pieces randomly flash before my eyes. I'm a parasite waiting to infect its next victim. If I die in this body and Enthor transfers me again into another poor host, I won't remember you. I'll lose you and everyone I hold dear to me. When someone dies, they have the right to rest. It's not fair that my soul is denied that. I can't put myself through that again. I won't."

I was shaking all over and tiny choked sobs escaped my lips. I hadn't wanted to act like that but once I started talking, everything seemed to break apart and I couldn't hold myself together.

Elric held me for a minute, and when I had regained some composure, he spoke into my ear. "You are not a parasite. What has happened to you I have no words to express how sorry I am for you, but it's not your fault. Yes, matters were taken out of your hands and terrible decisions were made but it was to keep you alive, and I will not say that I am not glad of it. If things had happened differently than we never would have met and my life would have a lot less meaning. I can't promise you that I will not let Enthor help save you, but I will promise you that it will be your decision. You're not alone any more; I will always be here for you."

I held him for a few moments more and then released him. I drew strength from his words and the love I saw in his grey eyes.

I let Elric help me up into my saddle and watched as he did the same. We all gathered together on the fresh mounts the Kannarah had provided.

Deneoes, however, remained with Fang, saying he much rather preferred her company to the uncomfortable gait of horses. This took a lot of persuasion on my part because my feline friend wanted to stay with me. However, I managed to convince her that Deneoes needed her more. She was not happy about it but I felt she understood. Oh, I was going to miss that creature, I hoped we were making the right decision to separate.

I looked around at my small group, and my eyes came to rest on Miara's mother. She had been the only one not to say anything through the whole of our plans. I had actually thought that she had changed her mind and decided to stay behind. She must have felt me staring because she turned suddenly and our eyes met. I still could not read anything from them. She was cold and devoid of emotion. She gave me the creeps. I shook the feeling away and told Miara to lead the way.

We all said our goodbyes to Enthor and Deneoes and watched them slip away into the forest. Then, with the sun at our backs, we headed out toward the cliffs and toward hope.

CHAPTER 22

King Edwin

Blinking my weary eyes, I tried to clear the fog of sleepless that had been plaguing me these past few nights, to no avail. I had come to my study early this morning, long before dawn in hopes of escaping whatever it was that haunted my dreams at night. Images of war and famine flashed across my mind and I shuddered, rubbing at my bloodshot eyes.

Standing up and stretching my taut muscles, I walked over to the window and looked out over my kingdom beyond. The pre-dawn air was heavy with heat, which was unusual for this time of year. Light here and there came from shops and homes preparing early for the day. My people would all be awake soon, starting their simple lives, comfortable in the fact that they were safe and depending on me to keep it that way.

I have worked hard to protect the people of Gareth, assuming the role of my ancestors with blind faith. I protected my own and stayed away from the troubles of the outside world, but with the revelations of the past weeks, I was terrified that my sanctuary would soon be breeched. I wondered anew how my son was faring in the world that he knew next to nothing about. There were so many dangers he was unprepared for, and I couldn't help but feel a twinge of guilt at not telling Elric more about what was out there, although truthfully I wasn't sure that I could have told him what to expect outside these walls, knowing so little myself.

Images of the dark, fanged beast that attacked my home came flooding back into my mind and I shuddered. A beast which had been absent for over 300 hundred years and thought extinct. I had known what it was the moment I saw it, but I tried to deny the truth. There was a *dragon* alive and well in the world and my stomach dropped at the thought. How could it be possible? How could something so terrifying exist? Why had my father not warned me? I had often wondered as a boy as most children did about Gareth's past and about the events that had led to my kingdom coming to be, but when I went in search of answers in my family's library, all I found was a locked door. Plenty of stories had been passed on through the generations but I wanted proof, I wanted to see them with my own eyes, to know about dragons.

I remembered the day I had asked my father why there were no writings about Gareth or even Eiddoril before the time of salvation. Being a young boy, I was fascinated with the tales of great battles and of dragons. I remembered my father being quite angry about my curiosity and the beating I'd received for trying to sneak into the library. He told me that what had happened in the past didn't matter, that what happened in the present was most important. My father had told me I would find no answers in the library that would aide in my life now and all I would find were lies and deceit. There were no such things as dragons or mighty warriors who had fought and won against impossible odds. There was only the Dark Lord and his rules, and if I wanted to be king someday I had to follow them. All that mattered was how I protected my people and my country, and that I could rely on no one but myself; nothing else was important, nothing else was worth knowing. My father made me swear on my life that I would never enter the library and I left my curiosity buried after that, along with my childhood innocence.

I grew up fast after that, always trying to be the man my father wanted me to be, but after that day he became more distant and critical of me. Nothing I did ever impressed him and I was left alone to grow up in a world plagued by distrust and war.

I inhaled deeply, trying to shake the horrors from the past, and I tried to remember what I had been doing only a moment before. A soft knock at the door brought my attention back to the present. I turned to see who was knocking, and the door smoothly opened.

The queen entered wearing a worn smile on her face. Anora was still in her light nightclothes, evading the heat from outside. Gods she was beautiful, and my heart still ached every time I looked at her. She had saved me from the bitter despair of my emotions, and without her I would not have become the man I was now.

My father had died suddenly during the night, and the healers said his heart had simply given up. I was at a loss. I didn't know how to grieve for my father and was so angry at being left alone to ensure the survival of Gareth.

It was during my father's burial that I met Anora. She had come from Clorynina on behalf of her father, King Harold. Now there was a man I was grateful for never having met. He had been a cruel man living in his ancestors' shadow of a doomed city. Clorynina was a large kingdom, second only to Gareth, but its reputation was horrible. The city had mainly been used for trading and selling slaves from across the sea. I was told that that was how so many of the races, as well has several species the Dark Lord employed for his army, namely the Litui, had come to dwell in Eiddoril. Poison festered in that city, and the only bright spot was Anora.

I remembered the first time I saw her and how I knew that day, I would love no other. Anora had boldly walked up to me beside my father's pyre and with her head bowed had offered her condolences. I was not able to help myself that day and I reached out and brushed her hand. It was the simplest of touches, but it caused her to look up and stare into my eyes. They were beautiful and seemed to glow with an inner light. I had invited her to stay for a few days before she made the long trip back to home. She had accepted and, as they say, the rest is history.

She walked over and handed me a hot cup of tea. I took it gratefully and turned back to the window, hoping against all odds that our son would suddenly appear and tell us that it was over and that we could go back to the way things were before. Anora joined me; for long minutes we both just stood there staring into the approaching dawn, neither wanting to disturb each other's thoughts, but it was the queen who spoke first, and worry hung on her words like a thick fog.

"I see you could not sleep again. Neither could I. Dread fills my heart. Something is wrong; I can feel it in my soul. Why do you not send out a small party in search of our son and Karah? We know where they were going. Why must we wait to hear word from them? They may need our help."

I looked at my wife's hopeful eyes and sighed, turning away from her and then walking back to sit at my desk. "You know I can't risk sending men out to look for Elric. We need every soldier here to protect Gareth. I would love nothing more than to help our son but I can't, I have a kingdom to worry about."

Anora's eyes fell. This was an old argument, one that she has lost many times. There have been many occasions over the course of our reign when small communities had sent out word that they needed help, but every time I would say that I could not spare enough men to make a difference. I hadn't wanted to leave Gareth unprotected so I did nothing, leaving the survivors to seek refuge here where I said it was safe, that it would always be safe as long as we stayed out of things. I always found a logical explanation for my seemingly heartless actions, but I was starting to believe that maybe I had been wrong. Anora had agreed most times, even when it meant turning her back on her own brother, which I knew she still had not forgiven me for, but Clorynina was stained, and I didn't want to get my hands dirty.

However, this was different. Anora was asking for men to go help our son and adopted daughter, not go save a city, but I still found it hard to justify the cause. I inwardly cringed at myself. I was a coward, not a king, and no matter how much I wanted to help my son, I just couldn't take the risk.

An insistent pounding on the study door interrupted the heavy tension in the room. I stood in front of my desk, recognizing the urgency in the knocking. "Come."

Duncan, my commanding officer, came through the door looking as though he had just seen the Dark Lord himself. He bowed deeply, and without waiting for an invitation, his words left his mouth. "Sire, mistress, I bring grave news. Early this morning we tracked a lone rider coming into our borders. He was dressed as a Dark Lord soldier but was alone. We stopped him just before he could cross the main bridge. We were able to detain him without incident. He said that he came here in peace and that he was a member of a secret faction within the Dark Lord's army sworn to protect the people."

My eyebrows rose at this news, but I shook my head in disbelief. "It must be a trick. I have heard of no such group. I hope you arrested him and threw him in the dungeon. I would like to speak to this wretch myself."

Anora spoke before Duncan could answer. 'Forgive me, my husband, but why it is not conceivable that this man could be telling the truth? You don't know what goes on outside these walls. It's a practice that you have become too comfortable with."

I turned my hot glare on my wife has she continued her attack. "Why is it so hard for you to believe that there are some who choose not to hide but to take action, even in the smallest of ways?" Anora was defiant and angry as she faced me.

My face paled, except my eyes, which were bright with fury. "How dare you speak to me this way? I have always done what I felt was right to protect you and this kingdom. What right do you have to question my actions? I am your king."

Anora did not flinch at my outbreak; instead, she placed a soft hand on my cheek and spoke quietly but with authority. "My right as a mother and your wife gives me cause to speak this way. You are a good man and I love you dearly, but please listen to what Duncan has to say. Act with your heart and not the logic that has run your decisions for most of your life."

I reached up and placed my hand over Anora's, letting my eyes close. Doubt filled my mind again. Was my queen right? Have I been wrong all these years? After a moment, I gently moved her aside and faced Duncan again.

"Continue. Duncan. What else did this man have to say? Why did he come here?" Duncan cleared his throat and the very air seemed to still hanging on his response. "Sire, he came to warn us. The Dark Lord has launched an assault. The whole of his army will be here before the next new moon."

I stared at the tattered piece of parchment Duncan held out to me. He spoke quietly. "I would not have believed either, Sire, if not for this note, which he produced. I am not sure of what it all says, but the soldier said that it was from Prince Elric. I recognised our seal so I believed him."

I reached out with a steady hand and unrolled the message.

Father,

I am writing this message under the direst of circumstances. I have received information pertaining to an imminent attack from the Dark Lord upon our city. The information is sound, so please do not dismiss it. This letter comes to you by way of a Dark Lord soldier, and I am sure this will be confusing. He is part of a secret militia that has been operating under the Dark Lord's nose for years. They are dedicated to the protection of the free peoples of these lands and are now in league with my companions and me. They will aide you in the defence of our city, but you must trust them. Much has happened since last we saw each other, and I must admit I am none too happy with what I have learned. It pained me deeply to know that the other realms of Eiddoril view Gareth as merely a nation of cowards and refugees. Your blind eye to the rest of the world may very well cause the demise of a home you tried so hard to protect, but that is conversation for another time.

I am on my way back to you, hopefully with reinforcements. We are travelling to Clorynina to speak with my uncle. I pray he holds no ill will toward us. Keep a sentry on the lookout down by the shores of the Forever Sea, which is where they will be headed. I am not certain who will come, but rest assured I will do everything in my power to find help. Until we meet again, Father, keep well and be prepared.

Prince Elric of Gareth

I folded the small piece of parchment and handed it to my patient wife. Anora read it without comment, but relief at the knowledge of her son's condition was plain to see on her face. We locked eyes, and although no words were spoken the gravity of our situation passed between us.

I pushed away the guilt and worries I felt for my son and got to the business of defending my city. "Where is this soldier now? I need to speak with him at once."

Duncan straightened and nodded. "He is in a holding cell. I thought it would be wise to detain him there until I had a chance to talk to you, Sire."

"Fine. Now we need to send word to the men at the docks to expect visitors. The prince is acquiring aide, who he has directed to converge at Aserah's docks. I want to know the minute anyone comes within miles. In addition, I want our own scouts to be sent in search of this army. I want to know how big it is and when exactly it will be here. Send out word to the surrounding farms and villages of the upcoming attack. Bring as many as we can hold over the bridge behind the walls. You will also need to inform the city residents to be expecting company. Once I have spoken to the soldier we can then begin to set up Gareth's defences."

"Yes, my king; I will update you as soon as possible." Duncan bowed once more and hastily exited the study, off to complete the tasks he had been entrusted to.

I was right on his heels, but Anora reached out and grabbed my arm. I did not turn but waited to hear her thoughts.

"This attack is not your fault. You did what you thought was right, just as you always have." Anora's voice was kind, but I could hear the anger behind it.

"Your words are appreciated, but we both know they are not deserved. I have been a blind fool, but I will not let that break me. This city will remain just as it always has. I promise you."

I gently shrugged off my wife's hold, and without a backward glance quickly retreated down the halls to speak with the Dark Lord soldier.

Chapter 23

Enthor

Twilight had come to the Kannarah forest. We crouched behind some bushes at the base of a tree, totally concealed from the soldiers we knew were out there but also in plain sight of the huge tomb that was now the Temple of Ashia. Deneoes and I had travelled swiftly, only stopping to rest our animals and quickly eat and drink.

The Kanarah Forest was west from where we left our companions and deep in the heart of the territory the Dark Lord now controlled. We had made good time and arrived in the majestic woods shortly before sunset on our third day. These woods were different from the rest of the forests in Eiddoril. The trees that grew here were tall and wide. Sometimes you could find the base of one of these trunks and it would take at least five minutes to walk its circumference. These trees did not grow close together like in a normal forest. They were spread out like giant towers, allowing for their massive limbs and trunks.

Their bark was a deep brown but the wood underneath was dark red, resembling the colour of blood. I had always thought these woods were the life centre of Eiddoril, each tree pumping its life energy into the earth around it. I reached up and touched one of the trees, and a shiver of power ran through my veins, but something was off. It felt sluggish and in pain. I snatched my hand back and hid the dread on my face from my young friend. We had enough to worry about right now, but the sickness I felt surging through this tree was not a good sign.

I turned my attention to the reason we had come: the temple. The once proud and beautiful structure was now decimated. The walls that had once shined a brilliant white were now green and cracked, covered in forest growth among other things. The exterior had been badly vandalized, and it was hard to tell that this used to be a beautiful place where people came to find peace. I stifled a roar in my throat and motioned to Deneoes to circle around the building to see what we could expect.

Twenty minutes passed before Deneoes and Fang returned. Deneoes spoke barely above a whisper, but the impact of his words hit me like a brick. "There is a large group of those lazy bastards camped out at the front entrance. I would say maybe 15 men, all armed, and not very happy looking. Even if we had the rest of our group it would be a hard fight that would no doubt attract more attention."

I motioned toward the back of the temple. "There used to be a back entrance for the mage disciples to use when they were in training. Did you see it? Were any guards stationed there?"

Deneoes had a small smile on his face that made him look juvenile, but I knew that the little Ywari was anything but a child. "I'm way ahead of you, old man. The back door is also guarded but there's only two of them back there. I guess they figured not too many people would know about a back entrance. We can handle them and then sneak in and out before anyone's the wiser."

It was a good plan, but I had no idea if there would be any soldiers inside. Unfortunately, it was our only option, so we prepared to move out.

Then chaos broke out.

Deneoes and I ducked back behind the cover of bushes just before a massive shadow blocked out the moon overhead. A stab of instance fear speared straight through my soul, and I found myself cowering for no apparent reason.

Deneoes beside me and likewise was not faring well. I could see the whites of his eyes and he held his head, stifling a scream of terror.

The soldiers ran this way and that trying to escape the unseen foe who threatened, but a single roar, like thunder, shook the ground, freezing the men in their tracks. Then everything once again was quiet, and the crippling fear subsided.

A lone figure strode out of the darkness carrying himself with smug indifference. He stopped before the temple's front entrance and examined his soldiers. The Dark Lord was not impressed. "Get up, you worthless, snivelling fools. How dare you act like children in my presence? I should have you all flailed! Where is Reaper? I need to speak with him immediately."

Fearing their lord's wrath no one spoke, which on their part was bad judgment. The Dark Lord, masking his fury at his men, pointed at one of the soldiers and bade him to come forth. I had to give the soldier credit. He could not have been more than 20 years old but came before his lord on steady legs and bowed his head respectfully.

The Dark Lord lifted the boy's chin, looked into his eyes and then grasped him around the throat, lifting him into the air. The soldier kicked and grabbed at the hand that was enclosed around his throat like an iron vice.

The evil dragon's voice again cut through the air. "I asked you a question, soldier. Where is Reaper?"

The scared boy tried desperately to answer his master's questions but didn't have enough air, and his struggles were starting to subside from lack of oxygen. The Dark Lord made a disgusted snort, snapped the boy's neck and dropped him at his feet.

A soldier standing in the back found his nerve and quickly made his way to his lord's side. Ignoring the dead body of his comrade, he quickly bowed his head and spoke. "My Lord, forgive me, but Reaper is not here. He came briefly four days ago, he said to speak with the guardian on your behalf. He was here for no more than an hour and quickly departed, leaving no message or clue as to his intent. Forgive us, my lord, had we known otherwise we would have investigated further."

The man kept his head lowered, as if waiting for the deathblow that would surely follow his bad news, but it did not come. I was surprised; the Dark Lord was never one to take bad news well. "That is most unfortunate. I don't understand. I told him to wait here for Ililsaya. He was supposed to gain her trust and trap her for me. Does this mean that no one has been here, not even that horrid creature and her band of idiots?" The Dark Lord shook with rage.

The young soldier kept his head lowered. "No, my Lord, no one has been here. We have kept a constant watch, and no one has entered and the guardian inside has not made a sound."

Deneoes and I looked quickly at each other, making sure that we heard the same thing. So it seemed the interior was not so unguarded after all. I glanced back at the Dark Lord and saw him standing very still with his eyes closed, as if listening for something. Dread filled my heart because I knew what the other dragon was doing—searching for Karah. I glanced down at the band wrapped around my wrist and was suddenly thankful for it. As long as I wore it, the Dark Lord would not be able to find me, but I wondered if he could still find Karah. Now that she could control her powers, she was not using them without her knowledge. Was that enough to keep her hidden from him?

The Dark Lord clenched his fists in frustration, and when his eyes flew open there was nothing human about them. "Who's in charge here? I need to be elsewhere but there are things that must be taken care of here first."

The officer who had spoken to him raised his head and saluted. "I am in charge of this unit, Master. What is it that you need?"

The Dark Lord nodded. "It seems that Reaper has been detained for reasons I am not yet aware of. I can sense him through our blood bond, but it has grown too weak to communicate with him. All I can tell is that he is near the sea, close to Clorynina. I can only assume that my prey has gone there instead of making her way here, which does not make sense to me—nor does his lack of communication. I must go there at once to make sure she is captured and ready for the sacrifice."

Deneoes stared at me with fearful and questioning eyes. I held up my hand to still him, but my own fears and realizations of what must be happening were causing me to shift nervously as well.

The evil dragon continued with his orders. "There are artefacts deep in the keep of this temple that need to be packed and ready to transport to the borders of Gareth. There is a powerful magic that surrounds them, so do not touch them until the guardian has released the spell. Be careful with them; they are extremely fragile and the power they contain are needed for the battlefield. After you have successfully removed them, kill the guardian and pull the rest of your men out. I have no more use for the pathetic creature, and it is time that this temple is buried in the past where it belongs."

The Dark Lord handed the soldier a jewelled dagger that glowed a faint red. "Use this to dispatch the guardian. It has enough magic in it to destroy her, but be careful not to touch it yourself or you will find the effects most unpleasant."

The soldier gingerly took the blade and handed it off to one of his other men. He bowed deeply and with confidence faced his lord. "Everything you command will be done. We will begin our tasks immediately. We will not fail you."

"No, you won't, if you wish to continue breathing." The evil dragon turned and left the clearing in his human form, the way he had come. Breaking tree limbs and a deafening roar were the only signs of his departure.

Deneoes and I did not move from our spots for several long minutes, making sure the other dragon was indeed gone. The soldiers at the front entrance wasted no time in carrying out their orders. Half went into the temple while the other half made preparations to move out.

We quietly backed away and made sure we were completely out of the soldiers' earshot before we discussed what had just happened.

My young friend said, "We need to go back and find Karah. If what that overgrown lizard said was true, then the others are walking into a trap. What does he need her for anyway? What sacrifice was he talking about? And who is this Reaper, another dragon?"

Deneoes looked to me for answers. "No, Reaper is much worse, and his hatred for Karah runs as deep as the Dark Lord's. He is a Hautur and this is not the first time he has been sent to capture Karah. As for the sacrifice, I have no idea, it is the first I have heard of it. I always just assumed the Dark Lord wanted Karah dead.

This news is most disturbing." Once again, I was left with more questions.

Deneoes threw his hands in the air in frustration. "But that means this Reaper character could be anyone. He could have been travelling with us the whole time."

Deneoes paused, and anger crossed his delicate features. "You said the ambush in Delroth was a setup, so what if one of those Kanarah giants is this Reaper?" He tapped his finger to his head as if he had just thought of something important. "I'll bet it's that tall hulking beast of a man, Jaitem. I never heard him speak two words the whole time we were together, and he just plain gave me a bad feeling."

I closed my eyes. Everything was going so terribly wrong. What was I supposed to do now? How was I going to get out of this mess this time? Separating from Ililsaya had been a gamble on my part, and now I wished I could take it back. When I opened my eyes again they were my dragon eyes, and they glowed with malice.

"You may very well be right, but there is nothing we can do about it now. We are too far from them and even if we could find them I doubt we would be of much use anyway. Well, I wouldn't be. We just have to trust that they can take care of themselves. Karah's fate is in her own hands now and if we have any hope of helping Gareth we need to find out what's going on in there." I pointed into the direction of the temple and then regarded my small friend.

He crossed his arms over his chest and seemed resigned. "Fine. I don't like this, but I guess you're right. I just hope you can get that thing off your wrist in time to go help them. They may be able to fight off a shape-shifter, but when that very angry beastie finds them, I'm not sure that the outcome would be in our favour."

I nodded my agreement. "I don't think so either. Even if I did make it in time to help, it would not be an easy battle. The Dark Lord is much larger than I am and he has the advantage of being in his dragon form more. Let's just get into the temple and see what we can do."

I pulled the Ywari closer. "There are many different paths down into the caves that riddle the underground of the temple. There is one direct path that leads to a main chamber where I'm pretty sure these artefacts and this guardian are. The other chambers are smaller, used for practicing with elemental magic. They all connect, however, and there are other entrances into the main chamber."

I started to move, with Deneoes close at my heels, but the little warrior stopped and grabbed hold of my arm. I turned my questioning gaze on my friend and saw fear and anger across his features. My heart dropped.

"What is it? What's wrong?"
"It's Fang. She's gone."

*

Fang

She ran with intense need through the trees and thick brush. She felt bad for having left her friends alone but needed to get back to her. No other thought ran through her mind, and she did not quite understand why. She had been happy living among the trees and her kind, but that had changed. They told her to protect the girl who smelled nothing like the regular humans she had encountered. They told her that this girl was important, that she would make the world safe again. She didn't understand but would do what the maker asked. She had grown to like the girl and the strange beings she surrounded herself with.

So she ran as fast as her feline legs would carry her, back to where she had left her, and she followed her scent to where she knew she would be in danger. Nothing mattered to the beast now, nothing but the girl.

CHAPTER 24

Enthor

"Maybe the creature has just gone off to hunt. I'm sure she'll return."

Deneoes looked at me with frustration and shook his head at my suggestion. We had both spent a few minutes searching the surrounding brush as best as we could but the wild cat was nowhere to be seen. But of course, if she didn't want to be seen she was quite capable of being right in front of your nose.

The young Ywari could barely contain his agitation. "You know as well as I do that this is too much of a coincidence. That animal always seems to know exactly what's going on. It just isn't natural."

Deneoes paced back and forth, growing more agitated. I tried to calm him. "You're right, but Fang saved Karah more than once, so we have to trust that she is here to protect her, not harm her."

I placed my hand on his small shoulder and squeezed hard. "We have to go. It will not take long for the Dark Lord's men to get organized. If we have any hope of this working, we need to act now."

Deneoes shrugged off my hold. "I hope you're right. Come on, let's get this over with, I really need to hurt something right now."

The Ywari unslung his bow and notched an arrow. He pushed past me and took point, leading the way to the back entrance of the temple.

As luck would have it there were still only two guards posted at the hidden door. However, they were both armed heavily and were on edge. Every movement in the forest caused them to flinch and stare into the deep abyss that surrounded them.

Their words eerily floated through the forest. "I don't like this. I feel like this creepy forest is going to come to life and swallow us whole. I don't see why we need to be back here anyway. No one can get through this damn door—if, in fact, that is what it is. Personally I think this place is haunted."

The taller Dark Lord soldier shivered and drew his cloak more firmly around his shoulders. He looked on in disgust. "Oh would you shut your babbling mouth? You're worse than a scared serving wench. We have our orders. I for one have no intention of crossing our lord. Just be patient, and when this is over we'll be sitting in the throne room of the mighty Gareth Empire, drinking ale and feasting till our bellies our full. You worry too much."

A low whistle sounded in the night, piercing the silence and making the soldiers look off to the right. Neither man moved, listening for signs of life. The whistle sounded again but now it seemed to come from their left. The two men moved out from the protective enclave of the doorway and stared in the direction of the noise. Two glowing golden eyes materialized out of the darkness and held the soldiers' gazes.

The pair drew their weapons, but before they had a chance to move, a sudden gust of wind slammed into them, knocking them both to the ground. One scrambled to his feet quickly but only succeeded in tripping over his companion's body. He glanced down and saw his friend's sightless eyes peering at him. An arrow was imbedded so deep into his throat that he could only see half the shaft. Blood trickled out of the man's mouth and quickly covered the front of his armour.

A snapped branch directly behind him caused him to swing his sword blindly behind, only to find that he had missed his target, and what looked to be a small child stood before him with a wicked grin on his face. He stared for a moment, trying to process what was going on, but before he could come up with an answer, I neatly snapped his neck from behind. The dead soldier dropped like a bag of bricks close to his fallen comrade. I flexed my taut muscles and rolled my shoulders, my dragon eyes still burning gold with an inner fire.

"Well, that wasn't so hard. Remind me not to get on your bad side." Deneoes smiled up at me and together the two of us dragged the bodies into the brush and hid them as best we could. We hurried back to the enclave of the temple door and Deneoes stared at it in confusion. I'm sure he was puzzled by the fact that all he saw was a solid wall of stone no handle no locks, nothing that would suggest it could be opened.

He looked up at me, frowning. "So I'm guessing you have a key, 'cause if not we are seriously screwed."

I frowned back at him and stood off to the side, looking for something. Deneoes watched as I gently scrubbed away moss and dirt from one of the stones that protruded slightly from the wall. It looked as though it had once been rose coloured but years of neglect and forest growth had dulled the true color. I gently placed my hand over the stone and prayed that this would work, while a strange bluish glow started to form a symbol on its smooth surface. The door began to shudder and then silently dissolved, as if nothing had been there at all. A dark hallway opened up before us, the end hidden in the total darkness of the interior. Stale air wafted out into the night, and I got the feeling we were walking into a tomb.

Deneoes shivered, no doubt feeling the same. "Neat trick. How did you do that without your magic?"

I ignored him, stepping inside the temple, and took a deep breath. Memories from another time came flooding back, and I fought hard to control the unexpected feelings.

Deneoes followed me and whistled in awe as the door rematerialized behind us and looked like part of the wall again.

We were thrown into complete darkness, but our night vision was adequate enough to find the torches that lined the walls. I reached up and removed one from the rusted sconce. Deneoes produced a flint from his pack, and soon fire lit our surroundings. I waved the torch around and took in the tomb-like scene. This particular hallway was narrow and the ceiling was quite low. It had only been used for mages to enter and exit the temple without disrupting the main activities in the main hall; it also provided access to the mages' private rooms. Many had called this home for a time including myself and I was haunted by their faces as I passed each door.

Surprisingly nothing seemed to have been disturbed here, for which I was thankful. I did not know how I would have reacted if I had seen my fellow mages' belongings desecrated like the rest of the temple. There were no footprints in the dust that lined the floors, and the signs of vandalism outside were nowhere to be found.

I let Deneoes catch up and answered his earlier question. "I am assuming the Dark Lord never made it to this part of the temple. The door we passed through can only be opened by someone who follows the elements. It is keyed to our spiritual and elemental magic. I can't use mine right now but this device could sense it"—I pointed at my wrist—"so it allowed me access. I'm betting the Dark Lord spent many frustrating days trying to get through that door."

My voice echoed and bounced off the walls, creating the effect of people carrying on a conversation.

Deneoes shrank a little at the intrusion of sound and spoke softly. "I would have liked to have seen the look on his ugly face when he realized he couldn't get through there, but could he have gained access somewhere else? This hallway must lead to the rest of the temple."

I gestured toward the end of the hall. "It does, but there is a similar door there too. To an outsider it would merely look like part of the wall."

Deneoes looked thoughtful. "Why didn't the Dark Lord just knock it down? He is a dragon after all, so why not just smash this place to bits?"

I shuddered at that comment, not wanting to think about what would have happened if my brethren had been capable of doing that. However, my sudden ill feeling had more do to with the secrets I kept hidden.

I paused and looked around once again at the beautiful artwork and artisanship that made up this temple. Many races had come together to build this structure and it was the evil work of one that could have caused it all to come crashing down. I glanced at Deneoes, who was patiently waiting for me to reply, and I suddenly made a decision, a very human decision that appalled me. My inner daemons were getting the better of me and perhaps that was good thing.

I continued walking as I spoke. "This temple is very powerful. It is protected by all four elements and long ago served as a place where all the races could come and be with their makers. Once you could walk these halls and feel the connection to the very world around you and it filled you with a profound peace. Everyone was welcome here, and it was the only place where you could be and see all the different races of this world in one location."

I turned to Deneoes. "Many, unfortunately, do not exist any more, the wars between good and evil proving to be too much for them. Others went into hiding, which you already know, and still others turned their backs completely on the elements and their magic." I gestured around the hallway. "No amount of dragon magic or sheer force can break these walls. They were crafted and infused with the elements' powers, and this structure will long outlast any mortal beings, but I am glad the elements chose to still protect this place even though most of the races chose to forsake them."

We had stopped walking, and Deneoes's confused face, lit eerily by the torchlight, looked to me for answers.

I looked off down the hall. "The loss of dragons in this world did more damage than the elements or even I could have foreseen. When we first came back here, none of the mortals understood or made any attempt to understand what the elements truly were. They all merely existed and were quite happy in the knowledge that everything you had would always be there. But we knew different."

Sadness filled my voice, and I found it hard to stop talking even though my dragon logic told me I should. "We should have left things alone and let the mortals exist on their own terms, but we decided to take it apon ourselves to teach you and to control you, but mortals were afraid of dragons. So we discovered a way in which we could deceive you . . . we took on human forms. In time, mortals adopted us as their gods with the help of us spinning tales of how we and not the elements created life in this world. We pushed the elements into the background, where they remained watching, letting our doomed scenario play out. We led everyone to believe that magic came through us, that without us the elements would not listen, and that we were your true gods."

I stole a glance at Deneoes, but his face was unreadable as he waited for me to continue. "Once again our arrogance ended in disaster. The elements returned and there were no more second chances. We were banished again and without guidance. After the other dragons' departure and the disappearance of their fake gods the mortals believed they could no longer wield magic, so elemental power was forgotten by most and things returned to the way they were before we came here. The elements were ignored and taken for granted once again and magic for the most part disappeared from Eiddoril."

Self-pity—another disgusting human emotion—washed over me. "When the other dragons left, it was I the elements turned to for help. They were the reason I stayed, not Ashia. I didn't know their reasons at the time for wanting me to stay, but they became painfully clear in time. Somehow they had known what was going to happen to Karah, and thanks to my unique abilities, I was the one chosen to keep her safe and hidden. I made myself believe that keeping Karah safe was the only thing that mattered. It was the only thing I could control that I had the power to do, so I abandoned the mortals and my oaths made as a mage and left you to your fates, knowing that the other dragons may never return, and leaving you and the others defenceless. I let the memory of dragons, your gods, fall into myth and legend, and my fellow mages were hunted down and slaughtered."

I raked my hands through my grey human hair. "I became bitter and lost. I didn't care what happened to creatures that were lesser than I was. I wanted my life back, I wanted my *mate* back, and I was determined to not let anything happen to the child who could help me do these things."

I turned away from my friend's accusing, hurt gaze. Of course there was more to this story, much more, but my human side was not that much in control yet. I needed this Ywari as my friend, and divulging my past dealings would only destroy that.

I placed my empty hand against one of the wooden doors that led to a bedchamber beyond and tried not to remember the faces who had trusted me without question. The faces I'd abandoned for a greater power.

My voice shook with pent-up emotion. "Being forced to be human for so long has affected me in ways that I never thought possible. I *regret* so many of my decisions and find myself seeking forgiveness. These feelings are foreign to me, and I can honestly tell you I don't like them." I remained facing the door, unable to look at Deneoes. "I don't expect you to understand, nor will I stand here and defend my actions. It may be too late but I will try and fix things. It is not in me to fail. I think too highly of myself."

I hunched my human shoulders in defeat and was suddenly exhausted. Never had I opened myself up to another creature this way, and if I was being honest, I didn't really understand why I did so with Deneoes. There was too much at stake and I was taking a stupid risk, all in the hopes that just maybe there was a chance for me, that maybe my soul would not be doomed.

I faced the young Ywari and waited for the angry accusations that I knew would come. Deneoes simply grabbed the torch out of my hand and started walking again. I fell silently into place beside him and let him express his thoughts. "I'm not going to tell you that I am not angry with you because I am, but you are here now and that says something. I've always thought that we are strong enough not to have to rely on a higher power to fix our problems for us, and unlike most mortals the Ywari always knew what the elements were, and we never lost faith in them. I am grateful for the life that this world has given me, but it is my own and no faith or following would ever take me off that path."

He turned fiery eyes up to my face. "What your kind did was wrong, what *you* did was wrong, but we were just as at fault, we let it happen. Let's just do what we came here to do and then we can figure out where we stand."

I thankfully agreed and let the matter drop. There would come a time when I would have to answer for all of my mistakes, but it wasn't now. I just hoped we would all be alive when that day finally came.

We came to end of the hall, which Deneoes complained seemed to take forever. In reality, we had only been inside the temple for maybe 15 minutes but it was like an eternity for him. It turned out that Ywari did not like to be confined. Deneoes quietly doused the torch with water from his water skin and joined me in the darkness at the wall. We both tried in vain to listen for any movement on the other side but it was impossible to tell what was going on beyond the safety of the hall.

Deneoes stood very close to me and kept his voice low, hoping he wouldn't give away our location. "Now what? Do we go in and hope no one is on the other side waiting to take our heads off, or do you have a plan?"

I crouched so I was eye level with my friend. "Fortunately, this entrance did not open up directly into the main hall. It opens into a small room on the opposite side of the library. It is in the library that we will find the pathways that lead down into the depths of the underground caves. When I bring down the doorway we should be concealed enough to take a look around and see where the soldiers have positioned themselves."

Deneoes nodded. "Well, I wouldn't exactly call that a plan, but I guess it will do. After you." Deneoes stepped aside and unslung his bow.

I stood and drew my short sword as well. I located the magical switch and gently placed my hand over the top of it. The same blue glow illuminated our small enclosure and then dissipated. The wall shimmered silently in front of us and then as before dissolved into thin air, leaving us staring directly at a very startled Dark Lord soldier.

CHAPTER 25

Karah

It had taken two hard days for our small party to reach the cliffs of the Forever Sea. We left the flat plains behind heading east back towards the coastline and followed the steady incline of land surrounding the sea. Lush forests and other plant growth made it difficult for the horses to pass, and we'd had to dismount several times to navigate the treacherous paths. These times were particularly painful due to my still healing leg, but I managed. Avada had done an excellent job stitching me up and the wound was quickly healing, but I still winced a little whenever I put too much weight on it.

I would have become completely lost, but the Kanarahs had no trouble finding their way. At least we didn't have to worry about pursuit; I doubted anything would be able to track us. The Kanarah race had chosen their hiding place well.

During our journey, I became rather close with Miara. She was a vibrant, strong-willed woman, and her compassion for her people made me ache inside. I was determined to find out more about my host human body and its background, which she seemed to appreciate. The story of how the Kanarah people came to live in the Forever Sea cliffs was not a pleasant one. She told me they had once been a strong people, living in peace in the Kanarah woods. They were true followers of the great Ashia, my mother. She protected them and taught them how to speak to the earth. It came naturally to them, and their ancestors were great magic wielders. But that all changed the day Ashia and the other dragons left, leaving them at the mercy of the Dark Lord.

Miara explained how things had been fine for a time, becoming allied with the kingdom of Gareth, and a strong bond had been formed. Their ancestors fought many battles together and they survived, but then 300 years ago, after the Great War, their most trusted allies turned coat and ran. I refused to tell my new friend that I had been part of the reason King Gareth had chosen to uproot his people. I was ashamed, and having Miara's accusing eyes on me was not appealing.

She continued to tell me how they had barely defeated the Dark Lord, and many losses had been suffered on their side, but instead of staying and trying to rebuild, Gareth left. He had asked them to come but they could not leave their homes, which were a part of their very existence. Their ancestors and many others who had fought with Gareth begged him to stay, but it was said that he was broken, that there had been no more life left in him. He turned his back and left, never returning and never caring what had become of them.

So after Gareth and his people had left, they were alone. The Dark Lord had been greatly damaged and had suffered many casualties, but he was still a dangerous foe. He launched a brutal campaign with the sole purpose of destroying anyone who had been aligned with the kingdom of Gareth. On top of that, the elements, which had been so good to them, abandoned them as well. The Kanarah could no longer wield magic as they used to. Some of their more powerful still could, but it was as if the elements had gone into hiding and were afraid to help. The Kanarah fought bravely, but it had become apparent that if they did not do something drastic, their entire race was going to be destroyed. So like their departed companions, they ran and hid.

They came to the cliffs of the Forever Sea. It was such a complete turnaround of their existence that they thought it would be a good place to hide. They adapted to the hard life and found new ways to survive. Many did not make the transition easily, and they lost a great number of their people to starvation and exposure, but in time, they survived. The Kanarah cut off contact with the outside world for more than 100 years, letting their race fall into history and be forgotten, but even though they could survive in the cliffs, they missed the forest, which called to them daily. It was time for them to return home but they just didn't know how.

*

It was still fairly early when our conversation ceased and we plunged yet again into thick, almost impassable terrain. We remained silent, saving our energy, and just when I thought I couldn't go any further, our small company emerged from the thick growth of vegetation and stepped into a different world. My breath caught in my throat as I took in the vast expanse of the sea. It extended farther than my vision reached, touching the horizon and then disappearing to the lands beyond.

I took a few tentative steps toward the cliff's edge and stared down and across, absorbing the dangerous, breathtaking scene. I wasn't sure of the distance to the beaches below, but the height was enough to make me feel a little dizzy. The cliffs were covered in vegetation, and here and there small waterfalls flowed and were swallowed by the sea. Giant birds darted in and out of the mist around the falls. I looked closer and recognized the shape and size of the animal. It was the same bird I had seen carrying the Dark Lord from the battlefield. I stifled a gasp and rested my hand on my sword.

Miara was beside me and noticed my alarm. "What is it, child? What are you looking at?"

I pointed. "Those birds circling the waterfalls—what are they? I've seen one before in Gareth. It carried the Dark Lord away after I'd wounded him."

Miara shook her head. "Really, you must have been mistaken. Those beasts are called Ristiapers. They are native to these cliffs. They make their nests behind the waterfalls where they are hidden. They would not venture far from these coasts. Their source of food is here, and as far as I know the particular type of fish they eat can only be found here. Perhaps what you saw was one of the Hautur. You had said they were present at that battle."

Miara's words sent shivers down my spine. I had forgotten about the shape-shifters.

Elric now stood with us, and he glanced at the huge birds. "Shape-shifters, evil bastards. I can't say I would be upset if they had never existed."

I leaned a little closer to him, letting his presence calm me a little.

Miara suddenly looked sad, and her voice was quiet. "They were not always evil, you know. There had been a time before the Dark Lord when the Hautur lived in peace with everyone. There are stories and legends that tell of a great partnership the Hautur had with our people, but like so many others they became seduced by the Dark Lord's promise of power."

Miara turned away and joined the others, helping them secure the horses and belongings. I let what she said sink in and couldn't for the life of me see any goodness in the Hautur. I gave one last quick look at the massive birds and sheathed my sword.

After we secured our mounts and belongings, Jaitem took point, and we started to descend to the beach below. It did not take him long to find a path that seemed to have been cut into the rock itself. It took us parallel of the shoreline and cut and wound its way through the rock and pockets of vegetation.

We walked in silence for a few miles, each of us lost in the wonders that surrounded us. The cliff face was alive with a magic of its own, and I was drawn to everything around me. It was hard to believe that something so beautiful existed in a world so full of hate and despair. I walked in the middle of our group, not really paying attention to anything but the music of the waves crashing against the shoreline far below. My absent-minded behaviour as usual ended up leading me astray, and I was roughly pulled back from the edge of the path by Avada, Miara's mother.

"It would serve you well to pay more attention to your surroundings. I would hate to see anything happen to you." The woman gave me a menacing look and then proceeded to pass me and catch up with her brethren at the head of our party.

I shook the feeling of dread that woman caused me and caught up to the rest of my group, who had all halted. As I got closer, I heard unfamiliar voices and saw that we were no longer alone. I quietly moved away to stand beside Nalin and asked him what was going on.

"We are near Miara's old village. Those two men"—Nalin gestured at the two hulking, unfriendly looking Kanarah warriors blocking our path—"are sentries for their village. They are not happy to see us, and I think we may have a problem."

Miara was in fact having a very heated discussion with them and looked like she was about to cause a fight when her mother moved her aside and spoke to the two younger warriors. They seemed to cower in her presence, and after only a few words they turned and Avada bade us to follow. Miara looked like she was ready to spit venom, but without arguing she signalled the rest of us to follow. Nalin and I fell in step beside Elric, leaving the Kanarah people to themselves.

"What was all that about?" Elric kept his voice low, but Nalin had no problem hearing the prince.

Nalin shrugged. "I'm not sure; they were speaking in their own tongue. It's a language that I am not too familiar with any more, but from what I could understand and from what I know about Miara and her tribe, Miara is not a respected member any more. She chose to leave after her sister's death and see what was out there in the world, much as her sister before her had done. Turia was disbanded from the tribe as well."

That statement caught my attention. "But Avada told me Turia gave birth here in the cliffs. If she was an outcast, how did she end up back here?" The story of my human body's birth still haunted my dreams, but I shrugged the feeling aside.

Nalin turned to look at me, and for a moment I saw such longing and sadness in his eyes. He looked away quickly and spoke softly. "I wasn't sure if I should tell you this or not. I wanted to but Miara said I shouldn't, that it would just complicate things more. But I think you should know, I think Turia would have liked you to know."

Oh boy. I felt another earth-shattering secret coming on. I was beginning to think that I should just keep my mouth shut and not ask any more questions. I think my sanity would appreciate that.

Nalin swallowed, and he looked very uncomfortable. "You see, I know so much about Miara and her family because I was once part of it. I was Turia's husband . . . and I guess you could say your father."

Well, as life-changing secrets went, that was definitely huge. I didn't know what to say. My mouth was suddenly dry and my mind froze. I was amazed I was able to keep walking. Elric gripped my hand, and I squeezed for dear life. How many more pieces fit into this puzzle of my life?

Nalin didn't seem to notice my discomfort and kept on speaking from his memories. "I met Turia in Delroth. I was barely a man, trying to find my way in these hard times, and I guess she saw something in me others didn't. I was captivated by her. I had never seen another woman who looked as she did." Love shined in his eyes but his voice was dark.

"We tried to make a living for ourselves, joining the local mercenary guild, but it was not what we wanted. We bore witness every day to the death and deceit that plagued these lands and we wanted to change it, not add to it." Anger flashed in Nalin's eyes, and he clenched his fists until the knuckles were white.

I placed my hand on his shoulder, and some of that anger left him, but contempt still laced his words. "The Dark Lord's men made monthly visits to Delroth, recruiting men into their ranks, and the women . . . well, you can imagine what became of most. It was during one of these raids that Turia's and my luck had run out. We had always been so careful to avoid them, but we were good at what we did and they personally sought us. They smashed their way into our home late one night and demanded that I join the Dark Lord's army, and of course, as you can imagine when they saw Turia all thoughts of recruitment left them. We did the only thing we could—we fought them, and we would have lost if it were not for the involvement of the group that I am now part of. Two out of the five men who 'attacked' us that night were not Dark Lord soldiers at all, and they quickly helped us dispatch the other three men. When they explained who and what they were, we were given a choice: join them or leave, never to show our faces again in this part of the world. For us it was an easy decision. This was our chance to do something against the evil that was swallowing our lands whole. So the two remaining officers staged the attack to make it look like we had murdered the three Dark Lord soldiers and the other two had escaped. Turia and I had no choice but to disappear for a few months anyway. We were wanted felons, so we went back to her tribe."

He laughed a little then, recalling some private memory. "Let me tell you, our reception was not a welcome one. Not only had Turia disobeyed her father by leaving the safety of their home, she also returned with a common man who had gotten her pregnant. I was more scared of her mother than any Dark Lord soldier, but in the end we were accepted into the tribe. Her mother bore no love for me, but she would not turn her daughter away, especially since she was with child."

Nalin stopped then and turned to look at me with sadness and regret. "I was away the night Turia gave birth and your soul was placed inside our child. I had been summoned to aide in a mission. I was furious and devastated when I returned, only to find that my mate had died during childbirth and that our daughter had disappeared. I vowed that someday I would find you and your mage and make you answer for what you have done."

I stared at the man who was in a sense my stepfather and held my breath. He had every right to be angry, but nothing could compare to the contempt I held for myself.

I started to speak but Nalin held up his hand. "Please let me finish. I carried that rage around with me for a long time, and it helped me get where I am today, but when I saw you the other night, it all just went away. I saw my Turia in your eyes. I saw our daughter, and once I got to know you and know your story, I couldn't hold any ill will toward you. Turia made the right decision that night. Even through the pain and despair of losing her child, she saw the chance to do something to make a difference in this world. Because of you, our daughter has lived. I believe she shares your spirit because you are so much like Turia. I am proud of you even though I have only met you. You must have gone through so much to get here, and I am proud that my daughter was given a chance to live and make the difference her parents had tried so hard for."

Tears streamed down my face as Nalin embraced me. All the guilt I had been holding inside let go a little, and I breathed in a heavy sigh. He released me and wiped at his own eyes.

Elric's arm replaced Nalin's around my shoulder, and together we started to walk again to catch up with the others.

"Thank you for sharing that with me. I know how hard it must have been. I promise your daughter's sacrifice will not be in vain. We will win this somehow, I will find a way."

"I know you will, we all will. We have no choice."

We walked the remainder of the journey in silence, and it wasn't long before we came to Miara and Avada's old village camp. I was amazed and truly in awe at the way these people lived. The Kanarah had literally made their own villages inside the cliffs. A network of underground caves snaked throughout the cliffs, connecting different tribes. It was not the ideal living arrangement but it was a brilliant hiding place.

After some major negotiations on everyone's part, we were permitted to stay, and they heard our story. Many were sceptical, and I noticed that Avada did nothing to convince them otherwise. Everyone in that tribe knew her feelings on the matter, and she did not hide them. I wondered why she had bothered to come at all. However, in the end, some were convinced of the gravity of our situation and promised to do what they could to help. Some travelled that day with Jaitem to the other tribes who inhabited these cliffs, and I could only hope that at least some would also be persuaded to our cause.

We decided not to stay in Miara's childhood home for the night, so we made the long journey back to the top of the cliffs were we had left the horses and made our own camp for the night. We would wait for Jaitem to return and then continue on our way to Clorynina in the morning.

It was nearing the end of the third day since I had separated from my friends, and I wondered not for the first time if we had made the right decision to separate. There was no hope for it now, but the nagging feeling that something was wrong clung to my soul.

I stood alone on a rocky outcropping watching the sun slip down. Everything was washed in the vibrant colours of the sun reflecting off the water. I had never seen anything so beautiful. I watched as the dark sea silently swallowed the last rays of the day and my thoughts drifted to earlier events. I wasn't sure how I felt about everything that had transpired today. We had gotten our message across, but we wouldn't know the outcome until dawn, when Jaitem returned. I hoped it would be good news, but my heart wouldn't allow me that pleasure.

A call from my companions drew me from my thoughts and I retreated back to our campsite. I took a seat next to Elric and watched the fire as my friends got ready for the evening. I decided I should probably to the same and started to make my way to my horse, but Avada was blocking my path.

"How is your leg, child? Do you need anything for the pain?"

The sound of concern in her voice seemed genuine but it did not follow to her face. I stepped back a little to give us space and regarded her with caution. "No, thank you, it's fine. You did an excellent job healing me, although I have been questioning why."

We faced each other, and a look of surprise crossed her features when she realized I was not backing down. "No, I don't suppose I've given you much reason to trust or even like me. I apologize. Come sit down next to the fire. I was just about to brew some of my famous mint tea. Will you have some?"

She gestured toward the fire where Miara, Elric and Nalin were sitting, and I reluctantly obliged. I returned to my spot next to Elric and shook my head at his questioning gaze. I watched in silence as Avada brewed her tea and then offered some to everyone. Once the steaming cup was in my hand, I had to admit that the aroma was quite relaxing and I let the tin cup warm my chilled hands.

I took my attention off my cup and glanced over at Miara, who in turn was staring at her mother with a strange look on her face. I turned to speak to Elric about it, but to my surprise he had fallen asleep where he sat. His quiet snores filled the suddenly silent night.

I gripped my cup a little tighter and looked at the rest of my friends. Each one had fallen into a deep slumber, their cups abandoned and spilled in front of them.

Avada remained where she was, across the fire, staring at me with hatred. I felt like a wild animal trapped by a hunter. She made no move against me and her predatory gaze did not waver from my face. I willed myself to be calm and started to search for my small hidden power within, as Enthor had taught me. It sprang to me instantly, trying to break free and protect me because it sensed the danger too.

It was at that moment that I realized who was with me. "Your name is Reaper, isn't it? You're a Hautur and are very good at deceiving me." I had gone completely still and my mind was focused. This was the creature who had killed my love, brought me before the Dark Lord and had been hunting me ever since. Anger, not fear, beat through my veins. This would end tonight, one way or another.

Reaper's look of shock was quickly replaced with smug indifference. It stood, and the form of Miara's mother slowly disappeared and was replaced with the shell of the Dark Lord soldier I knew all too well. He was as tall as Jaitem, and now that I was paying attention, I noticed he wore the same markings and other physical features of a Kanarah warrior.

I stood also and drew my sword from its scabbard. The water blade gleamed in the moonlight, and its transparent form seemed to move in time with the waves below. I felt my facial symbol grow hot as a wind started to blow and the campfire snapped and crackled with pent-up fury. "You have no right to wear the skin of the Kanarah. They are a good and strong people. You are a slug, a poor slave serving a lowly god. I'm not afraid of you, and you will not take me back to him this time."

Reaper laughed at me, a deeply evil sound that echoed around us. "I have no intention of taking you back. You would already be in his clutches if that was my intent. You do wrong to mock me. I am well aware of the Kanarahs' attributes. I know who they are and what they stand for. It is something that I have respected and loved for years. However, you destroyed that. It was your fault, and now, after all these years you will pay for it with your life."

Reaper unsheathed his own sword, which had appeared at his waist, and he began to circle the fire.

I did the same, all the while keeping the flames at the ready. They hissed and popped, eagerly waiting for me to unleash it.

Reaper smiled cruelly at me through the flames. "You really are a stupid creature. Do you think your muted powers can protect you? I'm not here on my master's orders. I was supposed to wait for you at the temple, capture you and bring you to him. But not this time; this time I will kill you."

Reaper's smile faded, and he regarded me with distaste. "The game has changed for the Dark Lord. He wants you alive to help fulfil his master's plans. He has no idea I am here, but if you keep throwing around your magic, he will. So I leave it up to you. Try to face me now on your own, without your magic, or fight me with your power, perhaps beat me but only have to surrender yourself when the Dark Lord appears and watch your friends die in the process, because I guarantee you he will not let them live."

I faltered, letting my magic die. The wind returned to a gentle breeze and the fire was reduced to a few burning embers. I was trapped and didn't think I could win a one-on-one confrontation with the shape—shifter, and I also didn't want the Dark Lord showing up and killing me or my friends.

"Why? Why are you doing this? Why do you hate me so much, and why after all these years of your master trying to kill me does he wish to keep me alive?" I kept a firm grip on my sword and never let my eyes drift from the Hautur.

He smiled at me and kicked at the remnants of the fire, burying it under the dirt. The moon was the only source of light now but it was enough. It glinted off the sea, reflecting its pale light around us. "You don't remember, do you? I guess that memory was not significant enough to grace your mind. Well, let me enlighten you. We have time before the end."

He pointed his wicked blade at my face. "You are the reason my love is dead. She died protecting you and your foolish notions of peace. It was because of you that a strong woman died with the knowledge of betrayal in her heart. She died hating me, and for that I will hate you until one of us stops breathing." Hate made Reaper's eyes burn a ghastly red, and I shrank back from those piercing orbs.

"As to why my master wants you alive, I'm not sure exactly what his plans are, but what I do know is that the god of Death is preparing for his return and he needs your power to help open the portal."

I had no idea what Reaper was talking about, but I pushed my questions aside. I had to make it through this before I started worrying about my true father. I fixed my eyes on the Hautur and braced myself. "I do remember that day; a vision of it came to me not too long ago, and I wept for the loss of life in my name. Do you honestly think I wished that? Do you really believe it's my fault? I have been hunted and murdered countless times. Do you think I enjoyed that, that I had a choice?"

I was furious. Images of this creature beating me and dragging me to the Dark Lord ran through my mind, ending with the image of a young prince slain in the bushes. My voice rose louder and I began to shout. "And what about you? If I wanted to play the blame game, I could easily place this whole mess at your feet. It was *you* who brought me to your lord to have my spirit torn from me and shoved down a mortal's throat, and it was *you* who killed the human *I* loved and left him in the bushes to die. So you tell me who has committed the greater evil."

Reaper paused and confusion stole across his features. He squeezed his eyes shut as if trying to remember something, but he violently shook his head, and when he opened his eyes again they were still filled with hate. "Enough of your lies! Nothing you can say will make me change my mind. I despise you and will have my revenge."

I threw up my hands in frustration and anger. "I didn't raise that blade and kill her, your *lord* did. He removed her head from her shoulders as if she was cattle waiting to be butchered. Can't you see all of this is *his* fault! You were just stupid enough to make yourself believe that it was mine. You are too much of a coward to face him, so you use me as an excuse to ease your pain."

There was no warning, just pure rage and instinct. Reaper came at me, leaping over the remains of the fire pit and slashing down with his blade, trying to cleave me in two. I managed to take a step back and balance myself before the crushing blow came down on my raised sword. Magic flared as my whole body convulsed with his impossibly strong strike, and I realized his was no ordinary sword. It pulsed with magic, making the blade glow a deep blood red, and gods, he was strong. The force of the blow left my arms shaking, and not leaving me any time to react he kicked me in the midsection and sent me stumbling backward, struggling to breathe. I heard him breathing hard, trying to control the anger that welled up in him. I remained bent over, holding my abdomen, waiting for him to get closer, but a shocked intake of breath whipped my body up.

Miara pulled her pole staff from Reaper's back.

She was a vision from nightmares. Fury and rage contorted her body and I no longer saw the woman I knew. I saw a warrior, a tool for destruction.

I waited for Reaper to fall to the dirt, waited for him to die, but to my horror he straightened and turned toward the Kanarah woman. "One of the perks of being a shape-shifter is that you can put your internal organs pretty much where you want, and we can regenerate incredibly fast. Sorry, my dear, but you missed."

Reaper came at Miara impossibly fast, and she was left in a defensive position. Her weapon was no match for his sword. They stood facing each other, locked in a deadly embrace.

Miara's face contorted with anger. "How? How did you deceive us? Where is my mother?"

Miara tried to pull away but Reaper held her close. "You won't believe me, but I wanted none of this. Your mother was a strong and good woman and died a warrior's death. I have hidden in your tribe for years, not only as your mother recently but as others as well. I wish I could explain to you why I've done what I have, but anger and despair is clouding your judgement and you wouldn't understand. I will mourn you; you should have just drank the tea."

Reaper pushed Miara away, catching her off guard, and smashed down on her weapon, snapping it in two. I ran to her defence but was too late. In the same motion, he pulled back up and drove the blade right into her stomach. He pulled the blade out in one fluid motion and turned to deflect my raised weapon.

My anger took control of my body, and I felt my power boiling inside. Storm clouds suddenly blew in from the sea, and lightning ripped through the sky. I came at Reaper repeatedly but he deflected every time, and his joy grew. Flashes of red and blue light lit up the night as our blades collided. I came at him again but this time he grabbed my wrist, leaving our magical blades locked. Mine shimmered with the power of the sea and his shined red with blood.

He held me there and stared into my eyes. "You can't win! It's over. You're losing control and your pathetic storm doesn't scare me. Goodbye, Ililsaya, may your soul finally be free."

Instead of pushing me back so he could deal a killing blow, he spread his legs and twisted his body, dragging me with it. I found myself flying through the air and then falling right over the edge of the cliff. I slid down a couple of feet before I somehow managed to grab an outcropping of rock. I dug my bleeding fingers in deeper and tried desperately to find a foothold. The waves crashed below waiting to swallow me and I fought not to panic.

I looked up and saw Reaper staring down at me with triumph. "I must admit, you are a fighter. I think I'll miss these times we've had together."

I spit my contempt at the Hautur. "The Dark Lord will kill you when he finds out what you have done. You've signed your own death sentence."

My fingers were going numb, and I ceased my struggles. Now that I was faced with death, my release from years of pain, I found I didn't want to go. I couldn't leave this world to creatures like Reaper and the Dark Lord. I wished for Enthor now; he would know what to do.

Reaper crouched down and was within reaching distance. "I know the Dark Lord will want to end my life, but it was a chance I was willing to take. Even though you believe I am a mindless, evil creature, I do love the world I live in and do not want to see it destroyed, which is exactly what will happen if you are allowed to live."

I stared up at him in confusion, but before I could say anything, a black blur slammed into Reaper's side, knocking him on his side and sending both forms skidding across the edge of the cliff and out of my sight. Snarls and a deafening roar was all I could hear, and then a scream of pain tore through the night along with a loud crash through the bushes. Silence followed, and then in the next heartbeat I heard the sound of beating wings.

A giant Ristiaper flew out above me, circled once and then disappeared into the night. I heaved a sigh of relief, but it quickly vanished when my fingers finally gave up their battle and I let go—but I didn't fall. Just in time, a strong arm grabbed me around my wrist and hauled me back up to the side of the cliff. I drew a shaking breath and opened my eyes to see Jaitem standing over me.

He handed me my sword and helped me stand. "What did I miss?"

I gave the larger Kannarah a huge smile, but it quickly vanished as a gentle moan from across the campsite brought our attention to the figure sprawled on the ground.

Jaitem and I ran together and knelt beside Miara. Jaitem gently placed her head in his lap and I held her hand. She was so cold and pale. Her blood was everywhere. She kept her other hand pressed against her stomach as if trying to hold her life inside. Her thick red hair hung limply across her face, hiding the dimming light in her lavender eyes.

"You stupid woman, what have you gotten yourself into this time?" Jaitem did not speak very often so his words startled me, but there was no heat behind them. He gently pushed Miara's hair out of her eyes and placed a kiss on her forehead.

"You know me, my love; I could never mind my own business. Is he gone? Did I wait too long to strike?"

I nodded as I gripped her hand tighter. "Yes, he's gone, and thanks to you I will live another day. But how did you know not to drink the tea?"

Jaitem looked at me questioningly and Miara choked on a laugh. "I hate my mother's mint tea; it always made me break out in a rash. She used to threaten me with it when I was younger."

She coughed and closed her eyes, trying to regain herself. When she spoke, again it was forced. "I've had a feeling something was not right since we broke camp outside Delroth, but I couldn't figure it out. So when she offered me that tea like it was a natural thing to do, a bad feeling crept into my soul, and I knew something was wrong."

Miara coughed again and gasped in pain. She gripped my hand tighter, and some of the fire returned to her eyes. "Don't give up, child; you are strong enough to defeat the Dark Lord, and he knows it, otherwise he would not be trying so hard to be rid of you. Free the people of these lands. Do what you born to do, be who I know you can be." Miara's strength faded and her hand slipped from my grasp. Jaitem closed her lifeless eyes and spoke a few words in their own language into her ear. A curse off to my left made my numb mind aware of my other two friends.

Elric and Nalin approached the sombre scene rubbing their heads as if they had just awaked from a nightmare. Elric reached out his hand and I took it, pulling myself up into his arms. I felt the tears coming, but I pushed them aside and told myself I would mourn later. I was done crying; it was time I took action.

I pushed away from Elric and looked down at Nalin crouched beside Miara's lifeless body. His words were like steel and full of contempt. "What happened? Where is Avada?"

I quickly filled them in about how Reaper had been disguised this whole time and how he had drugged the tea. I told them of Miara's bravery and lastly of Jaitem pulling me up over the cliff before I fell to my death. Then I remembered something else.

I ran back to the spot where I had gone over the side and searched the area. I followed the pattern of disturbed rocks and dirt and spied off to the right an indent in the bushes, as if something had fallen into them. I ran over to the ruined foliage and gasped.

There, lying among the broken leaves and twigs, was Fang, with Reaper's sword lying next to her. A long gash in her side glowed a faint unnatural red that matched the sword's pulsing magic. She was still breathing but it was laboured and came in quick succession. I bent down to move Reaper's still glowing sword but a hand grabbed my arm and pulled me away.

Nalin stood beside me, along with Elric and Jaitem. "Don't touch that sword. It's a blood blade. The Dark Lord fashioned them himself. When activated they can drain the life energy from its victims. All it takes is a simple scratch and the blade can draw out the energy. Fang is physically fine but her soul is being eaten alive. There's nothing you can do."

I looked down at the animal that had saved me more than once, who had given her life to protect a creature that was not of her species. How could I possibly just stand here and let her die?

And then I realized I didn't have to. I pushed past Nalin and drew my sword. The symbol on my face burned so brightly I could see the blue outline illuminating the night. Without thinking, I lifted the sword above my head and sent it crashing down on top of Reaper's blade. The force of the two magics colliding shattered it into pieces, and I stepped over them to kneel before my feline friend. I placed my hand on her mighty head and closed my eyes. I remembered something, something that not even Enthor or any of the other dragons knew about. My magic was much more than the ability to use all four elements at the same time. I could *heal*; I could manipulate life energy. I didn't know how to do this, and I wasn't even sure if I had enough power, but I let myself go and went in search of Fang's damaged life force. Surprisingly it was easier than I thought. My magic was drawn to Fang's soul. I could see it in my mind as a small white flame slowly being extinguished by a thick, murky mist.

I reached out and touched the mist with my powers, and at first nothing happened—my magic simply passed through the curtain of mist and did nothing to dissipate it. I felt a twinge of panic as I thought that my power was too weak to do anything, but I pushed harder, with all my strength, and felt something snap. Pain like I had never felt before washed through my body. My magic surged forward, evaporating the mist and wrapping itself around Fang's nearly depleted life energy. Her flame began to grow in size and intensity, using my magic to heal. When Fang's soul finally released me, I felt nothing but agony. I felt as if my body would burst apart.

I woke from my trance with a scream torn from my lips. Elric caught me in his arms and tried to still my convulsing body.

"What's wrong, what's happening to her?" Nalin stood close by.

"I'm not sure, but I think she used her power to heal Fang's life energy. But it's too strong for her human body to handle. It's killing her."

I thrashed against Elric, trying desperately to ease the pain that flowed through my body. I opened my eyes and found we were no longer alone. Dozens of spirits clung to the surroundings, all edging closer to me, trying to touch the healing power they needed. I cried out again, terrified of the creatures who wanted me. I tried to flee, pushing on Elric, trying anything to make him move so I could get away from the hungry, gaping mouths of the dead.

Elric roughly grabbed my face in his hands and forced me to look at him. "Listen to me! You have to let go. Push it back down; remember what Enthor has taught you. Please, I know you are strong enough. You have to try."

I forced my eyes shut and tried to breathe deeply. I tried to remember a song or poem, anything that would help me focus, and then out of nowhere a memory came to me. I don't know which life it was from, but I felt a warm embrace and a soft, soothing voice. She sang to me over and over and all of my fears and pain started to ebb. My power reluctantly began to recede back to its prison, but the walls were now fractured and it would not stay contained for much longer.

I drew in a shaky breath and opened my eyes. The spirits were gone and the night was quiet again. Elric was still holding me with a tired smile spread across his face. Fang, back to herself, padded over, placed her beautiful head on my stomach and began to purr. I stroked her head but even that small movement caused me intense pain. My nerves felt raw and flailed. Every muscle and bone in my body felt bruised. I had done a lot of damage to myself; I only hoped I still had a little time left. I wasn't finished yet.

"You did it, you're safe." Elric stroked Fang's soft fur too, but she wasn't purring any more. She was growling and then started to make a strange crying sound. She bolted out of my lap and stared out across the ocean with eyes glazed over in fear. I tried to get up to calm her, but I noticed that Fang wasn't the only one acting strangely. Elric, making no move to try to help me stand, began to shake. He gripped himself around his arms and started rocking back and forth on his heels.

I scrambled to my feet despite the protest my body was making and found that Jaitem and Nalin were holding their heads in pain and cowering in fear. Then it hit me. The feeling of dread and complete hopelessness drove a stake through my heart. I started to tremble with terror, not only because of the magical fear coursing through my mind but because of the fact that I knew who was causing it.

A dark shadow flew overhead and blocked out the moon. The Dark Lord came into view and dropped the shroud of fear that he held over us. I stood alone and defiant as he drew closer to cliff's edge. He roared a scream of triumph and roughly snatched me in his claws. I was exhausted and in too much pain to stay conscious, and the last thing I remembered was seeing my prince watching helplessly as I was carried away through the cold dark night.

CHAPTER 26

Enthor

Without hesitation, I plunged my short sword into the surprised soldier's throat, effectively silencing him. Deneoes caught the dead man's weapon before it clattered to the floor, and together we caught the corpse and dragged it silently into the shadows.

Deneoes was about to say something, but I held up my hand in warning. Voices could be heard just outside of where we were concealed for the moment.

"Randall? What's taking so long? I told you there's nothing back there but broken pots and dust. Get out here now, or I swear I'll leave you here with the rest of this garbage."

Deneoes and I held our breath as we listened to the men's exchange.

"Let's just go outside. Randall can catch up with the others when they come back up from the caves. This place gives me the creeps. The sooner we're done here the better."

I heard movement, like feet shuffling across the hard stone floor, making my nerves stand on end.

"No . . . something's not right. Why isn't he answering me? Randall? If this is some kind of joke, it'll be your head on a pike."

We stood motionless in the shadows as two more soldiers peered inside the small alcove.

"See? He's not even here. He must have already gone back outside. You worry too much. Let's go."

The larger of the two men held out his arm and blocked his companion from leaving. "Wait—what's this?" The first soldier knelt to look at something on the floor, which brought his companion back inside the entranceway.

"What?" He bent down has well and examined the sticky substance on the floor.

"That's blood. Now are you going to tell me nothing's wrong? Go get the commander. Something's not right here."

The second man rose to carry out his orders but found, to his astonishment, a "child" blocking his way. Deneoes winked once at him and launched his tiny muscled body at him. The soldier had no time to react as he stumbled backward and tripped over his still-kneeling companion. The wiry little man secured his hand over the soldier's mouth and deftly switched his position so that he was on the soldier's back. The sickening pop of his skull being dislocated from his spine seemed to echo throughout the small space.

The second soldier, confused by what was happening, didn't even get a chance to see who was responsible for his death. A strong hand from behind was placed on his mouth to silence him as a sword was plunged deep into his back, piercing his heart. The man slumped forward and lay close to the other soldier.

Deneoes regarded me with admiration and a little fear. "Come; it will not take the others long to discover some of their own missing. Keep to the walls and stay in the shadows next to me. The entrance to the caves is on the other side of this audience room and through the library. Be silent and try to keep up."

Deneoes gave me an obscene gesture but I ignored him, turned and headed out of the alcove. Much to our relief there seemed to be no other soldiers in the immediate vicinity. We made our way across the main audience room without incident and soon found ourselves in a trashed library. Huge towering shelves lined the walls, and what once were filled with thousands of books now lay broken and splintered on the floor.

Volumes lay strewn everywhere, all ripped apart. Stacks of books covered in dirt and filth lay against the walls while others were merely thrown into a pile in the middle of the floor, ready to be burned.

I stopped inside the ruin of this once-great library. I knelt and picked up a discarded book and gently held it in my hands. The front cover had been torn off but the pages were still relatively undamaged. It was a history from a race that had long since disappeared from these lands. I held in my hands the only thing keeping their existence from vanishing completely from Eiddoril.

I gripped the book tighter until my knuckles turned white. "This is my fault. I should have stayed and protected these relics of time. Without these books, we have no knowledge of what passed before us. Whole civilisations were stored safely in these pages, and I let them fall into ruin. I helped destroy worlds." My hands shook with anger, and all traces of human had left my eyes.

Deneoes boldly walked up to me, took the book and gently placed it back with the others. "So what are you going to about it now? Standing here pitying yourself will do no one any good, so snap out of it, old man. Where to next?"

There had never been a moment when I wanted to strike someone so much before, but I knew the little Ywari spoke the truth, which is why I refrained from decorating the walls with him.

Instead, I pointed toward the other end of the room. "Over there, on the south side of the room—do you see where the shelves have been torn from the wall?"

Deneoes nodded.

As we approached the wall, we saw that there was no wall there at all but a gaping hole that disappeared into darkness. Deneoes stuck his small head in through the opening and strained his eyes. Only darkness and the smell of decay greeted him.

He pulled back and gestured at me. "Please, after you, sir dragon."

I practically snarled at him but walked past Deneoes and led the way into the catacombs of the temple.

We had not gone far before the light in the passageway changed. The soldiers who had come down here before us had lit torches, and their soft glow illuminated our surroundings. We followed a path that was on a steady decline for several minutes and then it levelled off. Several other paths led off the main one, and I led us down one of these.

We were once again plunged into darkness, but our night vision allowed us to continue, albeit slowly. We made no sound as we travelled through the keep of the temple, so it came as quite a shock when we heard a roar tear through the silence. It shook the very foundations of the tunnel, and we feared we would be trapped down here by a cave-in.

The vibrations subsided, and Deneoes said, "What was that?"

I had stopped and was still facing ahead of us. Deneoes stood beside me and looked up at my face. I couldn't hide my look of shock and pain. "That was a dragon, and she's dying."

All sense and reason seemed to leave my body, and I sprinted for the end of the tunnel. Deneoes let out a curse and pumped his legs hard to try to catch up. He was already taking aim with his bow when we burst from the tunnel into the cavern beyond. What we saw stunned even me.

A huge dragon lay on its side against the wall. It was massive and took up most of the far side of the cave. The beast was the colour of the forest with flecks of gold throughout her shining scales. She was beautiful—and she was dying.

Several soldiers stood by watching the poor creature wither in pain. The rest were busy packing up what looked to be large rocks into crates. My eyes grew wide at the realization of what they truly were. Dragon eggs, and a dozen at least.

I returned my focus to the enemy. There were seven men, three by the dragon, three packing up the eggs, and one more standing watch at the other entrance into the cave. Deneoes and I did not have numbers in our favour, but rage and animal instinct were quickly taking over my human emotions.

Without stopping and before any of the soldiers knew we were even there, I signalled Deneoes and pointed him toward the soldiers with the eggs. I headed off in the direction of the downed dragon. I stole a quick glance and watched as Deneoes wasted no time and fired several consecutive shots at the man by our escape route. A powerful wind aided their flight and each flawlessly met their mark. The force of the magical wind left the soldier impaled on the stone wall. The other three, startled by our sudden appearance, quickly regained their wits and dropped the egg two of them had been carrying. It fell to the floor with a loud cracking sound, which brought another cry of anguish from the injured dragon.

That was enough for me, and I lashed out in fury at the three soldiers surrounding my dying brethren. I had two of them taken out before they knew what was happening, but the last one was proving to be a bit of a problem. He had regained his wits more quickly and while I was busy killing one of his comrades and knocking another out cold, he had come around behind me and smashed me in the back of the head with the pommel of his sword. I dropped like a sack of flour and fought hard to stay conscious. A swift kick to my ribs blew the air from my lungs and I dropped my sword, hugging my midsection. I cursed my weak human flesh and felt my dragon within fighting to get free, but it was useless. I turned my gaze up to the pompous fool who meant to end my life and tried to brace for the killing blow, but it never fell. I watched as the terrified, screaming soldier was lifted into the air by the jaws of a very angry dragon. She clamped down hard with her razor-sharp teeth and sent his blood spraying everywhere. With the last of her strength, she threw him against the wall of the cavern. I smiled at the sickening slap his dead body made against the cold stone, and then the poor dragon collapsed and lay still.

A shout from across the cavern brought my attention back to Deneoes. Damn, he was good, but even he couldn't last long against those odds. It turned out that those three men were not as stupid as their friends had been. They quickly closed the distance, leaving Deneoes little time to get off another shot. He dropped his bow, launched himself into the air like a cat leaping at a mouse and landed directly behind the trio. He spun on his heels and drew his twin daggers, throwing them at two of the soldiers. He didn't have the power of the wind to aide him, but his aim was true. One dagger struck the hand of one man, causing him to drop his sword in pain, and the other embedded itself in a soldier's groin. Not exactly the ideal shot, but it did the trick. The soldier dropped to the ground in agony.

Unfortunately, Deneoes only had two daggers, and there was still one soldier left. I quietly made my way closer to the pair, all the while being careful not to alert the soldier of my presence.

"Out of tricks I see, you little freak." The soldier smiled in triumph, but as Deneoes and I prepared for a final attack, the soldier suddenly dropped his sword and grasped the point of blade protruding from his midsection. He tried to speak, but blood bubbled up through his lips. I watched in disbelief as the sword was torn from him and he dropped face first in front of the surprised Ywari.

The other soldier with the injured groin tried desperately to stand to defend himself, but the rogue soldier quickly dispatched him as well with a quick thrust to his chest. He turned to face Deneoes, who had already armed himself with the fallen soldier's sword. It was too large and awkward for the small warrior but he managed to handle it. They stood facing each other for a moment trying to decide whether to should kill each other, but I decided that the Ywari had had enough fun for one day.

"Deneoes, if you're through playing around, I need your help. That man is not an enemy. He's one of Nalin's men."

Surprise marked the soldier's face at the sound of his commander's name, and he made no move to stop Deneoes from retrieving his weapons. Deneoes sprinted over to me while I knelt by the head of the wounded dragon.

Another figure stood close by and handed me a wicked-looking dagger. The blade glowed a blood red and seemed to pulse with an inner life. I looked up and was shocked to see the man I had knocked unconscious.

"This is a blood dagger. The Dark Lord created them. They have the ability to drain life force just by a single cut. This creature is dying from the inside out. There's nothing you can do."

I took the dagger with contempt and tossed it to the ground beside me. I placed my hands on the rough scales of the dragon's head and spoke soothingly to her. "I'm sorry, my sister, I didn't know you were here, but you did well, the eggs are safe. I will protect them now."

A strange guttural voice invaded our thoughts, along with a mocking, choked laughter. *"Enthor, you fool, I see you have been in human skin for too long. Your human faith and optimism are misplaced. None of us are safe, not even our creators."* She shuddered and convulsed in pain, which she shared with the mortals in her company. The two soldiers and Deneoes shook their heads trying to rid themselves of the intrusion, but it was no use. Even while dying the dragon was powerful, and she was determined to tell her secrets.

I spoke aloud for the benefit of my companions. "Tell me, Kimlryn. What has happened? Tell me how you came to be here with these eggs."

The mighty dragon sighed and lay very still. *"It does not hurt so much any more, you know. My life energy is almost gone. Being immortal is not a blessing but a curse. I am glad to have an end."* Kimlryn closed her amber eyes and seemed to fall asleep, but her voice came through to the minds surrounding her. *"I did not go through the portal with the others. Like you, I was in human form hiding, but not of my own accord. Mareth approached me two days before and showed me that he had stolen our brothers' and sisters' eggs, including my own. He gave me a choice. He would allow me to stay and live to protect the eggs until the other dragons returned, or watch him while he destroyed every single one. I had no choice; I had seen enough genocide; our race needed to survive. His hatred for Ashia was immense. He wanted her to suffer and planned to do it through their daughter."*

I stared in surprise and shook my head while Kimlryn's eyes opened and bore into my soul. *"The two of you were foolish to think he did not know the truth. He knew it from the very beginning that Ililsaya was his daughter, and he was prepared to do anything to control her. He knew how powerful she was, possibly more powerful than himself, but he needed to get the others and her mother out of the way to complete his plans."*

I stared at her in confusion. "I don't understand how you know all this. Why would Mareth confide in you?"

Kimlryn's rage and pain washed through her audience. *"I knew these things because I am his mate. I was Ashia's replacement."*

The shocking revelation stuck a spear through my soul. How could I have been so blind?

Kimlryn could not mask the contempt in her voice. *"The details of our arrangement are not important, but you need to know the rest. I am almost out of time, and if you have any hope at all, you need to hear what I know. My loyalty has ended. Mareth's plan was to overpower Ashia as soon as they crossed over to the immortal plain. He had secured an army of followers by holding their eggs hostage, but that was only part of his plan."* Kimlryn's voice focused on me. *"You were there when we travelled for those millennia. You saw the creatures that inhabited the other immortal realms. He went back to raise his own army, one that would promise power and revenge on their creators. Mareth is filled with so much hate for the elements and their creations here, especially the humans. He is bringing back an army of monstrosities to destroy this world and all who inhabit it. He has become powerful, more so than you can imagine. I can feel it even now through our bond and it terrifies me. He has drained entire pockets of the immortal plane of life, leaving them dried, dead husks. This world is the only one left with the power he craves, and he means to take it too."*

I shuddered at the thought and tried not to let my human fear show in my mind. "I don't understand. The Dark Lord has been trying to kill Ililsaya for centuries, so if Mareth wanted her alive then why did he permit it?"

Kimlryn's voice seemed to lower in our minds, and I knew she didn't have much time left. *"Mareth had no idea what Nubossa, your Dark Lord was doing in his absence. Mareth gave him no such order; he was only supposed to trap her in a human host, erasing her presence from mortal existence, but Nubossa's hatred for her and her allies ran deep. He took it upon himself to rid the world of her. It wasn't until Mareth sent Ashia back through the portal that he learned of Nubossa's actions, and he was not pleased."*

I froze and clenched my fists. "What did you just say? Ashia is here, alive?"

"I do not know if she is still alive, but yes, she was sent back. Mareth wanted the elements to see that he had the power to open the portal on his own without their help, and he wanted them to be afraid. Ashia was used as an example of what he was capable of doing to their beloved creations."

Kimrlyn's link with the others was fading, so she spoke only to me. *"Through all of Mareth's careful planning, the elements believed he ran into a flaw. He used too much of his own power when he sent Ashia back, and the elements have somehow reinforced the gates on this side, but he planned for that as well. That is why Mareth needs Ililsaya alive. When she is reunited with her true form, it will cause a huge flux in elemental magic and a major surge will be thrown out into the world, allowing Nubossa to perform the spell to open the portal on our side. It was his backup plan from the beginning, and without her he cannot come back."*

My heart sank at the female dragon's words.

"It was genius really. The spell he has placed on her is almost at an end. She was never meant to be trapped forever, only until this precise moment, but you have to make sure that never happens. Nubossa is heading his attack to the lands of Gareth. They will be there on the next full moon, which will also mark the autumn solstice. The elements' power will be at one of its highest and most easily available. He is bringing with him Ililsaya's true form, and when the moon is at its highest and the mortals are locked in battle, Mareth will open the portal from his end, and the joining of Ililsaya's soul and body will open our end, and then all hope will be lost."

Despair filled my voice. "What you're asking of me I cannot do. If Karah is not rejoined with her body, she will die in her current human one. Her power can't be contained in human form. My whole life has been spent keeping her alive and safe and now you're telling me I've been helping Mareth. I can't just let her die. And what about the dragons on the other side? They deserve a chance to live. I can't turn my back on them again."

Kimlryn shuddered and breathed out a final sigh. Her dying thoughts lingered in my mind for a long time after. *"It makes no difference to me what you choose to do. You have our eggs—my egg—so our species will not be lost. It is up to you to decide what happens now. My time here is done, but if you want to survive, if you want Eiddoril to survive, Ililsaya must die."*

The silence that followed Kimlryn's death was oppressive. I bowed my head and whispered a few words and then stood to face the others in the cave.

Deneoes was furious. "What exactly was that last bit you were talking to her about? Did I hear right? She wants you to kill Red? Tell me that's not what I just heard."

I glared at Deneoes but made no attempt to answer him. I couldn't. What could I possibly say that would make things better?

One of the soldiers—the one whose hand Deneoes had stabbed—cleared his throat. "I will not stand here and pretend I know what's going on. I'm still trying to process the fact that I just had a conversation with a dragon, I think, but some of what the creature said makes sense to me." He gestured to the eggs behind him. "We were ordered to take what we thought were rocks to Gareth. The Dark Lord told us that a great magic was contained in them and they would aide us in our victory. We had no idea that these were eggs; even the presence of this beast surprised us. We were only told that there was a guardian down here, and that it could not harm us because it was held by a powerful spell."

The man faced me. "When we came down here, she looked human. We were ordered to kill the creature with that dagger. The rest of the men were sceptical but I knew the lethal power of that blade. I am sorry, but I'm the one who killed your friend. She just sat there staring at me with hatred. She practically made me stab her. It was then that she transformed into this beast you see before you."

The soldier stared me in the face without fear or malice. It was his bravery and honesty that saved his life because it took me a considerable amount of self-control not to rip his throat out.

"I appreciate your honesty. You had to keep up appearances, and I must also thank you for aiding us today. Nalin would be proud of you."

He bowed his head. "Thank you, and I am glad to hear of our commander's well-being. We had heard many rumours but did not know what became of him. Where is he now?"

I was about to answer but Deneoes pushed past the soldier and grabbed me forcefully by the arm, making me look at him. "Maybe you didn't hear me the first time, but I asked what you planned to do about Red. I'd suggest you answer me because I'm done playing these games."

I almost laughed at the absurdity of this little creature threatening a dragon but the look in my young friend's eyes reminded me of the strength he had in his soul, and I had no doubt he meant every word he said.

I placed my hands on his shoulders and looked at my friend. "I have no intension of harming Karah, but we have a problem, which I'm not sure we have the power to fix."

Deneoes's shoulders slumped, and for the first time I saw fear in his eyes. "What aren't you telling me? Why did that dragon want you to kill Red?"

I kept my golden eyes fixed on the Ywari. "Kimlryn told me that this has been Mareth's plan all along. That Karah is the key to releasing him from the portal that he is trapped behind. He has amassed an army and is bent on destroying this world, no matter the cost. When Karah regains her true from at the right time the gate will open and Mareth will be free to wreak havoc."

Deneoes's eyes lit up. "Well what's the problem? We just have to convince her that she has to stay human, which I don't think she will mind anyway and we keep her away from the dark lord. Why do we have to kill her?"

I chose my word carefully. "Because the spell that is holding her powers captive is failing. It was meant to fail at the exact moment when the next full moon is at its zenith during the autumn solstice. Whether it is by our hand or not, she will die if she is not joined with her true form. Her powers are too great to be contained by mortal flesh. No matter what we choose to do there are horrible consequences, which I am not sure I can face."

Deneoes swore and stalked off to be alone with his thoughts, leaving me alone with Nalin's men. I was glad for the slight reprieve and let my friend be.

I turned back toward the other two men. "I find that I am in need of your help, if you are willing to give it. I am afraid that we do not have much time before your other companions realize something is wrong."

I held up my wrist. The metal bracelet I wore on my left arm glittered in the torchlight. "Do either of you recognize this device? It's blocking my powers, and I'm unable to shift to my proper form. Do you know how to take it off?"

The soldier who had spoken earlier came forward and touched the manacle. He then turned to his companion. "Go to the surface and see if the others are ready to leave. Stall them for as long as you can. I will figure something out down here."

The soldier left to carry out his order while the other turned back to me. "I've seen these before. The Dark Lord makes his warlocks wear them when they are not being used. I am not a magic expert, and frankly, it scares the hell out of me. I believe they work similarly to the blood blades. It drains your power instead of your life energy and stores it until it is disengaged."

"How was it disengaged? Did you ever witness it?" My hopes flared, but they were pounded back into the ground when I saw the look on the man's face.

"The only way I know to make the clasp release is with a drop of the Dark Lord's blood, right there on the symbol of death. That was how he always did it. I'm sorry."

My shoulders slumped and I held in a cry of frustration.

Deneoes, who'd been listening from a distance walked back over and examined the bracelet himself. His small almond-shaped face became very thoughtful. "Maybe it's not that complicated; maybe it's simpler than that. What if all it takes *is* dragons blood? Not necessarily one particular dragon, but any dragon. It would be the perfect prison."

I stared at my friend and resisted the urge to hug him. Could he be right, could it be that simple?

The soldier to my left stared at us in bewilderment. "Are you saying the Dark Lord is a dragon—and that you're a dragon? How is any of this possible?"

Deneoes stifled a laugh and patted the man's arm. "Wow, you guys really are slow. But I guess it's not all your fault; most humans tend to not see what they don't understand."

The soldier took a swing at Deneoes, but the wiry Ywari easily jumped out of the way and hid behind me. I was in no mood. "Enough! Stop acting like children. Yes, the Dark Lord is a dragon and so am I, so was the creature you killed. We are magical creatures that have lived since the birth of your world. We have been absent for a long time, but we are not myth or legend, we are real, and if this world stands a chance of surviving you mortals need us."

Disbelief shined in the man's eyes, but I had no time to argue. I took out one of my own daggers and pricked my finger. I then held it over the manacle and watched as a single drop landed on the metal surface. It snapped open and fell to the ground.

Deneoes cheered and punched me in the arm. "Finally something good happened. Now go all toothy and figure us a way out of this."

I shook my head in amazement and flexed my muscles, letting all of my power flow back into me. I bent to pick up the bracelet, which had closed again, and carefully placed it in my travel bag as I focused back on Nalin's man.

"First things first . . . er, I'm sorry, what's your name?"

The soldier continued to stare at me but managed to loosen his tongue. "I am called Radac, and my partner is called Tiaos. We have another with us as well but he remained up in the main audience hall. His name is Randall."

I paled while Deneoes looked away. "I'm sorry, but we surprised him when we emerged from a secret passageway. We had no idea . . ."

Radac's face flashed anger for a moment but he quickly recovered. "That is unfortunate. He was a good man. It is a risk we all take when we enter this fight. He will be remembered."

Radac put some distance between us and stood tall. "Now, what is it that you need us to do? As you say, we do not have much time. It will be rather difficult if not impossible to get you and your eggs out of here safely without further conflict."

I nodded. "I know, but I have a plan . . ."

A strange sound interrupted the conversation. It sounded like glass cracking into tiny pieces. I scanned the cave and my eyes came to rest on Deneoes, who was standing watching one of the eggs. It was the one that had fallen during his scuffle with the soldiers.

"Umm, Enthor, what's going on? Is it doing what I think it's doing?"

As if in response to his question the large multicoloured egg burst open, and there, covered in fluid and huddled in a tight ball was a baby dragon. It was the colour of midnight with golden flecks decorating its scales. Dark green spikes trailed down its back, and two small horns adorned its head. My heart jumped into my throat. I couldn't believe what I was seeing.

No one spoke—or breathed, for that matter; everyone's eyes were on the miracle unfolding before them. I feared that the creature was dead, and maybe that would be for the best. The eggs had been suspended in some sort of magical limbo for centuries. I couldn't be sure if that would affect the new life inside. I had never been present for a hatching. It was a highly private and spiritual affair for the females, so I had no idea what to do next. Deneoes, being the closest and most curious, crouched down and examined the hatchling.

"I don't think it is alive; it doesn't seem to be breathing. What should we do?"

Again, as if answering the question itself, the small hatchling uncurled its long neck and stretched out its legs. Its small wings, still wet with fluid, hung limply along its back. It made no attempt to rise but swivelled its head, opened its eyes and looked straight at Deneoes. Deneoes stared back. The creature then made a strange noise that sound almost like a dove cooing. Its bright intelligent eyes fixed on the Ywari and slowly picked its body up and sat on its hind legs, looking very similar to a newborn puppy. Even its tail moved back and forth a little, expressing its happiness.

Deneoes was horrified. "Oh no, no, no. I am not your mother. Enthor, *do* something."

I was doing my best not to laugh as I stood beside my friend. I crouched also so as not to frighten the creature and looked into its eyes. The young hatchling bowed its head and seemed to panic. It started to retreat backward into the shadows of the cave.

Deneoes rose and followed the poor beast. "Nice one, Grandpa. You scared the hell out of him."

I stood and shook my head in wonder. "It's amazing that even at its young age it can mentally communicate. It doesn't know words but it's projecting images and feelings. I'm afraid that because you were its first contact, its natural instincts lead it to believe you are its caregiver."

Deneoes shot me a venomous glare and continued to try to calm the beast. "Great, that's all I need. So what do I do now? I can't take care of a dragon. I have a hard time taking care of myself."

"Well, you seem to be doing just fine. It's very fond of you. You are, in fact, doing something that has never before happened. A mortal has bonded with an immortal. This creature will be loyal to you for the rest of your life and beyond. Nothing can sever that tie. You should be honoured."

Deneoes looked at his new friend and cautiously placed his hand in the middle of the dragon's head. It gently pushed back and closed its eyes, making that strange cooing sound again.

A shout of alarm brought everyone's attention to the main entranceway into the cave.

Tiaos burst through the opening. "The rest of the men are coming. I told them we were having some trouble with the guardian and that we suffered a few casualties. I tried to assure them that it was under control, but they insisted that they come down and help. They all would have been here sooner but we discovered the bodies of three men upstairs in an alcove. A secret passageway had been revealed. They know someone is in the temple, and they are conducting a search of the new hallway. I managed to slip away and come here ahead of them. And, sir, one of the dead men is Randall."

Tiaos shot an angry glance at me but otherwise remained silent.

I turned away from them all and made my way to the centre of the room. "Stand back. I don't want to harm anyone."

Without further explanation, I transformed into my true form. Where a man once stood was a massive blue and sea green creature

238

with malice in its eyes. I went for the two dead soldiers near Kimlryn first. I speared one with my golden horns where I had earlier struck him with a blade in my human form, erasing any evidence that the man had died from a sword wound. I tossed the corpse aside and rubbed the blood off on my dead brethren's horns. The second soldier needed no doctoring from me. His broken body still lay almost tore in two against the cavern wall. The man Deneoes had impaled close to the cave entrance was still hanging limply and staining the wall with his blood. I ripped him down allowing Deneoes to retrieve his arrow before I flung him back against the wall where he slid down to rest staring empty eyed at us. The final two soldiers were caught under my claws where I smashed at them until their features were unrecognizable. Then, as if I had not been there at all, I melted my features back into that of a man, but this time I resembled one of the dead soldiers. The whole ordeal took fewer than two minutes, but the importance of haste nagged at me.

"There—that should be a sufficient cover story. Now let's get the rest of these eggs packed up."

Nalin's men backed up and gave me a wide berth. They regarded me with fear and awe but did not argue, and they got to the task of storing the rest of the eggs.

Deneoes approached me with his new charge close at his heels. "That was gross and very disturbing. A little warning next time might be nice, and I see that you are nicely disguised again, but what about me and toothy here?"

I looked back and forth between the young dragon and the Ywari and came to a decision. "You're not going to like this, but I need you to take the hatchling with you. Go back to your people and tell them what has happened. This is no longer a fight to defend Gareth, it's a war to defend our world. Your people must believe this."

I placed my hands on Deneoes's shoulders and squeezed tightly, holding him with my gaze. "I am going to try and steer this group toward your village and meet you there. Yaleon will not be pleased with me, but I need somewhere safe to hide these eggs. They must not be allowed anywhere near Gareth; they are far too important.

The future of my race depends on us and I need your help. The Dark Lord must not find out about this young dragon either because I have no doubt in my mind that this is Mareth's other offspring that Kimlryn spoke of. You must keep the hatchling safe. I know this is a lot to ask of you, my friend, but I need to stay with the rest of these eggs. I need to get them to safety."

Deneoes's eyes widened as he understood the importance of the new dragon and then he nodded in agreement. "I'll do what I can, but what are we going to do when we all get back to Gareth? What about Red?"

I looked away and tried to sound reassuring. "I don't know what we're going to do, but I'll think of something, don't worry. Just go quickly out the way we came in. There will be no one outside, so use the main entrance. Be careful. We'll see each other soon."

We clasped hands and then Ywari and the dragon disappeared to safety down the side tunnel. I turned in time to see the rest of the detachment come running into the cave from the main entrance. They skidded to a halt as they took in the gruesome scene.

Radac gave them all a quick explanation of what had happened, which was surprisingly easy considering the carnage that surrounded them. The commanding officer gave Radac, Taios and me praise for being brave in the face of such danger.

With the rest of the men's help, the remaining eggs were quickly packed up. What few questions were asked were quickly explained away with mutterings about strange magic. None of the soldiers liked or trusted magic so the matter was dropped. They all wanted to get as far away as possible from the dead monster that they thought only existed in their dreams.

We left the cave with our special cargo and at the same time were briefed on what had happened above. They reported that a search of the hallway had produced nothing but several impassable doors and a dead end. Whatever had happened to the soldiers was being considered an act of rogue bandits looking for loot and that the sooner they were away from this place the better.

It was nearing dawn when the Dark Lord's men were ready to make their way to Gareth. Disguised as one of their own I watched in horror and despair has they carried out their lords final wish . . . torching the temple. The ancient volumes ignited hungrily and I held back my fury as the interior of the temple was destroyed. No amount of fire could ever destroy the temple itself but the contents were gone and I secretly mourned. I took position at the end of the group and tried to think of a plan to get these fools near the Ywari village.

We had not gone far when I suddenly held my head in pain. A surge of power rushed through me, causing my form to shimmer but it quickly settled back down so that I still looked human. The feeling was gone as quickly as it had come and no one had noticed anything. I forced myself to keep moving, but I wanted nothing more than to shift and fly far away. What I had felt was Karah, and she had just used a tremendous amount of power. Enough power that it was strong enough for me to know that it was her, and that could only mean terrible news. My heart filled with dread as I wondered what had caused her to use so much power and of the fact that it had been available to her. The spell was fading quickly now and I was running out of time.

I retreated into myself as we trudged on to our destination. My thoughts drifted to the news I had heard earlier. Ashia was here somewhere, and I desperately wanted to find her, but the safety of these eggs was my first priority. As soon as I had the chance, I would tell Nalin's men of my plan and then I could get a message off to Nalin himself. I needed to send word to Elric and the others to keep Karah away from Gareth. It tore at my battered soul knowing that I was signing her death sentence, but what choice did I have? What choice have I ever had? I knew eventually it would come to this but I was hoping I would find another way.

If Mareth succeeded in returning to this world, thousands would suffer and die, and it would not make any difference what deals I had struck. I'd abandoned the creatures of this world once, and I would not do it again. I was not sure if redemption was possible for me, and knowing what I still had to sacrifice made me wish I didn't care, but I did and I could hide from it no longer.

I pushed my dragon self back down behind human skin and continued to follow my path toward death.

CHAPTER 27

Prince Elric

The sea crashed and pounded the docks and ships below, showing the humans who worked there that it was nothing to be trifled with. All different sizes of ships, from a small, one-man skiff to a massive cargo vessel bobbed up and down in the unsettled waters, making the day's work all that more difficult. I stood at the window high above in my uncle's castle and watched as people busied themselves down at the docks. There seemed to be no end to the chaos that associated with harbour trade. I glanced up at the sky and saw storm clouds rolling in, which explained the behaviour of the sea. Before, I wouldn't have given the storm a second thought, but now my thoughts drifted to her, and I wondered anew if I had made the right decision to come to my uncle's city and not try to follow her. I had tried to follow, and in my blind need to protect the woman I loved I nearly launched myself off the side of the cliff in pursuit of the horned bastard. My friends somehow managed to calm me down with a lot of shouting and fists, if I remember correctly, to the point of reasoning, and I let them convince me to complete my task of finding help for my city. The decision plagued me endlessly and I prayed she would forgive me.

The only solace I had was the fact that I knew Fang was out there somewhere searching for Karah. The loyal feline had refused to follow us into the human city, and I was not equipped to argue with the animal. I trusted in her abilities and knew somehow she would find Karah; I just hoped she wouldn't be too late.

Footfalls from behind brought me back from my memories. I glanced over at my much taller friend. Jaitem stood beside me and looked out to the sea as well. His thoughts were no doubt on his mate. Miara's death weighed heavily on Jaitem, and I could only imagine what he was going through. I knew if our roles had been reversed I would not be as well composed. Although for all I knew he could have been a lit fuse waiting to explode. I saw the pain in his eyes every time I looked at him, and I did not envy him.

Jaitem was an anomaly here in Clorynina. His sheer size stuck out like a sore thumb, but fortunately, remnants of different races that had been traded from over the seas still called this place home, so it was easier for the Kanarah to blend in. I had never seen so many different races. Humans of all shapes and colours populated this city as a result of my grandfather and great-grandfather's slave trade. I wondered where they all came from and what it was like across the great sea, but such fantasies would have to wait. I had bigger problems.

All the slavers were gone now thanks to my uncle's rise to the throne, but he was still under the Dark Lord' rule, and Clorynina's reputation was still tarnished.

Clorynina had asked Gareth for help in ridding itself of the Dark Lord. The two cities were the most powerful in all of Eiddoril and possibly could have caused the Dark Lord a considerable amount of trouble, but my father had been unwilling to start a war. He'd wanted nothing to with it and turned his back on my uncle—an act I now feared would jeopardize any aide coming from the grand port city.

Jaitem turned to face me and again voiced his concern with our current situation. "Are you certain your uncle will see us? We have been waiting for more than an hour. We should just leave and make our way back to your city. The longer we stay the more likely it is we won't make it back in time."

I nodded and gripped the window ledge a little tighter. "I know, and I agree, but I have to at least try. We have to wait for Nalin's return. Hopefully he'll have information from his contacts about what's going on."

Our conversation was interrupted by a throat clearing at the other end of the room. We turned from the window and looked toward the sound. A young girl of maybe 13 stood in front of the large double iron doors that led to my uncle's audience room. She stood there examining us for a moment, her eyes bulging at the sight of Jaitem.

Her voice was almost musical and held all the innocence of childhood. "I knew the Kanarah were tall, but I wasn't expecting this. No wonder you must stay in hiding throughout most of these lands."

I stared at the child, not knowing what to say, but Jaitem came forward and gently lowered his large frame before the girl. "Tell me, child, how is it you know what I am when so many do not?"

The girl blushed a little and took a few steps back. "I know many things, most of which my father tells me to keep to myself, but I have a bad habit of speaking before I think."

I grinned at the girl and tried to mask the sadness in my eyes. "You remind me of a woman I know. Her mouth always seemed to get her in trouble too."

The girl walked past a still-kneeling Jaitem and approached me, taking my hand in her own. She looked into my eyes, and what I saw had no business being in the eyes of a young girl. There was wisdom and strength, but beneath that was fear. "Your dragon friend is safe for now. The Dark Lord does not wish her dead, but I fear there are worse fates, especially for the rest of Eiddoril."

I involuntarily tightened my grip on the girl's hand, causing the child to yelp in surprise. "What are you talking about? What do you know about Karah?"

The brave front dropped, and the little girl seemed to retreat into herself. She could barely control her own voice. "I'm sorry, I meant no harm, I . . ."

A new voice in the room cut the tension, and the force of his words landed squarely on me. "Unhand my daughter immediately or so help me you will regret it, whether you are family or not." My uncle, King Darius Kelodem, strode toward us with authority.

I quickly released the young girl, who ran for her father, burying her face in his clothes. "I'm sorry, Father, but the dreams . . . I just had to know if they were true. It's all happening as they have told me, Father. What are we going to do?"

"Hush, Risbela, I'll think of something."

Risbela looked up into her father's eyes and sucked in a calming breath. "You must help them, Father. Please promise me you will."

"That's enough, my child, go and find your mother and have something to eat. I will speak to you later."

Risbela gave her father one last hug, and then, without another glace at her audience, fled to the interior of the castle.

King Darius watched until his daughter was out of sight and then turned his venomous gaze on me. "You scared my daughter to death. I should have you flogged and thrown out of here. Why I permitted you an audience still baffles me. You deserve nothing from me." We stood facing each other, my uncle ready to spit nails, but I was in no mood for confrontation.

"Please, Uncle, forgive me. I didn't mean to frighten your daughter . . . it's just that what she said surprised me. She seems to know so much, and I don't understand. I thank you for seeing me. I know what my father has done, and you are entitled to your hatred, but I'm not him and I'm the one asking for help."

I sighed and ran my hands through my hair. "I've seen so much since I've left my home, so much pain and suffering. I just want it to end but I can't do it alone."

Darius studied his young nephew and came to some inner conclusion. "Yes, I see you are indeed not your father's son—more of my sister clearly burns in your veins, and of that I am glad. Come, there is much to discuss and I prefer to hold council in my private chambers. Even here in my own castle I am not free from the Dark Lord's ears."

The king turned on his heels and bade Jaitem and me to follow, but a commotion at the end of the audience room pulled our attention toward it. Three Dark Lord soldiers pushed their way past the king's home guard and boldly came to stand in front of us. The lead man, whose face was covered by his helm, was not playing games.

Darius was outraged. "What is the meaning of this? The Dark Lord may control my city, but he has no rights in my own home. You will wait like everyone else. I have business to attend to."

The shorter officer laughed in the king's face. "You truly are a stupid man. My lord allows you to keep your home to keep this city running smoothly. Do not think that he can't take that away and find someone else to do it for him. It would serve you well to remember your place in the grand scheme of things."

The soldier's attention shifted to Jaitem and me, leaving the cowed king to stare at his back.

"Our business seems to be related, in fact. These two are of great interest to my lord." He turned back to Darius and gave the king a mock bow. "If your highness will permit, I would like to join you in your discussions with these two men—that is if you have the time."

Darius forced his rising anger down and managed to bite out a response. "Of course. Please—after you. We will take council in my private chambers."

I exchanged a worried glance with Jaitem, but we did not put up a fight. If we were going to get out of this without any more trouble, we needed a plan.

The soldier gave orders to his other two men to remain here, and together with the king and his two guests we shut the large double iron doors and made our way to the king's rooms.

We walked in silence down the long hallway, our footfalls echoing, and finally came to a large wooden door with the crest of Kelodem on it. We all waited for the king to open the door and step inside the spacious outer greeting room.

I followed my uncle, but not before giving Jaitem a secret nod. Jaitem did not respond but acknowledgment flashed in his eyes as he bowed toward the Dark Lord soldier, implying the soldier should precede him.

The soldier paid little attention and entered the room with the very large Kanarah warrior at his back. Jaitem entered last, kicked the door closed with his foot, and in the same motion grabbed the soldier by the throat, pinning him against his large chest.

I was on him just as fast, my sword pointed at the soldier's throat.

Darius was aghast. "Stop! What do you think you're doing? This is not the best solution."

I ignored my uncle's warnings, and reaching over with my free hand removed the soldier's helm. There, turning quite blue in the face from lack of oxygen, was Nalin.

"It's all right, Jaitem, it's Nalin. Let the poor bastard go before he passes out." Jaitem released his friend from his bear hug and dropped him several inches back to the ground.

Nalin bent forward with his hands on his knees, sputtering and coughing, trying to catch his breath.

I approached him and extended my hand. "I'm sorry, my friend, but I had to be sure. Nice job, by the way. I can see now why you're in charge."

Nalin glanced up at me and gave me a devious smile, and then he straightened and clasped my hand. "No apology required. I would have done the same. I'm sorry about the intrusion, but what soldiers remain in the city were given strict orders to detain any outsiders. When word got out about you two, a unit was dispatched to investigate. I made sure I was one of them."

My uncle cleared his throat and placed his hands on his hips. "I hate to interrupt this little reunion, but could someone please explain what's going on?" King Darius, who had grown quite red in the face, stood a safe distance from us.

I gestured toward Nalin. "Uncle, this is Nalin, commander of the Order of Freedom, and my friend. He is not part of the Dark Lord's legions, and if you will permit us we will explain everything."

The king nodded but did not relax his stance. He led us to another room and closed the door behind us. "These are my private rooms; no one can get in here but me. Speak freely but do it quickly, because no matter how good this little charade of yours may be the Dark Lord is not stupid, and I am not willing to take any chances."

The king's room was not lavish but it was quite large. A long wooden table accompanied by six chairs was off to the side underneath a large window. The rest of the room was filled with a desk, several other chairs that looked more for show than for sitting, and a huge fireplace, which was lit, giving off warmth that somehow comforted my soul.

Darius led the three of us to the table by the window and bade us all to sit. When we were seated, he took a chair at the head of the table and listened to our tale.

A half hour passed before I finished summing up our current situation. When I finished I looked at my uncle, who had said very little throughout the conversation, and watched him get up from his chair and walk over to the window.

His voice drifted softly to our group. "I never dreamed this day would come. *Dragons*, of all the foolish legends. Why did the dragons have to be real? She's been telling me for years all these fantastic tales but she is just a child, too small and fragile to know such things."

Darius bowed his head, leaving me to wrestle with my impulse to question him about his daughter.

When again the king turned to face us, he had strength and determination in his eyes. "I will help you, Elric, if for no other reason than for the honesty and sheer bravery that I see in you. You will make an excellent king one day; let's just hope we all have kingdoms to still rule. Now down to business."

The king took his seat again and leaned forward, encompassing the group.

"Now, thanks to your mother, who I have never been able to say no to, I have been preparing for this meeting for several days, although I must admit I had my doubts about her message."

I raised a questioning eyebrow about my mother's involvement but did not put voice to it. I was just thankful that at least one of my parents responded to the letter I had sent.

Darius ignored my questioning gaze and continued. "It hasn't been easy, but I've managed to come up with a plan. I've had to mask the whole endeavour as an exploration of sorts. I am founding a journey across the sea to find new trade, or so the Dark Lord soldiers think. We have lost contact with several of our trading partners, and frankly, it is disturbing, but that is another problem I will deal with later. I have four large ships on standby waiting with supplies and able to smuggle in the hold at least 100 men in the gallows per ship. It will be a horrible journey, but thankfully it is only a four day sail down the coast to the boarders of Aserah."

My uncle focused on me. "I wish I could go with you personally, but if things go the way I think they will I need to be here to prepare my own home for defence. Once the Dark Lord discovers my involvement in this, he will waste no time striking against me."

A small smile graced his lips but there was no humour in it. "You may just have to turn around and save my skin, so just promise me you won't feed me to the wolves like your father did."

I stared at my uncle, feeling very uncomfortable, but he didn't seem to notice.

"So if there are no questions, may I suggest you get underway? The two soldiers you left behind are not going to be patient much longer. They may not truly know who you are, but that will not stop them from being suspicious."

We all rose, and I took my uncle's arm into a firm hold. "Thank you, Uncle, for everything; it is more than I could ever have expected. And don't worry, when the time comes to aide you there will be no hesitation. But I must ask you one more thing before we go. Your daughter, Risbela—how does she know these things? How did she know about Karah?"

King Darius replaced his warm, giving visage with that of a bear protecting its cub. "That, my boy, is a question I can't answer. I will do anything to protect her, and right now, her secrecy is doing that. Just know that she is very special and trust that what she says is true. Perhaps when this is over I will be able to tell you about her and you and your friends can help her, but for now I am asking that you respect our privacy, for her safety and our kingdom's."

I hated doing it but I let the matter drop. There was nothing more I could say to make my uncle talk, so instead I turned to Nalin. "So how are we getting out of here? By the sounds of things, the Dark Lord has his men looking for us everywhere. How are you going to convince those two that we are not the right men they are looking for?"

Nalin shrugged and replaced his helm. "Don't worry about those two; they're not the sharpest tacks, if you get my meaning. Most all of the soldiers have been pulled out to march on Gareth. The ones left behind are either very fresh recruits or stupid brutes. I can handle them. You two just meet me at the docks in an hour. There is a tavern there called the First Mate. Ask for a serving girl named Kiz. She will keep you safe until I get there."

Nalin bid his farewell to the king and his two friends and made his way back to the main audience hall.

Darius gave me a ring with the crest of Kelodem on it. The Ristiaper's head surrounded by a ring of thorns stared menacingly at me. "Show this ring to the dock master at dawn tomorrow, and he will show you to the ships and introduce you to my commanding officer, Isver. He will be accompanying you and will be in charge of my men. I will fully brief him on what you have told me today, and he will be under orders to follow your command. I'm sorry I could not do more. I look forward to seeing you again, dear nephew, under better circumstances."

We clasped hands again and the king led us out of his chambers down the other way of the hallway we had come. We made several twists and turns, and by the time we emerged somewhere behind the castle, I was completely disoriented.

Jaitem and I said our farewells and made our way to the first mate.

CHAPTER 28

Karah

Intense pain that I never knew could exist greeted my conscious thoughts. I felt as if every bone in my body had been turned to jelly. I didn't open my eyes for fear of seeing where I truly was. I remembered being taken away by the Dark Lord, and I could guess that he would be the first thing I saw when I opened them.

However, to my surprise it was a woman's voice that made me open my eyes. She spoke in hushed, soothing tones, which eased my pain a little. I realized I had my head in her lap and that she was smoothing my damp, sweaty hair. I couldn't see her face, which was turned away from me and lost in shadows. It was very dark where we were and I couldn't tell but I was pretty sure we were in a cave, a very large one. The stone beneath me was unusually warm.

I suddenly realized it was hard to breath. The air was stifling and I started to choke on my own intake of the humid air. The unknown woman helped me sit up and brought a shallow, stone bowl filled with what I hoped was water to my lips. It was warm, but thankfully it helped clear my throat. I held the bowl in both hands and tipped it, sending the water into my mouth and over my face. It hurt too much to sit up so I lay back down in the lap of my unknown companion. She leaned forward a little, and what light there was in the cave allowed me to see her face for the first time.

She was human with a fairly dark complexion. Her long hair hung in tangles and I couldn't be sure but it almost looked silver, like the colour of metal. She had a warm smile, but it was her eyes that drew me to her. They were bright and golden and full of fear. They were dragon's eyes.

"Hello, my daughter, I am glad to see you made it through the night. I was afraid that you wouldn't." The woman stared at me with concern and something else that I had not seen in a long time: love.

"Ashia? Is that really you?" Tears of joy quickly started to fill my eyes but dread dried them before they fell. "I thought you were trapped on the other side with . . . oh no, Mareth. Is he here? Are we too late? Where am I?" I started to panic, which did my body no good. I instantly felt worse, if that was possible.

"Calm down, child. You've done a lot of damage to your human body by using your magic; you must try to lie still." She settled me back down into her lap and went back to smoothing my hair.

She looked off into the darkness of the cave and sighed. "I'm your mother, Ashia, and no, Mareth has not yet returned, but he will. It is just a matter of time now. We are in Nubossa's lair deep within the Barren Wastes. I'm so sorry, my daughter, that I was so foolish and blinded. I never should have left you here alone. I never should have thought Mareth would change, and I never should have been so foolish as to think that I could beat him. Now it's too late. He has amassed an army on the other side and is bent on the destruction of our world. There is nothing to stop him. Not even the elements have the power."

Ashia looked back down at me and it broke my heart to see her in such inner pain.

I managed to shake my head in confusion. "But I don't understand. How did you get back here? And what about the other dragons? Why didn't they help you?"

"The others who followed us through the gate were deceived into going. Mareth and Nubossa—I believe the mortals call him the Dark Lord—had stolen all the eggs and threatened them with their destruction. As soon as we all crossed over they turned on me, and I didn't stand a chance. I became Mareth's prisoner like the rest of my kind, and I watched him destroy whole pockets of the immortal realm and amass his army. He has grown very powerful and somehow was able to open the portal by himself. He sent me through to Nubossa with a message for the elements. He wanted them to see what he was capable of and that he no longer needed them."

My heart sank with every word my mother spoke, and I fought hard to keep the tremor from my voice.

"Why didn't he just come back through then? Why give the elements a chance to retaliate?"

Ashia's golden eyes burned with hate. "Because Mareth is an arrogant greedy creature, he wanted to leave the elements cowering in fear. He wanted them to know that there was nothing that they could do to stop him from returning and completing his plans. I had thought that his arrogance would be his downfall because the elements were able to reinforce the portal on this side. Only a great amount of elemental magic can open it, but Mareth tricked us again. It seems that he had plans for that too."

"What plans? How could he possibly know that it would play out this way?"

Ashia paused and looked into my eyes. I could see the conflict there and I was afraid that she would not tell me the truth. I reached for her hand and squeezed it gently.

"I have seen that look before. Fitch had it many times when he was telling me about myself. Please do not keep things from me. I have the right to know. I think I have earned that."

Confusion crossed my mother's face. "Who is Fitch?"

I mentally kicked myself. "Oh sorry, I forgot. You know him as Enthor."

Ashia seemed to straighten a bit; concern and confusion filled her voice. "Enthor is here? I wondered what became of him but no one knew. I assumed he perished during Mareth's war."

It was my turn to look confused. "That isn't what he told me. He said that you asked him to stay behind to protect me."

"No, I had no idea that he had stayed behind, but I am glad of it. None of the dragons were supposed to stay, but I felt that I owed the mortals of Eiddoril something for ravaging their world. That was why I asked you stay. I wanted you to rebuild the trust lost between the elements and us. I only discovered afterwards that

Mareth had hidden someone also and that I had left you to your doom."

I closed my eyes in frustration. Enthor had lied to me again and I was finding it very hard not to be angry.

"Is Enthor all right? How did you get separated?"

I opened my eyes to find my mother staring down at me with concern for Enthor. I was too tired to be angry and decided to let Enthor's horrible communication skills be our secret for now.

"Enthor is fine as far as I know. We separated a few days ago. He went on to your temple to try to discover some answers while I continued south to Clorynina. We had planned to get help from Elrics uncle, but . . ."

I stopped talking. Thinking about Elric hurt almost as much as the pain that flowed through my body. I hoped he had not been foolish and tried to come after me. I hoped he had realized that there were more important matters to deal with and that he found the help Gareth so desperately needs. Ashia saw the hurt in my eyes and squeezed my hand back.

"I am glad that Enthor is still alive but it puzzles me why he did not tell me his plans. I'm sorry also for the heartache you are going through now. I know how much this man meant to you. You spoke of him often in your unconsciousness."

Ashia drew in a steadying breath. "I will not lie to you; I can see that you have lived with enough lies already, so I will tell you Mareth's plan for you. The spell that he had Nubossa place on you was never meant to last forever. He planned it that in the event that the elements tried to block the way back for him that you would be his key."

I didn't understand. "What key? What are you talking about?"

Ashia grabbed one of my hands and squeezed it gently. "You, my dear daughter, are an extremely powerful dragon, stronger than me and Mareth although he would not admit it. You have fascinated me since your hatching. You were so different and so powerful even at your young age. I knew you had a higher purpose I just didn't know what. Mareth knew from the beginning that you were his daughter. Enthor and I were fools to think otherwise. He watched you, watched your powers grow, and he saw the way in which you could control all four elemental powers simultaneously. He knew you would never turn on me or your fellow dragons so he designed a spell, a spell that would trap your spirit in a human body until he needed it again."

I shook my throbbing head. "None of this makes sense. The Dark Lord has been trying to kill me for centuries."

"Yes, which is something Mareth was most displeased about. When I was sent back, it was the first time that Mareth had been able to communicate with Nubossa since we had left. When he discovered what he had been trying to do to you, he was furious. Mareth gave Nubossa orders to cease his death pursuit of you and merely keep it up for appearances. He then made Nubossa participate in a blood bond ritual which would allow him to communicate with him in the immortal realm."

"Okay, so why am I the key? What is it that I am supposed to do?"

"During the autumn solstice which is in less than a weeks' time the elements power will be at one of its fullest. The gates to the different realms can only be opened during the solstices. That is the night Nubossa plans to attack the Kingdom of Gareth, it's also the same night that Mareth will open the doorway on his side. Nubossa is taking you and your true form back to Gareth where the spell that is holding your powers captive will finally end. Your power will be too much for your human body and it will parish. Your life spirit will be drawn back into your true form and the immense flux of your power and the elements together will give Nubossa's warlocks the power they need to open the door from our side, and then all will be lost."

I closed my eyes and tried to swallow the lump of despair in my throat. My quest that I had thought would save the world was only preparing me to destroy it. Reapers words suddenly came flooding back to me and the weight of them came crashing down. I opened my eyes and looked up to see my mother crying. It seemed so odd to me to see something as strong and powerful as a dragon crying, which brought another thought to my mind.

"Why are the elements allowing this? They have the power to destroy the Dark Lord, they always have. Why did they let this happen? Why won't they help us?"

Ashia rubbed at her eyes and reddened a little at her emotional outburst. "That is a difficult question to answer. My relationship with the elements runs deep so I know more about them than most, but I do not know all. I can tell you that they are fully capable of emotion; and they care very deeply for their creations and this world."

I found that very hard to believe. How can you care about something and not lift a finger to help. I held my tongue though and let my mother finish. "What happened after the dragons returned to the immortal realms is a mystery to me. I could not communicate with them there so I had no idea what was happening, back here in Eiddoril. When I was sent back, I was visited secretly by the element of Earth and he told me some of what had been happening. I was furious when it told me about you and how they did nothing to protect you and about the power and control, Nubossa held over the realm. I asked why but I didn't get an answer. Earth faded back into the stone and I never heard from any of the elements again. They are acting like scared children afraid to take action. I don't know what is going on but I feel that there is something more, something that is stopping them from acting."

I couldn't believe my ears. I was furious. "Are you trying to tell me that the creators of the worlds, the very essence of life are no more than scared children? What right did they have to create in the first place?"

"What else could they do? That is there purpose, to create, that is all they know. We all have a purpose. Sometimes we don't understand it or want to accept it but we can't deny the fact that we were all created for a reason. The elements merely do what they know how to do."

I was baffled; this was just too much for me to handle right now. I needed to get out of here; the only trouble was is that I didn't have the slightest idea how I was going to accomplish it. I looked up to Ashia.

"Why are you still here? Why haven't you tried to escape? Enthor told me that you were very powerful. Why didn't you fight the Dark Lord?"

"Because of this." Ashia held up her left hand and I noticed for the first time that she was chained to the wall. I also saw something familiar gleaming in the faint light. It was one of the Dark Lord's bracelets.

Anger filled my words. "I know of this device, it is how the Dark Lord managed to capture me in the first place. Enthor also has one on currently. We were ambushed in the town of Delroth. That is one of the reasons why we separated; he went to the temple to see if he could find any information on how to remove it."

Ashia shook her head in dismay. "He will be greatly disappointed. The only way that I have seen to remove these is by the Dark Lord himself. A single drop of his blood placed here on this symbol is the only way to release them."

I closed my eyes and thought; something was nagging at my pain-filled brain. "How were these manacles created? Where did they come from? Do you know?"

Ashia looked thoughtful and nodded. "I am not quite sure but I think they were created during the war which forced the elements to banish us. I believe Death created them as a way to control us but they were never used. They were made from pure dragon's blood and iron. When the iron shackle was placed in a pool of dragons blood Death infused it with its own magic combining all the powers together, creating a device which drained and stored magic."

I wasn't sure if it was the pain or my desperate need to have something go right for a change but I sat up abruptly and turned to look at my mother. "Have you ever tried using your own blood to release the shackle? Since it was forged using dragon blood maybe any dragons' blood would work. Maybe that's why they were never used against you, they were flawed."

Shock and hope filled Ashia's eyes as she glanced down at the prison she had been trapped in for years. She found a jagged piece of rock and gouged her finger on it. She then held her shaking finger over the shackle and let a single drop fall on the appropriate symbol.

With a snap, the shackle released and fell into my lap, where I carefully placed it whole again inside my torn tunic. Ashia gave me a hug but quickly put a finger to my mouth, someone was coming. Ashia quickly positioned herself more in the shadows and hid her now free hand behind her back. I did my best to sit up and together we waited for our guests.

The Dark Lord, flanked by two of his warlocks, came into the cavern. He was in human form, and seeing him was like reliving all of my nightmares.

His cold black eyes glittered with hate as he fixed them on me. "So you're awake. How was your little reunion? I thought you might like to see your mother before the end. I'm sure she has filled you in on everything so I'm not going to waste my breath."

The Dark Lord then came forward and roughly grabbed me by the shoulders and hauled me to my feet. He turned me toward the warlocks and shoved me into their arms. I gasped in pain as I stumbled and landed into their stick like embrace. I shuddered as one of them looked at me with dead eyes.

The Dark Lord came toward us, leaving Ashia forgotten. I needed to distract him, anything to buy us time to escape here. I sucked in a painful breath and tried not to look like I was about to puke. "So have you heard from Reaper, or are you still trying to get the knife out of your back!"

I shrank back at the look of sheer hatred in the Dark Lord's eyes. He closed the distance between us and grabbed my chin forcing me to look up at him. I could feel the warlock's sickly frame pressing against my back, leaving me wondering which was worse.

"It would do you well not to push me, whelp. The only thing saving you right now is the fact that my master needs you alive, but don't think that I will not make the journey to Gareth as painful as possible."

It probably wasn't one of my best moments but I decided to taunt him further. "You mean you're more afraid of Mareth than me? And here I thought that the big bad human girl pulled your strings."

Yep that did it. The Dark Lord sucked in a ragged breath and brought his hand back to strike at me, but he never got the chance. Ashia—who, by the way, can shift to dragon very quietly—grabbed the Dark Lord's arm in her massive golden jaws and flung him across the cavern where he hit the wall and crumpled to the ground.

I dived out of the way, leaving the two warlocks staring at the open maw of a very angry dragon. White-hot fire burst from her open jaws and incinerated the two hapless creatures, freeing their tortured souls at last. I tried to get up but my broken body just didn't want to respond.

Ashia's voice intruded my thoughts as she gently gathered me into her claws. *"I need to get you out of here. Nubossa will not be down for long and I am not yet strong enough to take him on. Do you know where your prince may be? We need to warn him and tell him of Mareth's plans."*

"In Clorynina, I hope. That is where we were headed."

Without further communication, Ashia carried me to the mouth of the cavern, and with a mighty push we were off to find my prince, leaving the Dark Lord screaming in anger.

*

Nubossa

Dragging my broken human body through the mouth of my lair, I watched in fury as my prey vanished from sight. I shifted to my true form and roared my anger to the darkening skies. I at least knew where they were headed thanks to Ashia's sloppy mind communication. I would just have to get there first.

Movement to my left stalled my leap into the air and brought my attention to one of my Litui soldiers. I waited as the creature made its way up the path and then knelt before me. I was in no mood for idle garble so I quickly invaded its mind.

"Speak quickly, I am needed elsewhere."

The Litui kneeled, scraping its claws along the rock beneath him. "Forgive me, Master, but I received a report from a Clorynina spy. It appears that the king is sending out an expedition across the seas. He thought it would be important to learn more for you so he followed the dock master. He met with the captain of the king's guard, who was heading the expedition along with two other strangers. There are four ships in total and all are packed with armed soldiers. Your spy did not think this a normal procedure for an expedition and found it of utmost importance to immediately inform you."

The Litui bowed his head further, trying to hide the fear in his eyes. Something else was on the creature's mind, and I was not about to play guessing games. I lost the hold I had on his feeble mind and yelled at the creature.

"Speak your mind, you snivelling beast. What else do you have to say?"

The Litui cowered in my shadow and held his head in pain but managed to finish his report. "We have received word from your army . . . there are complications. When General Qued reached the village of Emroth, they were met with a surprise. The town was completely deserted, and all of the supplies they needed were gone. Someone had warned them. At first he didn't think this important, but as he drew closer to Gareth, he discovered more and more villages were abandoned. When he reached the final town before Gareth, Holsten—I think that was the name—they found more of the same: empty houses and no supplies. General Qued decided to set camp there for the night, which ended in disaster. Many of the human soldiers sabotaged the camp during the night, and by morning nearly one third of the human soldiers had fled to join ranks with Gareth. Apparently, Master, they are part of a group called the Order of Freedom, who have been secretly operating under our noses for years."

The Litui shrank back against the cavern wall to avoid being impaled by my claws. I screamed into the air, causing chunks of rock to come loose and tumble down the side of the cliff. I turned and pushed the unfortunate creature further against the wall with my snout and opened my maw, exposing the razor-sharp teeth. My evil red eyes bored into the Litui and my voice drilled painfully into its mind.

"How? How has this happened right under my nose? And how many are involved?"

The Litui was beyond terrified and most likely now deaf so he couldn't speak, but I had no trouble hearing his panicked thoughts. *"Forgive me, Master, but I'm just a messenger. All I know is that they were successful in interrogating one of the deserters. I am not sure of their numbers but they are widespread and have all come to the aide of Gareth and—"* The Litui's thoughts froze.

I opened my jaws further and slid my forked tongue down the side of the Litui's face. "And?"

The Litui gave into his fears and started blurting everything that came into his mind. *"Gareth has other allies as well. There is a strange tribe of smaller beings covered in strange markings. They look like human children but are strong and longer-limbed. In addition, other warriors that are giants have been spotted. They have red hair and are built like Ngogar."*

The Litui closed his large, bulbous eyes and waited for the end but it didn't come. Instead, I withdrew and stood silently gazing out to the skies.

The Litui sighed heavily in relief and waited for my wishes. I did not make him wait long.

"You have done well and so have my spies, but there is one more thing that I require from you."

The obedient Litui bowed and awaited my request.

With a mighty push of my sharp claw I impaled the helpless creature, pinning it face down against the rock. I relished in the life force flowing through me, healing my injuries and soothing my angry soul. When there was nothing left to take I removed the corpse from my talons and pushed off into the skies, headed toward the Forever Sea.

I couldn't believe what I'd just heard. All my careful planning seemed to be blowing up in my face. How was it possible that two entire races had managed to escape my genocide? Moreover, this order of freedom, it was apparent that I had underestimated the humans once again and it seemed that my puppet king was attempting to cut his strings. I always knew he would eventually get tired of being under my control. I had no doubt that the king of Clorynina was attempting to aide Gareth and not commencing an expedition.

I would first head to the ships and take care of them before heading into the port city itself. I would teach this human king the price of disobedience. No matter how hard these mortals tried, they were just prolonging the inevitable. Mareth would again grace these skies and I would be there at his side.

It was time to show the humans who I truly was and watch them flee for their lives.

CHAPTER 29

Prince Elric

The ship swayed gently along the sea currents while the rising sun cast its brilliance over the sparkling water. It was a calm and peaceful scene, which did not match the turmoil in my stomach. I gripped the railing tightly at the stern of the ship and closed my eyes. It was not only the fact that I had discovered sea travel did not agree with me, but also the news Nalin gave me before we departed. Nalin had discovered a lot of information in a short period of time.

The Dark Lord's massive army, consisting of human and other creatures including his warlocks was moving swiftly, cutting a path of destruction across Eiddoril. The towns and villages that lay directly in their path were completely destroyed. The Order of Freedom warned who they could but the sudden attack took them unawares. There had been no hope for the settlements closest to the Barren Wastes. Many people had died, and it weighed heavily on the rebel leader's heart. Fortunately, the farther north the rebel army travelled, the less resistance they encountered. Most villages heeded the Order's warnings and fled before the Dark Lord army got there. However, most who fled were headed straight for Gareth. It seemed all their efforts to keep people safe were merely resulting in gathering everyone in one place to be slaughtered.

The outcome of this battle was not going to be a good one, and to top it all off Nalin had received a message from Enthor, who had successfully found what he needed to know at the temple, but none of it was good news. Mareth was preparing to return during the battle, and Karah was the key. Enthor had made it quite clear that I was to keep Karah as far away from Gareth as possible, but that was out of my hands now and it was pointless to tell the older dragon. There was nothing any of us could do but wait.

Once the ships docked in Aserah, which would be the day before the solstice, I would have to find Karah and get her away from the battle. Leaving Gareth's defences to others was not appealing, but I trusted our allies' skills, and really, there was no else I would allow to find Karah.

Opening my tired eyes once again, I squinted against the sun reflecting on the waves when something strange caught my gaze. It was an abnormal shape moving in fast from land. We had to travel far enough from land to be out of sight before turning course and heading back down the coast toward Aserah, so I was sure I wasn't seeing part of the cliffs or another boat. I didn't think it was a bird, either—the Ristiapers did not travel this far out to sea.

My anxiety rose as did my alarm as the object got steadily closer. I knew of only one creature that was that big and could move at that speed, and if I had any hope of saving these people, I had to act fast.

I ran from the railing, skidding and tripping over ropes and cargo boxes. I took the stairs three at a time that led to platform where I would find the captain at the wheel. I all but barrelled into the captain's back, causing him to curse.

"What the hell's the matter with you, boy? You look like you've seen a spirit."

I tried not to scream in the man's face. "Commander Ivser, where is he? I need to speak with him right now!"

A voice from behind made me turn my back on the bewildered captain. "I'm here, Prince Elric. What's wrong? You don't look well."

Instead of speaking, I grabbed Ivser, spun him around and pointed out to sea, back the way we had just sailed. "Do you see that dark shape moving toward us?"

Ivser nodded stiffly. "Yes, but what is it? I've never seen anything like it. Is it a bird or a storm cloud?"

I turned the man back toward me and stared into his eyes. 'No, it's a dragon, and we're in serious trouble."

Ivser didn't know what to say. I think he would have laughed at me but there was wildness in my eyes that made him question. "Elric, calm down. I think maybe the sea air has gotten to you. Go below deck and take a rest. I'll figure out what that is."

I was furious. "I don't need to rest! I need you to get your men up on deck and prepare to fight. You need to signal the other ships and try to warn them. We're all sitting ducks out here in the open, but we have to try something."

The commotion between Ivser and me was drawing attention. Both Nalin and Jaitem were soon flanking Isver and looking questioningly at me.

"What's going on, Elric? You're causing a scene." Nalin sounded annoyed but I could see alarm in his eyes.

I pushed past Ivser, who shot me a scowl, and pointed off into the sky. The large mass was even closer now and starting to take on a definite shape.

Nalin's breath caught in his throat and Jaitem drew his blades, which instantly were consumed by fire.

Nalin faced my uncle's commander with his own authority. "Commander Ivser, listen to Elric. That is no bird or anything that you have ever seen before. It is the Dark Lord and it is our deaths."

Ivser's face paled as he stared into the sky, and even he could not deny what he was seeing. "You mean the stories are true? What we were told as children about a great dragon destroying everything is true?"

I turned to face the commander again. "Yes, and if we don't do something quickly we're next."

Ivser snapped out of his fear and signalled the now terrified captain to sound an air horn. They used the horn to communicate between ships. Two long alarms followed by a short one was picked up and returned from the other three ships. It was a call for defences and to prepare for an attack.

Ivser was right back in my face. "Please tell me you have a plan. Do you know what that beast is capable of? What can we do to defend ourselves?"

I swallowed the bile in my throat and drew my own sword. "Unfortunately not much, like I said we are sitting ducks. I have only battled him once and the fact we escaped with our lives was dumb luck. The Dark Lord is capable of projecting fear directly into your mind, causing panic and chaos. At close range he can spray a corrosive acid from his mouth and drain life energy just by touch."

Ivser's eyes bulged. "So what you're saying is that we're screwed." Ivser pointed at Jaitem. "Your friend there seems to be able to wield magic—is there nothing he can do?"

I furiously shook my head and tried to calm my racing thoughts. "Jaitem has an elemental artefact imbued with the power of fire. I have a shield able to control the earth, but the weapon that would be most helpful right now is my friend's sword. It can control water, which would be extremely helpful right now."

Ivser, I knew, was confused. "What do you mean? If you can use the other two weapons, why not the sword?"

I sighed, hiding my annoyance with all the questions. "The artefacts are keyed to specific individuals. We are the only ones capable of using these weapons, and my friend was the only one who could use the sword, so unless you have a mage on board, just forget I even mentioned it."

A small female voice coming from the deck below caught our attention. "I can help you."

Ivser swore as he pushed his way past us and came down the stairs to kneel before the girl. "Risbela, what are you thinking? This is no game; your father and mother will be worried to death."

Risbela swallowed hard and looked past Ivser into my very surprised eyes. "I can help you. You said you needed a mage. Well, now you have one."

I stood beside Risbela and took her small hand. "I knew there was something special about you, and now I understand why your father has being trying so hard to keep you a secret. This is no game, child. Do you know what will happen if the Dark Lord sees that you are a mage? You will be captured and transformed into a warlock. I can't let that happen, not even to save us."

Jaitem had joined us as well and was studying the girl with great pride. "Elric, you cannot deny this child the chance to make a difference. Were we so different at that age? I see strength in her and the need to do what's right. If we do not let her help, we will not only distinguish her flame but doom us as well. What do we possibly have to lose?"

I could think of many things, but I kept the argument to myself. My friend was right. If we had any hope at all of surviving this we needed all the help we could get.

I reached back and unstrapped a scabbard from my back. I handed it to Risbela, whose eyes nearly popped out with excitement.

Isver rose and confronted me. "You can't be serious—she's just a girl! How do you even know she can wield that thing without taking her own head off?"

In answer, Risbela drew the water sword and held it out in front of her, balancing it in her delicate hands. The sword instantly reacted to her and the blade became transparent, moving in time with the sea below. She demonstrated a few mock thrusts and parries and then drew herself up to face Isver. "My father taught me how to use a sword since I was five. He always wanted me to be able to protect myself if my magic failed. He knew my life would always hold danger, and he did his best to prepare me. I can do this. Please let me help you."

Isver snorted but didn't argue; instead, he stalked off to the main hatch where his soldiers were massing. Staring into the sky he turned briefly and pointed. "Well, whatever it is you plan on doing, I suggest you do it now because we have company."

All eyes fell on the beast that was now within a mile or so. Isver signalled to the archers on board and sent them to the stern. Jaitem went with them, ready to set the arrows ablaze when the Dark Lord came into range. Nalin, Risbela, and I stood below the main mast. I had no fantasies about the outcome of this encounter. I had no doubt that I was going to die today, but maybe I could buy Enthor and the others some time. I hoped we could injure the Dark Lord enough to delay his plans in Gareth. If he didn't get Karah there in time, then Mareth would stay safely locked away. It was a long shot, but what else could I do?

I looked out toward the coming dragon and could just start to make out its features. I blinked a couple of times and strained my eyes. Something was different. The closer the dragon got, the more I realized it was the wrong colour. This dragon was a brilliant gold and the sun's rays glistened and shined on its scales.

Before I could form a conclusion, a greeting filled the minds of *everyone* on the four ships. *"Please do not attack. I apologize for the surprise and the mental intrusion but this is the only way I can communicate with you while I'm in my natural form. I had to wait until I was closer to speak with you. I am no threat to you. My name is Ashia, and I have finally returned to help you."*

"Ashia . . . as in 'Ashia, our missing god of light'? You've got to be kidding me."

Ivser whirled on me. "Are you telling me that one of our gods is a bloody dragon, a giant winged monster that at any moment could possibly be the end of us? You can't really believe any this—can you?"

I ignored the flustered commander and slowly made my way to join Ivser and the others at the stern. I didn't know if it would work, but I sent out my own mental message.

"Can you hear me? Is that really you? How can we trust you? No offence, but I was under the impression that you were in another realm fighting for your life. This does not make sense".

I held my breath and was grateful when a reply came.

"Prince Elric, I presume. I've heard a lot about you. I have someone with me who is in need of your help. I would have her speak to you but she is unconscious. Please trust me, and I will explain everything when we are on board your ship."

My heart caught in my throat. *"Karah? You have Karah? She's safe? Where is the Dark Lord?"*

She said, *"Yes, I have your Karah, but we do not have much time. Please tell your captain to lower his sails. I will try to come in close enough to drop Karah on deck, but the updraft from my wings will only push the ship away from me."*

I glanced at the captain to see if he heard, and by the look on his face I could tell he had. But he still looked to Ivser for the order.

I moved so that the commander of my uncle's men and I were face to face. "You heard her; lower the sails. We need to get Karah on board. You can trust her. She's no friend to the Dark Lord. She will help us."

Ivser squared his shoulders and stood his ground. "And how do you know that? A minute ago you wanted me to protect the men on this ship by any means necessary, and now you are telling me to trust a monster, something from my nightmares? You are insane! Why my king is helping you fools is beyond me."

Before I could form an argument, Risbela was between us looking up into Ivser cold eyes. "Please, Ivser, listen to Elric, and listen to Ashia. She is who she says; she is our god of light. I have dreamed about her and know what she looks like. They have told me to trust her. I know you do not believe what she says but I do know you believe in me, I have proven that to you many times. So trust me now, and let her on board this ship."

Ivser stared at the young mage, shaking his head. He closed his eyes. When he opened them again, the ice had melted but mistrust still brewed there. "I hope you're right, little one. Your father is going to kill me."

Ivser turned and signalled the captain. The captain then used the same horn and sent out the signal to stand down, and then he sent out his crewmembers to lower the sails. The deck instantly became alive with activity. Men quickly hauled on the halyards, pulling down the sails, the main and fore masts. Yards were then secured with riggings, and the sailors all returned to their posts. It all took fewer than ten minutes, leaving me thoroughly impressed.

Ashia, who had been waiting and circling above saw that the humans were ready, and she carefully glided closer to the ship. Even with the sails lowered she still caused the ship to rock and pitch in the waves. Most of the men were well back from the impossible aerial display and watched mesmerized as a dragon dropped a human girl into my waiting arms and then shimmered and transformed into a human woman, letting a gust of wind gently carry her rest of the way down to the waiting deck like a glorious ray of sunshine.

All eyes were on the beautiful creature before them. She was dark skinned, and her long silver hair flowed down her back almost to her feet like a waterfall. She wore a long gown coloured much like her dragon scales. The golden fabric caught the sun's rays and cast brilliance across the ship. There was no denying why we thought of her as a god, but my eyes were for Karah.

I gently pushed Karah's red curls out of her eyes and willed them to open, but she remained unconscious. Her shallow breathing was the only indication that she was still alive.

Ashia quietly stood beside me and knelt down, placing her hand on her daughter's forehead. "This body can no longer hold her; we must get her to Gareth as soon as possible so she can be reunited with her true form."

I looked up at her with alarm. "No, we can't. Look, I don't know how much you know about what is going on, but Mareth is planning to return to Eiddoril to destroy it. Enthor sent us a message to keep Karah away from Gareth because she is some kind of key. He asked me to keep her safe until after the autumn solstice, and that is what I intend to do."

Murmurs of shock and disbelief ran the course of the ship. Every person aboard was gathered near us and listened intently, not daring to interrupt their newly returned god of light. Only tiny Risbela dared come close to us. She sat down cross-legged beside Karah with her sword in her lap. Karah's symbol on her face flared a faint blue but that was the only response.

Ashia looked at me and her deep golden eyes pierced my soul. "Are you certain that is what Enthor said? If he has been to the temple, then he has spoken to the guardian there. She would have told him everything. I can't believe he is willing to sacrifice her after all this time."

I gripped Ashia's arm, not caring who the hell she was, and took on a fierceness of my own. "What are you talking about? What do you mean 'sacrifice her'? We've been trying to save her."

Ashia did not have a chance to respond. Panic broke out on deck. Men raced across the deck, holding their heads and yelling in fear. Some even jumped off the ship into the cold depths of the sea trying to get away from whatever was terrifying them. I wasn't sure if I was used to the fear attacks or if I was not affected but nonetheless I knew what was going on.

I spied Nalin and Jaitem desperately trying to get the captain to issue orders. Jaitem finally gave up and simply punched the man in the face. It was quite effective, really. The fear was still there but he was no longer controlled by it. The captain began issuing orders and delivering his own punches. Some of the sailors responded and went to the task of raising the sails so that we could try to get out of here.

Ivser, a wild look in his eyes, found me. His sword was drawn and he was ready to fight. "What is it, Elric? I can't see it but my mind is telling me it is there. My men will not last long against this kind of attack."

I reached out and grabbed another soldier as he was about to pitch himself over the side. I quickly looked at the commander. "It's the Dark Lord. Get anyone who can't handle the fear below deck and prepare the rest of your men. It looks like we are going to get that fight after all."

Ivser didn't argue. He turned and raced along the deck, trying desperately to control his men. I turned back to Ashia, who was holding a terrified Risbela.

An inhuman scream filled the morning air along with cries and crashing timber. Seemingly from out of nowhere the Dark Lord appeared and attacked the lead ship. He smashed through the main mast, splintering it in two and at the same time smashing down his tail, tearing a hole along the hull. Screams of the dying filled the air as they were smashed into the sea or caught in the Dark Lord's unforgiving jaws.

I bent down and grabbed Risbela out of Ashia's arms, ignoring the hateful look I got and shook the little girl. "Listen to me. I know you're scared, but you sneaked aboard this ship to help, so I need you to that now. Do you understand? Can you hear me?"

Risbela's glassy, fear-filled eyes came into focus and she did her best to stop shaking. She focused her full attention on me, and I could have sworn I saw a hint of gold sparkle in her eyes. "Yes, I can hear you. I'll do my best. Stand back."

Risbela walked on shaky legs over to the side of the ship and stared at the now-sinking vessel that was once part of their party. She steadied her breathing, raised her arms to the sky and began to chant. The sea instantly became alive. It frothed and swirled at her call. The power of the sea gathered in force, and I was amazed at how much power the little girl had. With one mighty push of her hands, Risbela sent a wave of seawater directly at the Dark Lord, causing him to pitch and fight to stay airborne.

The Dark Lord fixed on our ship and raced toward it, screaming his anger into the air.

Risbela raised her arms again but Ashia stopped her. "No, child, this is my fight. Get these people out of here. I will distract Nubossa."

Ashia turned to me as her body started to shimmer and said to me mentally., *"The spell that holds Karah is failing. It was designed to fail during the autumn solstice. She can no longer be contained by a mortal body. She must be reunited with her true form or she will be lost to us forever. This has been Mareth's plan all along, and I am sorry to leave this to you. If my daughter is to survive, you must take her to Gareth, but know that in doing so you may seal your world's doom. I don't know if she is strong enough to stop him but she was created for a purpose and I have to believe that stopping her father is her destiny. I do not wish to see this world destroyed, but I can't, unlike Enthor, sacrifice my daughter to do it, so I leave the choice up to you. I'm sorry."*

Without further communication, she launched herself, her form transforming in midair and met the Dark Lord head on. The collision of the two massive bodies rocked the ships. Ours pitched dangerously and I had to grab Risbela and Karah to keep them from sliding into the cold water.

The dragons gained altitude and fought each other in midair, raking at each other's undersides and tearing at one another with their jaws. Blood and scales rained down around us as the battle between immortals consumed the sky.

Risbela tore her gaze from the gruesome scene and began to chant again. The wind responded this time and filled the sails of the remaining three ships. With the Dark Lord's grip of fear released, the captain and his sailors got to the task of operating the ship. The captain steered the mighty vessel back on course and with the force of a gale storm, the three ships sped away from the fighting dragons.

Not everyone was needed to run the ships, and the others stared at the unbelievable battle, until finally both dragons plunged and disappeared into the sea, leaving everyone in awe wandering if what they had just witnessed was merely a dream.

I stayed long after the others had left, staring blankly at the spot where they had gone under, but pleading coming from behind me brought me from my dark thoughts. I turned to see Ivser begging Risbela to stop. The young mage was visibly trembling and her head hung slack between her shoulders. I hurried over to her and raised her chin so I could look into her eyes, which to my horror were blank and completely gold.

"Risbela, honey, let it go, let the magic go. You did it; we're safe. There is nothing more you can do. Come back to us, let the wind rest."

I waited and was afraid that she had not heard me, but the wind died down to a gentle breeze, causing the ship to lurch almost to a dead stop. Then she collapsed into my arms.

Ivser knelt beside us with fear in his eyes. "Is she . . . is she alive?"

I brushed her long damp brown hair from her face and felt her neck for a pulse. It was strong and steady. "Yes, but she is exhausted. She will more than likely be unconscious for several hours. Take her below deck and make sure she is kept warm." Ivser gently gathered Risbela into his arms and disappeared below deck.

I rose and walked back to where Karah lay. I sat beside her, leaned my head against the railing and closed my eyes, thinking about what I had just seen but also about decisions that I would soon be forced to make.

Creaking in the floorboards gave way my friend's presence. I opened my eyes and looked up at Nalin, who was bent over Karah, worry etched across his features.

"She's dying, isn't she? Why did Ashia bring her here? What are we supposed to do? We must not take her to Gareth."

I closed my eyes again and kept silent. I wanted to tell Nalin the truth but knew the soldier would only talk me out of what I had already planned to do. Nalin wanted to protect the people and so did I, but not at the cost of Karah's life. It was too much to bear and I would curse the name Ashia until the day I died for making me make this choice.

Without opening my eyes I spoke to my friend. "She brought Karah here so we can save her. We need to get her back to Gareth and to her true form. That is the only way she will survive."

I could hear the alarm in Nalin's voice. "But Enthor told us to keep Karah away, that she would help release Mareth."

I opened my eyes and leaned forward so that I was in Nalin's face, who was still kneeling beside Karah. The look in my eyes caused my friend to blink in surprise and back away.

"Enthor did not know everything. Ashia told me that Karah is only part of the key, the Dark Lord and his warlocks were always needed to perform the final spell. Ashia has taken care of the Dark Lord, and without him his warlocks are puppets with no strings. The door will remain closed." I was, of course, making guesses and hated lying to my friend, but I had no choice.

Nalin studied me for a moment and then nodded. "If that is what you believe to be true, I trust you. I know you would not needlessly put people's lives in danger. I will go tell the captain to remain on course. Thankfully, thanks to Risbela, we should arrive two full days before the intended attack. I just hope you are right and Ashia truly has taken care of the Dark Lord, because if she failed we are all doomed."

Nalin left me to my dark thoughts. I looked down at the woman I was risking the world for. A woman who in reality wasn't even human, but I didn't see her that way. I would never see her as anything but the fragile young woman I saw now. I wanted so badly to see her beautiful green eyes smiling at me. I wanted to tell her that everything would be all right, but all I could do was watch her chest rise and fall in an unsteady rhythm. I rose to my feet and gently picked Karah up and followed the same path as Isver down below decks. We had a healer on board; maybe she had something that could ease Karah's pain.

I bent and kissed Karah's cold cheek and whispered in her ear. "Hang on, Karah, please don't leave me. I told you I would always protect you no matter what and I meant it. Please forgive me but I am breaking my promise I made to you. I can't let you die, not even to save the world. I have to make this choice for you even though you may hate me for it. Just remember I love you and nothing will ever have the power to change that, not even you."

*

The Element of Water

Deep below the surface of the sea, we watched the two beasts fight for their lives. The battle did not last long and I watched as the dark one finally swam away toward shore, trailing blood and large welts caused by the water. He would survive but it would be several days before he was healed.

We then focused our attention on the creature lying at the bottom of the sea. Her golden red scales were dull now, and we watched as her life's blood pumped into the water. She was not dead yet, but her magic was quickly fading, and without help she would die.

I began to float closer but I was quickly blocked by a wall of sand. "What are you doing, Sister? We cannot interfere. Mother has forbidden it."

I rippled in agitation and paid my sibling no attention. "Mother is wrong, as she has been with a great many things. She does not even keep to her own rules; look at what has happened with that evil, dark creature. I am tired of watching our creations suffer and die. They think we don't care, that we just create them and leave them, only getting involved when we are bored, like some kind of spoiled mortal. When will this stop? I'm tired; I want a home where I can rest. Mother's undying appetite for power and destruction is consuming her. Something needs to change, and the balance needs to be restored."

The essence of Earth shifted aside and watched me go the rest of the distance to the injured dragon but he did not remain silent. "You know the others will not be happy. They have indulged your little rebellion up until now but they fear her; she is too powerful for us and will destroy us."

I did not turn to look at my brother; I simply went to the task of saving one of my favourite creations. "I don't care what the others think. Fire is a bully and air just does whatever he is told. In the end, they will side with us. They do not say it but they know what needs to be done. Besides, Mother would not dare destroy us, she needs us. She may have made us but that was with help. Her power lies in destruction. Without us to create, what is she going to destroy? So do not fear for our safety, fear for our creations' safety because that is what everything will come down to. The portal needs to be opened; he needs to be found and set free."

Earth silently shifted to my side and began building up the sand and dirt under the dragon. Together we steadily began to raise the dragon to the surface.

"What if you're wrong? What if he won't help? He abandoned us. What makes you think he even has enough power to control her again? And what about that monstrosity trying to get back here—are you certain it is wise to let him return? You must know that Mother has been helping him all this time; she wants this world destroyed too, and she wants us to start over again."

The three of us broke the surface of the sea and the mighty dragon began breathing normally again. I began the long journey back to shore while my bother followed silently. When I finally reached our destination, I gently beached her.

Now that the dragon's magic wasn't being used to breathe and keep her alive, it went to the task of healing her wounds. It would be a slow process, but she would survive.

I returned to my natural domain and watched as my brother concealed the dragon with dirt and rocks, making her blend in while she healed. When he was satisfied that nothing would discover the dragon he then came to the shoreline and sank back down into the sand.

My voice again filled his thoughts. "He did not abandon us, he was tricked, and you know this. Don't worry, Brother, he will help us—he has to, we are his children too. He has been trapped for a long time, I know, but once he comes back through the portal he will feel life again. He will restore the balance and then we can rest, we can stop creating new worlds and just enjoy what we have. Letting that greedy immortal back through is a risk, but we have to trust in the mortals. Our creations are strong and just. She will find him and bring him home, that is her purpose, she can't ignore it. Everything we have done, every piece we have put into place has come down to this; you can't back out on me now."

The sand gently rippled, moving in time with my movements. "She must be told, she must know the truth of her creation. She needs to know the truth about everything, even us."

I blended into a current and began to be swept along the same path as the human ships. My voice echoed through the dark water. "I know, and I will take it upon me to do this. I will go now and visit her. I will make sure she understands. Everything will work. It has to."

Earth slowly sank to the bottom of the sea as he watched me disappear, and his thoughts followed me. "I hope you are right, Sister. For all sakes, I hope you are right."

CHAPTER 30

King Edwin

I stood alone in front of the massive double iron doors that led to the library. It was locked, secured with heavy chains and an iron clasp. I stared at it with the key in my hand. How many times had I stood here as a child? How many others had stood in this spot thinking the same thing? With my heart pounding, I reached forward and inserted the key. At first the clasp wouldn't budge, time and neglect freezing the locking mechanism shut, but I was persistent and kept at it until finally a loud click echoed through the halls. I glanced around timidly. I felt like a child, snooping where he didn't belong, but it was hard to beat old habits. I took a deep breath and grasped the clasp holding the chains. I pulled it apart, letting the chains clatter against the door. I carefully pulled them through the two handles and dropped them in a pile on the floor. Then, with sweaty palms I released the latch on one of the handles and pushed the door inward.

Stale, musty air greeted me, along with darkness. I tentatively stepped into the large room and scanned the back walls, trying to see what I was looking for.

There, almost directly in front of me I saw a tiny sliver of light coming through what must be a window. I let my eyes adjust to the darkness, and then, with the help from the light in the hallway, I gingerly made my way to the window. I knew I should have just lit a torch or lamp but had no idea what was in here and didn't want to risk damaging anything. I finally reached the window with only a couple of bumps, against what felt like a table, I presumed, and I slid the heavy curtain across the window. The noonday sun spilled into the room, revealing a treasure, which was both priceless and powerful.

Volumes of dusty books lined shelves along three of the walls, and what couldn't be placed on shelves had been piled on a single large wooden table in the middle of the room. It was by no means a large collection but it was the most books I had ever seen or even heard of in hundreds of years. I found that I couldn't move and emotion overwhelmed me. I angrily wiped at my eyes and started to walk around the room, touching the dusty volumes, trying to read what was on the spines. Some words I could make out, but because the written word had been beaten out of us for so many years, I just didn't have the education to be able to read them all.

A stifled gasp from the doorway brought my startled attention to Anora, who was standing stock still with her hand over her mouth. I beckoned her into the room and turned my focus back to a particular book that had caught my eye.

My wife stood beside me and looked down at the worn cover. We could tell it was very old, much older than any of the other books here. The front cover seemed to be made from some kind of animal hide, and the pages were yellowed and brittle-looking.

Anora ran her hand carefully over the front of the book, taking off years of dust, and my heart jumped into my throat. There on the cover, drawn in what looked like blood, was a symbol, the same symbol our adopted daughter carried.

I stood motionless, staring at the treasure. "Is that what I think it is? Is that Karah's marking?"

Anora didn't respond. Instead she very gently picked up the book and opened it. I couldn't be sure but I would swear later that the very air in the room stilled, the stone walls seemed to lean closer and even the mighty river outside seemed to still, all watching and listening. Anora studied what was written on the pages, but neither of us could understand anything we were looking at. The whole book was covered in strange symbols and scratches that didn't even resemble any kind of writing we had heard of.

I snorted and began to pace. "Great. We find something that could potentially help us and we can't even read it. We're surrounded by our past but none of it is of any use. I should have listened to my father; I should have left this room alone."

Anora carefully closed the book but didn't return it to the table. It was as if something wouldn't let her, and although I knew nothing of magic, I felt something pulsing around us and centering on that book. I didn't like it one bit.

Anora clutched it close to her breast and turned to face me. "How can you say that? How can you stand there amongst these treasures and not feel a sense of awe? No one has looked upon these in several hundred years. Just think of the knowledge they hold, just think of what we could learn."

I was already on my way back out the door, ignoring my wife's words. Anora quickly followed and paid no attention to my alarmed look when I saw the book still clutched in her hands. I shut the door behind us but did not lock it.

Irritated, I faced my wife. "What good is knowledge if you can't use it? I need help to win this battle, not to teach history lessons."

I knew Anora would have argued further, but Duncan came into view. The soldier stopped before us and bowed. "Sire, forgive my intrusion, but I have just come from the main audience hall. Master Fitch has returned, and he is not alone."

Anora's cry of joy interrupted my response. "Elric, Karah—are they here as well?" Anora's smile faded at Duncan's words.

"No, my lady, they are not with him, I'm sorry." Duncan stopped speaking and had a strange look on his face.

I was in no mood for games. "Spit it out, man. What do you mean he's not alone? Who's with him?"

Duncan just shook his head with wonder in his eyes. "I think maybe you should just come see for yourself."

*

So that was what we did, all the while my frustration growing. The closer we got to the audience hall the noisier it became. It sounded like a large group was gathered in the room, some of which did not seem very happy.

The scene that we finally came upon was nothing I'd expected. Fitch was in the middle of the room surrounded by what seemed to be small children, but they looked nothing like any child I had seen before. One, in fact, held a large bow that was easily as tall as he was slung across his back. He was making obscene gestures toward one of his guards. Fitch had to restrain the boy, causing the other three "children" to raise their voices.

I was in no mood for this and immediately put a stop to their nonsense. "Enough! Master Fitch, although I am happy to see you alive and well, I am not pleased that you have brought this ragtag group of children into my castle. We are in the midst of preparing for a battle; this is no place for them."

The mouthy one with the bow sprung like a cat and landed right in front of me. His strange, almond-shaped eyes threw daggers at me. "That does it! Look, *friend,* for the last time, we are not children! Do we look like children to you? I don't know what your kids look like—I'm guessing by the looks of you not very good—but I'm pretty sure they don't carry weapons, or have hair down to their ankles, or are covered in tattoos, or have eyes the size of plums. Open your damn eyes, man! And I swear the next person who calls me a child is going to get a black eye."

I stared open-mouthed while Anora put her hand over hers to hide her grin.

Fitch, looking quite frustrated, put his hand on the small creature. "Calm down, Deneoes. This is King Edwin and Queen Anora, Elric's parents. Let's everyone calm down, and I'll explain everything."

Deneoes looked up at me and then at Anora. He pointedly ignored me and took Anora's hand in his and gave it a quick kiss. "I can see where Elric gets his looks from—and probably his brains too. I'm glad he had at least one smart parent. My name is Deneoes, and I am a member of the Ywari. I am pleased to meet you."

Anora bowed to the young man. "And I am pleased to meet you. Please forgive my husband, he has been under a lot of stress, as you are well aware."

Anora smiled warmly, but I'd had enough. "Someone better tell me what's going on right now or so help me I'll throw you all in irons."

Fitch came forward and bowed before me. "Your Grace, please forgive all of this confusion. When we arrived today I had no idea that we would cause such turmoil."

The old man turned and encompassed the group standing behind him. "Let me introduce to you Yaleon and his wife, Emtai. The other with them is their son Ossian, and this poor excuse for a mortal is Deneoes, their youngest. They are members of the Ywari, a race long believed extinct. They were once strong and trusted allies with the Gareth Empire. They are here today to offer their assistance."

Although I did not voice it, I was sure everyone could see the doubt on my face. The eldest of these strange creatures, Yaleon, was not about to let it slide. He stepped forward from behind Fitch and came to stand directly in front of me. His voice was deep and full of passion. "King, you lead your people with blind eyes. You don't believe what's standing directly in front of you, a poor trait that runs in your species. Many events have led my people here this day, and it has been brought to my attention that without cooperation among our races, all will be lost. I'm here today to let go of our past and aide you as we once did. Do not doubt our skills or integrity. We will stand with you, but not without your respect."

We stared at each other for long moments, and then, to everyone's surprise including myself, I addressed the Ywari leader. "I'm not going to apologize for actions in the past that were not my own, especially actions I am not aware of, but I will acknowledge the fact that I have been wrong in great many things. I will gladly accept your offer of aide with great thanks and promise that if we make it through this alive, we will try to rebuild what was lost."

Yaleon nodded and returned to stand beside his wife. I then addressed the people in my audience hall. "Now I'm sure you all have work to do. The Ywari people are my guests, and I expect them to be treated the same as any citizen within my borders."

I looked at Fitch and Yaleon. "If you would, gentlemen, there is much that needs to be discussed. Meet in the council chambers in 20 minutes. I will have a representative from the Order of Freedom there as well."

I was about to take my leave and prepare for the meeting, but Anora could hold her tongue no longer. "Master Fitch, please tell me—where are Elric and Karah? Are they well? Did you discover what you needed to save us?"

I stood patiently beside my anxious wife as Fitch said some words to Yaleon, and the remainder of the audience hall emptied out. Fitch came over and stood before my distraught queen and a surprisingly subdued Deneoes. Fitch took her free hand in his as he glanced curiously at the book she clutched to her chest with the other.

I swore I saw his eyes turn golden, but the illusion disappeared when he started to speak. "My lady, I'm sorry that your son is not with us, but the last we saw each other they were both well. It should just be a matter of time before they return."

Fitch's words trailed off as he stared at the book Anora held. He could not seem to take his eyes off it, which was giving me a bad feeling in the pit of my stomach.

Deneoes, however, had no trouble speaking. "You're a real piece of work, you know that? Are you seriously going to stand there and lie to her? After everything we've been through, you still don't know what it's like to be human. I'm starting to think we would all be better off if dragons had never come to our world."

Fitch whirled on the Ywari, causing the young man to jump back. I put my body protectively in front of Anora and waited listening. Fitch's voice rattled the artwork on the walls as he confronted who I thought was his friend.

"This is not the time or place to discuss this, and I've had it with your insolent behaviour. Get out of my sight before I do something I'll regret."

Deneoes stood tall and defiant but the wounded look in his eyes could not be masked. I found myself wanting to defend the little Ywari, but I held my tongue. I had no doubt that he could take care of himself.

Deneoes pulled a mask over his features and his voice was ice as he spoke to Fitch. "My guess is that you already have."

Without another word, Deneoes left the audience hall, leaving Fitch alone with Anora and me. Fitch stood there heaving, trying to calm his raging anger. He drew in several deep breaths and made sure he was composed before turning toward us again. Guilt was written all over the man's face, and it made me wonder what he was hiding and what that display had been about.

Fitch faced Anora once again. She had moved from her spot behind me and stared at him with a mix of fear and anger.

I was the one who spoke for both of us. "What was he talking about? And what the hell just happened?"

Fitch's eyes narrowed and I knew this man was not the same man I had known only days before. This man was cunning, ruthless and not someone I was entirely sure I could trust. His voice was emotionless as he spoke. "Please, I will explain everything, but not here. My friend has a very straightforward approach to things, and I sometimes have a hard time dealing with it. Come, let's go and prepare what is needed for our meeting."

Fitch stole a glance at Anora. "And may I ask, where did you get that book? Is it a personal journal? May I see it?"

Anora kept the book pressed to her chest and backed away from Fitch.

Fitch looked at her with a bemused gaze. "What? After all these years, you don't trust me?"

Anora steadied herself and walked toward the council chambers. I fell in step beside her with Fitch coming to stand on her other side. She took my hand and squeezed it hard. I took that as a signal that she wanted to handle this, so I let her, for now.

Her words were guarded as she spoke. "Forgive me, Master Fitch, but a lot seems to have changed since we last saw each other. You are not the same man I once knew, and until I know what you are keeping from me and from my husband, my secrets remain with me also."

I could tell Fitch didn't like it but he swallowed the argument. "Very well, my queen, I understand."

Our conversation ceased and we made our way to the castle's council chambers.

*

Enthor

The group, which included the king and queen, Duncan (accompanied by several of his officers), two officers from the order of freedom, Yaleon and a few representatives from the general populace all stared at me, unable to speak. The king, shaking his head in disbelief, was the first to voice what was on everyone's minds, I was sure.

"So let me get this straight. One of our missing gods, Mareth, is returning after all these centuries bent on Eiddoril's destruction. The army that is laying a path of death and devastation straight to my doorstep is merely a ruse for the main event. The leader of this marching death is a dragon along with yourself, Karah and all of our other gods we once put our faith in."

The king got up from his chair, placed both hands on the table and looked down the length of it at me. "You bring in these allies that we know nothing about, claiming they once helped us, and more unheard of allies are still yet to arrive? You've put my son in danger by allowing him to travel with a walking time bomb who could at any minute lose control over her power and harm anyone around her?"

The king moved from his place at the head of the table and made his way to where I sat unmoving. Each step Edwin took echoed through the chamber and I watched his anger grow. "You are apparently a creature who has lied and deceived the mortals of this land for centuries, and now you come to us expecting—what? That we should trust you? That I should let you have any say on how to save my people? Forgive me if I have my doubts, but tell me why I should listen to a damn thing you say."

Edwin stood directly beside me looking down, seething with anger. I pushed myself away from the table and stood. I closed my eyes and breathed deeply and when I opened them, again they were not human. My golden reptilian eyes encompassed the gathered group and then came to rest on the king. I had to give him credit;

he didn't even flinch. Edwin and the others watched as I let my body shift only somewhat to my true form. Where there once had been skin was now covered in deep blue and sea-green scales. Claws replaced my fingers and hands, but it was my voice that sent fear through the gathered mortals. It boomed and echoed throughout the room, causing the walls to tremble and the table to shake.

My focus turned on Edwin and I smiled inwardly at the shock rolling off his features. "What I have told you is true. I wish it were not so but it is. I have made many mistakes, but I am done apologising for them. You can either accept what I say as truth or not, I honestly don't care anymore, but know this: if you have any hope of surviving these next few days, I urge you to heed what I have said. Eiddoril needs to change, and it needs to start here."

A small but strong hand gripped my arm and brought my attention down to the Ywari standing beside me. I was happy to see that Deneoes had forgiven my earlier outburst. "Let it go, old man; they haven't had as much time to get used to you as I have, but eventually they will and they too will realize that in your own twisted way you are just trying to help."

I smiled at Deneoes and relaxed. My dragon hid back under human skin and I released my anger, which didn't last long when I saw what Deneoes had brought with him. Everyone in the room gasped and bolted from their seats. They were yelling and pointing at the very scared young dragon trying its hardest to hide behind Deneoes. It was a futile and comical thing to witness.

I yelled for everyone to be still and remain quiet, and then turned my fury on Deneoes. "Are you out of your mind? Of all the pigheaded stunts you have pulled, this has to be the worst. What were you thinking?"

Deneoes, not looking at all concerned, smiled up at me. "Will you relax and trust me for a change? Just listen."

Deneoes turned and spoke quietly to the young dragon. Its eyes instantly brightened and it seemed to get a look of concentration on its face. Suddenly I was hit with images in my mind. Some were from the escape in the keep of the temple. Some showed a young Ywari teaching a dragon how to hunt for food and stay hidden. I saw the short battle that took place when we arrived at the Ywari village carrying with us the hope of my race. Other images were more feelings, feelings of joy and trust that the creature felt around the Ywari. Feelings of wonder that the young dragon felt every time he found something new, and lastly, a feeling of love and a bond that would never be broken. The images and feelings faded, leaving everyone in the room quiet. I looked to all the faces gathered and knew they had just experienced the same thing. I looked back to Deneoes, who was patting a very proud-looking dragon.

I reached out and squeezed Deneoes's shoulder. "Nice job, my boy; well done."

The king looked visibly shaken but like a child who had just discovered a treasure. He leaned heavily against the table and sighed. "I don't know how much more of this I can take. I find myself daring to believe everything you have just told me, but that does not erase what you have done. However, you are right, something needs to change, and I think a small step toward that goal was taken just now. I can't even begin to express how I am feeling right now, how we all must be feeling. I never thought dragons existed, but here I am standing not five feet from one."

Edwin shook his head and went back to his seat at the head of the table. He was still the king and had a job to do no matter how strange it was becoming. I had to admit he was stronger than I had thought, and I was glad to see he was indeed not his ancestors.

Edwin said to me, "All right, dragon, you have our attention. Now that we know what the true threat is, what do we do stop it?"

A breathless messenger burst into the room and nearly fainted from fear at the sight of the startled dragon. The young creature sidestepped, trying to avoid the terrified mortal but only succeeded in scaring him more. The messenger started to back pedal but only managed to knock over a large potted plant and landed square on his backside.

Duncan was closest to him and reached down his hand to help the young man up. "Calm down and look at me."

The young man did not look at Duncan but instead stared fearfully at the baby dragon.

287

Duncan had had enough. "Soldier! So help me if you don't pull yourself together, I'll make sure you're the next thing that dragon eats!"

I stifled a laugh and watched the man's face twist in horror but it brought his mind back to reality and why he had come in the first place. He shakily saluted Duncan. The king's commander tried to control his frustration. "Now tell me why you have come. What has happened?"

Without taking his eyes from his commander the messenger spit out his words through chattering teeth. "Ships sir . . . three of them . . . coming into the docks . . . and redheaded giants, hundreds of them. They are taking over the beach. They say they won't speak to anyone except Prince Elric."

Duncan looked to me for conformation. I stiffly nodded. "It's the Kanarah warriors that I spoke of. Elric must have convinced them to help. As to the ships, I am afraid I do not know who that is."

Anora rose from her seat. "The sails, what colour are they? Did you see any kind of markings?"

The young soldier raised his voice so his queen could hear his words. "They are still too far off to tell, but what looks like a giant bird head decorates the bow."

Anora's voice raised an octave as she tried to contain her nerves. "Those are my brother's ships—Clorynina has sent aide. I was so afraid he would not heed my message."

Edwin looked at her sharply. "What message? I did not approve any message to be sent to Clorynina. I did not even want our son going there to seek aide. Your brother is in the Dark Lord's back pocket. What makes you think we can trust him?"

Anora's face flushed a deep red, and she balled her hands into fists.

I spoke before she could explode on her husband. "Forgive me, Sire, but you should not be looking for enemies where they do not exist, we have enough problems. Let's get down to docks and see if we can sort out what's going on."

Deneoes was already heading out the door with his dragon right behind him. "Yeah, I agree, we need to let Elric and Red know what's going on. They're not going to be happy."

I lowered my face so Deneoes did not see the guilt in my eyes. I had not yet told my friend that I had already sent word to Nalin to keep Karah as far away from here as possible. I prayed they had listened or this was going to be a very difficult reunion. I wasn't sure what I was going to do if I was forced to take care of this myself. It was a horrible, selfish thought but I couldn't help it.

The crowd in the council chambers began to disperse. Anora stormed past her husband and hurried to catch up with Deneoes. The king started to protest but I stopped him.

"Let her be. Your words hurt her deeply. You need to give her time to calm down. There is something I need to ask you though. That book she is carrying, where did it come from? It surprises me that the two of you are so openly displaying the fact that you even have any books, but I suppose under the circumstances now it does not really matter."

Edwin pulled his eyes away from his wife and looked at me. I could see the conflict in his eyes and knew he no longer trusted me. He hesitated for only a moment and then decided to tell me what he had done.

"I thought I would find answers in the family library. We were in there this morning. I must admit I was spellbound by what I saw in there but quickly realized I honestly don't have a clue what most of the books say. Anora found that one lying on the table. It's very old and strange. It gives off an energy that I can't explain. Frankly, it gave me the creeps, but Anora was captivated by it. We could not understand anything that was written inside. They were some sort of symbols and random scratches, nothing like what I have ever seen to depict a language. There's something else that you might find of interest. On the front cover, written in what seems like dried blood, is the symbol that Karah carries on her face. Do you know where this book came from? Have you have heard of it before?"

My eyes widened and glimmered a little and the king stepped back, afraid I suppose that I would lose control again. I was not angry though, only intrigued. "This is a great mystery because no mortal alive knew of that symbol. The only reason people came to know of it is my made-up prophecy. I know of no recorded writing that matches your description of the known mortals of this land. It almost sounds like . . . No, that couldn't be possible."

I left the room and entered the hallway. The king practically had to run to keep pace. His voice trailed behind me. "What? What are you thinking? Is this something I should be worried about?"

I continued on my hurried pace out of the keep and toward the stables. If we were going to get to the docks before sunset, we needed to hurry. I paused long enough to grab two fresh mounts from the stable hand who had apparently been expecting us, and helped the king mount up. My bright dragon eyes fixed on the king.

"If this book was written from when I think it was, then Anora may very well hold the key to saving us all. I don't know how it got here or how it survived all this time, but I am willing to bet that it was written by a dragon and it may hold the answers I have been searching for centuries. I need to see that book."

I left out the part that I suspected it to be Ililsaya's, and if I was correct it could hold the key to finally discovering what was so important about her.

Without further discussion, we took off and made our way to Aserah's small port.

CHAPTER 31

Karah

Something wet kept splashing my face, and my feet kept getting wet as if I was lying on a beach letting the waves tickle my toes. I opened my eyes and sat up, feeling surprisingly well. I glanced around and found that I was indeed on a beach. My fingers sank into the pure white crystalline sand, and I looked out to sea as far as my eyes would reach. The sun was low in the sky and was rapidly disappearing. The scene was peaceful and beautiful but very *wrong*. I started to panic as the memories of my current life came back to me. Was I dead, or was I having another vision from my past? A voice off to my left made me jump, and I turned to look upon a small girl—made out of water.

"Do not be alarmed, Sister; I am not here to frighten you. We have been searching for you for a long time. You are dreaming, and I come to you with the answers you have been searching for."

I blinked hard and made my mouth work. "You are the element of water but are not what I expected. Why did you call me 'sister,' and why have you waited all this time to help me?"

The element of water moved until it was directly in front of me. It reminded me of my sword and how it moved with the sea. Her words flowed from her like lazy waves lapping at a shore. "This will be hard for you to accept, especially now that you have been corrupted by mortal flesh for so long. You were always very stubborn, and even when you knew who you were you wouldn't accept it. It was your actions to avoid your purpose that caused this prison to happen, but I am here to rectify those mistakes. You are needed to destroy the dark dragon. He has become too powerful, and you have helped him gain the power to hurt us."

Nothing this floating bubble of liquid was making any sense, and it was beginning to tick me off. "Look, kid, I've had a hell of a past few weeks, so if you don't mind, could you please just spit it out? This whole dragon secrecy thing is getting old."

Water actually smiled and then carefully came closer to the beach. She reached out her watery hand and touched my forehead. A wave of peace settled over my mind and I focused on nothing but the water.

Then it spoke, and the sense of peace vanished. "Fine. You want the truth, Sister, then I shall give it to you."

There was a long pause as the element stared into my eyes. "You are our sister, travelling in dragon skin. You are the fifth element."

My eyes widened and I tried desperately to pull away from water, but I couldn't move and the watery hand remained fixed on my forehead.

"I see that you must see things for yourself. I am sorry to do this to you, but it is necessary for you to remember. This will be painful."

Before I could even mouth a rejection, images started to slam into my mind. The wall that had stood for so long, holding back all of my memories came crashing down. Water released me, and I dropped to the sand holding my head and silently screaming in pain. I squeezed my eyes shut and watched as hundreds of memories, spanning centuries, flashed before my eyes. Friends I had known and loved died before me; sacrifices made to protect me danced in my mind. I saw everything, felt every emotion. I saw myself denying who I was, rebelling against my maker, all because I wanted a different life. My soul was ripped open and it lay inside me in tatters.

Finally, after what seemed like hours, my mind quieted and I opened my eyes. Water still stood on the sea watching me. I slowly sat up and gathered my knees to my chest. I looked up and stared at my brethren with contempt.

Water shifted anxiously. "Do you remember? Have you seen all that you must see? Do you know what you must do?"

I sighed heavily as the immense weight of my situation settled around my human heart. "Yes, Sister, I remember, and I will not run any longer. I have caused enough pain with my selfishness. I will find him, and I will bring him home."

Water nodded and began to sink into the sea. "Now you must wake up. I have been here too long. You are not alone, my sister; we will stand by you and our creations, we will protect them as best we can while you are gone, but you must explain to them that we are a part of destruction as well as life. We will have no choice but to follow our mother's wishes. We can resist some but she will use us to strike at you and the ones you care for. She has been waiting for this for centuries, and she will not be denied. The war of creation has begun."

I nodded my understanding and closed my eyes, welcoming the darkness and the peace that I would soon have to give up.

*

Enthor

King Edwin and I arrived at Aserah's small docks just before dusk. In the fading light, we could just make out the sails of the three ships that were anchored just outside the small cove. Several smaller boats loaded with people were already starting to unload on the shore. They were indeed from Clorynina, and the look on King Edwin's face did not bode well for avoiding a confrontation. The majority of the Order of Freedom were camped here, as well as the Ywari warriors that had come. The situation was not a peaceful one, especially now that they were joined by a large group of Kannarah warriors. One in particular I recognized as Tilan, Miara's brother, and he was having quite a heated debate with Duncan.

"Stand down, you barbarian. I will not have you speak to the queen in such a disrespectful manner. If you would only calm down I will find out what is going on."

Tilan bristled at the "barbarian" comment and looked as if he meant to strike at Duncan, but then he spied the two newcomers and focused his wrath on me in particular. "You—you're the cause of this mess again. We should have listened to our elders and not trusted you. Now my sister is dead, and we are here to fight for an absent prince. Where are Prince Elric and Jaitem? They said they would meet us here. Explain things now or I lead my people back to our home."

I dismounted and approached the distraught Kanarah. I looked up into his fierce eyes and tried not to be angry for being blamed yet again for all the troubles in the world.

"I am sorry to hear of Miara's death. She was a brave woman and her loss will be remembered. I am not aware of the arrangements that you have made with Elric. We have been separated for many days, but this is his father, King Edwin, and any plans you had with Elric you can trust them to him."

A new voice cut through the air with contempt, and rage flashed through my soul.

"*Trust?* That is an interesting word to be coming from your mouth. Do you even know what that means?"

I turned to see Elric, Jaitem, Nalin and several others coming toward the gathered group. Anora, abandoning her courtly appearances, flung herself into her son's arms. Elric hugged her back, but the heat in his eyes never left my face. He gently pushed his mother aside and continued his trek to stand before me. Everyone stood out of the way sensing the tension that hung between us. Not even Deneoes, who was overjoyed at seeing his friend, dared set foot between the prince and me.

I tried very hard to remain calm. "Elric, I am glad to see you well. You have done well, my boy. I'm proud of you."

Elric drew his sword and rested the tip of the blade under my chin. Several onlookers gasped and Deneoes stepped forward but I held out my hand and silenced all of them. No one was sure what was going on, but no one wanted to cross me. My eyes gleamed a brilliant gold as I faced the young prince. "It seems that I am in the dark about your hostility toward me. Why don't you calm down and we can talk?"

Elric didn't move, and I was rapidly losing control. Elric's words bit into my skin. "You know very well where my anger comes from. I know the truth about everything. I know the truth about Karah, and I know why you wanted me to keep her away from here. You abandoned her and took the easy way out."

My eyes widened briefly but I quickly regained control. I was curious to know how Elric had found this out.

Deneoes, however, was furious. "What the hell is he talking about? Does this have something to do with what that dragon told you in the caves? You told me not to worry, that you would figure something out. Damn! I never should have trusted you."

Resentment dripped from my mouth. "I had no choice. It was a decision I did not make lightly. I care for her just as deeply if not more than you do, but I had to think of Eiddoril, I had to try and save it."

Elric pressed harder on the sword and a small bead of blood formed under my chin. "Do not stand there and speak to me of love; you don't understand the concept. If you did you would not have willingly sacrificed someone you claimed to be your daughter without a fight. I should just kill you now and save Mareth the trouble."

I finally stepped back from the sword at my throat and started to grow in size. I did not try to mask the anger that was boiling to the surface. "We both know this is a fight you can't win. You know I'm right. If Karah is allowed to be rejoined with her true form, then all will be lost. She is not strong enough to stop him. No one is." I put force behind my words, "Step back, prince, or I will retaliate."

Elric raised his sword ready to strike, but a voice, which I had hoped would not be heard, penetrated the tension between us.

"Elric, stop. Enthor has been wrong about a great many things, but this is my fault and it is time I accepted that responsibility."

Everyone looked to see who had spoken, but I already knew the answer. Elric let his arm hang limp at his side as he turned to face the woman he loved.

"Karah! You're awake and walking. What happened? Your body was damaged beyond our healer's capability. They said you would not wake again."

Elric started toward her but she held out her hand to stop him. But it was the cold, uncaring look in her eyes that stopped him dead in his tracks. "Please don't, I can't do this anymore. I am not who you think I am. I am not Karah . . . not any more."

Elric threw his hands up in frustration, and I stood beside the wounded prince, our conflict forgotten for the moment. I looked at the woman standing before me. "Ililsaya, is that you? How did this happen?"

The creature before me sighed but I saw strength in her eyes that I had not seen for a long time.

When she spoke, it was with great emotion. "The element of water came to me and healed this body and restored all of my memories. I remember who I am, and most importantly *what* I am. There is much I need to tell you and much I need to do. None of it you will like, but most importantly you all need to know that Mareth and Nubossa are not your biggest threat."

Ililsaya looked at all gathered around her, her voice growing in volume. "There is a being who you can call Destruction, if you like, who is behind all of this, and she is nothing compared to what we have ever faced. She wants to destroy this world, as she has done several times before, and I am the only one who can stop her."

CHAPTER 32

Ililsaya

The main audience hall filled to capacity—along with my growing anxiety. Lost memories were still coming back to me in painful fragments and it was hard to look upon the different races that had once trusted me without feeling guilty. My selfish actions nearly sent whole groups of mortals into extinction, and now it was my job to convince them to trust me again. It was a task I was not sure could be accomplished.

Loneliness crept into my heart as I stood at the head of the table where the king should have sat; instead, the royal family, including my beloved Elric, sat on either side of me. I could feel the heat of Elric's eyes constantly upon me, but if I was going to get through this, I could not afford to have any more distractions—not now and perhaps not ever.

The room quieted and all eyes focussed on me. It was time. I closed my eyes and cautiously reached inside myself to touch on my power, the power that could change everything. When I opened my eyes I called to my brethren. Instantly the torches that lit the room roared to life. One in particular, the one closet to the door, grew in size until it was the shape and size of a Ywari. It stood rooted to the iron sconce, flickering and sputtering in agitation, its arms crossed in front of its fiery chest. A panicked cry from an innocent onlooker was the only warning that Earth gave for his arrival. A portion of the wall itself came to life and took humanoid form, leaning casually on the door beside fire. A small wind tunnel began to form to my right, causing debris and dust to form into the somewhat recognizable shape of air, and lastly I drew my sword, which was already rippling and flowing like the sea. All though the surface of the blade remained flat, the image of a young girl appeared on its surface. I bowed my head to each.

"Forgive me, my brothers and sister for this call, but if I am to gain these mortals' trust I need them to know and see the truth. It is time our story was told."

Water was the first to speak. "Speak quickly, my sister. We cannot be here for long, but I understand why you have called us here. The mortals should have been made aware of us long before this. I hope you know what you are doing."

I hoped I did too.

I encompassed the group gathered in the room and saw looks of terror and wonder. My gaze came to rest on Enthor, whose dragon eyes were bright with anticipation. He nodded once at me and then with the help of his magic I let everyone in the room see as well as hear my tale.

"I apologize for this sudden display, but it is necessary that you all understand what is at stake. This is not a cheap magic trick, but in reality the cause of your existence. These four beings—Earth, fire, water and air—are what keep this world alive, including all of you."

I let the magic take over, and everything disappeared as we were all thrown into the past.

Eons ago, before time itself, there was nothing, only space and energy. This energy would move through time and space uninhibited, never touching, but one day two of those energies collided with each other and a powerful chain reaction produced our world. One of these energies was a positive, creating life, and the other was a negative causing the other end of the scale, destruction. Each is needed to maintain a balance. You cannot have life without death, and through destruction comes new life. It is a continuing circle that should never be broken.

As this new world grew, the two energies started to become aware and they formed into sentient beings. They had this new creation but they did not know what to do with it so they created the four elements. Earth, fire, water and air were born and through these elements, creation was born.

The elements' sole purpose is to create, and that is what they did. They made the world the way they thought was best. The elements created and Life infused them with his energy, creating souls.

Lands, water bodies and creatures were created, the first being dragons. Dragons were the elements' first creatures, so naturally they wanted them to be perfect in every way, but they were not. They were greedy, selfish, cruel and arrogant, and the fighting that they caused started a chain of events that mortals and immortals have been trapped in ever since.

The chaos that dragons caused started to tip the balance to the negative side of energy. Destruction was pleased, and something unexpected happened: she grew fat on the power that fed her through the dying world. The elements tried to fix their mistakes. They banished dragons to another state of being, the immortal realm, and started over with new creatures, but Destruction was left hungry and she craved more. Life and Destruction had always agreed not to interfere with their children's world but Destruction broke that truce. She began to interfere with the elements' creations, causing them to fight and to destroy, feeding her uncontrollable need for negative power. The elements were forced to banish more and more of their creations to the immortal realm and rebuild this world over and over.

The positive energy, Life, had had enough. In his attempt to try to control Destruction he stopped creating immortal life energies and created something new, life energy much more fragile and weak but easily reproduced. He had hoped that Destruction would grow bored with the energies that could not provide her with enough power, but it did not work. If anything, it made things worse. Finally, in desperation Life refused to create any life energy in any form so that when Destruction destroyed everything one finale time she would have nothing left and would, in a sense, starve.

However, Destruction had already become too powerful, and she was able to create on her own a being that she alone could control. The being is known as Death, and his realm is the Duggati.

In this realm, Death was able to recycle life energy. Instead of it resting and having peace, the life energy is forced back out into the mortal realm to be used for something else, leaving Destruction with an endless supply of chaos to feed her. Life failed in his attempt to control Destruction.

Destruction became more powerful and Life became weaker. There was no longer a need for him and he became obsolete. Destruction was able to lock away Life on the immortal realm, and there he has been trapped for centuries.

That was how this world existed for a time. The elements were forced to create and destroy over and over, feeding Destruction, and all would have been lost if not for the timely intervention of dragons once again. Dragons came back to the world, which is now known as Eiddoril, and with them, they brought a weapon.

Life was fond of dragons, and through them he saw a way he could possibly help his children and the mortals of the world, so with the last of his strength and energy he created a being. This being was an extension of himself able to create life energy. Life knew that this being would be a target as soon as it re-entered the mortal realm, so he placed the being inside a dragon and hoped that in time that dragon would start to heal this world and have enough power to come back and save him from his prison.

My voice cut through the magic and startled everyone. "That dragon was me, and I have failed miserably."

Shocked voices and murmurs filled the room, shattering the images that Enthor and the elements were projecting. I looked Enthor in his golden dragon eyes and was surprised to see jealousy and contempt. The elements, seeing that they were no longer needed, faded back into their creations and left me alone to deal with the mortals.

No one said anything until Anora spoke. She reached over and squeezed my hand. "Tell us what happened, child. We deserve to know. Do not be afraid; it is not an easy task to hold the fate of so many lives in your hands. Believe me I know, but we do what we must even if we hurt the ones we love."

I looked down at my adoptive mother, gave her a sad smile and squeezed her hand back. I sat heavily in the chair and tried to justify my past actions. "Things did not go according to Life's plan. His first mistake was my vessel's parents. Mareth was a lit fuse ready to explode. He hated the elements for what they did to us, and nothing filled his mind but revenge. Not long after we crossed over back into the mortal realm, Destruction saw a potential new plaything. She was the one who allowed him access into Duggati, where he learned the power of life-energy manipulation. However, something happened that surprised her. Death, taking his role in this world very seriously, rebelled against Destruction and closed all access into Duggati except for him. He also barred any life energy access that had been corrupted by Mareth and then later Nubossa."

I nervously ran my fingers through my human hair. "That is why Eiddoril is dying. Mareth and Nubossa have been stealing and using life energy for centuries. What they don't use is not allowed back to Duggati to be reused, so essentially we are running out of souls, and without a source to create new ones this world will cease to exist and there will be no more rebuilding."

I looked out across my audience and saw the horror of my words sink in. No one spoke, so I continued. "Ashia, your god of light, saw what was happening and she pleaded with the elements to help her, because through her mating bond she was linked to Mareth. By this time she knew she was with child and wanted to protect it. Again Death surprised everyone, and for reasons of its own removed Ashia's immortal life energy and replaced it with one of his mortal ones."

I caught the expression on Enthor's face from the corner of my eye, and what I saw confused me. He was so full of anger I thought he was going to change forms right there.

I tried to ignore him but uncertainty filled my voice. "Her act of selfishness had more of an effect on me than even I wanted to admit. When I was born Ashia knew something was different about me. The first and most obvious was the marking that covered most of my face. Everyone assumed it marked me as part of Mareth and Ashia, but it was really a symbol of what I truly was—Destruction and Life combined into one. I was balance. I knew right from the moment I was hatched what I was and how to hide myself. I knew my purpose, what I was supposed to do, but I rejected it, I was afraid."

I hugged my human body as memories from that time all came flooding back. "I don't know if it was the mortal soul that Ashia gained that infected me or if I was just not like the other dragons, but I developed emotions and learned to love. I was so afraid of being discovered that I rarely ever used my powers. Mostly I used them to heal the tortured souls, allowing them access into Duggati. The elements tried many times to get me to do what our father had intended, for they realized who I truly was, but I was too afraid and stubborn, and then eventually I fell in love."

I stopped talking and drew in a shaky breath. My eyes fell to Elric, who was watching me with pain in his eyes. My human heart broke into a million tiny pieces and I leaned my head back shutting my eyes to the world.

"His name was Seth and he was at the time the son of King Gareth. I came across him dying in a field not far from his home. He had been ambushed by one of Nubossa's raiding parties and stabbed with a blood blade. The wound had not been fatal but his life energy was slowly being consumed. I should have left him, I should have just walked away, but I couldn't. Something drew me to him and I saved his life. We met in secret after that, trying to keep our affair from being discovered. He knew me only has Ililsaya the dragon, the saviour left behind by Ashia herself to protect the land from Nubossa; he did not truly know what I was. Others found out about us, and we were urged to end our relationship, but being the fools we were we ignored them, and it was that ignorance, that stubborn denial of my destiny that sealed my own doom."

I sat up and stared straight at Enthor. He held my gaze as I poured my soul out. "Then one day it all ended. Seth was killed, and I was captured, forced into a mortal body, sealing my powers away forever. It turned out that Destruction knew about me after all. Mareth had discovered things about me, and through those observations, Destruction was able to figure out what I truly was.

Therefore, she put a new plan into action. After Mareth returned to the immortal realm to raise her army, she focused her attention on Nubossa. She gave him the power to trap me in a human body, waiting for the time when Mareth would be ready to return to this world, bringing with him enough chaos to feed her for many years. Everything that has happened has been her design; she has been planning this for hundreds of years and I did nothing to stop her, all because I could not control my foolish tendencies. I would ask for your forgiveness but I know I do not deserve it. Because of me, many lives have been lost and have suffered and this world may never recover. However, I have a chance now to set things right. When the doorway again opens, I will travel into the immortal realm and find my father. I will bring him back, and together we will stop Destruction."

King Edwin, after remaining quiet this whole time cleared his throat and spoke softly. "And what of us? How do we stop Mareth *and* the Dark Lord without you? If you leave we will be defenceless. You must tell us what to do."

I tore my gaze away from the older dragon and rested it on the king. I was shocked that I did not see open hostility in his face and of those gathered around me. There was anger, yes, but there was also determination and comradery. I almost cried at the sight.

I said, "You will not be alone. You have Enthor, and the elements will help you where they can. They are ready to take a stand against Destruction, but you must understand that she is part of them as well. They will not be able to resist her call. The natural disasters that have been plaguing us will get worse. As for Mareth, I have no intention of letting him pass through that gate. Once I am joined with my dragon, I will have no problem keeping up with him. He has no idea what I'm truly capable of. I'm sorry I don't have more of a plan but the elements have been putting their faith in you for a long time. They have positioned you all and believe that you can win this fight, and so do I. Nubossa's army is your biggest threat; you must keep them at bay and give me enough time to gain access into the immortal realm."

Nalin, who was standing near the back of the room, asked a very good question.

"What about the Dark Lord? We saw him go down into the sea. What if he's dead? How will you get back if the gate doesn't open from our side?"

I shook my head. "I will not hold out hope that Nubossa is dead. Ashia is a powerful dragon, but she was trapped in human form for a long time. She may have failed, or they both may have perished, which is why I have come up with a secondary plan."

I paused and faced Enthor. "Nubossa is not needed for the gate to be opened. I know the spell that is required to open the gate, and all I need is my true form."

My focus again shifted to the king. "I need to get into the heart of Nubossa's army and bring the advantage back to our side. They are bringing it here and it will be heavily guarded. As for the spell, I can teach it to Enthor and with the help of the elements the gate should open."

"And just how are you planning on getting through thousands of armed soldiers on your own? You may be a super dragon, but I'm betting you still can't use your full powers. You're going to need some help." Deneoes sat on top of the table near the end and mischievously watched me while I tried to figure out how to keep my friends from getting involved. It was, as it turned out, an impossible task.

Jaitem, Nalin and even Elric came forward, but it was Elric who spoke for them. "No, you're not going alone. You will have a better chance with help. Besides, it will give us a chance to see what we're up against. The more information we know the better equipped we will be."

Elric didn't look at me when he spoke and his words were emotionless. I tried to ignore the horrible feeling in my mortal stomach and turned toward the king.

"King Edwin, this is your kingdom and you should have some say in this. I am going no matter what, but it is the defence of this city that concerns the rest of you. What are your thoughts?"

The king motioned toward his son. "My son is right. You can't go alone, and as much as I would like to there is no way I can keep him from going. As you have already pointed out this is no longer just my problem. What happens in the next 36 hours will ultimately affect all of Eiddoril. I stand behind you and the rest of the races gathered here today. It is time we fight and no matter what the outcome at least we gave everything we have."

Edwin rose and addressed the crowd. "I suggest we all retire for what is left of this night. First thing in the morning, we meet and go over a plan to get Ililsaya into this army. Final preparations are being made as we speak and the final defences of this city will be discussed then as well. Try and get some sleep, my friends, this may be the last opportunity for it."

The king reached down, gave my shoulder a squeeze and then made his way out of the council chambers. The room emptied pretty quickly with conversations of what they had just heard and witnessed, and I watched as Elric left without even a backward glance at me. I was not surprised. I deserved no better, but it still hurt and I found myself glued to my chair, unable to move, staring at the door he had just walked through. Even Enthor had ignored me, lost in his own thoughts.

A gentle voice beside me brought me back to reality. "Elric is hurting right now; give him time, and he'll come around."

I turned to look at Anora and fought back tears. Curse this mortal body and all its weaknesses. "I don't want him to come around. He's better off this way. We were chasing after a dream that simply cannot come true. My path lies different from his and I can't let myself be distracted by foolish desires any more."

I stood, fully intending to leave but Anora reached out and grabbed my hand. "Love is not foolish. Yes, fools may fall in love but it is not foolish. Love is powerful and sometimes it is the one thing that keeps us alive. Don't dismiss it because it is difficult, most things worth having usually are. The two of you will find a way. You must believe that."

The look of hope and sincerity in Anora's eyes almost made me believe, but I was done fooling myself. I couldn't bring myself to discuss it any more so I gently pulled away from her and said my goodbyes.

However, before I was out the door she came running after me. "Wait—I have something for you. I don't know how I know that it's yours, but I found something yesterday that you may want."

Curiously, I turned and watched as Anora brought forward an old book. I didn't recognize it at first, but I took it and turned it over to see the front cover and my breath caught in my throat.

My voice shook with emotion but I managed a response. "This is my journal; I thought it would have been lost when Gareth moved his people. I sent this to Seth. I . . ."

I couldn't finish. I gave Anora a quick hug and fled down the hall as quickly as I could toward my room.

*

Nubossa

Shifting and flexing my tight muscles, I did my best to move in the small confines of the cave. I was aware of my surroundings but could not remember how long I had been here. Memories of battling Ashia and then plunging into the sea filled my mind. I had finally beaten that meddling, useless beast and sought out shelter in a nearby cave. I went as far below the earth's surface as I could, searching for the warmth that comes from far below, and then went into a deep, restorative sleep, using my magic to heal my wounds. Now I was hungry and the need for revenge burned bright in my blackened soul.

I slowly made my way back out into world and scanned my surroundings. Night was deep along its path to morning and the skies were dark with clouds. The nearby sea filled the night with a constant beat, and I watched a Ristiaper circle once and then fly out toward the water to find food. Betrayal suddenly crossed my mind but I pushed the feeling aside. I had more important things to be concerned about.

I spread my massive dark wings and inspected my body, confirming that all of my wounds had healed. Ashia had surprised me. She had indeed been a powerful dragon, but thanks to being trapped in human form for so long, it had greatly diminished her strength. I still had no idea how she'd managed to escape my iron shackle but I had no doubt it had something to do with that wretched creature, Ililsaya. Just thinking her name made my blood boil and I screamed my fury into the night air.

Through my fury, I began to realize a strange buzzing sound charging the air around me. I shook my horned head to try to rid myself of the strange sound but it only got louder and even painful. It got so intense that I was forced down to the sandy beach covering my head with my front claws. At first I thought it was my master, but this felt different and was more powerful. Then, just as quickly as it had come, it was gone.

I stood with a renewed purpose. I didn't know how I knew but I realized I knew exactly where to find Ililsaya and what I should do next. It was like someone pulled back a curtain and the solution to all my problems was there smiling at me. My evil red eyes shined with malice as I took to the skies in search of energy. It did not take me long to come across a small farm. It looked as though they raised goats, the only animal suited to living this close to the cliffs.

The cries of the dying animals brought the residents of the home out into the night, and then all that could be heard was the agonizing screams of the doomed mortals feeding the soul of a hungry monster.

CHAPTER 33

Ililsaya

I sat cross-legged on my bed, staring at the book I held in my lap. I had only lit one candle, which was now throwing shadows around the room as it wavered in the breeze coming from the open window. It was an unusually warm night for this time of year but it was overcast. The moon and stars were hidden from view, making the night dark and bleak, kind of like the way my soul felt right now. I knew I should have taken the king's advice and tried to sleep, but sleep was the farthest thing from my mind.

I slowly opened my journal with shaky hands and began to skim through the pages I had written so many years ago. Images and memories came and went as I read. I don't really know why I ever started keeping a journal, it was such a mortal thing to do, but I must have felt it was necessary. At least an hour passed before I came to my last entry. I had written it to Seth. I had finally come to the decision that I needed to follow my destiny. The war with Nubossa was not going well and I knew I had the power to stop it. I was too much of a coward to face Seth and tell him the truth, so I sent my journal to him through a messenger. I should have known that something was not right when my messenger came to me that very same night and begged me to meet with the prince in the morning. She had said that I at least owed him a proper farewell. I hated myself for being so weak. Maybe if I just been strong enough to face him, he would have lived, but I guess I would never know. I wiped at my eyes and read my final goodbye to my prince.

My dearest Seth,

I am sorry, my love, that I do not have the courage to say what is needed to your face. If I were standing before you now I would not have the strength or the will to tell you that this has to end. Even writing it fills my heart with such sorrow I am afraid I will never recover. I have not been honest with you. My great difference from you has always been the fact that I am dragon, but there is something deeper. I was born for a purpose, a purpose that I have hidden from for centuries, but I can hide no longer. Nubossa is winning, but I know how to stop him. I can't tell you the details because it would put you in more danger than you are already in, but you must trust that I know what I'm doing and would not have made this decision lightly.

By the time you read this I will have already departed, but I will return as quickly as possible. I know the key to stopping this war and I know where to find it, I just need you to trust me. I will always keep you close to my heart and there will never be a day that goes by that I will not regret the pain I have caused you. I don't know if there can ever be a future for us but I promise that when I return, we can try. Farewell, my prince. Thank you for loving me and showing me that it didn't matter who we were, that as long as we had each other it was enough. Remember me, my love, and forgive me.

Till we meet again,
Ililsaya

I gently closed the worn book and held it close to my heart. I squeezed my eyes shut and willed the tears not to come, but a soft knock on my door made me wish for something else: to disappear. I knew who it was without even asking. I hesitated for only a minute before I swallowed my fear and told Elric to come in.

He silently pushed open the door and stepped inside and then quickly shut the door behind him. He walked over to my dressing table, pulled the chair over beside my bed and heavily sat down. He looked horrible. His hair was unkempt, and he still hadn't shaved. He had removed his travelling clothes and was now dressed in a plain white shirt with worn hide pants. However, it was his eyes that showed how much pain he was in and how tired he was. They were red rimmed and bloodshot, and they sent a dagger straight through my heart. His voice, however, was calm and steady.

"We need to talk, and I'm not leaving this room until we do. Now do you want to start or shall I?"

I put my book aside and sat with my head down.

Elric reached forward and gently lifted my face back up and made me look at him. "I guess that means I start. Okay, I can deal with that."

He gave me a small smile, which gave me the courage to unlock my tongue. I reached up and took his hand in mine and prayed I wouldn't start crying—not yet anyway. "No, I'll start; I at least owe you that. I'm sorry I was so cold to you today. I didn't know what else to do. I figured that once you found out the truth about me, it wouldn't matter anyway. I wouldn't blame you if you never wanted to speak to me again, and in a way I wish you wouldn't. This will never get easier, and, in fact, it will only get harder from here. My selfish acts have caused nothing but pain, and I will do it no longer. Please tell me you understand; please tell me you will not make this any harder than it has to be."

Elric studied my face for a minute and then stood and walked over to my open window. He was impossible to read so I had no idea what he was thinking. Elric sighed and swore under his breath. "I knew I should have started, but I was trying to be a gentleman. Now, if you're through being a martyr, I have a few things I'd like to say."

He turned back toward me, and for once I kept my mouth shut. "You, my dear, are one of the most stubborn, hot tempered, foolish women I have ever met, and I am quite sure that my life would have been much easier if we had never met."

My eyes widened at the sudden insults, but Elric wasn't finished. He sat beside me on my bed and stared down at his hands in his lap.

"But every day I thank whatever divine intervention brought you to me. I love you, and for reasons that I can't possibly explain to you, I will never stop. You fill a space in my soul that I had no idea needed filling and I will stand by you until Eiddoril crumbles around us. You can sit there and tell me the million reasons why we shouldn't be together and try to convince yourself that those reasons are true, but I want you to look me in the eye and tell me you don't feel the same way. Tell me you don't love me, and I will walk out that door and never bring it up again."

He looked up at me with tears and his soul in his eyes. I leaned forward so that our foreheads were touching and gently wiped his cheek with my trembling hand. "I can't. I do love you, more than I ever thought I could again, but what do we do now, how can we possibly make this work? I have to leave, and where I'm going you can't follow. I may fail and never return and because I was so selfish and scared to do what I was born to in the beginning, so many lives have suffered and been lost. I don't know if I can handle it any more. I can't lose you again."

Elric kissed my tears that were now freely running down my cheeks. He cupped my face with his hands and moved so that our bodies were almost touching.

"I don't know what we're going to do, but just for tonight let's pretend that none of it matters. Just for tonight, let's just be together. I'm not Seth; maybe we share some of the same qualities but I am not him. You won't lose me."

I hesitated for only a second and then gave in to my mortal desires. I closed the gap between us, and just for that one night I forgot everything—and it was enough just to be loved.

*

We gathered early the following morning in the courtyard. The skies were still overcast but thankfully it was not raining. A thick fog clung to everything and the morning air had an oppressive humidity to it that was quite unusual for this time of year. It was a very unsettling morning and did not bode well for things to come. I focused my attention on the king and Duncan as they ran down the list of preparations to make ready for war.

Edwin's voice carried through the morning air. "Now everything that could be harvested from the fields has been and is stored inside the keep. If it comes down to it, we should have enough rations to last us I'm hoping until spring even with all the extra mouths to feed. As of tonight, I am ordering everyone across the bridge and inside the inner ward behind castle walls. It will be tight and definitely not the best living conditions but it will have to do. The shops and other merchants have been cleared to make space for makeshift tents for housing and for the wounded. The Order of Freedom has conferred with my own soldiers, and they have been stationed at tactical points surrounding the castle. The Kanarah and the Ywari will be part of the main fighting force, but I am afraid it will not be enough."

The king turned worried eyes to me. "Enthor, Ililsaya, you have both been in battle with the Dark Lord before. What do you think his plan will be, and do either of you have any other ideas for defending Gareth?"

The elder dragon spoke first. "I'm afraid the sheer size of Nubossa's army will be your greatest obstacle. He will be relying on numbers to wear you down and deplete your resources. Due to the diverse species he has employed within his ranks, you'll have to adapt quickly to their various fighting skills."

I added my own opinion. "The Litui will be a grave threat. Not a lot is known about them because of their mysterious origin, but we do know they're able to fight both in the water and on land, so the river will offer no protection from them. The Hautur are always a guessing game. I have no idea which form they will take. They could be humans, Litui or other creatures that reside in the Barren Waste. But they are vulnerable during a change, which you already know."

Enthor nodded and picked up the conversation again. "The bulk of his army will more than likely try to storm the bridge using each other as shields. Their numbers will make it quite easy to get across and take control of the bridge, allowing the humans access across. I am going to suggest we destroy the bridge before they can make use of it."

The king was shocked. "Are you saying I need to destroy the only access into the city? We'll be trapped. The only other way out of Gareth is the underground tunnels that lead out behind the castle and into the mountains. If the castle is taken, how would we get the survivors out?"

Enthor tried to hide the disdain in his voice, but I noticed, which left me wondering again, what was bothering the older dragon. He began to pace in front of Edwin as he tried to explain his plan. "I know it seems like a drastic measure, but you need to take the bridge out of the equation. It will not stop them but it will slow them down enough to make more of an impact and give Ililsaya and me time to do what needs to be done. I suggest those tunnels be used to evacuate the woman, children and elderly. The mountains will provide protection, and if we fail, they will be all that survives."

I stood beside the king and gently placed my hand on his shoulder. "Enthor's right. Nubossa is ruthless, and he's had many years to train and mould this army. Any humanity these mortals had was driven out of them long ago, and they won't hesitate to do anything to fulfil their master's wishes. They will not stop until the castle is theirs or we are all dead. We need to save as many people has possible and this will be the easiest way."

Anora, who stood on the other side of her husband let her thoughts be known. "I will lead them out. I know the tunnels well and the leader in the village of Sunder is a good friend. He will not turn us away."

The king looked at his wife beseechingly. His words carried authority. "No, you can't, it is too dangerous. I will not allow this."

Anora's face reddened in anger. "Do not start this pompous attitude of yours again. You have a duty to protect these people and so do I. What do you expect me to do, sit up in my rooms watching my city burn while the people I care about fight to protect it? You can't tell me what to do and I won't be treated like some child."

I actually thought Anora would strike her husband but again the king surprised us. Edwin actually gave his wife a small smile and kissed her on the cheek. "I know you are not a child and I'm sorry for always seeming to say the wrong things to you lately. You are the bravest person I have ever met, and I would trust no one else with the safety of our people, but it will not stop me from being worried. I only wish I could be in two places at once."

A small voice from behind Anora startled everyone. "I can help her, Uncle Edwin; I will protect Aunt Anora and the rest."

Edwin bent down and grasped the young girl by her shoulders. His face softened, and he spoke with respect. "I know you can, Risbela, but I don't want you to try to be a hero. I know what you are capable of, but so is the Dark Lord. If he is still alive, he will be looking for you, so I need you to stay hidden. Only use your powers if you must and don't do anything rash or your father will kill me."

Risbela gave her uncle a quick hug and then retreated back into the folds of Anora's skirts. For all of her power and courage, she was still only a child and it showed on her face today. That child was very special. Not only was she a powerful human mage, the likes of which had not been seen in centuries, she seemed to have the ability to communicate with the elements. I was sure they had a deeper purpose for her but I couldn't imagine what it could be. She was fascinated with Enthor and he had already begun to form a liking to her. Perhaps there was hope for the dragon species. Even Deneoes's new charge showed signs of deep emotion. The young dragon, which he had named *Spike* (a name I hated and was determined to get him to change) continued to grow and show great attachment to the mortals around him. Enthor had told me who the young dragon's parents were, and I was at a loss about how I felt about having a half-brother. I only hoped that his behaviour was a sign that Mareth's evil was not hereditary and that he never discovered he had another offspring.

The king stood and resumed the meeting, bringing me out of my musings. "I will heed your advice, Enthor, but how do we bring the structure down? It has stood for more than 250 years. We don't have enough time or the manpower to do it."

Enthor bowed to Edwin. "Leave that to me, Your Grace. As soon as Ililsaya and her companions are on their way I will take care of the bridge and add some of my own defences along the shore. They will not get across that river without serious casualties."

The king nodded in agreement and then turned his attention toward me. "Now then, my dear, let's figure out how we are going to get you inside enemy lines and decide who is going with you."

I looked at all the faces and let my gaze rest on Elric. He smiled and nodded, giving me my cue to speak for my friends. "Deneoes, Jaitem, Nalin and Elric will be going with me. I would have preferred a smaller group, but I was informed that I have no choice in the matter."

Deneoes just smiled at me with those huge almond-like eyes glittering with mock innocence. I smirked back.

"As to how we are going to get in, we really haven't had a chance to discuss it. I was hoping that maybe one of your scouts could provide us with more information."

A new voice entered the conversation, drawing everyone's attention to the newcomer. "I may be able to help with that, if you will permit me to speak."

The speaker was a Kanarah warrior who had been standing near the back of the group, leaning against the wall. I hadn't noticed him before now, but there was something strangely familiar about him. The much taller male stepped away from the wall and the shadows that hid his face. My eyes grew wide at the sudden recognition, but before I had a chance to shout a warning, a flash of black fur materialized out of nowhere and slammed into the unsuspecting Kanarah. They rolled over top of each other several times before coming to a stop with the mighty cougar on top, her jaws firmly around the other's neck. I ran over to the two struggling masses and threw my arms around Fang's great neck, making sure to stay well away from her teeth.

"Fang, where in the world did you come from—and how did you know, my friend? How do you always know when I need you?"

Without taking her feline eyes from the Kanarah, Fang growled in acknowledgement. I crouched down and told Fang to release the soldier's neck. Long gashes on either side were visible but they were already healing.

I looked the Kanarah in the eyes. "You will not fool me this time, you foul creature. This is where it ends."

The others rushed forward to see what was going on. Jaitem, who was terribly confused, said. "Karah, call off your beast. I know this man. He's no threat to you."

I rose back to my feet but never took my eyes off the creature pinned to the ground. "This is no friend. This is Reaper, and I plan on getting rid of him once and for all."

Hatred that I have never seen before filled Jaitem's face as he drew his twin blades. They instantly became ablaze, which matched the fire that consumed his eyes. Elric was at my side as well with his own sword drawn. Its sharpened point rested directly against Reaper's throat where Fang had removed her jaws.

Surprisingly the creature laughed. "I am not here to fight you pathetic excuses for mortals. I could have killed any one of you in the time that I have been here but I didn't. I came here to offer my help, and by the looks of things you're in sore need of it."

This time I laughed. "You can't be serious! Why should I believe a damn word you say? I despise you and can't wait to rip your heart out."

Reaper's face became sombre. "If you do, you'll never know what really happened that day. You'll never know why your prince had to die."

The world went deathly still and my whole body stiffened. I spread my fingers and small bolts of energy leapt between them. The wind began to pick up and the already dark clouds grew darker. My companions took cover and didn't dare interfere with the raw rage they saw in me—all except one.

Elric was suddenly there in my face. He grabbed hold of my shoulders, careful to stay away from the energy that pulsed through my fingers, and he shook me. "Ililsaya, get a hold of yourself. You're losing control. He's lying; it's just an attempt to save his wretched life. Stop this before you hurt yourself."

I stared hard at Elric and even snarled at him, but he didn't release his grip and never dropped his gaze. It was his eyes and the terror I saw there that finally got through to me. I closed my own and forced myself to breathe. It took me a few minutes but when I opened them, I was back in control. I let the energy leave my fingertips and the weather around us returned to what it had been.

I moved Elric aside and again looked down on my prisoner. Fang no longer had her jaws at the creature's throat, but her huge front paws still pinned him to the ground. I placed a steady hand on her shoulder.

"Fang, let him up. If he tries anything, feel free to rip him apart. I want to hear what he has to say."

Jaitem was furious. "*No!* He killed Miara, and for that I will see him pay. You cannot dishonour her by allowing this thing to live."

Jaitem was heaving, trying to control the emotions that raged inside him.

I understood how the man felt but I had to know why Reaper was here. "I'm truly sorry, my friend, but I have no choice. I need to know what he has to say. This is bigger than you, me or even Miara, and we need his knowledge. Please understand."

From the look on my friend's face I knew he did not understand. He sheathed his swords, spat at my feet and then turned from me, exiting the courtyard. I would have to mend that later if I could, but right now I had other matters to worry about.

Fang had removed herself from the Hautur but she did not go far. Elric still had his sword drawn and I could see Deneoes had an arrow notched and aimed at Reaper's head. Enthor was there also, eyeing him suspiciously, ready to strike if needed.

I drew my own sword and rested the tip on Reaper's chest. "Talk fast and don't think for second that if I don't like what I hear that I will not hesitate to end your wretched existence."

A sneer marked the lips of the Hautur but he made no move to get up. "Of that I am sure. You have much to hate me for now that you have regained your memories, but I am not here to discuss that."

My eyes widened in surprise. Reaper had indeed been here for a few days. There was no other explanation for him knowing that I had regained my memories.

As if reading my mind, the Hautur spoke. "Yes, I was there when you got off the ship, and I was also present last night at your meeting. Many things were made clear to me, and I came to the conclusion that I can help you."

I shook my head. "No, you don't get to do that. You don't get to just turn off a switch and change sides. Why now? What's changed?"

"Many things have changed, starting with you. If you can truly do what you say, then what choice do I have but to help you? I told you before that despite my actions I do care what happens to this world. The choices I've made and choices my race have made were made to aide our survival." His vile gaze encompassed all who surrounded him.

"You and the rest of the inhabitants of this world are completely ignorant of our painful history. The Dark Lord offered us a new life, and for better or worse it was our best option at the time. I'm doing this to benefit my species and myself and has nothing to do with my hatred for Ililsaya. That is a flame that will never be extinguished but I see now that she is needed, at least for now." He returned his black eyes to me. "My race deserves the same rights and freedoms as the rest of the mortals . . . that is all we have ever asked."

I remained quiet, staring at the strange Hautur. If anyone could understand his feelings, it was I, but that still didn't excuse what he had done. There is always a choice.

Reaper was not finished. "I do not expect you to believe me, but I was not the one who killed your prince."

I pushed the blade harder against Reaper's chest, causing him to retreat a little. "You're right. I don't believe you. If it wasn't you, then who was it? You were the only one there when I was captured and you made no move to deny that it hadn't been you."

Reaper actually looked guilty and confused. "No, I didn't deny it because I don't *remember* it."

My eyes widened and something tickled the back of my mind. I tried to concentrate on the feeling but it disappeared. I lowered my sword a little and stared at Reaper. "Explain yourself. What do you mean you don't remember?"

"It is the spell that holds you captive. I can't remember anything clearly before that time. The Hautur can live for centuries but we are not immortal. I was a fledgling when the Dark Lord found me, but I should be able to remember life before that day. I was fed hatred from the moment the Dark Lord discovered me and I have fostered it ever since."

I gritted my teeth and gave Reaper a small nod, giving him permission to continue.

"I will not dispute the fact that I was there because since flashes of events have been returning to me. I did not understand them until last night, when I heard your tale." Reaper turned from me to hide the shame that covered his face. Shock stole my words and I just stood there listening to a creature who seemed just as lost has I was.

"The plan to capture you was mine, but the prince was never supposed to be there. When I arrived, he was already fighting with someone and the encounter did not end well. Whoever was responsible for the prince's death had the power to wield death magic, and the list of beings capable of that, as you know, is very small."

I was stunned and also furious. I shifted my blade to the right and plunged the sword deep into the tissue and muscle just below his shoulder. Reaper hissed in pain but he still made no move to retaliate.

I removed my sword and crouched until I was eye level with the creature. "I believe you. I don't understand why but I do, but don't think for a second that I don't know what you're trying to do. I will not lose focus of what needs to be done and I won't start looking over my shoulder. I know you had nothing to gain in telling me this and in a way I am glad to know the truth, and for that I thank you, but when this is over, and if we are both still alive, we are going to settle this one-on-one—the way it was meant to be."

Reaper smiled cruelly, all trace of vulnerability vanished, and bowed his head.

I stood and extended my hand. "Now get up before I question my decision and decide I have lost my mind."

Enthor flew between us, and I could feel his hot breath in my face. His golden dragon eyes burned with anger. "You have lost your mind! How can trust this creature? He has done nothing but cause you pain. He will try to kill you and this time I can't save you. You know how important you are! Why are you taking such a stupid risk?"

Enthor was breathing heavily and looked like he wanted to strike me. Fang crouched low to the ground, ready to pounce, but it was Elric who came between us and pushed the dragon off. "Back off, Enthor. If she thinks this is what needs to be done, then I trust her. She knows what she's doing, and besides, Reaper is right. He could have killed any one of us but didn't. Maybe it is a trap, but our options are a little limited right now. You're not in control any more, dragon. She can make her own decisions and I suggest you find a way to accept that."

Enthor couldn't accept it. Rage filled his face and I feared he would strike Elric. Instead, he hastily shifted to dragon and rose into the air, causing all of us to hit the ground or be crushed by his wings. I stared after him for a moment with dread as he disappeared among the clouds.

Deneoes stood beside me but made no move to put away his weapon. He looked up at me and sighed. "Don't mind him; he'll get over it. I have discovered that you dragons act before you think and your stubbornness is way worse than mine."

I stared at him open mouthed, and Deneoes laughed. "Well, maybe not as stubborn, but pretty damn close! So let's find out what this walking sack of slime has to say. It's getting late, and if we are going to get to that army before nightfall we'd better hurry up and decide what we're doing."

I looked around and noticed that our group had diminished. The king and Duncan were still here but he had sent Anora and Risbela back to the keep. So that left Nalin, Elric, Deneoes and Reaper.

I fixed my attention back on the latter. "You have gone to great trouble to be here, and I have put a lot of strain on my companions, so let's have it. How do you plan to help us?"

Reaper straightened to his full height and crossed his massive arms across his chest. "First, there is no way you will be able to get all of you in there without being seen. I suggest you go alone with me as your guide."

Shouts of protest rang through the courtyard and I had to raise my voice to be heard. "Enough all of you! Let him finish."

Reaper gave my companions a disgusted look and continued with his plan. "As I was saying, your true form will be kept directly in the centre of the army, surrounded by armed soldiers at all times. It will be impossible to sneak you all through and get back out with your lives. Now as you know, the Dark Lord is less than pleased with me, and he will be expecting me to redeem myself. Even if he'd been killed in the battle with Ashia, which I strongly doubt, he will have informed his acting commander of my actions. I purpose that I bring you in as my prisoner in the guise of a peace offering. Once inside we can find your true form and I can get us both out of there."

Elric spoke before I could. "That would be a perfect plan—if we could trust you. You're asking us to put all our hopes and chance for survival into your hands. I can't believe you think it would be that easy."

Reaper moved directly in front of Elric, and in his current Kanarah form, he looked down at the smaller prince. "You have no choice. If you want to take back some control in this fight, you have to trust me. However, since it seems that I still need to prove that I will not betray you, I will tell you one more thing. I will tell you how to detect and defend against my kind."

Deneoes's eyes brightened. "Hah, now that's more like it! Out with it, you giant piece of filth." Reaper curled his lip at the much smaller Ywari but made no move against him. "I find your constant jabs of humour very irritating and would love nothing more than to string you up by your tongue."

"Get in line." Deneoes puffed out his small chest like a peacock, but I was in no mood for this.

"Deneoes, knock it off . . . let him finish. This isn't the time."

Deneoes forced his mouth shut and instead focused on scratching Fang behind her large ears.

Reaper ignored him. "As I was saying, there is not much that can harm a Hautur. We can regenerate very quickly and are incredibly strong, but we are at our weakest during a change. I know you already know this, but I will add that the quickest way to kill us during that change is to behead us. That is the only definite way to be sure that we are dead. It is also an effective way to deal with us in our other various forms. It is more difficult to accomplish but I suppose you could get lucky. I will also tell you a way in which you can tell us apart from the other species that we mimic, which will be your greatest weapon. We have extremely acute hearing in whatever form we choose. This gift is very useful but can also be a hindrance. Because our hearing is so acute any high-pitched sound causes us great pain and makes us lose our focus. It can force a change, leaving us vulnerable and—"

Reaper never finished his sentence. He suddenly dropped to his knees, holding his head in his hands in pain. His form started to shimmer, and he was quickly losing the image of the Kanarah warrior. Then his discomfort stopped. Reaper regained the form of the Kanarah and focused his black, hateful stare on Deneoes. I followed Reaper's eyes and saw the young Ywari with a small familiar wooden whistle sticking out from between his teeth.

Deneoes simply smiled and shrugged. "What? I had to make sure he was telling the truth. Who knew the tool we used to scare away wild dogs and signal each other would work on other wild animals too? Good to know."

This time Reaper did try to get hold of Deneoes but Fang was instantly in his face. Reaper withdrew and seethed with anger. "If you all are done playing these childish games, I would like to know your answer. Will you let me take you in or should I just leave now?"

Elric and I exchanged glances and knew what each other was thinking. I spoke for us. "You could try to leave but I doubt you would get very far. I will go with you but we are not travelling alone. Elric is coming with us as far as the outside perimeter of the army, where he will wait for our return. That is the only way I will accept your offer."

Reaper nodded grimly in agreement. "Very well. I will meet you outside the castle gates. Be ready in 20 minutes." Without a final glance the Hautur disappeared behind the courtyard walls.

King Edwin clasped his son's hands and tried very hard to look hopeful. "Be careful, my son; do not let your guard down. That creature is an enemy no matter how helpful he has just been. Duncan and I will return to the keep and get the word out about the Hauturs' weaknesses."

He then turned to Deneoes. "And tell me, my young friend, how long do you think it would take you to make more of those whistles?"

Deneoes smiled and threw the one he had in his hands to me. "Just in case. I don't trust that slimy bastard either. Almost every Ywari carries one of these whistles, and I'm sure we can make more. I'll go speak to my father. I suppose I'd better go find Mister Grumpy Tooth as well. I want to see if he needs any help blowing the bridge up—it sounds like fun."

Nalin was the last to leave. "I'll go try and find Jaitem and see if I can talk to him, but I'm afraid it may take him a long time to forgive you. I'll also make sure that my men are ready as well. Be careful, my friends. I hope you know what you're doing."

Elric and I stood side by side and watched our friends go about their new tasks. As soon as everyone was out of sight I let my false courage fall and slumped my shoulders.

Elric took me into his arms. "You're thinking about Seth, aren't you? Do you really think that what Reaper said was true?"

I let him hold me as I tried to deny what I felt in my heart to be true. "Yes, I think he's telling the truth; what reason did he have to lie? I don't understand his motives but I do believe him when he says he wants to help save Eiddoril. I just can't help thinking where

323

Seth is now and who could have possibly done that to him and why. If his spirit is here somewhere on the mortal plane, how do I find it? How do I help him find peace?" Elric moved us apart far enough so that he could kiss the top of my head and look at my face. "We'll find a way. When this is over we'll find a way. I promise."

We left the conversation at that and together with Fang close at our heels, we went in search of supplies and Reaper.

CHAPTER 34

Ililsaya

Thunder rolled and lightening flashed through the dark clouds. The rain that had been threatening all day finally decided to make an appearance, making stealth nearly impossible. We stayed low to the ground and slowly inched our way forward through the slick grass and mud until we could see over the hill and into the valley below. My breath caught in my throat, and all I could do was stare in stunned silence.

Nubossa's army spread out below us like a swarm of insects. It was like looking at a huge blanket of death laid out over miles. I couldn't be sure of the numbers but I could see enough that I knew we would be outnumbered by at least ten to one. They were also closer than we had thought. They could have attacked us tonight, but it seemed they were holding true their master's wishes. The autumn solstice was tomorrow night and I could see no way to stop this tide of death from killing everyone I held dear.

Movement off to my left caused me to jump, but I relaxed when I saw that it was only a small rabbit seeking shelter in a nearby bush. It sat there for a moment staring at me, and then its form began to shimmer and almost liquefy. It took fewer than 15 seconds for Reaper to reform as a Dark Lord soldier. He silently crawled through the slick grass and came to rest beside me.

Despite my hatred for the creature I managed a small smile.

Elric said, "A bunny? Really? Nice way to instil fear into the hearts of seasoned soldiers."

Reaper ignored Elric's comment and kept his voice low. "The Dark Lord is not down there. No one I spoke to has seen or heard from him in several days. In addition, I think I found the location of your dragon form. It is in the centre, where you can see that cluster of tents. It is heavily guarded and I see no other reason for that kind of attention."

I nodded toward the Hautur and looked back out across the field of enemies. I had to do something to even these odds. "Look, I have a plan, but you're both going to have to trust me."

Reaper and Elric looked at each other and both scoffed at my words.

Elric pulled me back from the edge and sat up a little straighter. "What's your plan?"

I swallowed and found some courage. "We need to take out some of that army tonight or we're in serious trouble. I know how I can do it, but you're not going to like it."

Reaper had rejoined us from his spot and looked into my eyes. "You want to rejoin with your body tonight, don't you?"

Elric looked at me in shock as I slowly nodded. "Yes, and before you disagree with me, let me explain. Once we get close to my dragon, I can use my full magic, killing this mortal body. My spirit will be drawn to my original form and once we are re-joined, the flux of power will destroy a large area surrounding me. It will cause a lot of chaos and confusion and will wipe out a large amount of the enemy."

Elric shook his head. "No, it's too risky. How do you know your spirit will find your body? Enthor has always been there to guide it. And how do you know if you will have enough strength to get out once you are a dragon again? You haven't been a dragon for a long time, and you will be severely weakened."

I stood my ground. There was too much at risk here. "I am not a true dragon, I'm something stronger. I'll know how to get back to my dragon form, of that I am certain. And yes, I will be weakened, and that is why I will need Reaper to get me out."

Now it was the shape—shifter's turn to look shocked. "You're placing a lot of faith in a creature who would love nothing more than to see you die."

"Yes, but as you have said before, you need me. And trust me, there will come a time when we both can satisfy our need for revenge. I've seen you carry the Dark Lord off several times; it is not something that will be difficult for you."

Reaper remained silent, thinking.

Elric reached out and held my hand. "Are you sure about this? Are you sure it will work?"

I slowly shook my head. "No, but what choice do we have? That army is too powerful for Gareth, and even with the help of Enthor and all the others it will be a slaughter. It has carved a path of death and destruction straight here from the Barren Wastes with no resistance. We have to stop it or many others will face the same fate. I don't see any other way."

Elric bent forward and kissed me. "Fine, but I'm going as close as I can. I'm not putting all my faith in this creature to get you out. I'll be there as back up."

Reaper bristled and then put on an emotionless mask. "I'll get her out, if this crazy plan works. Come—we need to move. I will show you a place where you can see what is going on without being detected."

We all slowly made our way down the small hill and found the game trail that Reaper had followed into Nubossa's army. Before we got within sight of the mass of soldiers, Reaper silently pointed to another small hill dotted with brush that would give Elric an excellent vantage point. I handed him my sword and then offered my hands to the Hautur. My prince stood rigid and silent as Reaper loosely bound my hands behind me and then drew his sword, pointing it at my back. I could see the conflict in Elric, but before he could change his mind, he silently disappeared up the hill and was swallowed by the rain.

I took a deep breath. "I'm ready. Let's make this convincing."

In response, Reaper shoved me forward, causing me to slip in the mud and go down on one knee. He then roughly hoisted me up, and I felt his hot breath in my ear as he pulled me close. Dread filled me as I listened to what could possibly be my worst mistake ever.

"Convincing? I wouldn't worry about that. After all, I've had a lot of practice."

I sneered at him and tried to bash the back of my head against his nose, but he moved too quickly and shoved me forward again. I buried my anger for now and let Reaper push me into the viper's nest.

*

The rain was coming down hard by the time we made it to the centre of the encampment. My hair was plastered to my face and my clothes were dirty and torn. I was also sporting a bloody nose. My captor seemed to be taking his role a little too seriously. We had to pass through several checkpoints, but once the word spread of who Reaper was, no one gave us any trouble. I just hoped I wasn't making a huge mistake. If something went wrong here, which was a major probability, then we were screwed.

I kept my head lowered as Reaper spoke to the commander of Nubossa's army. "General Qued, you have done well in my absence; I am impressed. I have heard the reports that our master may not still be alive. I only wish that I could present this prize to him instead of his trusted officer. It would please him greatly to know that you have not failed in his great plans. We will make sure that tomorrow Gareth will burn to ground for the glory of the Dark Lord—and here is our assurance."

Reaper forced me down to my knees and I sank into the muddy ground. I chanced a small look up at this General Qued, and what I saw froze my blood in my veins. His large black reptilian eyes glittered with malice, and he smiled, wide showing his sharp teeth.

"Why don't you tell my lord yourself, traitor? I'm sure he is very interested in what you have to say."

The flaps of the main tent in front of us parted and out walked Nubossa, smiling cruelly. His soldiers bowed and made a path for him. He came to stand directly in front of me and looked down with his cold dragon eyes fixed on mine.

"Oh, Ililsaya, how it never ceases to amaze me at how utterly stupid you can be. Did you really think that poor excuse for a dragon could have beaten me? Your mother was weak, and I enjoyed every last moan of pain I crushed from her mortal throat."

Anger burned a hole in my stomach but I remained silent.

His hot glare went to my "captor." "And you, my trusted friend, did you think I would not discover your treachery? You are no better than the human scum you surround yourself with. The two of you make a fine pair."

I struggled to my feet and looked up into the larger dragon's face. "Nubossa, you need to stop this. There are things you do not understand. There is something bigger that threatens all of us. You need to call off this attack or all of Eiddoril will suffer."

Nubossa's eyes widened in surprise at my use of his true name. Murmurs quickly ran through the ranks like wildfire, but the Dark Lord silenced them all with just a look. "So, you remember my name. Tell me, child, how much do you know?"

"I know everything. I remember that day you finally captured me and the way I laughed in your face. I know that without me, Mareth cannot return to this world and I know that if you continue on this path you will be helping a much more powerful being. She wants to see this world die, and unless you let me stop her, you and your pathetic reign of glory will come to an end."

Nubossa reached out, grabbed me by the throat and squeezed it painfully. Spots started to fill my vision and I tried desperately to move away from his iron grip. However, before he could finish the job he stopped and watched me drop to the ground, coughing.

He knelt beside me and removed the mud and water from my face with his rough hand. "Well, about that—there's been a change in plans. I have no intention of letting Mareth through that gate. And as for you, you and I are going to take a trip. You will be far from here when the spell that holds your powers at bay ends. Your spirit will have nowhere to go and you will be doomed to rot in Duggati. Your friends will all die at the hands of my army, and this time there will be no survivors."

I tried to get to my knees but Nubossa pushed me back down. Fury started to build in my soul and my powers instantly sprang to life. Spirits formed around us, sensing my power. They didn't frighten me any more, and they seemed to know that I was back in control of my power. They waited patiently, fading in and out of reality, waiting for me to release them.

I pulled my gaze from them and looked to the sky. Lightning flashed and hurled down to protect me. Dozens of soldiers were thrown back, leaving only Nubossa and Reaper close to me. Nubossa rose and stepped away. I pushed myself up and stood on shaking legs. My hands had already come free from their false binding, and I held them in front of me like a shield. I let my power build inside me and I felt the walls crack even more. Just one more push and they would be free.

But a figure was thrown at Nubossa's feet and I fought hard to contain the tide of magic flowing inside me. The evil dragon held a blood blade to his throat. Elric looked up at me through swollen eyes. He was covered in blood and had been beaten badly. He mouthed the words *I'm sorry* and my heart plunged into the ground.

Nubossa laughed through the raging storm. "It seems that no matter how many lives you live, you still can't shake your human weakness. Swallow your power or your prince will forever walk this world in pain."

I closed my hands into fists and forced my power back behind its wall. The storm died down and it even stopped raining. The spirits around us wavered in agitation but didn't disappear. I stared at Nubossa with hate.

"You have no idea what you are doing. Why have you changed your plans? Mareth will kill you when he is not able to come back through. He can still communicate with you and cause you pain. You are not strong enough to stop that."

Nubossa never took his gaze from me, but he also never stopped pointing that horrible blade at Elric.

"You know, it was a funny thing. After I killed Ashia, I had to heal myself so I went into a deep sleep. During that sleep, many things became clear to me. I had a visitor in my dreams. At first I thought it was Mareth, but this being was far more powerful than anyone I had ever encountered. She didn't speak to me, but when

I awoke I felt stronger, different. I knew that I now have the power to block Mareth from my mind and end our blood connection. I also knew what I needed to do." His voice rose as he tried to contain his excitement." You must never be allowed to be reunited with a dragon host. You must be trapped in Duggati, where Death can control you. In addition, there must never be dragons in this world again, except for me of course. She has promised total control over this world and it will be me the mortals will call God."

I shook my head in amazement. "And you call me stupid. Do you really think something with that much power would ever let you control anything? Did you not learn anything from being under Mareth's heel? You are a puppet, nothing more, and it will be you who dies first when she puts her own final plans into action."

Nubossa reached down and hoisted up Elric's limp form. He held the prince's body against his with his blade at his throat. "What is your answer, Ililsaya? Do you stand and watch your prince die or do you unleash your power? You can't save him and control your spirit at the same time. So decide. I will release him if you come with me now. It makes no difference if he dies now or during the battle to defend his city. Either way he dies, but at least you can *choose*. That is what you have always wanted, isn't it, the right to choose your own path? Here it is, but make it quick because I'm in no mood to wait."

I stared into Elric's eyes and saw what he wanted me to do, but I couldn't, I couldn't let another love die because of me. I would find another way into the immortal realm.

"Elric, I'm sorry, but—" My words came out in a gasp as I stared down at the blade protruding from my chest. Blood pumped from my pierced heart and I cried out in pain has the prison walls inside me finally gave way.

Nubossa threw Elric to the side and dived to catch my body. Nubossa caught it, but it was already too late. My human host was dead and my life energy was free.

*

Nubossa

I tried in vain to grab hold of Ililsaya's energy to consume it, but it slipped through my human fingers. I looked up with my dragon eyes into the face of my betrayer.

Reaper sheathed his own bloodied blade and his form started to shimmer. "I will be a slave no more, Master. I will not see you help destroy this world."

Before I could strike, the Hautur took to the skies as a giant Ristiaper and disappeared into the dark clouds.

I roared to the skies in my pathetic human form and couldn't contain my anger. I started to shift to my dragon form. Human soldiers stood by, stunned, not knowing what to do as they watched their leader transform into a thing from their nightmares. I stretched and flexed my massive dark wings and then tore off the tent that concealed Ililsaya's dragon form. The humanoid form of the dragon that I tried in vain to destroy for so long was now surrounded by bright white energy. It pulsed and the energy started to spread out in all directions. Dozens of spirits clung to her form, trying to feed off her energy. I stared in horror not knowing what was happening. I had never seen a life energy act that way.

I tried to get close to her but lightning struck from the skies, narrowly missing me. A wind began to blow that was so strong that even with my claws dug firmly into the ground I was losing purchase. The ground around me shook and cracked, causing upheavals of dirt. I sent a mental message out to my troops: *"Get back, all of you, as far as you can. Move now!"*

I took to the skies but not before an enormous explosion of pure energy slammed into me, knocking me into a group of my own fleeing men. The white-hot energy moved out in a circle, creating a massive bubble, incinerating anything within its path. It grew until it seemed that it would engulf the whole valley but the pressure inside was too much and it burst, spilling pure elemental energy into the air. It felt as though the world collectively inhaled as the massive amount of energy was absorbed into the earth and sky. Night was turned to day and chaos reigned from the skies.

The stillness in the air that followed was peaceful. I gathered myself, but it was as if I no longer existed. The men and creatures alike who survived the blast stood stunned and disbelieving, but it was not me they were staring at.

They stood on the outside of a deep crater staring down at the lone figure in the center. She was beautiful. Her long, fiery-red hair draped down to her feet and flew behind her like a flag. Her skin was the colour of the earth and her eyes were the colour of the forests and were full of hate. She was dressed in a long gown that clung to her lithe figure. The fabric was the colour of the ocean and seemed to flow around her like water, but it was her face that captivated the crowd. It was completely covered in a strange tattoo that shined a brilliant blue. As it began to fade to a light golden colour, we could see that the lines formed a pattern: the sun and the moon joined as one.

She stood tall and proud and stared directly at me, her voice ringing through the valley. "Your men now know what you are, and they are afraid. Their fight is not with Gareth or with me but with a being that threatens their very existence. If you continue on this path, you will all die, along with this world. Dragons are not your enemies; we are not all like your Dark Lord. Remember that in the days to come because you will find that dragons will be the only ones that can save you."

I hurled acid at the woman standing below me, but she merely raised her hand and a wall of dirt sprang in front of her to protect her. I fumed at being embarrassed in front of my men, but I never got the chance to retaliate. Everyone, including me, watched as a Ristiaper glided down, snatched the human form of Ililsaya and flew off toward Gareth, leaving me with failure again.

All of the gathered soldiers turned as one and looked at me with fear and uncertainty. I gathered myself, seized the closest Litui and drained him dry of his life energy. My men scrambled out of the way of the rampaging dragon.

Two more soldiers gave their lives before I sent out another mental message to the remainder of my army: *"Be still, or I will finish all of you."* I put force and persuasion behind my words and the soldiers stopped to listen.

"Do not be fooled by that witch's words. She was trapped for a reason and she cannot be trusted. I am not your enemy. I am the one trying to stop an evil being from coming here."

I paused for dramatic effect and was pleased to see that I held everyone's attention. *"Your gods left for a reason. They were evil dragons who lied and deceived you. Mareth and Ashia were not truly your gods but greedy, lazy creatures who only thought of themselves. They went away to find more power so that when they returned they could rule you without opposition. I have always been honest with you, and yes, some of my methods have been cruel, but it was all in an attempt to keep this day from coming to pass."*

I lowered my reptilian head in mock shame. *"Yes, I did lie to you about my true nature but that was only to protect you. I was ashamed to be part of the dragon race and wanted only to redeem myself and do what's right."*

Murmurs of agreement and pity filled my mind and ears, filling my soul with elation.

"The humans of Gareth follow this false god with blind eyes, but they must be made to see the truth. We must stop her from letting evil back into this world, and we must do it by force."

I raised my horned head and roared my triumph to the skies that were now accompanied by thousands of mortal voices. Their need for a cause had been fulfilled and they would do their mindless duty even if it meant their deaths.

"Now gather your weapons and your wits—we are moving out now! Gareth will pay for this strike with their lives. Follow me and I promise you will have everything your hearts have ever desired! You will know the great rewards of heeding a dragon's wishes. If not, then step forward now and end your pathetic lives at the end of my claws." I did not have to wait long for a reply. A chant of thousands strong filled the scorched valley. All were in awe and regarded their leader in a new light. I smiled as I fed the mortals with fear and persuasion. It was so easy to toy with their simple minds.

I spread my black wings to their fullest and launched myself into the air, and from the skies I sent my final command. *"Now go, bring death to the people of Gareth! Burn the city to the ground and swim in their blood!"*

A wild, hungry cheer rose into the night sky. The army moved as one with a renewed spirit and headed across the valley toward a sleeping and unaware Gareth.

Chapter 35

Enthor

Standing on the bridge that led into Gareth I let my mind wander to recent events. I was angry at not being told what Ililsaya truly was and I was at a loss as to how to proceed. I had tried to contact my employer but it seemed that he was also preoccupied with the coming war. I now understood why he wanted her so badly, and I was having second thoughts.

Deneoes's impatient huff drew me from my dark musings and I watched the young Ywari look up to the dark sky. He wiped the water out of his eyes and turned to watch me pace up and down the length of the structure. I could tell by the tone of his voice that the Ywari was losing patience.

"Oh, would you just smash it to bits already! Why must you analyze everything to death? You are a bloody dragon, just shift and smash it. I don't see the problem here."

I stopped pacing, gave Deneoes a withering look and sucked in a calming breath.

"No, that's your problem. You never stop to think about anything. There are a lot of factors to consider, like—" I stopped in mid-sentence and cocked my head to the side, listening.

Deneoes stood beside me and did the same thing. Even though we were the only ones out here, Deneoes still lowered his voice. "Hey, the rain stopped—and does it seem strangely quiet to you? It feels like the whole world has suddenly gone still and is holding its breath."

I silenced Deneoes with my finger and pointed out across the fields toward the hills and valleys that marked Aserah's borders. Lightning flashed through the sky and touched down somewhere off in the distance. The strange phenomenon occurred excessively too many times in the same spot to be a coincidence, and then as we watched, a massive ball of light exploded in the sky, shattering the silence of the night. The ground shook, causing the stone bridge to pitch underneath us. The river began to rush under the bridge in a frenzy and the wind fiercely blew around us.

We raced to get off the bridge and then stopped to look back across the fields. Whatever that explosion had been had lit up the sky and was now painted with fire. The elements around us seemed to inhale the power swirling in the air, and then they were gone. The water returned to a normal flow and the earth settled back down. The wind calmed to a gentle breeze and the fire in the sky dispersed. Everything was as it was before, but I knew what had happened.

My form began to shift and shimmer and where once stood a middle-aged man was now a mighty dragon. My blue and green scales glittered in the moonlight, which had finally made an appearance.

Deneoes had to jump out of the way before he was knocked over by my tail. His confused voice drifted up to my ears. "Hey, what the hell's going on? What was that?"

I stared across the field for a moment longer and then brought my mighty head down to look at the Ywari. My mental voice intruded his thoughts. *"You must go to the keep. Tell Edwin, Nalin, your father and Jaitem to prepare the men. Nubossa is in his dragon form and is very close. His army is on its way. That explosion of energy was Ililsaya. She has been rejoined with her dragon form, which was not their plan. Something terrible has happened and we must be ready."*

Deneoes didn't say anything, which surprised me. He just turned and ran for the keep. It didn't take long for his small body to get lost among the empty farmhouses and fields.

Launching into the air I set my sights on the bridge, but movement across the fields caught my eye. After a few seconds, I realized it was Fang, and she was carrying something on her back. Her powerful feline limbs pumped fiercely as she ran for the bridge and the safety of the keep. As the mighty cat got closer, I could tell who she was trying to save. Emotions and memories warred inside me, making me physically sick, forcing me to fiercely shake my horned head to clear my thoughts. I hesitated for only a moment before I concluded that I had a job to do and very little time to do it, and I was tired of mortal delays.

Without a second thought, I sucked in a huge breath and shot a fireball at the bridge. The force of the impact tore a huge hole directly in the centre of the bridge. Huge chunks of stone fell into the river, sinking below the surface. Then with my tail, I smashed down on the bridge, cleaving the structure in half. More debris fell into the water 10 feet below and was quickly lost to the bottom of the river. I rose into the air again and concentrated my efforts on the near side of the bridge closest to Gareth. I blasted my fiery breath at the end of the bridge, completely destroying the supports, and turned the stone to dust. With one final swipe of my tail, the remaining pieces of the bridge fell into the river.

I touched down on the bank, transformed back into my human form and watched as Fang came racing toward the damaged bridge. Without stopping, she mounted the other end of the span and with a power and momentum I never knew the creature possessed she launched herself out and over the large expanse of water. She easily touched down on the other side with her massive claws digging into the dirt for purchase. She paused for only a moment and regarded me with those too-intelligent eyes. Then with a roar she continued her journey with her injured party toward the keep.

I stood and watched the mighty feline while wrestling with the impulse to finish what I had started but I couldn't, not yet. I angrily shook my head again and turned to complete the defences. I extended my hand toward the damaged end of the bridge that still stood and with my eyes closed said the language of the elements. The ground rumbled with the force of my words, and when I again opened my eyes, the former empty space now projected the illusion of the bridge.

I pointed my hands next at the shoreline surrounding the river. I focussed my magic and called to the elements for help. They responded, and quickly I turned the ground surrounding the river into slick mud, which with the slightest amount of weight would go sliding into the river below. It was on the river itself that I focussed my next spell. I sent a blast of cold air into it, making the temperature drop well below the freezing mark. A thin sheet of ice was visible as the waters rushed by underneath, but unless you were paying attention, you wouldn't see it. Anyone who fell into the water would be caught up in the swift current and slowly die from exposure to the frigid cold.

Satisfied with my work I prepared to go and search for Ililsaya. It seemed that she indeed needed my help after all, which I knew she would. I should never have let her go through with this foolish plan. Now, after all these years, all of my plans could be ruined and I would never be granted what I sought.

A mental intrusion interrupted my dark thoughts. It was Ililsaya.

"Enthor, we need to talk."

*

Ililsaya

I watched the elder dragon from the night sky as Reaper circled him. The Hautur flew close enough to the ground so that he could drop me without causing me too much discomfort. I stepped gingerly, still not used to my body, and came to face my oldest friend. He did not look happy and said nothing as he watched Reaper shift to something more suitable. The Hautur came to join us in the guise of a common human. The Hautur and I stared at each other for a minute, I think trying to decide whether we should attack each other. I still wasn't sure how I felt about him killing my human host earlier, and I was questioning his motives. Thinking about that night brought up another painful moment, which I quickly buried. Now was not the time to mourn. I would face those terrible consequences later.

I pulled my glare from Reaper and spoke to Enthor. "It is good to see you, my friend, but I'm afraid we need to get back to the keep as soon as possible. There are things I need to discuss with the king."

I swallowed the lump in my throat and was shocked to see the hostility in the elder dragon's face. "I'll bet you do. What the hell happened, and where is Elric?"

An ache filled my soul and I lowered my gaze. My voice was full of pain and I fought the tears that were rapidly filling my eyes. "I had a plan, but Nubossa's army was too many. There was no way they could have stood their ground against them. I had to try to level the playing field so I sacrificed my human host and rejoined with my dragon form. I took out a lot of soldiers, but Elric was caught in the blast . . . he didn't make it."

I shook visibly trying to hold in my grief. I lifted my head and studied Enthor. He had the same look he would get when he was trying to decide whether or not he should tell me something, which left a sour feeling in my stomach.

Reaper, who was standing beside me, laughed.

Enthor forcibly tried to control his anger as he regarded the shape-shifter. "What is so amusing, Hautur?"

Reaper shrugged and then crossed his arms across his chest. His words were mocking. "I find it funny that the one creature she should be able to trust is hiding things from her. I am very good at reading body language, and what I read off you stinks of guilt. What are you hiding, dragon?"

In response, Enthor started to shift into dragon form, causing us both to retreat. His giant snake-like body grew until I had to strain my neck to look up at him. I stood my ground in front of Reaper as Enthor's massive reptilian head lowered until I could look into his golden eyes.

His mental voice dripped with hate as it drilled into my skull. *"Move, Ililsaya, and let me end this mistake before it gets worse. You can't trust him; he will betray you in the end."*

I didn't move and I gathered my power around me. "I don't know what's going on with you, but I intend to find out. I am not a lost human child any more and I have accepted my path—perhaps you should do the same. As for Reaper, I have no doubt that in the end he will try to kill me but that is something I will deal with, so for now he stays. This is not the time for us to be fighting amongst ourselves. Nubossa is on his way and we need to get to the keep."

Enthor blew smoke out of his nostrils in response and lifted off into the rapidly lightening sky. Dawn was coming and there was still so much that needed to be done. I watched Enthor fly off toward the keep and put my ill feelings aside. Something was not right but I didn't have the time to figure it out.

Reaper regarded me with mischief on his face. "Do you still need me to carry you, or are you ready to proceed on your own?"

Instead of answering Reaper's snide remark, I closed my eyes and focussed my powers. It had been so long since I had been in my true form that I had forgotten the rapture I felt every time I let the power take over. I started to shift slowly at first and then once I was comfortable I let my full power flow through my body. The humanoid shape vanished into a lengthening reptilian body. Deep red scales with golden flecks covered me, followed by two massive wings sprouting from my back. The bony spikes that led from my forked tail to the base of my crest were black as midnight, and my silver horns spiralled around my long head. With my transformation complete, I lowered my head so I could see myself in the shifter's eyes. The symbol that marked me pulsed with a faint blue and then faded into a golden colour.

Reaper actually smiled and bowed his head. "You truly are a magnificent creature. It's a shame that I must kill you someday."

I laughed inside his head, feeling a little giddy. *"We shall see. Now let's get going, and try to keep up."*

I launched myself into the predawn air, and for that brief moment, I revelled in the joy of being a dragon.

CHAPTER 36

Ililsaya

It was a quick flight by dragon wings to the keep's courtyard. The sun was just starting to peek over the horizon, so I was shocked to see so many people scrambling about. I circled around the perimeter a few times and could see that everyone was awake and moving. Soldiers and warriors from three races prepared for the battle I had just instigated. Shouts of alarm and notched arrows made me remember that I was in dragon form. No one knew what I looked like so I quickly spied someone I knew. Nalin and Jaitem were standing atop the turrets, preparing men to attack.

I focused my thoughts toward them. *"Hey, it's me; tell them not to shoot. I don't want them wasting their arrows."*

Recognition lit their faces and Nalin threw me a friendly but confused wave. Jaitem, however, only turned away and called to the others to stand down. I guess he was still upset with me. I didn't blame him really, but I had enough to worry about.

The courtyard wasn't exactly the best-suited place for a dragon to land but I managed. Everyone stepped out of the way and waited while I shifted back to human. I was greeted by many stares and open mouths, which made me feel very uncomfortable.

I searched around for Reaper but didn't see him, but that didn't mean he wasn't there. Enthor stood by the base of the stairs that led up into the keep. He only nodded at me and made no move to communicate with me.

Edwin and Anora were the first to approach me. They were both dressed for battle. The king wore his armour with his sword and shield strapped to his back. Anora too was ready for the upcoming encounter. She wore light chainmail covered with a leather shirt. She now wore pants instead of her customary gown and even sported a wicked-looking blade strapped to her belt. I actually had no idea she even knew how to use a sword, but by the looks of her, I was sure she could take care of herself.

She was the first to reach me and embrace me. I tried so hard not to break down, but when I tried to speak, no words came out.

Anora immediately noticed my discomfort. "What's wrong, child? I'm sorry for all of the stares, but you are rather stunning. I'm afraid it will take us some getting used to."

"No it's not that . . . I have something to tell you . . . it's Elric, he's . . ."

Anora smiled. "He's fine, thanks to that wild cat of yours. He was pretty banged up but I'm sure he will be much better after he hears you are safe. We practically had to tie him to the bed so he would stay still for our healers to look at him."

Relief and confusion washed through me. I gripped Anora tightly and smiled. I saw Deneoes and Fang come out of the keep. The large feline bounded toward me with my sword clutched in her jaws and almost knocked us over. I bent down, took the blade and stroked her soft, silky fur.

"Thank you again, my friend. I don't know what I would do without you. I thought I lost him. I thought I'd failed again."

Deneoes placed a gentle hand on my shoulder, which brought my attention to him. He looked very confused. "I don't get it, Red; you didn't know Fang had Elric?"

I shook my head. "I thought he was dead. I thought he'd been killed in the blast."

Deneoes looked back at Enthor, who had not moved during our conversation. "But the old man was still at the bridge when I left. I took off here right after we saw the sky catch fire. He stayed to finish taking down the bridge and setting up traps. Fang must have passed over the bridge to get here. Why didn't he tell you he saw them?"

A voice that seemed to materialize out of nowhere came from behind the king and queen. "That's a very good question, you short little freak. Maybe you should ask him."

Weapons were drawn and all eyes trained on Reaper. He was once again in the guise of a human. but now he sported the armour of a Gareth soldier. He put his hands in the air and turned 360 degrees, showing us he wasn't armed.

Fang lowered her head and growled, but I wasn't sure if it was Reaper or Enthor she was upset with.

I stood between Reaper and the rest of the crowd. "That's enough, Reaper, I think you've caused enough trouble."

The Hautur shrugged and remained silent.

Enthor, who had been watching us this entire time, now stood close to the shifter. "This is ridiculous. When are you going to open your eyes and see that this creature's only purpose here is to cause trouble? We don't even know where he is half the time. How can you condone that kind of risk? You're letting your foolish emotions get in the way again, just like you always have. If you won't take control, then I will. Someone needs to think about the safety of Eiddoril."

He moved toward the shifter, but I turned so I was face to face with him and straightened to my full height. I was taller than Enthor, and I used my height to look down on him. My symbol that adorned my dark face in pale gold started to flare blue, and my green dragon eyes glittered with anger.

Enthor stood his ground, but his dragon came to sit just under his skin. His golden eyes dared me to act.

I was not intimidated. "I don't know what's going on with you, but it scares me. You have never acted like this and I was actually starting to think that being forced to be human for so long had changed you. All I see in your eyes lately is hate, and I don't understand why. I know I have made mistakes but so have you, and trust me, I remember everything now. I know the decisions you've had to make to keep me safe and they weren't always desirable."

I softened my voice a little and touched Enthor's arm. "I trust you with my life, just as I always have, but you need to trust me. I will not falter and give in to my fears as I once did. I will save this world from extinction."

Enthor's eyes lost a little of their anger and I saw shame and guilt on his face for an instant. But then it was gone, replaced with an unreadable mask.

"Everything I've ever done was to protect you, so that someday you could save us all, and yes, I made some grave mistakes to achieve that goal. You're right, being human has changed me, and most of the time I hate it. I don't want all these emotions. I don't want to feel the way I do. I'm a dragon, an immortal, and if I could turn it all off I would."

Enthor stepped back from my touch and motioned toward Reaper. "You are making a mistake, but I will not question you on it any more. You are no longer the young dragon I once looked out for, and if you wish to be allowed to make more mistakes, so be it. I only hope that this time you think of others and not just yourself."

Enthor's words deeply wounded me. I didn't want to ask but I needed to know something. "Look, I understand why you did the things you did. Perhaps when this is over we can sit down and talk about it so we can both heal. But there is something I need to know and I want the truth." I paused, fearing the older dragon's answer. "When I saw you earlier at the bridge, had you seen Fang and Elric? Did you know he was alive?"

Enthor looked me straight in the eye—and lied. "No. She must have crossed somewhere else. The only creatures I saw were the two of you."

I quickly turned away from him to hide the betrayal and confusion on my face, but Reaper saw, and for a moment our eyes locked and I thought I saw pity there, but it was gone in an instant. I buried everything deep down and retreated behind my dragon. I felt safe and in control and knew I had a job to do; I would deal with Enthor later.

I walked with authority to the top of the steps and put a little power behind my words to project my voice. "Listen to me, all of you. My actions earlier may not have been part of the plan but I did succeed in causing some causalities and chaos. I made the choice to join with my true form last night because I saw what you are up against. Nubossa's army is immense and they are driven by lies and false promises."

The courtyard was silent as I spoke.

"Nubossa's plans have changed. Destruction has visited him and she is done playing around. She has given him the power to break his connection with Mareth and has convinced him to stop Mareth from returning. She knows I'm here and knows what I want to do. She wants that gate to remain closed. She wants dragons gone from this world permanently, with me trapped in Duggati where Death would be able to control me."

I paused and looked at each and every one gathered in the courtyard—including Enthor, who could not hide the confusion in his stare.

"What Nubossa fails to see is that once he has fulfilled his purpose, she will find a way of destroying him as well. With all the dragons gone, leaving me forced to create life energy in Duggati and eliminating the two dragons that fed from it, Destruction can then successfully turn her attention to the mortals and sit back and watch as you destroy each other and your world again and again without worrying about running out of life energy again."

Deneoes bristled at my callous comment. "Are you saying that we are too stupid to realize what's going on? We know the whole story now, Red. We know what not to do."

I didn't stray from my path; I needed these mortals to understand. "Do you? You may not be stupid, but you are mortal, and although your emotions provide you with your greatest strengths they also house some of your greatest weaknesses. Trust me, I know better than most. You have been led by mistrust and hate for many years, and it pains me to say it but humans are the worst culprit. You seem to hate and mistrust anything that is different from yourselves and what you don't understand. I'll admit that some' of your mistrust was fostered by the dragons, but after we were gone you let yourselves be taken by your worst emotions. Many races died or fled because mortals couldn't find common ground. You have all been contributing to your extinction for years."

I lowered my voice and filled my words with compassion. "What you have gathered here today will be your ultimate weapon: use your friendships and comradely as a shield. You must never go back to the way things were or Eiddoril will be lost and there will be nothing for me to return to."

There was silence throughout the courtyard as my words sank in.

I felt a presence at my back. I didn't need to turn to see who it was. Elric silently came to stand beside me and placed his hand in mine. I turned my head a little and smiled at his battered face, which didn't look quite as bad as I thought. The blood had been washed away and a long gash along his forehead had been neatly stitched up. His beautiful grey eyes were visible but one was surrounded by purple and black bruising. I resisted the urge to hold him, suddenly feeling self-conscious. This was the first time he had seen me in my true form. Some of my features were similar but I definitely was not the woman he'd fallen in love with.

Elric noticed my discomfort, mouthed the word "later" and nodded back toward the crowd.

I opened my mouth to speak but the behaviour of those gathered around me made me pause. They all looked terrified and were looking to the morning skies, all except Reaper. He caught my attention and I nodded in understanding. I had to do something before total chaos irrupted.

I raced down the steps with Elric close at my heels. My dragon voice boomed across the courtyard. "Edwin, Anora, you need to start the evacuation now."

I pointed to the skies. "It's Nubossa. He's projecting fear and is trying to scatter our forces. You need to control these people. Their fears are not real; you must do whatever it takes to keep them from losing their minds."

Just to confirm my thoughts a dark shadow flew overhead, blocking the sun. Nubossa screamed into the morning air, throwing another attack of crippling fear and despair. Shouts of terror and alarm sprang from everywhere. People scattered in every direction.

Enthor ran for the gates to get to the outer ward. "Try and calm these mortals down; I'll take care of Nubossa. He is only returning the favour and trying to cause turmoil. Have Anora get these people out of here and then get everyone in position. The army will not wait for nightfall."

Enthor cut off his communication and quickly shifted to dragon. He took off into the sky and headed right for the dark dragon. They collided briefly, each beast raking each other with claws, but Nubossa broke off first. I watched as the evil dragon ducked and avoided all of Enthor's attacks. The last I saw was the evil dragon heading back out toward the valley with Enthor close at his wings. I hoped Enthor knew what he was doing.

With Nubossa distracted, the fear that had gripped everyone lifted but damage had already been done. People were running everywhere and all sense of order was gone. I did the only thing I could think of: I roared. I'm sure that if anyone had been watching me it would have looked quite comical, but my deafening voice echoed throughout the courtyard and froze everyone in place.

Deneoes, who was nearby trying to knock some sense into some soldiers, smiled at me. "Nice—you know you could have done that earlier."

I grimly shook my head. "It wouldn't have worked. I had to wait until Nubossa's hold on them had passed."

King Edwin came to me red-faced and exasperated. "Yes, about that, is there nothing you can do to protect us from that attack? I don't see how we will be able to defend ourselves if we're too busy being afraid of unseen forces."

Again I had to shake my head. "Unfortunately there is nothing I can do to block his attacks, but as Elric and some of the others can attest to, it does get easier to control once you recognize the cause. Enthor will keep him distracted has much as possible, but it will be up to your men to overcome their fears. Now that they have been exposed to it, hopefully next time it'll be easier."

I drew in a calming breath. "We need to get moving. If Nubossa is brash enough for that kind of display, that can only mean his army is not far behind. We need to get the innocents out of here and prepare the men for battle."

The king nodded and ran off to find Anora to get that part of their plan into action.

Elric and Deneoes were quickly at my side. "Where do you want us?"

"We need to find Nalin and Jaitem. Deneoes, where's your father?"

The Ywari looked toward the main gates. "He's with our warriors outside the gate. You'll probably find the Kanarah there as well. I'll go tell them it's time. My little dragon friend is waiting for you at the top of the east tower. He knows what you want him to do. You just have to tell him when."

Deneoes grasped my hand and squeezed hard. "Watch your back, Red."

I nodded and Deneoes left, leaving Elric and me headed toward the tower where I had seen Nalin and Jaitem earlier. It turned out we didn't have to go far. The leader of the Order of Freedom met us halfway, out of breath and on edge.

"No matter how many times that bastard does that, it hits me hard. I came down to tell you we spotted the Dark Lord's army. They're coming over the last hill before the farm fields and the bridge. My men are already positioned among the abandoned farmhouses, and half the Gareth and Kanarah warriors are headed to the riverbank. If they get through, the rest of us, including the Ywari, are stationed outside and inside the castle walls. We should be able to hold them at bay long enough for you to get that portal open. I have to ask though: now that you are back to yourself, will you be able to open the gate? I know you were relying on the transfer to help fuel the spell."

I had hoped to, but I didn't reveal my doubts to him. "I hold enough power inside me to accomplish what needs to be done. I will also have the aide of the elements. The gate will open."

Elric looked worried. "What about the other dragons and creatures that plan to come through? They've been trapped for a long time and have had nothing but Mareth feeding them stories of revenge. How are we going to convince them not to attack?"

We kept walking as I told him my plan. "Mareth will send the dragons and other immortals through first. He's powerful, but he's also a coward. He's always made others do his dirty work. He will be relying on the chaos that they cause to beat down our defences. Once the dragons come through, they will be disoriented and will not immediately attack." I gestured toward the east tower. "I've got Deneoes to position his dragon in the east tower closest to where I plan on opening the portal. Once he sees all the dragons come through, I want him out there to face them and to project the images of the eggs and where they can be found. I'm hoping that it will be enough to see one of their offspring alive and well and to see their eggs unharmed to lead them away from here."

"What about Spike? won't he be in danger?"

I couldn't help but smile a little thinking about the young dragon. "I'm not worried about Spike; he is perfectly capable of taking care of himself. He's had the advantage of being raised by a very devious Ywari, and I'm sure he knows some tricks to keep him out of trouble."

Nalin rolled his eyes. "Yeah, or get into it. What about the other creatures? Do you have any idea what will come out of there?"

I shook my head. "No I don't, and I'm afraid that will be a wild card. From what Enthor and the elements have told me, most of the creatures will be scared and confused. The elements were forced by Destruction to banish them, so I'm hoping they will just be grateful to have a real home again. However, there will be some that will be a grave threat. There are far worse things than dragons and they have had a lifetime to think about revenge. I will have to be the main weapon against those beings. Mareth is not expecting me to be fully aware of my strength. He is counting on the destruction of my joining and my disorientation that follows to aide in his attack. When he discovers I am not only capable of fighting back but am, in fact, more powerful than he is, he will be greatly surprised."

Nalin nodded and grasped my hand in his. "Be careful, my friend, and hurry back."

I stood and watched as Nalin ran for the outer ward and was passed by a very angry and out of breath Enthor. "I hate that dragon! The sneaky bastard disappeared into storm clouds. There is a bad one rolling in, and I think she knows what you are planning. Nubossa's army is cresting the last hill and is approaching the river. Its time. Are you ready?"

In response, the skies suddenly turned dark and became filled with deep purple, green and black storm clouds. The sun disappeared, and thunder shook the courtyard walls. Gale-force winds picked up, and we had to fight the flying dust and debris. The sword on my back began to vibrate and felt too warm against my back. I drew it from its scabbard and looked into my sister's eyes.

"I've come to warn you. Mother knows what's going on. Our game has come to its climax. We will be torn between helping her and her allies and you and yours. This storm is only the beginning, but we will resist her as much as possible. When it comes time to open the portal, I will come to you and help you channel our power through you. After that, you are on your own. Once you are through you will be naturally drawn to our father, you are a part of him, and your soul will find him."

My sister's childlike eyes shined with fear. "I don't know what you will find on the other side. Mareth has done his master's biddings well and there may be very little life left in the immortal realms. You will not be able to survive long. You must find our father quickly and return as soon as possible. We will open the portal again during the winter solstice, so be ready. We will do our best to keep these mortals safe until your return. Be safe, Sister, and do not fail."

My sword darkened and returned to normal. I left it unsheathed and looked up toward the deadly sky.

Elric grasped my hand and made me look at him. He had to shout to be heard over the wind. "Are you sure you want to do this? We can find another way."

I faltered for a moment. Did I want to do this? Did I want to risk my life and happiness for a world that may never recover? I looked from my prince and Enthor, whose golden dragon eyes burned with fury. Yes I was sure. This was my choice, my destiny and I planned to win.

I gave Elric a gentle kiss and hid my fears. "Yes, I'm sure. There is no one else, and if we are to ever have a chance at happiness, I have to do this. Now go find your father; he will need you. Enthor and I will head out toward the army. We need to find the warlocks and take them out. Meet me at the tower tonight. I will need your help when the portal is opened. Make sure Deneoes and Jaitem are there as well. We will need all the elemental weapons in one spot to help defend against whatever comes through the portal. Just remember, don't attack unless they strike first. I want to try and avoid as much confrontation as possible."

Elric kissed me back with passion and then reluctantly let me go. I watched him leave the now deserted courtyard. The marking on my face began to burn blue with magic and I turned my dragon gaze on Enthor. I didn't know what to say to him. I didn't trust him any more and it tore at my soul. He seemed to sense this but made no move to console my fears. We simply turned and together made our way in silence out of the courtyard and ran through the abandoned houses in the outer ward toward the front gates.

It took us at least 15 minutes of hard running to reach the main gates, but it felt good to get my body moving. As soon as we passed through the doorway, the portcullis was dropped and Gareth was sealed behind solid stone. We ran tirelessly down the worn road. I looked past the empty farmhouses and the waiting soldiers and beyond to the river. Humans and Kanarahs lined the riverbank waiting with arrows, shields and spears. A solid line of fire could be seen cresting the final hill into the farmlands of Aserah, burning a pathway straight to us. The dark clouds had turned the day into night, further hampering our defences. There was no sign of Nubossa, which made me worry.

I grabbed Enthor by the arm, pulling him to a stop in front of one of the farmhouses. "What happened to Nubossa? Where did he go?"

Enthor ignored my question and started to shift into dragon. I did likewise and launched into the sky just in time to avoid a fireball rocketing toward the empty farmhouse I had just been standing next to. Wood and debris exploded everywhere and the soldiers stationed nearby scattered. I whipped my gaze back across the river and saw more of the fiery missiles headed our way. The warlocks had dropped the line of fire and were now hurtling it across the sky.

I yelled into Enthors mind. *"I need to stay in my human form; I can control the elements better that way. You go and find those damn warlocks."*

I dodged another firebomb, which landed in the fields, instantly catching the dry grasses ablaze. Soldiers and warriors scattered trying to avoid the fire raining from the sky. I dropped back down to the earth close to the riverbank and instantly changed back to my humanoid form.

Enthor took off toward the bulk of the army, searching for the evil magic users, but he was quickly intercepted by their dark leader.

Nubossa didn't bother to communicate through our minds and his dragon voice shook the skies. "It's time for this game to end. I have waited a long time for this moment and I will not be denied."

The Dark Lord screamed at Enthor, throwing acid toward him. Enthor barely made it out of the way before Nubossa was on him. Enthor fought hard trying to free himself from the larger dragon, but sheer strength wasn't going to win it for him.

Nubossa grabbed Enthor by the shoulders near the base of his wings and sank his claws into him. Enthor cried out in pain and then used his unique body shape and curled around Nubossa like a snake. Before the dark dragon could free himself, Enthor erupted a stream of fire into Nubossa's face. The black dragon screamed in pain and fury and clamped his fierce maw around Enthor's neck. I sent a blast of wind at the pair, knocking them both off balance, managing to break them apart. Enthor used the advantage and headed for the lake with Nubossa right behind him.

More fire came soaring over the bridge and continued to pummel my surroundings, all the while leading Nubossa's army closer. The first wave was almost at the bridge and now the fire was accompanied by shouts of war. Arrows flew from our side finding multiple targets, but unless I did something about those warlocks, no amount of arrows would help.

I focussed myself and let my power guide me. Everything seemed to disappear and all I was aware of was the elemental magic that was being violently tossed around. I stood near the river's edge and called to my sister. I held my arms out toward the water, and instantly the icy liquid sprang to my outstretched limbs. I pivoted so I was facing the fields and threw the water around me like an erupting geyser. In the same motion, I completed my turn so that I was facing the river again and caught a fire blast in my hands before it could harm anyone. I held it for a second, letting the power rush through me, and then I made it grow and I sent it flying back to where it had come from, leaving a smoking crater. Cries of triumph from our side filled the air but I held no such joy. This fight was far from over.

Nubossa's army had reached what they thought was the bridge and started to push their way across. I watched dozens of soldiers fall through the false bridge and plunge to the icy depths below. Some tried to climb out but were held back by slick, muddy sides that proved impossible to traverse. I sent my power again into the water and the current sped up, carrying bodies past me, trapping them in an icy grave.

Gareth's men continued to hammer Nubossa's army with arrows and the Kanarahs attacked with their spears, but the enemy were now countering with missiles of their own. Once they figured out that the false bridge was a trap, they pulled back and formed protective barriers with their shields.

Movement coming from behind the human soldiers brought cries of triumph from the enemy lines. Ngogar came into view pulling massive battering rams and catapults. Then I watched, startled, as part of the shore started to slide rapidly down the embankment into the water. The earth was filling in the bottom of the river. The warlocks were trying to form a dam and their own bridge across.

I tried to focus my attention on the magic-made bridge but was knocked to the ground. The body covered me as dozens of flaming arrows sailed overhead. I lay there stunned as recognition hit me. Reaper, his black eyes glittering, gave me his hand and hauled me back up. Fang was at his side, also dodging arrows and growling at the Hautur.

"No one gets to kill you but me, so I suggest you focus and figure out a way to stop those warlocks."

I stared at him in amazement but managed to get my mind straight. "I can't take them all on at the same time. As soon as I try to stop that bridge, our soldiers will be hit with something else. I have to protect them. I need another magic user or at least I need to know how many of these bastards I'm dealing with. Nubossa has more than I thought and they are very powerful."

Another wave of fire came at us and I pushed Reaper out of the way while raising my hands in the air. A powerful gust of wind caught the fire midair, and I swept it away down river where it popped and sizzled and then extinguished.

Reaper looked across the river and made a decision. "I'll go see what I can find out. I'll see if I can discover how many there are and where they are."

Without waiting for my reply, he shifted to a small rat and scurried past the soldiers who were already starting to come across the warlocks' bridge, and now that the water was dammed, Litui began to jump in and swim their way across as well, seemingly impervious to the frigid temperatures. Hand-to-hand combat ensued everywhere. I drew my sword and fought hard to hold my position at the earth bridge. I tried to focus my power again while keeping attacking men at bay on the growing structure, but a wave of fear and terror blanketed the area. I looked up in time to see Nubossa diving down through the dark clouds and stood frozen as he snatched me up into his claws. My sword fell from my hands and I watched helplessly as the men below fought for their lives.

Nubossa gained speed and altitude as he closed his bloody claws around me. He changed his flight and started to fly away from the battle and Gareth. He was taking me from the battle. I tried to struggle free but he squeezed painfully and I resisted the urge to cry out. Instead, I closed my eyes and went deep inside myself. I drew my brothers and sister to me. Rain started to pound down hard, hampering the dark dragon's wings and impairing his visibility. I hoped it would interfere with his magic and cause him some pain distracting him further. I grasped hold of Nubossa's talons and sent a bolt of lightning charging through his body, causing his whole frame to shudder. He released his hold on me. My human form plunged through the stormy sky as I once again called to the elements for help. The wind slowed my descent and I shifted to dragon in midair. I searched the blackened sky for my enemy but he had disappeared again, the bloody coward.

Stopping the rain, I changed my course and headed back toward the battle. Nubossa had carried me quite a distance and I was growing fatigued by the time I returned. I swallowed the horror I felt as I viewed the carnage below. The warlocks had been hampered by the rain also so they let up on their fire attacks, but they had completed their bridge and now the bulk of Nubossa's army poured over it. Our men were being overrun, and unless they fell back, there would be no one left.

I flew down closer to the earth bridge and blasted the enemy with all four elements. A stream of pure blinding white elemental energy flowing from my open maw incinerated the occupants coming over the bridge, and chunks of dirt and mortals flew into the air.

I banked and circled back around looking for Duncan and the commander from Clorynina. I found them fighting side by side and invaded their minds. *"You must pull the men back. Get back to the keep. I will hold them off and cover your retreat, but you must hurry. I can't fight their warlocks and Nubossa at the same time".*

Right on cue the evil magic users sent fire streaking across the sky right for me while at the same time another earthen bridge began to from quickly across the river. I darted out of the way but one of the fire shots grazed my belly, searing off my scales and exposing the tender skin underneath. I bit back the pain and flew closer to the ground, skimming the edge of the shoreline, knocking Dark Lord soldiers into the water. I banked off, landed back on our side of the river and quickly shifted back to human, ignoring the flesh wound in my abdomen, which was wet with blood, and tried to cover our own soldiers' retreat.

I stretched out my arms and called to the water. The again dammed river rose quickly up the banks and spilled over the shore. I reached down, plunged my hands into the freezing liquid and lifted my arms back up. The water followed my motion and looked like I was pulling a blanket up out of the river. I extended my reach to its fullest and the giant water curtain rose higher into the sky. The force of the water completely obliterated the warlocks' Earth bridge for a second time and successfully cut off the bulk of Nubossa's army from our defenders, allowing them to regroup and head for the keep. The only problem was that I was injured and using a considerable amount of power, and I wouldn't be able to keep this up for long.

The temporary delay in action from Nubossa's men didn't last long. They spotted their target through the wall of water and took aim. I sent another wave of magic through the water and ice began to form. It spread quickly but not before two arrows found their mark. One lodged itself into my bare shoulder, the other in my thigh. Pain and fatigue flooded my body as I strained to keep the wall of ice up. Movement to my left caught my attention as my furry fanged companion came into view. She was soaking wet and her maw was covered in gore. She padded toward me and leaned against me, trying to push me towards the keep.

"I can't, not yet; I need to give our men more time."

The decision was taken away from me when two large firebombs struck my wall of ice, shattering it and sending shards flying everywhere. The force of the blast sent me flying and I landed hard several feet away from the river's edge. Several more arrows came sailing toward me and I barely had enough strength to push them away with wind.

Fang, who was crouched beside me looked to the dark sky and roared. It was almost as if she was signalling something. I didn't have to ponder long because out of the clouds flew a familiar form. I let the giant Ristiaper gather me in its talons and I watched from above the earth bridge rebuilding and my feline friend headed toward the keep. I listened to the shouts of mortal rage at losing their prey, and as the cries of war slowly faded, I let exhaustion take me.

CHAPTER 37

My temporary reprieve was roughly interrupted by shouts and feline roaring. I opened my eyes to find myself back in Gareth's main courtyard surrounded by violence. I was lying on my back on the rough cobblestone.

Elric was standing right above me with his sword pointed at Reaper's throat—who was again in the guise of a Gareth soldier. Anger flashed in the Hautur's eyes as he reached up and grabbed the prince's sword in his hands. The sharp blade dug into his skin but he didn't flinch.

"How many times do I have to save her before you believe you can trust me? I didn't shoot her full of arrows, nor did I throw the firebomb that lacerated her stomach. I am trying to help here, but if you don't want my help, then I'll leave. I don't know why I have stayed as long as I have anyway."

I propped myself up on to my elbows. "Why have you stayed? And don't feed me that garbage about wanting to kill me yourself. There is something deeper going on here, and I want to know what it is."

Elric lowered his sword and crouched beside me, but I kept my gaze on Reaper.

He flexed his hand and his wound began to close over and heal. I watched the conflict of emotions warring in his eyes. "My reasons are my own and someday soon I will explain things to you, but for now you have bigger things to worry about. You're not healing. Why?"

I let the matter drop for now and winced at the pain I felt in this human form.

Elric made me drink some water and then smoothed my hair out of my eyes. "What can I do?"

I moaned a little in pain and shifted my body weight. "I can't heal in human form. I need to shift."

I took Elric's hand in my own and squeezed. "And you must trust Reaper. We can't afford to have everyone fighting with him every time he appears. He will cause no harm, and besides, Fang seems to have already made her choice. She seems to be content with his presence, and I trust her instincts beyond a doubt."

Fang sat on her haunches close by watching us. Her gaze fell upon me, and just for an instant our eyes locked and I felt something so familiar, but it flickered from my reach. Fang shook herself as if she was trying to rid herself of a bug and then proceeded to pace impatiently along the wall, her fur shifting to match the colour of the stone.

Elric's voice brought me back from my thoughts. "All right, I'll do this for you, but I still have a bad feeling about it." Elric stood and motioned everyone to get back.

My human female body disappeared and elongated into my dragon form, filling up the limited space in the courtyard. When my transformation was complete, I looked down at the wound that covered most of my underside. My symbol on my face pulsed with magic and I felt myself begin to heal. It would not be long before I felt myself again.

I took a moment to survey the courtyard. It was not a pretty scene. Injured soldiers and warriors were everywhere, crammed into the confines of the courtyard walls. I quickly estimated that fewer than half had made it back from the river, and with those odds I had a terrible feeling in my gut.

I swung my massive head around to where Elric stood with his father, Nalin, Jaitem, Reaper and Deneoes and spoke to their minds. *"Reaper, what did you find out about the warlocks? There are too many for me to handle on my own and with Enthor possibly gone I don't know how I can fight them and Nubossa."*

Reaper's words were sombre. "The warlocks were a major secret within the Dark Lord's plans. Even as close as I was with him I did not know all that involved them. I can tell you that there are at least ten I could see and they are very powerful, but I may have a solution to at least part of your problem."

Reaper waited for the rebuke from my companions, but surprisingly none came, so he continued. He untied a small sack from his waist and brought something from it. Its dull metallic surface brought back bad memories. I hissed at it.

Reaper nodded. "Yes, these are the bracelets that were used to suppress your magic. The Dark Lord uses them to control his warlocks. If enough of these can be placed on the warlocks, they would be easy to take out and would level the playing field to more even ground."

Deneoes walked forward and looked inside the bag. "Sounds like a good plan, but how do we get them on them?"

Reaper's words were shrouded in secrecy. "I have already spoken to my people who are within Nubossa's army. They are ready to carry out this plan. They will no longer be a threat to you and will no longer serve the Dark Lord."

We all stared open-mouthed and disbelieving, and something again tickled the back of my mind.

Deneoes looked up at the shifter, shaking his head. "Whoa, whoa, whoa—now what are you trying to tell us? Are you saying that you somehow convinced a whole race of slime bag enemies to suddenly switch sides? I was starting to actually like you, but now I think you might be off your rocker."

Reaper almost smiled. "As I have said before, there is much about my people you don't understand, and trust me when I say that they are *my* people. They will do what I command. They will not fight for you but they will not fight against you either."

Reaper looked up at me, and for the first time I saw vulnerability in him that I never expected. "Our faith and our calling have been lost and forgotten for a long time, but I swear to you that I will not betray you again."

That's when it clicked. The tickling in the back of my mind became a pounding and sudden recognition and memories flooded my mind. It was like a physical blow and I had to take in several calming breaths before I could communicate. I remembered.

I lowered my massive head and spoke to everyone's mind making sure they all heard but my focus was on Reaper. *"I remember now. I'm not sure why this memory took so long to resurface but I remember. You and your people were my guardians. You worked with the mages and we fought side by side. You were at one time one of my closest friends, but your feelings toward me changed. You were so young and I was in love with another."*

Reaper silenced me with his hand and a look of genuine regret. "I'll finish the story, although I wish you had left this memory buried."

Reaper inhaled deeply and I thought he would not continue, but Deneoes of all people nodded at the shape-shifter, urging him to continue.

Reaper's eyebrows rose and he looked back at me. "I was devastated and full of hate when you chose the human over me. You were the only creature who ever gave our race a chance. You were never repulsed by us and you helped the other mortals accept us as well . . . all but the humans."

Anger filled Reaper's voice as he avoided the stares of the humans gathered around him. "I couldn't bring myself to understand your thinking in choosing a human so I retreated into myself and fled. As you said I was very young and I couldn't control the emotions that warred inside me. The Dark Lord found me and polluted my mind with his fear and evil. He saw in me the perfect weapon and exploited my pain to its fullest. I would like to say that it was he who controlled me with his magic, that it was his entire fault, but I would be lying. I let myself be controlled and gave in to my jealousy. I betrayed you and helped trap you and stood there and watched with joy in my heart as your human lover died at someone else's hand."

Reaper's eyes met mine, and they were filled with so much sorrow and regret. His voice shook with emotion. "You pleaded with me as I dragged you before the Dark Lord, but it was too late, my soul had been stained and I didn't know how to fix it. Then the spell was cast and everyone forgot who you were, including me. My people fell into the dark, because without you the rest of the mortals shunned us. We fled to the Barren Wastes and let the Dark Lord take care of us. I had no idea who you were, only the hatred and lies the Dark Lord told me and the hate I felt for you after the Kanarah woman died was all I knew. I followed the Dark Lord blindly leading my people in a war that wasn't our own but as I found out more of his final plans, I knew I had to try to do something. I still cared for my people and wanted a better life for us. I came back to Gareth with the full intent of killing you, but your speech stirred something in me. I didn't know what it was, but I decided to wait and help you. Then last night, when you finally regained your dragon form, the spell was broken and all of my memories came back to me . . . and they almost destroyed me."

Reaper paused and took a steadying breath. "I would say that I am sorry, but it seems too empty a gesture. I will not ask for your forgiveness because I am not sure I can ever forgive myself, but I pledge my life to you and swear I will never betray you again."

Silence fell across the courtyard. Thunder cracked and rolled through the dark sky, and the fire in the torches spit in agitation, reminding everyone of the danger we were still in.

All eyes were on me and I closed my own to calm my anger. When I opened them again, I was still and focused. My mental voice betrayed my emotions though. *"I remember now, and yes, it would be useless to ask for my forgiveness. What you did caused so much pain and what you and your people did afterward is shameful . . . you have much to atone for."*

I straightened my neck to its fullest and looked down on Reaper. *"However, so do I. I accept your pledge and am grateful for the Hauturs' support again. As for our past and our future, that is something that will have to be dealt with later."*

I lifted my head and addressed the crowd. *"I suggest we get moving. Nubossa's men will not take long to reach the front gates. We need to keep them out of the outer ward. If they succeed in penetrating those walls, then it will be easy for them to smash through the city and reach the inner ward and the keep. It is nearing evening and the moon will be high soon. I will do what I can to fortify the walls, but I am counting on you to keep those soldiers out of Gareth. With the warlocks neutralized, they will be without magic and on even ground with you.*"

Duncan came forward and held out my sword. "I retrieved this from the battlefield. I saw you drop it when the Dark Lord took you."

I shook my horned head and gestured toward Reaper. *"I can't carry it any more; I don't want to chance losing it again. Give it to the one it rightfully belongs to. Give it back to Reaper—or should I say Ranjir?"*

Surprise lit Duncan's face, but he did has he was asked. Ranjir reached out and took the water sword from Duncan's hands and it instantly flared to life. He stared at it momentarily, emotion clouding his eyes, and then he strapped it to his back with his other weapons.

An out-of-breath messenger burst into the courtyard and ran straight for the king. "Sire, they're here! The army has reached the main gate. The outer ward is under attack."

A large boom echoed throughout the courtyard, signalling the arrival of Nubossa's men. I instantly took to the sky, trying not to knock people over in the process and headed for the front gate.

They were not using magic yet but they didn't need to. The Ngogars had dragged along the battering rams and catapults I'd spotted earlier—and they brought something else. Four huge siege towers hastily made from bits and pieces of what looked like houses were being pushed closer to the castle walls. The warlocks must have made them from the destroyed farmhouses—very clever. The large uprooted tree fortified with iron tips they were using for a battering ram was strapped between four of the Ngogars, and they rammed it relentlessly against the gates. Their massive bodies shook with the effort and the Litui soldiers whipping them into action had to jump out of the way to avoid their massive horns. The iron of the portcullis shuddered as a second blow rocked the structure.

Flaming debris periodically flew over the walls from their catapults, causing fires everywhere among the empty houses, while still other shots were chunks of solid rock that slammed into the walls. The enemy did not take long to spot me, and I was instantly assailed with fire and lightning strikes. I ducked, dodged and managed to land on our side of the gate. I quickly transformed and ran through the gathered soldiers on the ground.

Yaleon and Tilan saw me and came to my side.

Yaleon's dark eyes were wide, but he was in control. "There are too many, and with their magic, we won't last long. We've tried our arrows and spears but they are simply pushed aside by their evil magic."

I grasped his shoulder and tried to give him hope. "I know. We have a plan in motion to eliminate the warlocks. Save your weapons; you'll get your chance to use them shortly. As for these walls, stand back and I'll see what I can do."

I moved closer to the wall and placed my hands on the rough surface. I called to my brother and poured my power into the walls. The battered walls shimmered with magic and where once stood walls made from common stone now stood a nearly impenetrable wall of granite more than capable of withstanding elemental attacks.

I turned my gaze to the surroundings soldiers. "Hold on to something, I'm going to try and take out those siege towers." I plunged my hands into the ground beneath the walls and poured the power of Earth into it trying to guide it out and underneath our defences. The area around us began to shake violently and I fed the tremors as long as I thought it safe for our men.

Another blow to the gates brought me upright and I saw the walls start to change. The warlocks were attempting to counter my magic. Damn them! I retreated back from the soldiers and shifted again to dragon. I launched gracefully into the air and flew over the castle walls, and before they knew what was happening I blasted the battering ram and its operators with pure energy, leaving nothing but a smoking crater. The warlocks' attention was again drawn to me, leaving the castle walls intact. They resumed their elemental attack on me, forcing me into impossible aerial moves that I could not keep up for long.

With the evil magic users focused on me, that left our men free to attack the enemy soldiers. Yaleon gave a command and hundreds of Ywari who had been waiting below sprang to the wall and scaled it like a tree. Their tiny barbed hands and feet found purchase where there was none, and once they reached the top they began assaulting the enemy with arrows. However, no matter how many enemy soldiers they took down, three more sprang to take their place littering the ground with bloody corpses', and every minute those siege towers drew closer. They had survived my tremors and I could not target all them without leaving myself open. The warlocks were forcing me to stay airborne, and no matter where I turned, another wave of magic flew through the air.

I had no idea how long we had been fighting, but I was growing tired. Thousands of dead men and creatures alike lay strewn across my vision and still they kept coming with mindless determinations. We were not without our own losses. The castle walls were scorched with fire damage and our defenders on the wall were dwindling. Where were the Hautur? Why were they waiting so long to strike? I needed those warlocks neutralized now or we were finished.

I tried to circle closer to the ground, around a gathered group of soldiers where I was sure at least some of the warlocks were hidden, but an impossibly strong updraft grabbed my wings and sent me spinning into the night sky. I rose above the clouds and finally righted myself and saw that the moon was steadily approaching its position; the long day had finally turned to night and I was running out of time. I dived back down through the thick cloud cover and found the siege towers had finally reached the walls. Enemy fighters were pouring on to the turrets and engaging in combat. I could do little but watch as I tried desperately to avoid being struck again by warlock magic.

My patience finally ran out and I recklessly dived for the centre of enemy lines, but Nubossa had different plans. He tore through the night sky and headed straight for me. I had no time to react and we collided, each of us raking at the undersides of each other's bodies. Scales and dragon blood rained down as we both tried to gain an advantage. I winced in pain as Nubossa reopened the wound I had received earlier, digging his claws into my tender muscle. I tried to wrap my longer body around the dark dragon but he was not going to be fooled by that manoeuvre again. He bit down hard on the base of my wing, making me lose my balance. He released his painful grip and pushed himself away from me.

We hovered in midair for an instant before Nubossa's voice filled my mind. *"Now, my warlocks, attack! Take this useless excuse for a dragon down."*

I braced for the elemental attack, but it never came. I silently screamed for joy, left the battle to the mortals and launched myself at the bewildered dark dragon with vengeance. We embraced again in our deadly dance.

"It looks like you'll have to do your own dirty work for a change," I shouted in his mind. *"Come, let's see how well you fight on even terms."*

Fear and rage exploded into my mind, causing me to lose focus. I started to untangle myself and try to descend, but Nubossa dug his sharp claws into my back and dragged us up into the sky. My wings were useless so I went limp, and then, using my longer neck and body, I snaked my head around so that I was looking into Nubossa's face. My symbol flared a brilliant blue and I opened my jaws to blast the bastard with my power, but he suddenly dropped me and my shot went harmlessly into the sky. My back throbbed with pain, but at least my wings were free, and I beat them furiously and turned in pursuit.

The skies had finally cleared with the absence of elemental interference, and glancing at the moon I quickly changed my direction. I foolishly pushed Nubossa from my mind and raced to my rendezvous point.

My scream of pain echoed through the night sky as Nubossa landed on my back again and sprayed acid onto the base of my neck. I lost concentration and we started to plummet at breakneck speed to the ground.

Nubossa released himself from my back, but before he could fly from me, I rolled over, attached my body to his underside and flipped us around. Our momentum crashed us both into the earth below, causing the ground to shake and split apart. The impact separated us, and I was thrown a few hundred feet away from him.

I lay still as I watched the dust and debris settle back down around me. I couldn't move. I watched as my evil brethren pulled himself up out of the hole we had created and shook his body. He looked horrible, with one wing dragging limply along the ground, but he still managed to stay upright. I had not taken the brunt of the impact, but there was no way I could defend myself.

I lifted my head weakly and spoke to Nubossa as he stalked triumphantly toward me. "You need to stop this; you must see that you are being used. What will you do when you are no longer useful and she tries to destroy you? It will happen. Trust me, I know."

Nubossa sneered at me as he came steadily closer, his voice grating and booming across the night.

"You know nothing. If anyone has been a pawn in a game, it has been you. The only difference is that I know all the rules and the players, and you don't."

I closed my eyes, pretending to be in pain, when actually I was gathering my power for one last attack. I argued with the stupid, evil dragon. "What are you talking about? I know my purpose, I know why I was created, and I will save this world."

"You're so foolish, Ililsaya; you still do not understand the lure of the power. Power can control anyone, even the ones you hold most dear to you."

My eyes flew open along with my jaws, and this time my elemental burst hit its mark. My power hit Nubossa in the shoulder and tore his left wing almost completely off. It hung gored and useless by his side, matching the other.

All reason left the dark dragon and he charged. I tried to move out of the way and call to my power but I was too weak. But then the strangest thing happened: the ground below his feet became like quicksand, causing his front limbs to sink. He pitched forward, drilling his head into the soft ground not 10 yards from my snout.

I turned my head weakly to the side and saw Elric removing his shield from the ground. He was flanked by the rest of my friends and someone I wasn't entirely sure I wanted to see. Enthor came forward with his life crystal held out before him. The prism caught the moonlight and reflected it back around him.

Enthor was not without scars. He had an acid burn down the side of his face and left arm and he walked with a limp. However, when he spoke the power in his voice shook me. "It's over, Nubossa. This is where it ends. You have caused enough suffering. May you find peace in Duggati."

Nubossa pulled his head from the dirt and dropped it. His evil, cold red eyes drilled into my soul, and he laughed in my mind. *"You know, I almost feel sorry for you. Good luck, Ililsaya, I will see you soon."*

Before I could ask him what his cryptic message meant, Enthor activated the crystal and Nubossa's life energy was drawn into it. I saw the ghostly form leave the damaged husk of dragon flesh and flow effortlessly into the waiting prison. The prism faded and then went dark.

Enthor pocketed the crystal and stood before me. I gathered myself and sat on my hind legs. I stretched and flexed my wings and then went deep inside myself. I called to my brothers and sister and felt their power enter my soul, healing me and making me stronger.

When I was healed, I turned my cold gaze to my once-trusted ally. Now I was filled with so much doubt it made me angry. I quickly shifted to my human form and stood emotionlessly before Enthor. "I'm glad you're alive. I was afraid Nubossa had beaten you. What will you do with his life energy?"

Enthor eyed me suspiciously, trying to read my face, but I showed nothing; it was a trick I had learned well from him. He shrugged and turned from me. "It's not your concern; trust me, I'll make sure it gets where it needs to be."

I bet he would. I let the matter drop and instead focussed my attention on my prince. He came forward and swept me into his embrace. I saw the hate in Enthor's eyes and now realized I had to fear for my prince's life. Gently pushing away from Elric and never taking my eyes off Enthor, I began to draw my power to me, but something interrupted me. The hairs on the back of my neck and all down my arms stood on end. My hair started to rise, and when I went to smooth it down a small shock went down my spine.

Deneoes reached out and touched me, giving himself a shock as well. "Ouch, what the hell was that? It's like the air is charged with lightning."

And I realized that was in fact what was happening. I looked up to the sky and stared as a spot of light shined in the night sky. At first I thought it was a star, but then it started to grow and pulse. As it got bigger, it took the form of a vortex swirling quickly in the night sky. It felt as if all the elements' energy was being pulled into the vortex.

My voice cracked a little with anxiety. "It's the portal; Mareth is opening it from the other side. Its time! Quickly, I need all of you to surround me. I will need the power of all the elements and your weapons will act as conduits. Where is Ranjir?"

"Here." A voice came from behind me as the Hautur ran toward our group.

I sent him a quick mental message that only he could hear. *"Please act like nothing is going on. I need you to do something for me, something I know you will not like, but I am begging you to do it".*

Ranjir's eyes flashed with understanding as he slowed his pace, but he gave nothing away as I again spoke to his mind. *"When I'm gone, you need to protect Elric. I don't know what's going on with Enthor, but I don't trust him and I'm afraid Elric is a target. Please promise you will watch out for him—please."*

When Ranjir finally reached me, he grasped my hand as if in greeting and gave it a hard squeeze. He betrayed nothing with his eyes but I took the gesture as my answer.

"Thank you," I said.

I refocused my attention on the group gathered around me. "Ready?"

My companions all nodded.

"Good. Now form a circle around me and point your weapons toward me. Enthor, I need you to say the spell; it will leave me more of my mind to draw in the elements' power."

Enthor moved into position outside the circle several feet behind me. His words betrayed no emotion. "Of course. Whenever you're ready."

I looked up to the east tower and sent out another mental message. *"Spike, are you ready"?*

A small dragon's head poked its way over the wall and feelings of determination and excitement filled me.

The vortex was growing and slowly descending. It came to rest at fewer than 30 feet from the ground and pulsed with energy. The moon shined with magical brilliance, and I inhaled the raw elemental power surrounding me. Everything was ready but something wasn't right; I felt a presence trying to invade my spirit. I shook my head in confusion. It wasn't Nubossa—he was trapped inside the crystal and Mareth had no such hold on me, but I felt a connection . . . a strangely familiar caress, and my body shuddered at the intimate intrusion.

The storm clouds that I had kept at bay once again gathered, but this time they took on a form. My companions gasped as a humanoid shape formed of black and green storm mass appeared in the sky. Lightning continuously flashed through the form, illuminating its dark features. Eyes the colour of blood gazed lidless at the puny creations on the ground and she drilled into my mind. Her touch was intoxicating and I closed my eyes, moaning in rapture at the power she fed me. I heard voices, people desperately calling to me, but I raised my arms and threw them all back with a burst of power. Nothing mattered to me; everything left my mind but her.

The mother withdrew some of her power and I cried out in anger. She soothed my mind and then spoke, her voice eerily echoing through the night. "Young child, I have been searching for you for a long time. I have missed you, but now you can come home, now you can be with me the way it was always meant to be."

A fresh surge of power flowed through my body and I convulsed in ecstasy. "Yes, I will come with you, I will do as you say. Just don't take away the power. I have been in pain for so long; I just want to feel the power."

The mother laughed. "Excellent, child, I knew you would come to me. You are very special, and together we can feed off this world for eternity."

"Yes, I would like that," I dreamily replied.

"Now, daughter of the elements and life, prove yourself to me. Destroy these pathetic mortals. Bathe in their deaths and feed off their *destruction*."

I opened my eyes, which were no longer my own. I threw my arms to the sky and called to the elements and made them do my bidding. I felt their pain and their sorrow but nothing could penetrate the wall of power that smothered my soul. The earth shook and the wind howled. Trees were uprooted and lifted into the air and fire rained from the sky. Screams of terror and pain surrounded me but nothing mattered, nothing but the power. An ugly laugh poured from my mouth as I directed the elements in a dance of destruction.

Several mortals—I couldn't recall their names—tried to reach me but I flicked them away like flies, laughing at their screams of terror. I continued my attack on the mortals' puny existence until a large furry shape slammed into my side, and I fell to my hands and knees. The chaos around me subsided and I stared breathing heavily into the eyes of a creature I once knew. The great cat delved into my fractured mind and tried desperately to reach me. I knew this creature, had loved this being, but I couldn't remember why. I started to push the cougar away and then another presence was next to me. He grasped me roughly by the shoulders and made me look at him. He was injured and blood ran freely down his face. His clothes were singed and torn but his bright grey eyes were what caused me the most pain. I saw fear and betrayal, but underneath it all I saw love. I knew this man, loved him more deeply than anything in this world and I would die for him.

His voice cut me like a blade. "Please, Ililsaya, don't do this. We need you. I need you. Please come back."

Sudden pain racked my body as the mother tried to push more power into my soul, but something was resisting it. The small flame that burned deep within my soul flared and began to grow. The power that I had been born with fought against the pollution that raced through my body, and it burned as it cleansed my soul. I became aware of myself again and I shook with emotion. Destruction had played me well and all I held dear had paid the price. I tried to look away from Elric to hide in shame but he held me and I let his love, our love, feed the life energy inside me.

The mother screamed inside my skull but could no longer harm me. The power of Life now protected me and offered itself as a weapon. I stood and faced my enemy in the sky and raised my hands toward it.

Elric stepped back as my body began to glow a golden hue. It got brighter and brighter until all those around me had to look away. The tortured souls of the dead surrounded me, and I screamed my fury and hatred at the sky and sent my life energy rocketing into the night. The spirits followed it in a starving frenzy, cloaking the golden stream in black as it ripped through the mother, tearing a hole through her corporeal form and forcing her screaming back to wherever it was that she'd come from.

The night was calm again and the moon and stars shined down on me. I had not beaten her but at least she now knew I wasn't easily defeated and that I could harm her.

I turned back to my companions and took in the landscape. Destruction was everywhere and my heart sank at the knowledge of what I had caused. Small fires had erupted everywhere, and trees and debris littered my view. Even the castle hadn't escaped my wrath. There were large cracks spreading up the wall, and in one place part of the centuries' old structure had collapsed. I now understood Nubossa's message and it terrified me.

Elric limped toward me with a haunted look on his face and I backed away.

"Elric, I'm so sorry, I never meant to harm anyone. She was so strong, and I . . ."

Enthor came between us, snarling and pointed to the sky. The vortex was still there but it was shrinking, and unless I did something now we would have to wait until the next solstice. and there was no way I could defeat the mother on my own again. The next time she would be ready.

I grabbed Elric by the arm and together we ran to our positions. I was glad to see that all my friends had made it, but they looked at me differently and it hurt to think what they must now think of me.

Enthor shouted at me, "Hurry, you don't have much time. Gather the elements and open the portal."

Enthor closed his eyes and began to recite the spell. His dragon voice boomed across the fields and echoed off the castle walls. I stepped inside a ring of arrows from Deneoes and called to my brethren. The wind instantly swirled around me, picking up speed until I could barely see my friends. I stretched my hand to Jaitem on my right and fire leapt into my extended fingers. I reached out my other arm toward Ranjir and my sister joined me. Elric slammed his shield into the ground in front of me and Earth followed up through my body, completing the circle. Lastly, I turned my gaze toward the moon, tipped my head back and exposed my pulsing symbol. Pure energy rained down from the moon and bathed me. My symbol absorbed all of it, and in one final motion and at the culmination of Enthor's spell, I clapped my hands together sending all of that power shooting straight into the vortex, splitting it wide open.

The elements all died down around me and I nearly collapsed from exertion. Elric came to me and supported my weight and then together with the rest of our friends we watched the vortex absorb the power. It bent and flexed, growing larger. It began to expand and looked like a hole was being torn in the night sky. The swirling, colourful mass stilled and became a solid golden colour. I saw a desolate landscape and then shapes start to fill the void. They sped toward the opening and freedom.

We all scattered, leaving Enthor and me room to shift, and together from the sky we watched all hell break loose.

CHAPTER 38

Dozens of dragons poured from the portal, filling the night sky with vibrant colours. Under other circumstances, it would have brought great joy to my heart, but I knew that this situation was a bomb waiting to explode. The dragons hovered in midair and some even landed, each looking around in confusion. The transition between planes is not a pleasant one, and I took advantage of their discomfort.

I screamed into the young dragon's mind. *"Spike, now!"*

The dragonling wasted little time and launched its small body into the air. He flew around the others, dodging in and out of their line of sight, and then when he was sure he had their attention, he blasted their minds with images. Images of their eggs safe and unharmed filled the dragons minds, feelings of joy at being reunited with his kind, feelings of love that he held for a mortal, and lastly an image of Nubossa's capture. All the dragons started talking at once, and I roared to get their attention. All the dragons stilled but one.

"Ililsaya, is that you? You're alive? And who is that, Enthor? What is going on? Where did this young dragon come from? He looks like Kimlryn."

I exhaled and spoke to my brethren. "Zhyess, it is good to see you. I'm sorry, but I don't have time to explain everything right now. Just know that Nubossa is gone and is no longer a threat. Your eggs are safe and Enthor will take you to them as soon as this is over, but I'm afraid I need to ask something of all of you. I know Mareth has been plotting his revenge for a long time and I'm sure he has promised you glory, but I am asking you to turn on him now. Help me fight the horde that is about to come through that gate. Help me save our species and our world. Together you can make this your home again. The mortals are not your enemies, and as you have seen through the eyes of one of your own hatchlings you can all live here peacefully."

Zhyess eyed me suspiciously but she also made no move against me. "You keep referring to us staying here and living our lives, but I didn't hear what your involvement in all of this is. We were told that you betrayed us and that it was you that caused our banishment and that your mother, my sister, had been slain by Nubossa. How did you escape and defeat such a powerful foe?"

I fiercely shook my horned head. "Please, I know you have many questions, but I need your answer now. Can it not be enough to know that your offspring are safe and that I am offering you a chance at peace? I will handle Mareth on my own, but I need you all to help these mortals against the hoard that is coming. Only you know what they are capable of, and if any get past me I need you to try and talk to them, tell them we are not their enemies."

I waited and watched the dragons. Some grew bored and were just happy to be free of the immortal realm and took off into the night without a word. Others gathered around Zhyess and faced me.

"I'm sorry for what Mareth did to your mother. None of us wanted this, but we had no choice. I never believed what Mareth told us about you. I can't speak for all of us, but there are some who will help you. I must tell you that some of the creatures coming through that gate will not be swayed."

I shuddered at her words, but at least we were no longer alone.

Zhyess looked at me with doubt. "How are you going to stop them from coming through? No dragon is that powerful, not even Mareth."

I spread my jaws and let my magic dance between my teeth. White hot energy popped and sizzled, waiting to be used.

Zhyess put some distance between us and fell back to the rest of the dragons.

My voice echoed through her mind. *"Don't worry; I have a few tricks up my sleeve."*

It was a very human expression, one that was lost on the older dragon, but we didn't have time to discuss it. Dark shapes were already pouring through the gate. Some could fly but most simply dropped to the ground on shaky limbs. Creatures of all shapes and sizes re-entered a world that had banished them long ago. The other dragons banked off and separated, each taking on groups of newcomers. I was curious to see what they looked like but I didn't have time.

As I flew closer to the vortex I saw a large black shape blotting out the portal. I had thought it was Mareth, but this being made my soul shiver in fear. It clung to the sides of the portal and pushed its flat face out into the mortal realm. It spotted me and smiled, exposing large, razor-sharp teeth, and then right before my eyes it began to dissolve into fog. I shot a stream of elemental energy at the gate forming a barrier that spread to encompass the whole portal, but I was too late. The creature was gone and loose in Eiddoril.

I continued to pour my energy into the gate as dozens of creatures threw themselves against my barrier. The stream of immortals seemed to be endless and I wasn't sure how much longer I could hold the wall, but then the dragon I had been waiting for blocked out the background. He inhaled and blasted my barrier with his own energy stream. A black wave of power stained with electricity collided with my elemental power and shattered my barrier in a shower of sparks. The blast blew me back several feet, but I quickly regained myself and faced my father in midair.

He hovered inside the portal and stared at me with those evil red eyes. His voice hit me like stone, but I stood my ground. "Daughter. Well isn't this a disappointing surprise? I knew something had gone wrong when I could no longer communicate with that fool, Nubossa. I trust you killed him and rid me of that useless burden? I should thank you, but I don't think you would accept it." He paused and exposed his teeth. "You know I really don't see what all the fuss is about. I merely want to take back what is rightfully ours. Dragons—not those pathetic mortals—were meant to rule this world. They are weak and incapable of growth. I can rid this world of the filth that corrodes its power and rebuild from the ashes. I can be a god."

I shook my head and laughed at my father. "You are just as much a fool as Nubossa ever was. None of you understand what is controlling you. It's the power of Destruction; she is the one feeding you with magic, making you fat with greed and directing you like a good little soldier. You are no god. You are a puppet like the rest of them who has grown too heavy for its strings. She wants to cut you loose and watch you die to feed her hungry soul."

Mareth's eyes burned with anger. "What are you talking about? Who is this 'she'? No one controls me, I control them, and its time I taught you some respect for your father."

Everything happened very fast after that. I drew the power of the elements to me. The moon had reached its zenith and was now on its descent. The magic holding the portal open rapidly began to fade, and it started to close.

Mareth saw what was happening and launched himself forward, blasting his black energy straight toward me. I gained speed and momentum and started a collision course with the dark dragon. My own elemental energy burst forth from my gaping jaws and met his, causing sparks to fly everywhere. A magnificent light display lit up the night sky, causing everyone to watch the battle overhead.

Mareth poured more of his power into his stream and started to push me back. His head and shoulders were now visible to the mortals below. I reached down deep inside and pulled on my birth-given power. The power of life instantly came to my call and added its strength to my stream. The white-hot elemental energy mixed with the golden hue of life pushed Mareth back through the portal.

Mareth screamed in pain and cut off his stream, leaving mine to wreak havoc on him. My power hit him directly in the chest and knocked him fully back through the gate. I cut off my own power and followed my momentum toward the gate.

I sailed through on exhausted wings and as I came crashing down in a foreign land.

My prince's voice echoed through my mind: "Goodbye, my love, '*til we meet again.*"

Then the gate snapped shut and I was left alone, surrounded by enemies.

Epilogue

Ranjir

Prince Elric stood alone staring up at the morning sky, where just the night before he had watched his love enter a realm where she had no allies. Ililsaya had won: she had beaten Mareth and saved us from Destruction, but it had come at a great cost. More than half the allied soldiers had perished that night. They had fought hard, and in the end, with the help of the new dragons, they pushed the enemy back and sent them running to the Barren Wastes. I was not sure of all who perished, but I knew one of them was Ivser, the commander of Clorynina's men, and another was Tilan, Miara's brother. Sadness filled my heart as I thought about the Kanarah woman. Our confrontation flashed before my eyes and I held in the contempt I had for myself. I had so much to atone for, so much to fix. I knew that it may never happen, but at least I could do one thing right. I would heed Ililsaya's final wishes.

My mind drifted back to the present as I watched the prince. Word had been sent to the village of Sunder where the women, children, and elderly had been evacuated to, and Elric expected his mother would be returning soon with the residents of Gareth. It was going to be a long, hard winter trying to rebuild all that was destroyed, and with all the new beings to worry about, I was afraid still more of these people would perish. Everything had changed in our world over night and there were many pieces to pick up and still others that remained a mystery.

Fang stood beside the prince and I quietly approached them. I remained silent as I watched Elric stroke the large cat and collect himself. Elric turned and tried to be hospitable. I gave him credit.

"Is everyone accounted for? Have the dragons given you descriptions and names for the new beings?"

I eyed the prince with respect and nodded. "Yes, all those who have stayed. Ililsaya was right. Most of them just wish to live their lives and will be no threat to us, but I'm afraid there were others that escaped that may become a hindrance down the road. They have fled most likely to hide and explore their new home. I think it would be best if we targeted them sooner rather than later."

The prince nodded and started to walk past me toward the castle.

I felt I needed to say something. "Prince Elric?"

Elric stopped but didn't turn around. "Yes?"

"She'll be all right; she'll come back to you. We just have to make sure she has a world to come back to."

Elric didn't answer and instead continued his trek across the field.

I left him alone with his thoughts and followed silently behind, fulfilling the promise I had made. I sighed as I spied a great blue and green dragon circling high overhead, and knew that my task was not going to be easy.

CPSIA information can be obtained at www.ICGtesting.com
Printed in the USA
LVOW090712150612

286181LV00004B/1/P